Colette Caddle lives in Dublin with her husband and two young sons. She is the author of twelve bestselling novels. To find out more v[illegible] Colette's website at www.colettecaddle.com o[illegible] @colettecaddle.

Praise for Colette Caddle

'Charles Dickens once advised budding novelists [illegible] make their readers laugh, make'em cry, but most of all, make'em wait. And bestselling writer Colette Caddle does all three with an assured hand' *Irish Independent*

'If you like Marian Keyes, you'll love Colette Caddle' *Company*

'Will have readers laughing and crying every step of the way' *Irish Times*

'An engaging, warm slice of life with which all women will be able to identify. Highly recommended' *Publishing News*

'A warm, irresistible Irish author for all ages. Heaven knows how they do it, but they have that special magic' *The Bookseller*

'Caddle seems to know instinctively what women readers want' *Ireland on Sunday*

Also by Colette Caddle

FROM THIS MOMENT ON
EVERY TIME WE SAY GOODBYE
ALWAYS ON MY MIND
BETWEEN THE SHEETS
THE SECRETS WE KEEP
IT'S ALL ABOUT HIM
THE BETRAYAL OF GRACE MULCAHY
RED LETTER DAY
TOO LITTLE TOO LATE
SHAKEN AND STIRRED
A CUT ABOVE
FOREVER FM

Colette Caddle

Changing Places

SIMON & SCHUSTER

London · New York · Sydney · Toronto · New Delhi

A CBS COMPANY

First published in Great Britain by Pocket Books, 2005
An imprint of Simon & Schuster UK Ltd
A CBS COMPANY

This paperback edition published by Simon & Schuster UK Ltd, 2013

1 3 5 7 9 10 8 6 4 2

Simon & Schuster UK Ltd
1st Floor
222 Gray's Inn Road
London WC1X 8HB

www.simonandschuster.co.uk

Simon & Schuster Australia, Sydney
Simon & Schuster India, New Delhi

A CIP catalogue record for this book is available from the British Library

Paperback ISBN: 978-1-47112-733-5

Printed and bound by CPI Group (UK) Ltd, Croydon, CR0 4YY

For my boys, Peter and Seán

Changing Places

Chapter 1

'Good food, good wine and some lacy underwear – that's the way to a man's heart.' Mark Donnelly gave Anna a knowing wink before going back into his office, laughing to himself.

'Isn't he terrible?' Val said with a tolerant smile. 'What's the special occasion anyway?'

'It's Liam's birthday – he's thirty-three today.'

'So book a table in that new Indian place, it's supposed to be good.'

'Can't afford to,' Anna told her, pulling a face. 'I spent the last of my wages on a couple of DVDs for his present. I'll take him out next week when I get paid.'

'Then just go to some nice little wine bar for a drink,' Valerie suggested.

'And take the scenic route home . . .' Anna smiled as she remembered some of the detours she and Liam used to take when they were dating.

Val frowned. 'In the dark?'

Anna's lips twitched at the older woman's

innocence. 'Haven't you ever gone up a leafy lane with a guy, Val?'

'Not unless you count the time I went picking strawberries with Tommy O'Malley.'

'When was that?'

'When I was eleven,' Val said, her expression wistful. 'I suppose Mark's right. About the underwear, I mean.'

Anna chuckled at Val's blushes. 'Yeah, maybe we should just stay in. I could cook something nice and be decked out in a sexy nightie when he walks in.'

'Well, watch out for hot grease. You don't want any nasty burns in your privates. That wouldn't be very romantic.' Val switched off her PC and stood up.

'Are you doing anything this weekend?' Anna asked, conscious that they always seemed to talk about *her* social life.

'I'll probably bring Edna to bingo tomorrow night.'

'Oh. Nice.' Anna knew for a fact that Val hated bingo but her autocratic sister made Val take her every week. She was supposed to be an invalid, apparently riddled with arthritis, but she always seemed to be game for a night out, especially when her sister and minder had other plans.

'And I was thinking of visiting that new garden centre on Sunday,' Val went on.

'Sounds great.'

Val adjusted her scarf and put on her jacket. 'Well, goodnight, Anna. Hope you have a lovely time and

Liam appreciates the effort. Shouldn't you be making tracks yourself?'

'I just need a quick word with Mark before I go.'

'Don't let him keep you, now.'

'I won't. 'Night, Val.'

Anna tidied her desk, leaving out her list of Monday's appointments before going into Mark's office. He waved her to a chair as he finished a phone call. 'No, Jan, I'll be late. No, I'm not going gallivanting! I'll have you know, I have to meet a very important client.' He rolled his eyes expressively at Anna. 'Yes, yes, as soon as I can. Right, darling, bye.'

Anna shook her head as he replaced the receiver. 'You're a disgrace. You don't have any appointments tonight.'

'Excuse me, I have a very important date with a pint of the black stuff!' Mark rubbed his hands together. 'And you never know who I might bump into, in the pub. It's important to circulate in this business, I've made some of my best sales over a pint.'

'If you say so, Boss.'

'So, what can I do for you?'

'I just wanted to ask you about number seven, Marlboro Road. I have one couple coming back to see it a second time and I think they might make an offer.'

'Excellent.'

'Yes, but there's no way it will be for the asking price.' Anna handed him the details.

'Four hundred and twenty thousand Euros? That's

a bit steep. I thought we agreed it should go in at three-nine-five.'

Anna sighed. 'We did, but Mr Delaney wouldn't hear of it.'

'And you don't think he'll want to accept an offer under four-twenty?'

'He might take four-fifteen but no less than that. He is the most stubborn man I've ever met and he just won't listen to reason. There's no way this couple will offer four-twenty.'

'Want me to have a word with Delaney?'

'Would you? He's the sort that prefers to deal with men.'

'No problem. Let me know when this couple make an offer and I'll talk to him then.'

Anna stood up. 'Cheers, Mark, that's great.'

'And in return, you can do something for me.'

Anna lowered herself back into the chair. 'Oh, yes?'

'Yes. I have a client who's looking for a house on a bit of land – say an acre or so. And he'd like a view of the sea.'

'He's got money then.' Land was very expensive on the coast north of Dublin, and a sea view added several thousand to the price of even the most modest property. 'How come you're not handling this one yourself?' Anna asked. Mark made a point of dealing with the larger properties himself. Of course, he left it to Anna to do the measuring up and take the photos but he handled the clients.

'Let's say that unlike your Mr Delaney, Charlie Coleman enjoys dealing with the ladies.'

'Ah, you mean he's a lech. Are you using me?'

Mark handed her the file. 'Of course! Have a look through this and we'll talk again on Monday.'

Anna stood up. 'No problem. See you Monday.'

'Don't forget the lacy underwear.'

Anna grinned. 'Val's right. You're a terrible man!'

After a quick trip to the supermarket, Anna went home and started to prepare dinner. She'd agonized at the deli counter for a good ten minutes before finally buying two chicken Kievs. It was safer, given her limited culinary skills, and Liam loved it. She was just slicing some mushrooms when she heard his key in the door.

'Hey, Birthday Boy, what time do you call this?' she said as he wandered into their tiny kitchen, loosening his tie.

'The lads insisted on bringing me for a pint,' Liam replied, snaking his hands round her waist and pulling her to him. 'Mmm, you smell good.'

'Stop that,' she laughed, pushing him away. 'Let me concentrate on cooking your birthday dinner or you'll have to go out for chips.'

Liam shrugged out of his jacket and tossed it on the back of a chair. 'What are we having?'

'Chicken Kiev.' Anna turned to smile at him. He really was a fine thing with those wonderful green eyes and thick brown wavy hair that she always wanted to touch.

Liam grinned slowly and reached for her again. 'Sounds good. Have we time for a starter?'

Anna reluctantly pulled away. 'No, sorry, no starters.'

'You're no fun. Have I time for a shower, then?'

Anna glanced at the clock. 'If you're quick.'

'I'll be ten minutes.'

Anna quickly fried onions and mushrooms, wrapped them in foil and then popped them into the oven beside the chicken and baked potatoes. Once she'd opened a bottle of wine and set the table, she went into the sitting room and plumped the cushions.

She caught sight of her reflection in the mirror over the fireplace. Not bad. After realizing that she didn't actually *own* a sexy nightie, she'd decided that wearing sexy clothes was better than putting on her old Minnie Mouse nightshirt! Shaking back her long, auburn hair over her shoulder, she turned one way and then the other admiring the new purple top that clung to her small breasts and tiny waist. She was wearing it with her black suede trousers that hung low on her hips, and perilously high sandals that she only wore when she didn't have far to walk.

Going back out to the kitchen, Anna checked the chicken and turned down the heat. Just this once, she was determined not to burn anything. After making sure all was in order, she poured a glass of wine and carried it back into the sitting room. Curling into a corner of the large comfy sofa, she looked around in appreciation. The walls, sofa and carpet were all white, relieved by vibrant throws and pillows that were thrown carelessly around the small room, and the soft glow from the numerous candles she'd lit earlier.

'You won't be able to live like this when you have kids,' her sister, Rachel, had told her.

Anna loved this room but it wouldn't bother her if she had to change it tomorrow in order to make the place child-friendly. Not that this terrace house was designed for kids. The second bedroom was tiny, and they only had a small courtyard where she kept a few pot plants. They'd probably have to move into a nice sensible three-bedroom semi-d like Rachel's when they started a family.

She and Liam had discussed children a number of times but decided to wait until Liam got to senior management level. That wouldn't take long, Anna thought proudly. He was clever, a hard worker and very highly thought of. He was currently Production Manager in Patterson's Electronics, the firm where he had worked for nearly eleven years now, and he'd already been promoted twice. The owner, Ted Patterson, had hinted more than once that when he retired to his house in the west of Ireland, Liam would probably be the one to step into his shoes. But that was a long way ahead. Ted Patterson was a sprightly and quick-witted sixty-four-year-old who was unlikely to consider retirement for another ten years or so.

As for Anna, she was doing pretty well herself. After drifting from one job to another since she left school, she finally felt she'd found her niche when she came to work for Donnelly's Real Estate. Two years on, Mark was giving her more and more responsibility and he'd told her that he'd be reviewing her salary in a month's time. Anna was delighted. Now all she had to do was persuade him into taking on a junior. They needed to hire someone if they were to keep developing at the rate they had been doing over the last twelve months. Mark wouldn't want to, of course – the man was a skin-flint – but Anna was confident that she could talk him round. He was pleased with her work, but then why wouldn't he be after the money she'd brought in over the last couple of months? She thought with satisfaction of the house she'd sold that morning. A couple more sales like that and Mark Donnelly would wonder how he'd ever managed without her.

She was back in the kitchen checking the chicken when Liam returned.

'You're looking very pleased with yourself,' he said, pouring himself a glass of wine.

'I sold the house on Sea View Lane today.'

'The ramshackle hovel you've been trying to offload for months?'

'Yep.'

'That's great news – well done!' Liam grabbed hold of her and kissed her. 'I hope you're going to take me out for a slap-up meal when your commission comes through.'

Anna made a face. 'Don't hold your breath. You know what Mark's like. I'll be lucky if I see it this side of Christmas!'

'You can't put up with that. March in there first thing on Monday morning and demand it in your next pay-packet.'

'No, I plan to keep on his good side.' Anna snuggled closer into his chest. 'Aren't you going to ask me why?'

Liam chuckled. 'I've a feeling you're going to tell me.'

She looked up at him, her dark eyes shining. 'I think it's time we started a family.'

'I see.'

'Is that it?' She pulled back, frowning.

He shrugged. 'Pretty much. Just one question.'

'Oh?'

'Can we eat first, I'm starving!'

'Oh, you!' Anna pummelled his chest.

Liam sniffed. 'Do you smell burning?'

'Oh, shit!'

'So what do you think?' Anna asked when she'd rescued their dinner and they were seated at the table.

'About a baby? I suppose it's time.' Liam swallowed a piece of chicken.

Anna's eyes widened. 'Really?'

'Yeah. We may as well get started now, as it's likely I'm going to be made General Manager before long.'

'Liam, that's fantastic.' Anna leaned across to kiss him. 'It's official then?'

'No, but Ted Patterson was dropping very heavy hints today about changes and restructuring, so I read between the lines.'

Anna frowned. 'But if he's going to promote you, why not just do it?'

Liam rested his knife on his plate and took a drink of wine. 'From what I can gather, Frank Boylan is going to take early retirement so my position won't be public until that's signed and sealed.'

'You'll be a much better General Manager than Frank Boylan,' Anna assured him.

He grinned. 'You know what I love about you? You're so biased!'

'And we'll be rich,' she said happily.

'A few extra shillings and a bigger company car,' Liam agreed. 'Maybe we could even afford to buy a bigger house!'

Anna laughed excitedly as she raised her glass. 'Happy birthday, darling. I've a feeling it's going to be quite a year.'

'Gary, did you put the bins out? *Gary?*'

Rachel's husband didn't look up from his laptop. 'I'll do it later, I'm busy.'

'If you want to know what busy is, try looking after your son and this house for a couple of days,' she retorted. When Gary didn't bother replying, Rachel went back out to the kitchen and started to fling clothes into the washing-machine. It drove her mad when Gary behaved like this. As if he was the only one who worked while she sat filing her nails watching daytime television.

Gary Hanlon was the Sales Director of a small company on the other side of Dublin that supplied and fitted windows, doors and conservatories, and the way he went on, you'd think he had no staff at all! Rachel hated his job and hated how it took up all his time, even when he was at home. She knew he thought she had an easy life by comparison. As if minding an energetic five-year-old was easy – although Alex was a little darling – and the house cleaned itself. It wouldn't be quite so bad if Gary talked to her occasionally, but he always seemed to be working on that damn laptop or else had his head buried in a newspaper.

When they did talk it was about Alex or what needed doing around the house, and the latter subject almost always ended in an argument. Rachel knew Gary thought she was a nag, and the part that upset her most was that he was probably right. But she wouldn't be like that if he treated her better. If he came home straight from work instead of going for a drink with 'the lads'. If he didn't make her feel like a boring, drab housewife.

Slamming the door of the machine shut, she went upstairs to check on her son. Her face softened as she bent to tuck the duvet around him, first extracting a Power Ranger, stuffed elephant and a tiny racing car. With his long dark lashes resting on round pink cheeks, mouth slightly open and dark-blond hair brushed back off his face, he still looked like her baby. Her fingers moved to her stomach and she sighed as she thought of the baby brother or sister growing there.

Turning off the light, she crept out of Alex's room and went into her bedroom. Gary's suit jacket was on the bed, where he'd tossed it when he got in from work. Automatically, Rachel slipped her hand into the pockets and examined the contents. Some loose change, a crumpled-up receipt for soup and a sandwich in the pub across the road from his office, another from a bookshop, and his comb. Nothing to give her any reason to be suspicious, but she was. It had been a year ago now when she'd started to suspect that her husband was up to something. After *that* terrible night which still gave her the shivers whenever she thought about it.

She had been settling down to watch *Big Brother* when there was a bloodcurdling scream from Alex's room. She'd charged up the stairs and into his room to find him rolling around in agony clutching his side, his pyjamas and sheets covered in vomit. Feeling his forehead, Rachel realized immediately that he was burning up. She called the doctor, hugging the phone between her neck and ear as she held her son and bathed his forehead with a wet cloth.

'Call an ambulance, Rachel,' her GP had said as soon as she'd described the symptoms. 'The little man may have appendicitis.'

As she waited for the ambulance, Rachel tried to reach Gary but there was no answer on his mobile. He was at a business dinner and she knew that Bill Grant, his boss, was with him so she looked in their address book to get Bill's mobile number. Normally, she would never dream of interrupting Gary when he was out with colleagues, but she knew he wouldn't mind tonight. This was an emergency.

Bill Grant seemed slightly bemused at her frantic call. 'Oh hello, Rachel – no, you're not interrupting. I was just watching the golf on telly. What can I do for you?'

Rachel had quickly told him about Alex, conscious that there were blue flashing lights in the road outside. 'I must have gotten it wrong, Bill. I thought Gary had a business dinner this evening.'

'Nothing official, my dear, although he could well be out with a customer – probably is, in fact. A hard worker, your Gary.'

Rachel bit her lip as she went to open the door. 'Yeah, Bill, he is. Look, I must go, the ambulance has arrived.'

'Is there anything I can do?'

'Perhaps you could phone around and see if you

can track him down? Tell him we're on our way to Temple Street Hospital.'

'Consider it done. Now try not to worry, I'm sure the lad will be fine. Our lot were always getting one thing or the other. Looked as if they were at death's door one minute, right as rain the next.'

'Right, thanks, Bill.' Rachel hung up and went back to where Alex sat huddled on the sofa, his eyes closed and his face flushed. 'It's okay, darling, you're going to be fine.'

The rest of the night passed by in a blur. Within an hour, Alex had been in the operating theatre and when Gary arrived, several hours later, Rachel was sitting at his bedside, holding his limp little hand.

'Jesus, is he okay? What happened?' Gary sank to his knees at the other side of the bed and stared worriedly at his son's face.

'He's just out of surgery. They've taken his appendix out.'

'Did he wake up? Have you talked to him?'

'Just for a moment. He's on a lot of medication for the pain. They said he probably wouldn't wake again until morning.'

'Sleep's the best thing for him,' Gary nodded, his eyes never leaving Alex's face.

'Where were you?'

'What?'

Rachel watched him steadily. 'Where were you?'

'I told you, I had a business dinner.'

'You also told me Bill was going, but he was at home watching golf.'

'I didn't say that – you never listen.'

'Why didn't you answer your mobile?'

'I left it in the car by mistake.'

Rachel looked at the clock on the wall at the end of the ward. It was almost three o'clock. 'That must have been some dinner.'

Gary shot her an irritable look. 'Dan decided we should go clubbing. The client was all on for it; there was nothing I could do.'

Rachel knew Dan Horgan of old. He was in his early thirties, a dedicated bachelor and a man who liked the good life. He had often dragged Gary out with him, although Rachel didn't believe her husband needed much persuading.

'I would have called,' he continued, 'but it was nearly eleven when we left the restaurant and I didn't want to wake you.'

And Rachel had let it go at that. She hadn't been entirely convinced, but her mind had been on Alex and she didn't want to think about the implications if Gary *was* lying to her. However, that episode had made her suspicious and now she always checked his pockets and his wallet. Once, she'd even checked his emails when he'd gone to the loo and left his laptop open on the chair beside her. She felt disgusted with herself for snooping but she couldn't help it. If only he talked to her more, she wouldn't have to check up on him like this.

Rachel hung up Gary's jacket, took off her clothes and went into the bathroom in her bra and pants to remove her make-up. She studied her reflection as she applied her cleanser. She had the same eyes as her sister, Anna, but there the similarity ended. Though Rachel also had red hair, hers was dull and lifeless. The last time she'd gone to the hairdresser, she'd allowed herself to be persuaded to go blonde and had regretted her decision almost immediately. She'd also had it cut in a different, younger style, but the choppy cut did not flatter her. Rather it emphasized her plump cheeks and drew attention to the bags under her eyes.

Rachel hadn't slept properly since she'd been pregnant with Alex. In the last month of pregnancy, her back had ached and her bump had been huge and she couldn't find a comfortable position. Her mother told her that it was her body preparing her for motherhood.

'You're not going to get much sleep once the little one comes along,' she'd joked.

Rachel had laughed too. 'I don't care. It will be worth it.'

And it had been, Rachel thought as she washed her face and patted it dry with the soft towel. Alex was a wonderful little boy but he'd been a difficult baby and she'd spent many nights slumped over his cot while Gary slept soundly, oblivious to his son's screams. Even now, Alex wasn't a great sleeper and Rachel often ended up sitting on the edge of his bed in the early hours of the morning. God only knew how she'd cope with two. She did like the idea of a brother or sister for Alex, but the thought of looking after two children on a minimum amount of sleep overwhelmed her.

She hadn't told Gary about the baby yet, more as a punishment for being such a grumpy so-and-so than anything else. She knew he'd be over the moon at the news but she was finding it hard to get excited by the idea. Her life had only just started to settle down, and now that Alex was at school she actually had some time to herself again. She often had all her housework done by ten just so that she could go for a walk or have a wander round the shops. She'd also been thinking of joining a gym. She'd never managed to lose those extra pounds after Alex was born and she'd liked the idea of toning up and getting into some of those thin, body-hugging clothes that her sister wore. Now there was no chance of that. Rachel went back to the bedroom, took off her underwear and slipped into white cotton pyjamas. And when the baby was born next December, money would be too tight for her to join anything more adventurous than Weight-Watchers.

She was about to climb into bed when Gary appeared in the doorway. 'I've put out the bins,' he said.

'Oh. Right, thanks.'

'Sorry,' he said, taking her in his arms. 'I had a bitch of a day.'

Rachel thought of the mountain of ironing she had done and the shopping expedition in the lashing rain. 'That's okay.'

He bent his head and kissed her neck, his fingers moving to explore her breasts. 'Are you very tired?'

Despite herself, Rachel felt her body respond. 'Not too tired.' She closed her eyes as he started to open her pyjamas.

Chapter 2

Anna rummaged through the rack of clothes, pulling out a short suede skirt to examine it more closely. After a quick glance at the price tag though, she put it back – Liam would kill her if she spent any more on clothes. Her Visa bill was up to its limit and she didn't get paid until the following Thursday. Besides, if they were really going to start a family she'd have to be a bit more careful with her cash. Babies were expensive. She still remembered her shock at the final bill in Mothercare the day she went with Rachel to buy only the basics. Still, her sister would probably be able to lend her lots of stuff. Her attic was full of old baby toys, clothes and the pretty cot that had been a gift from their parents.

Walking back out on to the main street in Malahide, Anna psyched herself up to go to the supermarket but it was such a lovely Saturday morning, a walk around the marina was a lot more tempting.

'Hey, Anna!'

She turned to see her sister waving at her from across the road.

'Hi, Rache.' She crossed the road to join her. 'How's it going?'

'Yeah, fine. Where are you off to?'

Anna sighed. 'I should be doing the shopping.'

Rachel smiled. 'Not in the mood, eh? Tell you what. Let's treat ourselves to a coffee and a cake. We could go up to Café Provence.'

'Why not? Where's Gary?' Anna asked as they headed for the little coffee-shop.

'Golf. Liam?'

'Soccer.'

The sisters exchanged tolerant smiles.

'How come guys get to amuse themselves on Saturdays and we end up doing all the housework and shopping?' Anna moaned. 'Where's Alex?'

'He's playing soccer too – now that's a sight to behold. A gang of five-year-olds chasing a ball around a pitch for an hour, it's hilarious. I can't go and watch any more because Alex gets very cross when I laugh.'

As they approached the coffee-shop a couple vacated a table outside and Rachel made a beeline for it.

'I'll go and get some menus,' Anna said.

'I don't need a menu. A large latte and a gooey doughnut for me, please.' Rachel patted her thickening stomach. Cravings were a great excuse for indulgences.

Anna went inside and ordered lattes and doughnuts for them both before putting on her dark glasses and returning to sit down opposite her sister. 'Oh, isn't it a beautiful morning? I wonder what it's like where Mam and Dad are. I wonder *where* they are.'

'Pisa,' Rachel told her. 'Mam was looking at the tower when she phoned the other day.'

Anna chuckled. 'She loves to rub it in, doesn't she? The last time she called me was from a phonebox just across from the Trevi Fountain. I've always wanted to visit Rome ever since I saw that film with Audrey Hepburn – you know the one.'

'*Roman Holiday*, with Gregory Peck?'

Anna shook her head. 'No, it wasn't Gregory Peck, it was Cary Grant.'

'It was Gregory Peck,' Rachel assured her.

'If you say so.' Anna pushed her hair back from her face. 'They certainly seem to be enjoying themselves. You know, when they first told us they were selling up and buying a camper van I thought that senility was setting in early.'

'Yeah. I never really saw them as the adventurous sort.'

'You never do think about your parents like that. It's like trying to imagine them having sex.' Anna shuddered and then smiled at the startled waitress who was placing their order in front of them. 'Oh thanks, that's lovely.'

'I wonder where they're heading to next?' Rachel stirred sugar into her coffee. 'I suppose we'll have to wait until the next postcard arrives. What are they like! Wouldn't you think they'd invest in a mobile?'

'Mam always loved writing,' Anna said fondly. 'Don't you remember when we went to the Irish college in Donegal she used to send us a couple of cards a week?'

'God, I'd forgotten all about that. And she posted a congratulations card to me when I had Alex, even though she visited us in hospital every day.'

'She's a romantic,' Anna said. 'God, I miss them! Wouldn't it be great to hop on a plane and go out to see them?'

'Why don't you?' Rachel's tone was slightly sharper than she realized. 'There's nothing stopping you.'

Anna cut her doughnut down the middle. 'No money, and Mark would freak if I took time off. We're very busy at the moment.'

'Oh, of course, I was forgetting you were an important businesswoman,' Rachel sniffed.

'Oh Rache, don't start.'

'Don't start what?'

Anna sighed. 'Having a go. All I said was that I was busy.'

'Aren't we all? Just because I don't work doesn't mean I'm not busy too, you know. You don't have a life of your own when you have kids. You have to plan, plan, plan if you want to do anything or go anywhere.'

'Really?' Anna sipped her coffee, deciding it was probably best to let her sister have a rant.

Rachel always went on as if Anna had a great life,

as though, because they had no kids, she and Liam could hop on a plane whenever they liked. Mind you, when Liam got promoted they'd probably be able to do just that. Except, Anna reminded herself, they could hardly go gadding about if they wanted to have a family. They'd have to start putting some money by.

Saving had never been a big issue for either of them before. Liam had his pension plan and Anna's father had made both his daughters take out life and health insurance when they started work, but apart from that, they lived from pay cheque to pay cheque. Maybe now they should open a proper savings account.

'Anna?'

She looked up at her sister. 'Sorry, I was miles away.'

'I was just asking if you two have made any holiday plans yet.'

'Oh, we'll probably grab one of those last-minute deals later in the summer. What about you?'

Rachel sighed. 'I expect we'll take a house in Enniscrone for a couple of weeks.'

'That's nice,' Anna said, not totally convincingly.

'No, it bloody isn't! I'll still be cooking and cleaning, just in a different location. I would really love to go to Portugal or Spain. It would work out just as cheap, and at least we'd be guaranteed a bit of sunshine.'

'And Gary's not keen?'

'No, he hates the sun.'

'That's a pity.'

'Yeah.'

An awkward silence descended on them and Anna racked her brains for something to say that might cheer her sister up. 'I sold a house yesterday,' she blurted out eventually.

'That's nice.'

'Yeah, I was thrilled. It was in a bit of a state and Mark had been trying to offload it for months.'

'I should get a job.' Rachel stared gloomily at the people hurrying past. 'I miss the buzz of the office. You've no idea, Anna, how much easier it is than staying at home.'

'I don't know about that, Rache—'

'I do! Look, I've been there, remember? In an office you know your day will end at a set time and that you'll get a lunch break and a coffee break, and when you go home, your time is your own. But it's completely different when you're a mother. Sometimes I don't even get a minute to have a cup of tea, and then there are the broken nights.'

Anna shot her a look of disbelief. 'But Alex is at school until one, and you're not saying he wakes every night, are you?'

'He has nightmares.' Rachel waved a dismissive hand. 'And while he's at school I'm cooking and cleaning. A home doesn't run itself, you know.'

'I do know that,' Anna said. 'I have to do it all when I get home in the evening.'

Rachel gave her a hard smile. 'Ah well, you're quite the wonder woman, aren't you?'

Anna put down her cup. 'Oh, for God's sake! I think I'd better go and do that shopping.'

Rachel immediately stood up. 'I need to make a move anyway.'

'I'll see you, so.'

'When?' Rachel demanded. 'What about tomorrow? Alex hasn't seen you for ages.'

'Oh, we can't, Rache – sorry. We're meeting Helen and Tom for a game of tennis and then we'll probably go for a late lunch.'

Rachel's smile became even more like a grimace. 'Oh, well, drop in sometime when your busy schedule allows.' She leaned over to brush her cheek against her sister's. 'Bye.'

Anna groaned as she watched her march off towards the car park. Why was it that she always seemed to be in her little sister's bad books? Nothing she said ever seemed to please Rachel, Anna thought as she headed back towards the supermarket. And it wasn't as if she deliberately tried to antagonize or bait her sister. But Rachel seemed to resent her and was always making smart comments about Anna's job or lifestyle.

Anna went into the shop, grabbed a basket and wandered down an aisle flinging pre-packed vegetables into it. She felt really bad about turning down Rachel's invitation, although it had been more of a command! But, honestly, what was she supposed to do? Liam had made the arrangements with Helen and Tom ages ago. Anna opened a fridge door and rooted around the ready meals. Rachel could be damn irritating at times and today was definitely one of them. They were sisters, for God's sake, and with Mam and Dad away they only had each other.

Anna missed the old times. She and Rache used to be so close. Yes, there had been rows, plenty of them, but that was normal. It was especially bad once Anna left school and started working. Rachel developed a nasty habit of sneaking into her room to nick make-up, clothes and shoes – the ultimate sin in Anna's eyes. From an early age she'd always had a thing about shoes and once she'd started work, she'd spent every spare penny she had on them. Though usually quite easygoing, Anna would fight like a cat if Rachel took them without asking. Inevitably they would be returned dirty or, worse, scratched. Bridie, their mother, would have to intervene and Anna would usually forgive her sister in exchange for one of Rachel's hair-do's.

Rachel had a talent for creating elaborate hairstyles and had infinite patience, taking time and care as she piled Anna's auburn tresses high on her head. She would never let Anna look at her reflection until she'd finished, at which stage her sister would stare in amazement at the sophisticated stranger in the mirror.

It was Rachel who had done her hair the first time she met Liam. She had been an old married woman by then but agreed to call over to the house to do Anna's hair because she'd been invited to a charity Christmas ball.

'Everyone who's anyone goes to this ball,' Rachel had told her big sister. 'You have to look your best.'

Anna had been invited by a guy she'd just met. She hadn't really liked Baz and had no intention of seeing him again, but she couldn't resist the thought of going to a ball. She spent hours getting ready, with Bridie and Rachel's help, and was very pleased with the result.

The long black dress she'd bought for the occasion was a sleek and figure-hugging number with a plunging neckline. With her hair piled on the top of her head, tiny ringlets framing her face and the pearls her mother had lent her, she didn't look too bad at all.

'Gorgeous,' her mother had pronounced with tears in her eyes.

'You'll knock 'em dead!' Rachel had agreed.

The two women had stood at the hall door, waving as she and Baz had sped off in a taxi.

Anna had been a bit disappointed in Baz on their second meeting. He'd looked a lot better the night they met. Having said that, the club had been dimly lit and she'd had one too many glasses of cheap champagne. Still, despite his pallor and his bulging watery blue eyes, he looked quite nice in his black tux. Anna loved men in dresswear. Even the wimpiest guy could manage to look like James Bond in a dinner jacket. She was determined to make the best of the night and enjoy herself.

It didn't take her long to realize that this would be next to impossible. Without even introducing her to anyone, Baz had left her at their table and disappeared to the bar. Anna made the best of it and chatted to a couple of the other women. They were halfway through the starter before Baz finally returned, rather the worse for wear and without a drink for Anna. Ignoring her reproachful look, he proceeded to slag off the food, the band and then he'd launched into a series of filthy jokes. By the time Baz had knocked a full pint of lager over the woman on his right, Liam, who was sitting across from them, had had enough. Jumping to his feet, he'd strong-armed a somewhat bewildered Baz out of the room and handed him over to a bouncer, who promptly threw him out.

When Liam returned, he crouched down beside Anna to tell her what had happened.

'I'm sorry if I've ruined your night, but your boyfriend was way out of order.'

'He's not my boyfriend!' Anna protested, 'I only met him last weekend. God, what a prat! Thanks for getting rid of him, I appreciate it.' She looked at him from under her lashes, thinking he was even better-looking close up. 'Please, let me buy you and your girlfriend a drink.'

Liam grinned at her. 'She's not my girlfriend. Her

fiancé's down with the flu and she asked me if I'd like to come along instead.'

'I'm very glad you did.'

Liam's eyes twinkled back at her. 'I'm quite glad I did too.'

And that had been that. Anna had known within weeks that Liam was the man for her and the following Christmas, they got engaged. Rachel, who was eight months' pregnant at the time, had pestered her sister not to get married for at least six months, to give her time to have her baby and get her figure back. Anna and Liam had agreed to marry in August and although Rachel still hadn't been as skinny as she would have liked, they'd all had a wonderful day.

Anna continued to daydream as she stood in the long line at the checkout. She and Liam had double-dated with Gary and Rachel a lot at the beginning, although it was clear to Anna that Liam and Gary had little in common. Though Gary was the same age as Anna, he'd always behaved like a much older man. He was very involved in his career, followed the stock markets avidly and liked to discuss politics. He was amazingly proud of his home and its location, being in one of the more up-market parts of Malahide.

Liam, by contrast, was laid back and always up for a laugh; he never talked about his job or how well he was doing. He didn't seem to have a problem with Gary, but at the same time, he was never exactly relaxed in his company either. Still, as a foursome, they'd always had a good laugh. In fact, it was only in the last couple of years that the socializing had pretty much ground to a halt. Why or who was at fault, Anna really didn't know. She didn't think she or Liam had changed that much. She'd have to ask Jill what she thought.

As best friend to both sisters, their cousin Jill knew everything there was to know about the Gallagher sisters. At twenty-nine, Jill Clarke was two years younger than Anna and a year older than Rachel. Living around the corner from the Gallagher family home, she had grown up with them, fought, cried and laughed with them. She had always been the peacemaker in the sense that she could usually make both sisters see the funny side of even the most explosive situations. It was Jill who'd stepped in when Anna broke the head off Rachel's Barbie doll. Jill, who'd comforted both girls when their beloved dog, Homer, died. And Jill who'd stopped Anna killing Rachel the day that Rachel dyed her sister's hair orange instead of the platinum blonde she'd promised.

Now, as a high-flying advertising executive based in the centre of Dublin, Jill was still very much a part of their lives, although, Anna realized as she walked back to the car, Jill usually met the sisters separately now. When the threesomes had stopped, Anna couldn't quite remember. Feeling decidedly fed-up, Anna dumped her shopping in the boot of the car and went home to tackle the ironing.

*

Bloody cheek! Rachel fumed as she shoved the hoover around the living room. Her dear sister had as good as said that she did the same amount of housework *and* held down a job too. Well, that was just typical! Anna completely underestimated how hard it was, raising a child. Anyway, Anna wasn't as fussy about cleaning as she was. Rachel had always been the one to clean their room when they were growing up. Anna's idea of cleaning was to cram her clothes into the wardrobe, straighten the bed and give the room a quick hoover.

Rachel gave a snort of indignation as she hoovered the cobwebs from the ceiling. 'I bet Anna never thinks of hoovering up here!' she muttered. It was easy for her sister to criticize. She was married to a great guy, working in a job she loved and still blessed with the same figure she'd had at twenty. Unlike Rachel who was overweight already and now, with the pregnancy, it would only be a matter of weeks before she started to balloon. Still, when she'd been pregnant with Alex, Gary had treated her like a china doll. It would be nice if he did that again. She could do with some pampering.

Rachel had decided that she would tell him tonight. She'd organized a babysitter for Alex and booked a table at Gary's favourite Chinese restaurant. They could both do with a night out together. Maybe away from Alex, the television and Gary's damn laptop, they'd actually be able to behave like a normal couple.

She was just putting the hoover away when she heard Gary's key in the door and Alex came racing in.

'Hi, Mum, I scored a goal! What's for lunch? Can I have a biscuit while I'm waiting?'

Rachel pulled her scruffy son into her arms for a hug. 'I'll make you a sandwich and you can have yoghurt. No biscuits until after your lunch. So tell me about this goal.' She listened to Alex chatter nineteen-to-the-dozen as she made his sandwich, smiling briefly at Gary who'd joined them in the kitchen and was standing at the worktop reading the paper and drinking a beer.

'Good game?' Rachel asked him when she'd settled her son to eat at the kitchen table.

'Not bad,' Gary murmured without looking up.

'I met Anna in the village this morning.'

'Oh yeah?'

'I asked her over tomorrow but of course it was too short notice for her. They're playing tennis.'

'I don't know why you invite Anna over at all. Any time she's here you just snipe at her.'

'I do not!' Rachel protested, feeling her cheeks grow hot. Turning away from him she bustled around the kitchen, tidying and wiping down surfaces. How could he say that? She wasn't the sort to snipe. Sure, she and Anna had their moments but then didn't all sisters? Still, Gary was an only child and didn't understand the way families worked. You said things to brothers and sisters that you would never say to strangers, and you did it because you knew you would get away with it. Forgiveness was not asked for nor given; it was assumed. Idiosyncrasies were accepted, faults excused; it was all a part of being a family.

For the first time Rachel felt real happiness at the idea of the life growing within her. It would be good for Alex to have a sibling. And Gary would be very happy when he knew. She turned to face him. 'We're going out tonight!' she announced brightly.

Gary looked up, a frown on his face. 'Out? Where?'

'The Chinese. I've booked a table and a babysitter. I thought it would be a nice treat for us.'

'Oh love, I'm really not in the mood and the football is on. You don't mind, do you?'

Rachel forced a smile. 'No, of course not, it was just an idea.'

'Let's get some takeaway instead and I'll open a nice bottle of wine.'

'Yeah, sounds good,' Rachel murmured.

Chapter 3

'Game, set and match!' Liam dropped a kiss on Anna's cheek before bending to pick up the water bottle.

'Good game.' Helen joined them, mopping her brow with her towel. 'God, it's hot. I'm about ready for a nice cold spritzer.'

'Meet you up at the bar,' Tom told his wife. 'And don't hang around talking, I've booked Cruzzo's for two o'clock.'

Helen rolled her eyes at Anna. 'Should I remind him that we're usually ready first?'

The two girls headed into the changing rooms and quickly showered and dressed. 'Are you two in a rush today or can we have a nice leisurely lunch?' Helen asked as she combed her damp hair.

'Reasonably leisurely.' Anna made a face. 'I'd like to drop over to Rachel's later. She was only saying yesterday that it's ages since we've seen Alex.'

'Well, you can drop by straight after lunch and everyone will be happy.'

'I should make Liam drive,' Anna laughed. 'If

he has a couple of beers with lunch he'll nod off as soon as he hits the sofa and Rachel will be disgusted with him.'

'That sounds good to me. They can drive and you and I can share a nice bottle of wine. We're going to my darling mother-in-law's for tea so I could do with a drink!'

'What's she done now?' Helen was constantly giving out about Tom's mother and Anna loved to hear her friend's tales of woe. Although the woman couldn't be as bad as all that because though Helen seemed completely frustrated with her, her stories were usually tinged with grudging affection.

'She's only told Tom she'll do all his ironing for him while I'm away next week.'

'Oh, that's right – you're off to Cork, aren't you?'

'Yeah, lots of raw young things need computer training so muggins got the job. Still, I love Cork and with a bit of luck I should have time for some shopping. Anyway, I thought the break would do Tom good. You know what a lazy lout he is. A week alone would make him realize exactly how much work I do in the house. But now, his beloved mother is going to do the ironing and, don't you know, he'll be eating there most nights. So instead of appreciating me more when I get back he'll probably be telling me how well his mother irons his shirts and what a great casserole she makes.' Helen shook her head in disgust.

'Irish mothers have a lot to answer for when it comes to sons,' Anna agreed. 'Liam was totally spoiled. Do you know, he didn't even know how to work the washing-machine in his mother's house?'

'Ha! Tom still doesn't know how to work ours – or he claims he doesn't – and we've been together eight years! I'm as bad as his mother. I'm way too soft on him.'

'Next time you're going out of town, plan it for when his folks are away too,' Anna advised.

Helen paused, her lipstick halfway to her mouth, and stared at her friend in the mirror. 'What an excellent idea!'

Anna laughed. 'Just don't tell Tom it was mine.'

Helen was still smiling as they joined the men in the bar.

'What are you looking so smug about?' Tom asked.

'Oh, nothing, dear. Now, gentlemen, that's your first and last beer,' she added, eyeing the glasses in their hands. 'It's your turn to drive.'

'Probably just as well,' Liam agreed. 'I have to write a report when I get home.'

Anna looked at him in dismay. 'Oh Liam, it's Sunday. Can't it wait?'

He shook his head. 'I need to have it ready for tomorrow.'

'But I thought we'd drop by Rachel's later.'

Liam looked confused. 'But you told me that you'd told her we couldn't make it.'

'Yeah, I did, but, well, we could just drop in for an hour.'

'I can't keep up with you,' Liam said with a long-suffering look at Tom. 'One minute you're giving out about her, the next you want to go visit her!'

'I didn't give out about her,' Anna protested. 'Don't exaggerate.'

Liam shook his head and then drained his bottle. 'We'd better get to the restaurant, people. Come on.'

Nearly two hours later, feeling rather mellow after the wine, Anna sank back into the passenger seat and closed her eyes.

'Still want to go to Rachel's?' Liam asked as he pulled out of the car park.

Anna's eyes flew open and she turned her head to look at him. 'Would you mind? We won't stay long, I promise.'

'No problem.'

'Thanks, sweetheart.' Anna put her hand on his thigh and closed her eyes again. It seemed only moments later when she heard Liam calling her.

'Anna, we're here.'

Straightening up in the seat, Anna flicked down the sun visor and checked her appearance in the mirror. Apart from being slightly flushed after her doze, she looked okay. Not that it mattered. After the usual wrestle with Alex she'd soon be looking dishevelled anyway.

It was Gary who opened the door, quickly hiding

his surprise behind a smile. 'Anna, Liam! Come in – great to see you!'

'We're not staying long,' Anna said, exchanging kisses with her brother-in-law. 'Just dropped in to say hi.'

'Anna! Anna!' A little figure came hurtling down the hall and threw himself into her arms.

Anna grabbed the banisters to steady herself. 'Hey, big guy, how are you?'

'Fine. Have you brought me something?'

'Alex!'

The child froze as his mother came into the hall and gave him a stern look.

'Sorry.'

'That's okay, darling. I brought you some sweets.'

'Thanks!' Alex threw a triumphant look over his shoulder at his mother.

'How was the tennis?' Rachel asked coolly after kissing Liam and brushing her cheek against Anna's.

'Excellent,' Liam said as Gary led the way to the kitchen and handed him a beer.

'You won then,' Gary laughed. 'Some wine, Anna?'

'Just a small one. Liam, should you really be drinking that?' Anna looked at the bottle, eyebrows raised.

'We only have to go a couple of miles down the road,' he groaned. 'I've eaten a huge meal since the last beer and that was three hours ago!'

'Can I have a Coke?' Alex asked, hopping around the kitchen on one foot.

'Yes,' said Gary.

'No,' said Rachel at the same time. 'He's already had one can, Gary. You know what he'll be like if he has another.'

Alex's face fell but Liam gave him a gentle punch. 'Come on, you want to be a great footballer, don't you? All the best sportsmen drink water. They wouldn't touch that stuff.'

Rachel shot him a grateful smile. He was such a sensible man and would make a great father one day.

Alex happily accepted the glass of water from his father and returned to Liam's side. 'Will you play football with me?'

'Leave him alone, Alex,' Gary said.

'That's okay, Gary. Let me finish my beer, Alex, and I'll give you a quick game.'

'Deadly!' Alex drained his glass and hurried off to get his football boots on.

'He's getting so tall,' Anna murmured to her sister with an affectionate smile.

'Can't keep him in clothes,' Rachel said gruffly, 'and his feet have gone up a size in a month. You wouldn't believe the price of children's shoes, Anna. It's such a rip-off.'

'You should ask Mam to get some for you. Shoes are usually a lot cheaper on the continent.'

'That's not a bad idea,' Rachel mused. 'I'll mention it to her the next time she phones.'

Rachel poured herself a glass of water as she spoke and for the first time Anna noticed how peaky her sister was looking. The men were engrossed in a discussion about last night's football so Anna suggested they go out and sit in the garden.

'Are you okay?' she asked when they were alone on the patio.

'Sure, why do you ask?' Rachel looked wary.

Anna shrugged. 'You just seem a bit down and you're very pale.'

'I'm pregnant,' Rachel blurted out.

'That's wonderful!' Anna threw her arms around her sister and hugged her.

'Shush.' Rachel extricated herself and looked anxiously towards the kitchen window. 'Gary doesn't know yet.'

'Why ever not?'

Rachel led Anna down the garden, pausing beside the pink rosebush. 'I just haven't found the right moment.'

Anna looked at her, mystified. She knew that if she were pregnant she'd be shouting it from the rooftops. As for Liam, he would have been sitting there by her side waiting for that oh-so-important blue line to appear on the testing stick. 'How far gone are you?'

'Seven, maybe eight weeks.'

'Nearly two months!' Anna exclaimed and then clutched her side as her sister gave her a sharp dig. 'Sorry, but you really have to tell him.'

'Shush, they're coming.' Rachel started back to the house as the men emerged with Alex running ahead bouncing the ball.

'Rachel.' Anna hurried after her.

'Not now,' Rachel said through gritted teeth. 'Alex, come here and let me tie your lace before you break your neck.'

Alex stood impatiently while Rachel crouched over his boot. 'Watch me, Anna, I'm going to win!'

'I don't doubt it.' Anna smiled at him and sank on to a sunlounger. 'Come and sit down, Rachel.'

'I'll join you in a minute,' her sister said, not looking at her and heading back inside.

When Liam and Alex began their game, Gary came over to sit next to Anna.

'How's business?' she asked.

'Busy as always. Everyone wants to build a conservatory when the weather gets nice. How about you? How's the hectic world of property?'

'Hectic,' she joked, 'but I love it. Though I must say, you meet a lot of strange people.'

'And see some very weird homes, no doubt.'

Anna wrinkled her nose. 'Some very dirty, smelly houses. You wouldn't believe how some people live.'

'Oh, I would! You see a lot in the windows game as well, believe me. You should go to my mate Dan's house. That man doesn't even know what colour his carpet is!'

Anna grinned. 'I seem to remember Rachel mentioning him. He's the guy who has a library of porn in his loo, isn't he?'

'That's the one. Maybe we should fix him up with Jill.'

Anna looked at him, horrified. 'How could you even think of doing such a thing?'

'Well, it would be nice to see her settle down with someone. It's quite sad that she's still on her own.'

Anna spluttered on her wine. 'God, you're such a chauvinist! She doesn't need a man to be happy, you know.'

He rolled his eyes. 'You are so like your sister. All I'm saying is that she's a great girl and any man would be lucky to have her. What's so wrong with that?'

'Nothing, I suppose. Actually, she is seeing someone at the moment.'

'Oh, yes? What's wrong with this one?'

Anna's smile was rueful. It was a given that if Jill was dating someone, there would turn out to be something wrong with him. Liam said she was too choosy but Anna thought her cousin was afraid of commitment. Anytime a relationship lasted more than a couple of months, Jill started to find fault. With Stan, the last guy, it had been his feet. Despite showering every day, Jill maintained his feet smelled. Anna pointed out that this hadn't seemed to bother her for the first six weeks that they were together, but Jill had dismissed this.

'I can't live with a man with smelly feet,' she had said with finality.

'You're not living with him,' Anna objected but Jill had made up her mind, and Stan and his feet got the elbow a week later.

'She hasn't found anything wrong with him – yet,' Anna said now to Gary. 'You never know, maybe this is it. She seems very happy. Oh, great goal, Alex!' She cheered as her nephew fired the ball between the two plants that were acting as goalposts. 'He's such a lovely kid,' she murmured to Gary.

'He has his moments,' Gary replied, but there was pride in his eyes as he watched his son.

Anna glanced over her shoulder. 'Would you like more kids?' she asked quietly, knowing that her sister would throttle her if she overheard.

He shrugged. 'I suppose so, though I don't know if Rachel would agree.'

Before Anna could ask what he meant, Rachel appeared at the kitchen door. 'Come on in, Anna, I've made some tea. Alex, time for a break.'

'Ah, Mum!' Alex moaned.

Liam patted his shoulder. 'It's okay, big guy, we'll play again after tea.'

Mollified, Alex charged over to his mother. 'Can I have some cake?'

'Sure.' She tousled his hair and smiled at Anna. 'It's Madeira.'

Anna stood up and followed them inside. 'My favourite. Do you know, your granny makes the best Madeira cake in all of Ireland?' she told her nephew as they sat down at the large kitchen table.

'It's her recipe I use,' Rachel told her. 'Hands,' she said to her son and with a sigh, Alex climbed back down and went into the loo to wash them. 'Please don't say anything, Anna,' Rachel whispered when he was gone.

'Of course I won't but I really think you should—'

'Should what?' Gary asked, as he and Liam walked in.

'Come down to the spa in Wicklow with me some weekend,' Anna said hastily. 'The break would do her the world of good.'

Rachel stared at her, amazed at the sudden shift in subject. 'It would cost a fortune,' she said automatically.

'It would,' Liam agreed with a confused glance at his wife.

Anna reddened. They'd only been talking earlier about cutting down on their spending so that they could afford all the necessities that came with babies. 'Just a thought,' she mumbled with an apologetic smile.

They got up to leave after the second half of the football game – Alex won – and in the hallway Anna turned to her sister and hugged her tightly. 'Take care of yourself.'

'Yeah, you too.' Rachel smiled briefly. 'If you see Jill, ask her to call me.'

'Will do.'

'Bye, Rachel.' Liam kissed his sister-in-law and then grabbed Alex in a rugby tackle.

'Aargh, leave me alone,' Alex shrieked, giggling in delight. 'Will you come again soon?' he asked, when

Liam finally put him down and they moved out to the car.

'You come around and see us,' Anna said, immediately feeling a pang of guilt. 'I'll call your mum and arrange it.'

'When? Tomorrow?'

'You have school tomorrow,' Rachel reminded him, 'and Anna has to work.'

'So, when?' he persisted.

'How about next weekend?'

'Really?' Alex lit up.

'You bet,' Anna said, dropping a kiss on the tip of his nose.

Chapter 4

Jill stretched languorously as she listened to Andy singing in the shower. She would be late for work if he didn't get a move on but she didn't care. Making love was a wonderful way to start the week. Anyway, she'd been working hard all night, she realized, chuckling to herself. She and her team had been trying to come up with an idea for a sponsorship deal for a lingerie company for weeks and it had suddenly come to her – in a manner of speaking – when she and Andy were rolling around on her lambskin rug in front of the fire.

Grabbing her red silk robe, Jill swung her short but shapely legs out of bed and went into the bathroom. 'Come on, darling, I'm going to be late.'

He ducked his head around the shower door and grinned. 'Well, if you're going to be late anyway . . .'

Returning his smile, Jill shrugged out of her robe and walked over to him, enjoying his eyes on her body. 'You are a very bad influence, you know that?' she murmured.

'I certainly hope so,' he said, reaching out and pulling her into the shower.

An hour later, Jill climbed into her beloved Audi TT, popped on her shades and roared into the city on her short journey to ADLI Advertising. As she weaved her way in and out of traffic, she sang loudly and tapped the steering wheel in time with the song on the radio. Jill hadn't had any breakfast but didn't feel remotely hungry. That was the wonderful thing about sex. It seemed to satisfy her appetite in every way!

What a great start to her new diet. This one she knew would work, she'd read all about it on the internet. It was called the Neander-Thin and was based on what cavemen used to eat – meat, fish, nuts and berries. How could she fail? She pulled in her stomach and groaned as she thought of all the Naan bread she'd eaten and the wine she'd consumed at the restaurant last night. She hadn't meant to, but Andy had said he thought she was sexy and curvaceous and that had been the end of all her good intentions. But today, without the effects of wine clouding her judgement, Jill was determined to start her diet and lose a stone. She had tried numerous diets but none of them seemed to suit her. She was sure Neander-Thin was the answer. Of course, Anna would laugh at her for going on yet another diet.

'Just cut out the booze and sweet things, Jill,' her cousin advised on a regular basis but Jill knew it was much more complicated than that. Anna, a lifelong skinny, didn't understand. Rachel often agreed to join her cousin in her efforts to lose some weight but she was in a different league as far as Jill was concerned. Sure, Rachel was bigger than she had been before Alex was born, but Jill would bet she was still way under ten stone and that was cuddly rather than fat in her book. But it was impossible to convince Rachel that there was nothing wrong with her body. Once she got something into her head, Jill knew from experience, it was hard to shake it out.

Jill swung her convertible into her reserved parking spot, grabbed her Firenze tote bag and hurried through the door of the ultra-modern office block that housed ADLI Advertising. Breezing through Reception, she said hello to Lindsay, the receptionist, and flashed a smile at the cute courier standing at the desk. She passed the lift and took the stairs to the third floor. As she puffed her way up she concentrated on the calories she was burning and how gorgeous she'd look in that new red dress she'd bought at the weekend. When she arrived breathless outside her office, Karen her assistant was biting into a cream slice. Jill stared at her aghast. 'What are you doing? What about our diet?'

'But it's Bob's birthday – he bought cakes for the whole office. It would have been rude to refuse.' Karen tried to look guilty and failed.

'You are just so weak,' Jill said sternly.

'I kept you an éclair; it's on your desk.'

Jill beamed at her. 'Cheers.'

As she sat down at her desk and eyed the éclair with a mixture of relish and dismay, her phone rang. 'ADLI, Jill Clarke speaking.'

'Hi, Jill.'

'Anna, how the hell are you?'

'Not as good as you, by the sound of it. What has you so chipper on a Monday morning?'

Jill leaned back in her swivel chair. 'It's a beautiful, sunny day, I have my health – oh, and the most gorgeous man made me late for work.'

'It's still on with Handy Andy then?'

'Don't call him that, although I must admit, he's certainly handy.' Jill chuckled.

'I'm glad it's going so well. Just promise me that you'll give this one a chance?'

'I don't know what you mean.'

'Yes, you do. Anyway, enough about you, I want to talk about my sister.'

'Rachel?'

'Do I have another?'

'What about her?' Jill hedged.

Anna's voice dropped and Jill could imagine her hugging the phone to her ear in the tiny estate agent's. 'She told me something yesterday, but swore me to secrecy.'

'Oh yes?'

'She's pregnant,' Anna hissed.

'Good at keeping secrets, aren't you?' Jill murmured. 'Is she happy about it? I'd say Gary's chuffed.'

'Well, that's just it. She hasn't told him yet. Isn't that totally weird? Why on earth would she want to keep it a secret from her own husband? Unless . . . God, you don't think—'

'Don't be silly,' Jill cut her off. 'Rachel would never dream of cheating on Gary.'

'Still, it would explain—'

'Anna, don't be ridiculous! It's probably all been a bit of a shock. Give her a chance to get used to the idea.'

'You already knew, didn't you?' Anna said.

'I sort of guessed.'

'Crikey, you don't miss much, Sherlock, do you?'

'Elementary, my dear. Now, I really must go. I have a mountain of work to do.' Jill's eyes returned to the éclair.

'Promise me you'll talk to her?'

'But what do you want me to say? I'm not supposed to know, remember?'

'You can tell her the truth, that you guessed. Please, Jill?'

'Yes, yes, okay then. I'll call her tonight.'

'Angel.' Anna blew a kiss down the phone. 'Let me know how you get on.'

Jill hung up, wolfed down her cake and then went back to the doorway of her office. 'Karen, could you call the team working on the Cauldwell's Lingerie account and ask them to meet me in the boardroom in fifteen minutes?'

'Yes, Boss.' Karen continued to rummage in her bag.

'As soon as you can.' Jill bristled. It was probably a mistake being too friendly with Karen. She was inclined to take advantage.

'Yeah, yeah, just let me find a tissue, would you? Damned hay fever.'

Jill belatedly noted the girl's red nose and her watery eyes. 'Sorry,' she muttered and went back into her office. She knew she'd spend the rest of the day paying for this. How come she could be tough with them all, apart from Karen?

'Everyone can make it except Vinny,' Karen told her a few minutes later. 'He did stop by earlier to talk to you about it but you weren't in. He left you a note.'

'Ta.' As Karen left, Jill spotted the tiny yellow Post-it stuck to the edge of her diary. *Sorry I missed you. At meetings all day. Back at 5.30.* The note was marked 9.45.

'Bastard,' Jill muttered. Vinny must have been thrilled that she was late. And now he was making sure she stayed late, too – not that she'd any intention of leaving before six. No one could accuse her of not putting in the hours; this morning was a once-off. Most days she made a point of being in before her team and staying after they'd left. Bloody typical that the little toad Vinny Gray should come looking for her, today of all days. And she would bet a fiver that he'd mentioned it to her boss, Sue Boyle, before he'd left.

Not that Sue would take any notice of him, of course. She could spot a crawler like Vinny at fifty paces. Pity he was so good at his job, Jill thought with a sigh. It would be such a pleasure to get rid of him. But apart from rubbing her up the wrong way, Vinny hadn't put a foot wrong. He was definitely after her job. 'Not a chance, mate,' she said out loud as she thought of her brilliant idea for the Cauldwell's Lingerie sponsorship. She couldn't wait to tell the team and put a presentation together for Sue. This would definitely be a feather in her cap.

'So I think this is the perfect sponsorship for Cauldwell's Lingerie,' Jill said in closing. 'The Miss Ireland competition has everything Cauldwell's are looking for in a campaign.' She ticked the points off on her fingers. 'Very high profile, long duration and it exactly targets the lingerie market. What do you think?' She looked around at their faces.

'It's good,' Michelle said cautiously, not quite meeting Jill's eye.

Jill blinked. 'Good?'

'Yeah,' Gerry agreed, 'but I think Vinny's idea is better.'

Jill swallowed hard. 'Vinny's come up with an idea? He never mentioned it to me.'

'He did try,' Rebecca rushed to his defence, 'but you weren't in.'

Ollie nodded in agreement. 'So he gathered us together because he knew he'd be out for the rest of the day and he wanted to see what we thought.'

Jill forced a smile that was more like a grimace. 'Well, is someone going to tell me about this wonderful idea?'

Gerry coughed nervously before starting to explain. His nervousness disappeared almost instantly as he got carried away by his own enthusiasm, and as he talked Jill could understand why. 'So, to summarise: by sponsoring a breast cancer charity, Cauldwell's will get a very high profile, target women specifically, and I think the worthiness of the sponsorship speaks for itself.'

With a sick feeling in the pit of her stomach, Jill realized that Vinny's idea left hers for dead. 'Well,' she said when Gerry had finished, 'that sounds like a winner to me.'

A wave of relief went around the table. 'You like it?' Michelle asked.

'It's brilliant,' Jill announced. 'I think we should put a presentation together for Sue right away.'

Ollie frowned. 'Shouldn't we wait until Vinny gets back?'

Jill fixed him with a steady gaze. 'We work as a team here, Ollie. Vinny told you the idea so that it could be progressed. Let's not waste any more time. Our customer has been waiting long enough.'

For the next hour they discussed the charities they could approach and knocked together a shortlist to put before Sue. 'Right, guys, thanks.' Jill stood up and gathered her papers. 'I'll let you know what the boss says. If she's happy with it, we'll take it to the customer tomorrow.'

'Will Vinny be doing the presentation?' Rebecca asked.

'Not my decision, but of course, I will suggest that.' Jill nodded at the others and left the room.

She was back in her office before she let herself breathe again. 'Bastard, bastard, bastard!' she groaned as she slipped behind her desk, sat down and kicked off her shoes. She felt completely crushed by that little slimeball and he hadn't even been at the meeting. The realization that Vinny's idea was way better than her own was devastating. For the first time, Jill began to question her ability. Maybe she wasn't quite as good as she thought.

'Rubbish!' she admonished herself, recalling the dozens of excellent campaigns she'd come up with over the years. Maybe she was just tired or needed a break. Or maybe there were too many distractions in her life. She thought of Andy and how he'd made her late for work this morning. That wouldn't be happening again, she promised herself. She was going to have to watch Vinny Gray. She had underestimated him. Now she'd have to praise him lavishly to Sue, insist that he do the presentation to Cauldwell's and watch her back every minute of every day from now on.

Chapter 5

Despite her own worries, Jill did remember to phone Rachel as she'd promised Anna. 'How are you?' she asked.

'I'm fine,' Rachel said, sounding anything but.

'Let's go for a pint,' Jill suggested.

'Can't. Gary's out.'

'Then I'll come over.'

'Oh – okay then.'

Ignoring the lack of enthusiasm in her cousin's voice, Jill hung up and hotfooted it over to Malahide, stopping at an off-licence on the way. After some hesitation, she bought two bottles of wine.

When Rachel opened the door, she raised her eyebrows at the two bottles. 'It is only Monday, Jill.'

'One is non-alcoholic,' Jill told her, as Rachel led the way into the living room.

'Ah.'

'Now, where's the corkscrew?'

'Anna shouldn't have told you,' Rachel said when they were seated with glasses in their hands.

'She didn't have to,' Jill said gently. 'I'd already guessed. But why the secrecy?'

'Oh, I don't know. I just haven't found the right moment to tell Gary.'

'Don't you think he'll be happy about it?'

'Yes, of course. Don't worry, I'll tell him. Now, how are things with you?'

Jill allowed her cousin to dismiss the subject. She knew from experience that Rachel wouldn't talk until she was ready. 'I've had a pig of a day. I really screwed up.' She prattled on about Cauldwell's and Vinny and watched her cousin relax before her eyes. It never ceased to amaze her that Rachel seemed to accept her career without question but resented Anna's, visibly bristling when her sister even mentioned her job. But then Rachel had always been a bit in awe of her older sister. Jill sometimes thought that the only reason Rachel had got married and had Alex was because she wanted to beat her sister to it. She seemed to need to be first at something. Of course, Anna was completely oblivious to this.

Rachel had abandoned the non-alcoholic wine and gone to make some camomile tea. 'It calms me down and keeps me from strangling Gary and Alex,' she joked when she returned.

'Is Gary still working long hours?' Jill asked, topping up her own glass.

'Yeah, never stops, God love him.'

'You don't sound very happy about it.'

'Oh, I just get a bit fed up being on my own all the time.'

'You need to get out more. Stop depending on Gary for your social life. Do something different.'

'Like what?'

'I don't know – yoga, dance classes, bridge.'

Rachel stared at her. 'I'm twenty-fucking-eight, Jill. I should be out clubbing, for God's sake, not playing bridge!'

'Then do it,' Jill shot back.

'Yeah, right.'

'I'm serious. Come out some night with Anna and me. We could make a night of it. It's been ages.'

Rachel looked dubious at the mention of her sister.

'Oh, come on,' Jill urged. 'It would be fun.'

'Anna will probably be too busy to go out with us.'

'Of course she won't, I'll ask her. How about Wednesday?'

Rachel looked taken aback. 'What – *this* Wednesday?'

'Why not? If Gary's working you can always get a babysitter.'

Rachel looked vaguely surprised at the idea. 'I suppose. Linda next door is always offering to look after Alex and he worships her.'

'There you are then.' Rachel glanced at her watch and stood up. 'I'll call Anna in the morning.'

'Are you going already?' Rachel looked disappointed.

'I need to be in at the crack of dawn tomorrow,' Jill said, kissing her cousin's cheek. 'I have some knives to sharpen. But I'll call you about the arrangements. And Rachel?'

'Yes?'

'Phone me when you're ready to talk.'

'Talk?'

'About the baby, about Gary.' Jill shrugged and smiled. 'Hell, about the price of petrol if you like.'

Rachel hugged her fiercely. 'Thanks, Jill.'

Anna was waiting outside a small, drab terraced house in Kinsealy at ten o'clock the next morning when her mobile rang. Jill was between meetings and hurriedly filled Anna in on the proposed night out. Anna agreed readily although her enthusiasm dwindled when she heard her sister was going.

'It will be fun,' Jill said firmly and rang off.

Anna had her doubts, but she didn't have time to think about it right now as the young couple who had come to view number seventeen were getting out of their car.

'Hello, there,' she smiled and switched into business mode. 'Susan?'

The girl nodded. 'And this is Damien, my boyfriend.'

'Nice to meet you.' Anna held out her hand and after a moment's hesitation the man took it.

Anna withdrew from the limp handshake and turned to open the door. 'Shall we go in?' She led the couple around the small house, pointing out the marble fireplace (a very strange orange colour), the Aga (way too big and imposing for the small, plastic kitchen) and the wonderful storage (dark brown hulking great wardrobes that dwarfed the bedrooms and shut out the natural light.) 'Very well maintained,' she said as they stood in the tiny back garden. Well, that wasn't a lie. There was sod-all in the garden to maintain!

'It's a bit poky,' the man complained.

'Oh, but it's so cosy!' His girlfriend snuggled in against his arm. 'I'm sure I could make it into a wonderful little home for us.'

'It's overpriced,' he muttered, moving away from her, 'and what about that field at the back? They could build a bloody factory there for all we know.'

'It's actually zoned as a green area,' Anna told him with a pleasant smile.

'Huh, that's what they say *now*,' he snorted.

Anna kept the smile fixed firmly on her face. 'Shall we move on to the next house?'

'Yes, please.' Susan beamed at her. 'It's in Ashgrove Lane, isn't it? That's such a lovely road.'

Her partner frowned. 'I don't think we can afford a house in that area.'

'It's only five thousand more than this house,' Anna told them as she locked up and led the way out to her car. 'The owners want a quick sale.'

'Why, what's wrong with it?' he replied.

Anna suppressed a sigh. 'Not a thing, I assure you.

They're emigrating and they need to sell up before they can afford to buy a place.'

Poor Susan, Anna thought as she drove the couple down to the next property. There was no way this guy was buying this or any other house. He would come up with every excuse in the book, and after stringing Susan along for a while he'd dump her and move on to the next unfortunate. Anna had seen it all before. Dublin seemed to be full of women just dying to settle down with their partners even though they were patently Mr Wrongs. The men, however, were content to stay with their mammies. 'Do you have your own house to sell, Damien?'

'Oh no, Damien lives with his parents,' Susan told her and received a glare from her partner. Anna suppressed a grin as she pulled up outside 42, Ashgrove Lane.

This was going to be a complete waste of time but then that's what the property world was all about. She'd have these two back on the street in fifteen minutes and then she could concentrate on the three valuations that had to be done before lunch.

'I'll let you wander around on your own,' she said, ushering them into the hallway. 'Just shout if you need me.' She didn't normally let clients do this but the house was already empty and she could check back with the office while Damien came up with excuses of why this house wouldn't suit.

She dialled the number and Val answered in a

sing-song voice, 'Donnelly's Real Estate, Val speaking, can I help you?'

'It's me.'

'Oh hi, Anna. Any luck offloading that place in Kinsealy?'

'No chance. I'm in Ashgrove now but I don't expect a bite here either.' She lowered her voice. 'The guy has no intention of buying.'

'Poor girl,' Val said, immediately understanding the situation. Like Anna, she'd seen it all before. Sometimes she felt more like a social worker or counsellor than an estate agent. She was glad she didn't have to show desperate girls and reluctant boyfriends around properties any more. Running the office suited her much better and Anna was more than capable of doing the job on her own now. 'Well, I wouldn't waste too much time on them. I have a couple more properties for you to value this afternoon.'

Anna frowned. 'That may be a problem. I have three to do this morning, and then I think Mark was trying to arrange a lunch meeting with Charlie Coleman.'

'Was he? Hang on, let me check.'

Anna hummed along to 'Greensleeves' while she waited.

'Anna? Yes, Mark says to meet him in Cruzzo's at twelve-thirty.'

'Right, then you'd better phone those clients and put them off until tomorrow. I've a feeling this might be a long lunch.'

'If Charlie Coleman has his way, you won't get out of there before three.'

'You know him? What's he like?' Anna was curious about this client that Mark was so keen to impress.

'Nice lad, something really big in computers – don't ask me what. Seems to be loaded.'

'How old?' Val used the term 'lad' for men anywhere between fifteen and fifty.

'Not much older than you, probably, although he's a bit thin on top so that makes him look older.'

'How come you know him?'

'Oh, his parents live in Malahide and his grand-parents before them – lovely family.'

'Is he married?'

'I don't think so. There was some scandal a few years back about him getting a teenager into trouble, but as far as I know he's still single.'

'Interesting,' Anna murmured as she heard Susan and Damien coming back. 'Look, I've got to go, Val. Talk to you later.' She turned around as the couple joined her. 'Everything okay?'

Susan looked as if she might burst into tears. 'It's really lovely but probably not for us.'

'Oh?'

'A bit big for our needs,' Damien grunted.

'Just a few square feet bigger than the last house,' Anna said, holding his gaze.

'And I'm not keen on the redbrick front.'

'How unusual, most people love redbrick. Still, to

each his own. Sorry you don't like it.' She looked at Susan.

'Oh, I do! Still, it's important that we buy something we're both happy with.' She slipped her arm through Damien's and gave Anna a brave smile.

'I'll drop you back to your car then, but please contact me if there's anything else I can do for you.'

'Oh, we will. We're going to keep looking, aren't we, Damien? The perfect little place is out there for us somewhere.'

Damien muttered something unintelligible as they piled back into Anna's car.

The rest of Anna's morning passed in a flurry of measuring and negotiating. The number of clients who thought their houses were worth more than they actually were was incredible, and it wasn't always easy to persuade them to be a little more realistic. Mr Delaney and his dingy house in Marlboro Road was a perfect example. Mind you, if he gave his house a bloody good clean he might actually get four-twenty for it but Mark positively forbade her from telling him so.

Anna pulled into the restaurant's car park, and took out her make-up bag. She turned around the rearview mirror, reapplied her mascara and lipstick and ran a comb through her hair. Slipping out of her driving shoes and into her heels, she stepped out of the car, put her bag on her shoulder and went inside.

She was glad she'd worn her cream linen suit. While it was very businesslike, the tight skirt stopped just above her knee, showing off her slim, tanned legs. The waiter obviously appreciated the view.

'Good afternoon, miss, can I help you?'

'Hi. I'm at Mark Donnelly's table.'

'You're the first to arrive. Would you like to take a seat here or would you prefer to go up to the table?'

'Here's fine.' She sat down on a comfortable leather sofa and tossed her bag on the table. 'Could I have a sparkling water, please?'

'Of course, and I'll bring you a menu.'

The waiter had just returned with her drink when a man of medium height, with a receding hair-line and a deep tan walked in. 'I'm meeting Mark Donnelly,' he announced loudly.

Anna stood up as the waiter led him over. 'Mr Coleman? I'm Anna Gallagher, I work with Mark.'

Charlie grinned, showing off a row of even white teeth, and gripped her hand in his. 'Lovely to meet you, Anna. Please call me Charlie.'

'Can I get you a drink?' she asked as he took the seat next to her.

'A pint of Heineken, please,' Charlie asked the waiter and then turned back to Anna. 'So you work for Mark? You must be new.'

She shook her head. 'No, I've been with Donnelly's a couple of years now.'

'Strange we haven't met before. Mark and I go

way back. I played rugby with his little brother.'

'Then you might know my husband, Liam Harrison?'

Charlie frowned and shook his head. 'Name doesn't ring a bell. How old is he?'

'Thirty-three.'

'Ah, way after my time then,' Charlie chuckled. 'I must have been on my third job by the time he left school.'

Anna smiled and handed him a menu. 'I don't know where Mark's got to but we might as well have a look at the menu.'

'Sounds good,' Charlie agreed. 'I forgot to have breakfast.'

'Forgot?'

He shrugged. 'I work best in the early morning, and when my cleaning lady comes in she usually brings me some tea and toast. If she's not in, I don't bother.' He patted his waist. 'Probably not a bad thing.'

'So Mark tells me you're looking for a property with a view.'

'Oh, time for business, is it?'

His brown eyes twinkled at her and she felt herself blushing. 'If you'd prefer to wait for Mark . . .'

He shook his head and laughed. 'I'm just pulling your leg, Anna. Yes, a view of the sea would be nice.'

'And you want to stay close to Malahide?'

'Yes, well, this is where my folks are and now that

they're getting on a bit, I'd like to have a place nearby. Also, I need some land for my daughter's pony.'

Anna made a quick note of that in her diary. 'We have a couple of properties on our books that might suit you. I could show you them today if you like, or would you prefer to arrange another time when your wife is free?'

Charlie burst out laughing. 'Now you're fishing, Anna.'

She flushed again. 'I'm sorry, I didn't mean to—'

'I'm just teasing. Look, I'm not married. Sophie was the result of a drunken day out at a David Bowie concert in Slane Castle.'

'Oh.'

'Best mistake I ever made,' he said. 'Thankfully, our parents didn't try to push us into marriage so we agreed to raise Sophie as a member of both families. Jeri, that's Sophie's mother, is married now and has two other kids. They're moving to Galway next month – her husband has got some big job down there – but Sophie doesn't want to move to a new school so she's going to stay in Dublin with me.'

'That must be very hard on her mother.'

'Yeah, but Jeri's got her hands full with the other two, and once Sophie does her Leaving Certificate next year, she can decide whether she's going to go to college in Dublin or Galway.'

Anna frowned. 'So wouldn't it be better to rent somewhere until she decides?'

Charlie raised an eyebrow. 'If your boss could hear you trying to talk me out of a sale . . .'

'Don't worry,' Anna joked, 'if we don't sell you a property, we'll rent you one.'

'No, I'm not interested in renting,' he told her. 'I've been meaning to invest in some property for a while. God knows, my money isn't making anything in the banks.'

'Well, as I said, we have a couple of properties I think might interest you. One needs a bit of work, but it could be amazing.'

He shrugged. 'Work doesn't bother me. As long as the location is right and there's somewhere to keep the pony. Sophie's nuts about that bloody animal.'

Anna's mobile phone trilled and she excused herself as she answered it. 'Mark, hi.' She listened intently for a moment. 'Okay, that's fine. Yes, he's here, would you like a word?' She handed the phone over to Charlie.

'Mark? What's up? Oh, don't worry about it, Anna's looking after me.' He winked at her. 'Right, then. Okay, talk to you later. Bye.' He gave the phone back to her. 'Looks like it's just you and me.'

'Then let's order, I'm famished.'

Lunch was far from businesslike as Charlie entertained Anna with stories from his schooldays in Malahide, his travels in the States and his business. He had been working in the accounts department of a large retailer when he started designing websites for friends. It had brought in a little extra money and relieved his boredom, but through word of mouth it had taken off and now his company, D-ZineIT, was one of the top website design companies in Europe, employing sixty staff.

'So where's your head office?' Anna asked, fascinated.

'There isn't one. My staff are all over the place; a couple of them are in Dublin, a lot over on the west coast, and I've more than twenty people in Belgium, France and Germany.'

'Amazing. You must do a lot of travelling.'

'Not really. Most of my business can be taken care of over the phone or through email and conference calls.'

'That's fantastic.'

'You should have a look at my website and tell me what you think.'

'I don't think that my opinion would be of much value. Apart from email I'm not really au fait with the internet.'

Charlie's eyes widened. 'You mean you don't even shop? I'm going to have to take you in hand, Anna.'

She grinned. 'We'll have none of that, Mr Coleman, I'm a married woman!'

'Just my luck,' he sighed. 'Never mind, I will do my best to keep my hands off you and concentrate on houses.'

'I would appreciate that,' she laughed.

'Now, how about some coffee?'

She checked her watch. 'We should really be making a move if we're to view both properties today.'

He smiled. 'Then let's go.'

After a brief argument, Charlie allowed her to pay for lunch. 'It's on Mark's business account,' Anna assured him.

'I've never enjoyed business as much before.'

'That's because you're usually just sitting in front of a screen,' she told him, leading the way out to the car.

'Let's go in mine,' he suggested.

'Okay then, where is it?' She looked around the almost empty car park.

'Right here.' He pointed at the large Kawasaki bike parked outside the door.

'You must be joking.' Suddenly his casual white shirt, jeans and leather jacket made sense. She shook her head as he handed her a helmet. 'I can't go on that in this!' She gestured at her tight, knee-length skirt.

He grinned. 'Oh go on, it'll be fun.'

'Not a chance! I'll drive. You can either come with me or follow – please yourself.'

With a dramatic sigh, Charlie put back the helmets and followed her. 'Are you always like this with your clients?' he asked, climbing into the passenger seat.

'I don't have any other clients like you,' Anna assured him.

'I think that might be a compliment,' he mused.

'It is.'

Anna drove the short distance to the first house, pulled up outside and went to the keypad on the pillar to open the imposing gates.

'Very impressive,' Charlie said as they drove in.

'You ain't seen nothing yet.' She guided the car up the long driveway lined with fir trees until it curved sharply and the house was in front of them.

'Crikey!' Charlie stared at the large period house with three chimneys, long sash windows and steps leading up to the imposing front door. 'I never knew this place existed. How long has it been here? Who the hell owns it?'

'Believe it or not, it's only three years old.' Anna drove around the house and pulled up at a side door. 'It was built by an actress who wanted the period look without the hassle of renovating and with all mod cons.'

'So why's she selling?'

'She worked on a soap but her character got killed off last year and she's been "resting" ever since.'

'I see. Well, I can tell you right now that I absolutely hate the place.'

Anna grinned. 'Thought so, but fancy having a look around anyway?'

'Love to.'

Chapter 6

'Hello, you! I was about to send out a search-party,' Liam remarked when Anna finally arrived home at nearly seven o'clock.

'Sorry.' She bent to kiss him. 'I was with a very important and very rich client.'

He abandoned his paper and pulled her down on to his lap. 'Did you make a sale?'

'No. I showed him two houses and he hated both of them.'

'Hard luck.'

'No, it's fine. Now I have a much better idea of what he's looking for. How was your day?' Anna slid down on to the sofa beside him and kicked off her shoes.

'Pretty good. Patterson's been shut up in the boardroom all day with Boylan and the accountant.'

'And that means?'

'Well, it's obvious, isn't it? I'd say they were working out his retirement package.'

Anna gaped at him. 'I had no idea that things were going to move this quickly.'

'Well, I didn't want to get your hopes up but I'd say Boylan will be gone by the end of the month.'

Anna planted a kiss on his cheek. 'And you'll be the new General Manager! Oh Liam, this is wonderful. I'm so proud of you. You've worked so hard.'

'It will mean more responsibility and probably longer hours,' Liam warned her.

Anna sighed. 'That seems to be the price of success. Rachel's always complaining about the hours that Gary works.'

'It's the only way to get on.'

'And I suppose if you do get promoted you'll be taking up golf,' she groaned.

'Not if, when,' he corrected, standing up. 'I'll have to, won't I?' He did an imaginary swing. 'Maybe I should get Gary to take me out a few times. Don't want to look a total novice, do I?'

'God forbid,' Anna laughed, going out to the kitchen in search of something to eat. 'Okay, it's beans on toast, toasted cheese sandwiches or scrambled eggs on toast.'

Liam followed her out. 'Anything with no toast?'

Anna smiled sweetly. 'Cheese sandwiches?'

'Toasted sandwiches it is.' He opened the fridge to get a beer. 'Want one?'

'Yeah, why not? Though on top of the wine at lunchtime I probably shouldn't.'

'You were boozing at lunchtime?'

'Yeah, in Cruzzo's.'

Liam raised an eyebrow. 'I didn't know Mark's

budget stretched to treating clients to fancy lunches.'

Anna felt herself blush. 'This guy is loaded so Mark wanted to give him the red-carpet treatment.'

'I see. Well, it's good that he's willing to let you handle the bigger customers. Does this mean you'll get all the commission if you make the sale?'

Anna wrinkled her nose. 'I haven't asked.'

'You should, my love. Don't let him walk all over you.'

She turned to face him, bread knife in hand. 'I tell you what. You handle Patterson and I'll handle Mark, okay?'

Liam looked nervously at the knife. 'Yes, darling, sorry, darling.'

'Idiot.' Anna went back to cutting the bread and wondered why she hadn't told Liam that she and Charlie had had lunch alone. 'I'm going out with Jill and Rachel tomorrow night,' she said instead.

'Rachel?'

'There's no need to sound so surprised.'

He held up his hands. 'I'm not saying a word. If you and your beloved sister fancy a girly night out that's your business. I'm sure you'll have a great time.' He snorted.

Anna scowled at him. 'I'm sure we will too. Oh Liam, don't be so hard on the girl. She's having a tough time at the moment.'

'Oh – why? What's up?'

'Nothing, nothing,' Anna said hastily. 'Just women's troubles.'

'Oh, right,' Liam took his beer and wandered back to the television.

Anna smiled. 'Women's troubles.' The two words guaranteed to shut up every man! Though she wouldn't admit it to Liam, Anna wasn't really looking forward to tomorrow night. Normally she'd jump at the chance of a night out with Jill, but with Rachel tagging along it was bound to be hard work. And now they couldn't even pour a few drinks into her to loosen her up.

Anna slipped the sandwiches under the grill. It was very hard to understand why Rachel wasn't over the moon at the idea of another baby when she herself couldn't wait to start a family. She'd heard of women suffering from post-natal depression but ante-natal depression was a new one on her. And imagine not telling Gary she was pregnant. Anna would never keep stuff like that from Liam. They had always shared their problems, whether personal or work. Liam was her friend, her soulmate, her lover. What kind of marriage would it be if they kept things from each other? An image of Charlie Coleman suddenly came to mind and Anna dismissed it. That was different. That had been harmless flirting – something Liam probably indulged in on a regular basis.

Anna was shaken out of her reverie by the smell of burning and she hurriedly rescued the sandwiches, scraped off the black bits and called her husband.

'So where are you going tomorrow night?' he asked as they ate.

'Dunno, Jill is organizing everything.'

'You don't seem very keen,' he said.

'I'm not,' she admitted. 'It's just that I've a busy week ahead and I'd much prefer a quiet night in.'

Liam pretended to choke on his sandwich. '*You* want a quiet night in? Who are you and what have you done with my real wife?'

Anna laughed. 'Maybe I'm getting old.'

'That must be it. You're ready to stay at home and mind babies.' He winked at her. 'Never thought I'd see the day!'

'Are you going out after training tomorrow night?' Anna asked.

He shook his head. 'No chance. I've an early meeting with Patterson on Thursday.'

'So if I cancelled Jill and Rachel, you and I could have a quiet night in, I suppose.'

He stroked her knee under the table. 'If you play your cards right.'

'You are going,' Jill told her the next morning when she got the call.

'But Jill—'

'I don't want to hear it, Anna. See you at eight-thirty.'

'That's very early, I'm not sure—'

'Eight-thirty at Rachel's. Be there.' And Jill hung up.

'Thanks.' Anna put down the phone and glared out the window.

'Something wrong?' Val asked.

'Just being press-ganged into going out tonight.'

'How terrible,' Val teased. 'I hate it when that happens.'

'Oh, don't start,' Anna moaned. 'You've no idea what a difficult night it's going to be.'

'Why's that then?'

'Because my sister will be there,' Anna replied without thinking.

'And that's a problem?' Val looked concerned.

Anna gave an embarrassed laugh. 'No, it's just that she's a bit down at the moment and not much fun.'

'And isn't that when she needs her sister most?' Val chided her.

'It is indeed, you're quite right, Val.' Anna picked up some papers and escaped to the photocopier. She felt riddled with guilt now for saying anything derogatory about Rachel. She was her sister, for God's sake, and even if she was annoying at times she was family and you didn't talk about your family like that. At least Anna didn't.

She hadn't even told Liam how upset she'd felt when Mam and Dad decided to sell the house and leave the country to travel the length and breadth of Europe. There was something so final about the sale of their family home, and it had been hard to put on a brave face and wish her parents well. And Anna did wish them well, she really did, but she still missed them and often wished they'd been content to stay put and veg out in front of the telly like most normal parents. Anna had often wondered if Rachel felt the same, but had never asked. Her sister hadn't seemed bothered on the face of it, but whether that was for real or just a front, Anna had no idea.

'Oh Jill, I'm really not in the mood for this,' Rachel was telling her cousin.

'Don't even think about pulling out,' Jill ordered, distinctly fed up with both sisters. 'I organized tonight for your benefit, remember?'

'I'm not some kind of charity case,' Rachel retorted, stung.

'I'm not saying you are, but you did say you should be out clubbing, so tonight, you're going clubbing.'

'Okay.'

'Sorry, did you mutter something?'

'I said okay, okay?'

'Try to contain your enthusiasm. I'll call for you at eight-thirty. Be ready.'

Dragging herself upstairs, Rachel went into the bedroom and opened her wardrobe to see if she possessed any suitable clubbing clothes that could compete with her gorgeous sister or voluptuous cousin. As she trawled through the wardrobe, Rachel thought how old and dated everything looked. Sensible clothes of a stay-at-home mother. Sweatshirts, cotton tops, drawstring trousers and leggings. Stuff that didn't require too much ironing and that didn't draw attention to the thickened thighs or bulging stomach.

And when had she stopped wearing colours? Everything she owned seemed to be pale and washed-out and mumsy. God, it was depressing. She pulled out the pair of tailored black stretch trousers that she always ended up wearing when she had to get dressed up. She could wear the silky grey halter-neck top with them that she'd bought for Gary's Christmas party, but her arms were too fat and pale to be exposed. The red shirt was out because it showed off every lump and bump and accentuated her red cheeks – why had she ever bought it? That left the black V-neck velvet top – which made her boobs look nice, but velvet seemed a bit warm for Summer – or her white shirt, the Old Reliable. She'd have to leave the last button open but at least she didn't feel so bad about that now that there was a baby inside. With her high black shoes and plenty of make-up she should look reasonably presentable.

Rachel sank on to the bed with a sigh. Being presentable was all very well but she'd prefer to look like a babe. She'd prefer to make men's heads turn, to get chatted up when she went to the bar, maybe even be asked to dance. It would be so nice to feel sexy and fanciable. Gary sometimes told her she was sexy but that didn't count because it was usually said after a few drinks and accompanied by a hand on her leg. Men would say anything at a time like that.

Rachel quite enjoyed sex with Gary. He knew her body well and for a short time she could close her eyes and imagine she was sexy and beautiful. But even their adequate love-life would come to a halt once Gary found out about the baby. He'd been terrified to come near her when she was pregnant with Alex for fear of hurting the baby – as if! But, on the other hand, he had looked after her, cosseted her and been so tender and thoughtful that Rachel would gladly trade her predictable sex-life for some more of that.

Rachel decided to tell him about the baby tonight when she got home. She had to do it soon, now that Jill and Anna knew. All she needed was for Anna to tell Liam and Liam to say something to Gary and then she'd be in real trouble. He would be disgusted that she had confided in her sister before telling him. Rightly so, as she knew her mother would say. God, how she missed her mother! It was lovely getting her postcards every couple of weeks but it wasn't the same as sitting down over a cuppa and having a really good chat.

Rachel would have loved to tell her mam about the baby and confide her fears about having a second child but there was no way you could have a conversation like that on the phone. Perhaps when the school term finished she'd take Alex to visit her parents somewhere for a few days. It would be nice to have a break and Alex would be thrilled to see his granny and grandad. Rachel took the black trousers and went downstairs to press them, feeling slightly happier. The thought of seeing her mam suddenly made all of her problems seem manageable.

Chapter 7

'So where are we going?' Anna asked when they were in the taxi and heading for the city centre.

'I thought Renards – we could have something to eat there,' Jill replied as she checked her lipstick in a small compact mirror. 'And if it's too quiet we could head round to the Viperoom.'

'Where?' Rachel frowned, not having heard of either of these clubs. 'What's wrong with Club M?'

Anna giggled and rolled her eyes at Jill. 'Oh Rachel, you're *so* out of touch.'

'Well, I'm sorry but I'm a little bit busy being a full-time mother to keep up with all the trendy nightspots that I never get to visit.'

'Lord, you'd think you had a dozen children, to listen to you.'

'Ladies, ladies, please,' Jill cut in. 'We're going out to enjoy ourselves and let our hair down, remember?' She didn't think she could cope if the two of them started tonight. After having to sit smiling as that little shit Vinny presented his sponsorship plans to the ecstatic senior management of Cauldwell's, Jill felt exhausted and would have much preferred to curl up on her sofa with a large glass of wine and a box of chocolates.

The taxi pulled up outside Renards and she pushed 25 Euros into the driver's hand. 'Keep the change. Right, girls, let's go.'

'Let me give you something towards the taxi fare.' Rachel started to rummage in her bag.

'You can buy the first round.' Jill propelled her towards the door. 'Mine's a double.'

After they all had a drink in front of them, Jill did what she usually did when she wanted to relax the sisters; she steered the conversation around to their escapades when they were children.

'You were always causing trouble,' Rachel told her big sister, 'but Mum always blamed me. You could do no wrong.'

Anna looked incredulous. 'That's rich! You were always nicking my stuff and listening in when I was talking to my friends. You don't know how lucky you were, Jill, being an only child.'

'I had you two instead though, didn't I? Telling tales on each other, playing tricks on each other.'

'We weren't that bad,' Anna protested, looking at her sister for support.

'Not at all!' Rachel confirmed. 'Family rows are what prepare you for going out into the big bad world.'

'So how did *I* cope?' Jill asked.

Anna winked at her. 'Like you said, You had us!'

'Ah right, I see. Are you still drinking water, Rachel?' Jill signalled to a waiter.

Rachel made a face. 'No, get me one of those alcohol-free beers.'

'They're disgusting,' Anna said, wrinkling her nose.

'I know, but there's only so much water I can drink.'

'What about an alcohol-free cocktail?' Jill suggested.

'Oh, yes!' Rachel looked hopefully at the waiter.

'We have a selection,' he told her. 'I'll bring you the list.'

The cocktail list was impressive and Anna and Jill decided to try one too. 'Plenty of alcohol in mine,' Jill warned the waiter.

'Yes, madam.' He smiled and left.

Jill stared after him. 'Madam? God, do I look old enough to be a madam?' She leaned forward to examine her reflection in the glass table. 'That new cream isn't working. Look at all the lines around my mouth.'

'They're scratches on the table,' Anna told her. 'And you look gorgeous as always.'

Jill was wearing a very sexy wrap top that emphasized her cleavage, and a short tight black skirt that showed off her wonderful legs.

'I need a lot more than face cream,' Rachel complained. 'I'm the youngest and I look the oldest.' Anna, three years her senior, was looking impossibly young and beautiful in powder-blue cotton cut-offs and a tiny strappy top that revealed her toned, tanned midriff.

'Of course you don't.' Anna waved an impatient hand at her sister.

'It's true,' Rachel insisted. 'I've let myself go. I'm sure Gary thinks so.'

Jill and Anna exchanged glances. 'Why do you say that?' Anna asked.

'Oh, I don't know.' Rachel shrugged, relieved that the waiter chose that moment to deliver their elaborate cocktails. She took a sip of her drink and smiled in delight. 'This is gorgeous!'

'Mine's lovely too,' Jill agreed, allowing Rachel to dismiss the comment, but she knew it hadn't been an idle one. She saw Anna open her mouth to question her sister and shot her a warning look.

'So when are you going to tell him?' Anna said instead.

Rachel spiked a piece of strawberry with her cocktail stick. 'Tell him what?'

'You know what.'

Rachel abandoned the strawberry and sat back in her seat. 'Probably tonight.'

'Really? That's great!'

'He'll be very happy, Rachel,' Jill added.

'Yes, of course he will.' Anna's smile was encouraging.

'I know.' Rachel forced a smile and then excused herself to go in search of the loo.

'Do you think she's okay?' Anna asked Jill when they were alone.

'Yeah, but I don't think she'd planned on having another child, at least not yet.'

'I don't understand that. It's not as if she has anything else to do. Now that Alex is at school you'd think she'd be delighted. I mean, what does she do all day?'

Jill shook her head, laughing. 'Oh, please don't say that to her.'

'Of course I won't. I'm not completely insensitive, you know! But I'd go nuts at home all day on my own. It seems so, so . . .' Anna searched for the right word '. . . boring. She certainly doesn't look like she's enjoying herself, does she?'

'Shush, she's coming,' Jill hissed and smiled broadly as Rachel returned. 'So, girls, how about a dance?'

As the evening wore on, Rachel relaxed a little although it didn't stop her sister irritating the hell out of her. As usual, after just a couple of cocktails, Anna was tipsy, giggly and bumping into everyone. But with a toss of her pretty head and a wide smile she'd sing 'Sorry!' and receive the inevitable indulgent smile and a 'That's okay.' Anna could do no wrong.

Jill bopped her heart out with her two cousins, sang along to all the lyrics and watched Rachel watch Anna. Her envy was understandable, she supposed.

Anna could get away with anything simply because it was clear that all she was doing was having fun. Rachel looked so like her, but her grim face and distant manner meant she was nowhere near as attractive as her sister. What, Jill wondered, would it take to put the smile back on to her face?

Anna sat back in the taxi and closed her eyes. She was feeling pleasantly woozy from the cocktails and footsore from dancing in her high shoes but it had been a good night, much better than she'd been expecting. While Rachel hadn't exactly let herself go, they'd had a few laughs and relations had definitely improved. And when Anna got out of the taxi to say goodbye to her sister, Rachel hadn't even pulled away when, on impulse, Anna had hugged her. Maybe a few more nights out was exactly what they needed.

Rachel definitely needed to loosen up. She had been spot on when she'd said she looked older than her sister and cousin. Her solemn manner and clothes made her look closer to forty than thirty. Anna had seen her in the same clothes on several occasions and those black trousers were positively shiny at this stage. Rachel could well afford to buy clothes but she just didn't seem interested.

Anna remembered the wonderful Saturday shopping sprees the three girls used to enjoy before Rachel got married. They rarely came home without a new outfit. But Rachel had stopped meeting them after she married Gary. In fact, everything had really changed once Gary came along.

Rachel had been dating a mad, charismatic, slightly unpredictable guy before she met her husband. Bridie was a bit concerned about the relationship because Eric didn't seem the most reliable sort of boyfriend, but he was a lovable rogue and even she couldn't resist him for long. When he decided to throw in his job and move to the States, Bridie and Shay were terrified that their twenty-year-old youngest daughter would go with him. But they didn't have to worry about that because it soon became clear that Rachel didn't figure in Eric's plan.

Rachel was devastated. Anna and Jill did their best to cheer her up but nothing worked. They were all amazed and delighted a couple of months later when Rachel announced she'd met someone and was going on a date. Gary Hanlon was not what they were expecting. He was as different from Eric as it was possible to be. Older than Rachel by three years, Gary was serious, conservative and very ambitious. When he proposed just six months after they met and Rachel accepted, her family were stunned. But she seemed happy so they wished her well and it all seemed to have worked out for the best.

When Alex came along a year after the wedding, he had adoring, delighted grandparents in Bridie and Shay and a thrilled Aunty Anna, only too eager to babysit. Life went on, but Rachel had assumed a new role and didn't have the same time or interest for shopping or girly nights out. Anna and Jill had continued their weekly shopping expeditions for a while but the junkets had petered out a couple of years ago when Jill moved in with one of her boyfriends who liked to spend Saturdays in bed. It hadn't bothered Anna too much. She'd continued to shop, sometimes dragging her mum along too but now even she was gone.

'Right, love, where will I drop you?'

With a start, Anna realized that the taxi had just turned into her road. 'Number five, the one on the right with the white wall.' After paying the man, Anna climbed out and started to rummage in her bag for her key. When she got inside, she stepped out of her sandals, fetched a large glass of water and tiptoed, slightly unsteadily, up the stairs. As usual, Liam was on his back, arms outstretched, snoring softly. Anna slipped out of her clothes, leaving them in an untidy heap on the floor, and climbed in beside him. To hell with her make-up and teeth, one night wouldn't kill her. She snuggled up against him and kissed his chest.

'Good time?' Liam murmured, kissing her hair.

'Yeah, not bad.'

'Good.' Liam pulled her closer and promptly went back to sleep.

Rachel tucked the covers in around her son, kissed his forehead and then went into her own room. Gary was a silent heap on his side of the bed. Tiptoeing into the en-suite, she carefully removed her make-up, brushed her teeth and changed into her pyjamas. She climbed into bed, switched off the lamp and settled down beside her husband. It hadn't been too bad a night, much better than she'd anticipated, although she'd felt a bit out of place in that trendy club that Anna and Jill had seemed so relaxed in.

When had they got so sophisticated? When had they left her behind? It was the same when she went out to any of Gary's business functions, she always felt like the odd one out. It was easier to let him go out alone and she often used Alex as an excuse to stay at home. Gary used to get annoyed when she made her excuses but now he took it in his stride and almost seemed to expect it. If he did have the odd fling it was probably all her own fault. Maybe a new baby was exactly what they needed to get them back on track. It would bring them closer together and maybe Gary would spend a bit more time at home.

'Gary?' Rachel put a tentative hand out to her husband but with a groan he moved further away and buried his head under the covers. With a sigh, she rolled over on her side and closed her eyes. She could always tell him in the morning.

Jill was relieved that the evening was at an end and she could sink into her big soft bed. It was nice when Andy stayed over, but some nights it was even nicer to stretch out and relax and not have to worry about how you looked or if your breath smelled! This was definitely one of those nights. The stressful day, energetic dancing and too many cocktails had exhausted her. Setting her alarm, Jill switched off the light and put on her eyeshade. Time to get some sleep. She needed all her wits about her these days with Vinny Gray snapping at her heels.

Chapter 8

Anna glanced impatiently at her watch and then up and down the road. The Gardiners were supposed to have met her here at four and now it was twenty past. Liam was expecting her to meet him in the pub at five but there was no way she'd make it on time now. She pulled out her mobile and phoned Val.

'Donnelly's Real Estate, Val speaking, can I help you?'

'Val, it's me. Have you heard anything from Mick and Sara Gardiner?'

'Not a dicky bird.'

'Have you a mobile number for them?'

'Hang on, let me check. Er, no, just a home and work number.'

'Will you try them and call me back?'

'Of course.'

Val rang off and Anna paced the narrow hallway. She was back in the doorway looking up and down the road again when Val called back. 'They're not coming, I'm afraid. It seems they forgot all about it.'

'Oh, for God's sake!'

'I know, love, it's very annoying. You get yourself on home and have a nice cup of tea.'

'Okay, thanks, Val. Have a good weekend.'

Anna set the alarm, locked up the house and went out to her car. At least she wasn't going to be late now. Liam had asked her to join him and the gang from work because he thought it was important to socialize with them.

'I'm going to be their boss soon,' he'd told her, 'and I want them to know that they can always talk to me if there's a problem.'

Anna didn't think Liam's colleagues would ever have a problem talking. They were a feisty, outspoken bunch and most of them had been working for Patterson's since they left school. Anna often wondered what the older men thought of Liam's meteoric rise within the company. After all, he was only thirty-three and had been in nappies when some of the others had started work.

After she'd found a spot in the car park outside the Swiss Cottage, Anna ran her fingers through her long hair and touched up her make-up. As the future boss's wife she had to look the part, after all. Smiling at the thought, Anna went into the lounge and pushed her way through the Friday crowd towards the corner where the Patterson staff usually sat.

'Anna! Over here!' Sarah, Liam's secretary, waved at her and gave the man beside her a dig in the ribs. 'Move up, Greg and let Anna sit down.'

Liam stood up and gave her a quick hug. 'Hi, sweetheart, what would you like to drink?'

'White wine, please. Hi, everybody.'

'Howaya, gorgeous?' Greg Dunne, the Purchasing Manager, winked at her.

Ciara, the nineteen-year-old receptionist, grunted something and then fluttered her eyelashes at Liam. 'I'd love another Bacardi Breezer.'

Sarah rolled her eyes at Anna. 'What's she like?'

Anna laughed and squeezed in beside her. 'How's it going?'

'Grand. Your timing is brilliant. Patterson and Frank just left.'

'Yeah, it was like a bloody morgue,' Greg told her.

'Oh, yeah?' Anna thought it best not to join in the slagging. After all, Liam was going to be 'one of them' soon. Looking at him standing at the bar joking with Phil Johnson, the Accountant, she thought he'd probably miss being one of the lads. While he was the most senior manager here, because of his age and relaxed attitude he'd always been accepted as one of the gang. Anna wondered if he realized that this would all change. It wouldn't be long before it was him that they'd be moaning about, but then that was the price of success.

'Miserable old sod only bought one round,' Sarah was saying. 'No wonder he's rolling in it.'

'Hi, Anna, how's it going?' Phil brought over her drink and then took the seat across from her.

'Great, Phil – you?' Anna smiled at him. Phil

Johnson was one of the nicest guys she'd ever met and she couldn't understand why, at nearly forty, he was still single.

'Probably gay,' Sarah had said when she'd mentioned it to her one time. 'I mean, look at how well he dresses.'

'No chance,' Liam had scoffed when she'd told him what Sarah had said. 'Phil's as straight as I am.'

As Anna sat listening to Phil she couldn't help wondering. He had such gorgeous brown twinkly eyes, shiny black wavy hair and he was in great shape – tall and not even a hint of a paunch. 'So, are you doing anything nice this weekend?' she asked him.

'Yeah, I'm heading off to Wexford in the morning.'

'Oh?' Anna's ears pricked up. 'Have you family down there?' she asked as Liam came back from the bar and sat down.

'No.' Phil smiled easily but offered no further information.

'So it's a holiday?' Anna probed.

'Anna!' Liam muttered.

'Yeah, I suppose.' Phil drained his glass and stood up. 'Gotta go, guys. Have a good weekend.'

Liam shook his head. 'Well done, Anna. Are you planning to interrogate everyone?'

'I was just making conversation,' Anna said innocently.

'You're wasting your time,' Sarah told her. 'We've all had a go at Phil but he plays his hand very close to his chest.'

'I haven't had a go,' Eddie from the Finishing Department protested. 'He's not my type!'

'Will you all leave the man alone,' Liam told them.

Sarah frowned. 'You're very protective there, Liam. You and Phil aren't at it, are you?'

'Ah, now, please!' Anna protested, laughing.

'Okay, okay, I admit it.' Liam held up his hands and received a thump from his wife.

Eddie leered at Anna. 'If you need a shoulder to cry on, darling, I'm your man.'

'Thanks, Eddie, I'll remember that.'

'No one's that desperate,' Ciara told him.

'I'll have you know I'm very popular with the ladies,' Eddie retorted.

'They must be the ones with bus passes,' Ciara shot back.

'Or guide dogs.' Liam winked at her.

The girl smiled back at him and Sarah nudged Anna. 'You'd better watch her,' she murmured. 'She's got the hots for your hubby.'

Anna giggled. 'God love her, she'd need to dance naked on the table in front of him before Liam would get the message.'

'And don't think she's not capable of it,' Sarah muttered.

Liam caught Anna's eye as she finished her drink. 'We'd better head.'

Ciara pouted. 'But it's early.'

'And I'm starving. I booked a table in Silk's, is that okay?' he asked Anna.

She smiled. 'Perfect.'

'Have a nice evening, you two,' Sarah told them.

'Don't forget my offer, Anna,' Eddie winked at her.

'You behave yourself or you'll be making the tea on Monday,' Liam warned him.

'Bye, everyone.' Anna followed Liam outside, blinking in the sunlight after the gloomy pub. 'Crikey, you have a real admirer in Ciara, don't you? She fancies you like mad.'

Liam laughed. 'She's like that with everyone. Now, why don't we go to the house first and drop your car?'

'Great, I'll follow you.' Anna slid behind the wheel and waited while Liam walked over to his Peugeot.

'We shouldn't be here,' Anna remarked when they were sitting in the Chinese restaurant tucking into spare ribs.

'Why not?'

'We're supposed to be tightening our belts, remember? Saving our money. Getting ready for Baby.'

'We're not going to sit in every night either.'

Anna looked relieved. 'I'm so glad you said that. I think I'd crack up if we did. I mean, we're going to have to live a much quieter life anyway when we have a baby.'

'Why?' Liam looked puzzled.

'Well, for a start we'll be too tired to go out all the

time. I remember how exhausted Rachel was when Alex was small.'

'I think your sister exaggerates just a bit. I mean, for God's sake, it's only a baby. All they do is sleep, eat and—'

'Yes, why don't you stop right there.' Anna dabbed her lips with her napkin. 'Seriously though, life isn't going to be the same, Liam, don't kid yourself about that.'

'Kid myself, ha-ha, very funny.'

Anna made a face. 'It's true.'

'Are you having a change of heart?' he asked, eyebrows raised.

'No! Of course not!'

'Good, 'cos I'm kind of getting used to the idea.'

'Really?'

'Yeah, but I want you to be sure about it, Anna, before you give everything up.'

Anna looked startled. 'But I'm not going to give everything up.'

'Oh?' Liam topped up their wine glasses. 'I thought you'd want to stay home with the baby.'

'God, no! Well yes,' she amended, 'but not for ever. I thought I could work a three-day week or something to keep my hand in, and then when the child is older, I could go back full-time.'

Liam smiled. 'You love that job, don't you?'

'Yeah,' she admitted. 'I'd miss it if I had to give it up completely.'

'Who would mind the little one?'

Anna shrugged. 'He could go to a crêche or a babyminder.'

'He?'

'Or she,' Anna smiled. 'I won't be like Rachel,' she said after a moment. 'I'm thirty-one, I've given this a lot of thought and I know it's what I want.'

'I'm glad you feel like that, sweetheart. I mean, you're the one who'll be looking after the child most of the time, so this has to be your decision.'

'I hope you're not trying to tell me you won't change nappies,' she said, her tone severe.

'I'll change nappies, clean up puke, even watch bloody *Barney*, darling, whatever you want.'

Anna sighed happily. 'I can't wait.'

Chapter 9

'Alex, I won't tell you again! Go and brush your teeth and wash your face and hands, we're going to be late for school.'

'But I feel sick,' Alex whined.

'Then I'd better not give you a muffin for your snack,' Rachel snapped, dragging a weary hand through her hair. She had had barely two hours' sleep and was feeling nauseous and light-headed into the bargain. If Alex didn't start to behave himself she was quite likely to burst into tears.

'Don't want a muffin,' Alex sulked, digging his toes into the carpet.

'Fine.' Rachel grabbed his arm and frog-marched him into the bathroom. 'Now, brush your teeth or there'll be no muffins for the rest of the week.'

'But Mum—'

'Don't say another word, Alex,' Rachel warned.

The little boy looked up at her with mournful eyes, scrunched up his face and proceeded to throw up all over her slippers.

'Jesus!' Rachel kicked off her slippers, dropped to her knees and started to mop at her son with a towel. 'I'm so sorry, darling. Do you think you're going to be sick again?'

Alex nodded and promptly threw up again, this time into the sink. Rachel held his head. 'It's all right, darling, you're going to be okay. You'll feel so much better now.'

Alex leaned heavily against her, his eyes closed and his cheeks flushed. Rachel put a hand to his forehead – yes, he definitely had a temperature. 'Let's get you cleaned up and then it's back to bed for you.' Alex said not a word as she stripped off his pyjamas and washed away the vomit. Then she handed him a toothbrush. 'Brush your teeth, darling, and get rid of the yucky taste.'

Obediently, Alex brushed his teeth and then followed his mother into her bedroom.

'You climb up there while I get you some clean pyjamas.' When she'd settled her son in bed, Rachel went to fetch the Calpol. On her way back, she stopped off at Alex's room to collect his teddy.

'Thanks, Mum.' He gave her a shy smile when he saw it.

She hugged him. 'You're welcome. Now, is there anything else I can get you?'

He shook his head.

'Do you feel sleepy?'

'A bit.'

'Well, I'll pull the curtains and let you sleep.'

'Will you stay with me, Mum?' Alex's eyes looked huge in his small, frightened face.

'Of course I will.' Rachel climbed into bed and pulled him into her arms. As she held him, she closed her eyes and promised herself she'd be a better mother. It wasn't Alex's fault that she was miserable. She was giving the poor kid a tough time lately and, God knows, he didn't deserve it.

After Alex had fallen asleep, Rachel checked his temperature again and then slipped quietly out of the room. He seemed better now, probably something he ate or a bug he'd picked up at school. Going downstairs, Rachel brightened at the sight of a postcard in the hall. Snatching it up, she took it into the kitchen to read over a cuppa. She didn't even glance at it until she was settled at the kitchen table with her mug of tea and slice of toast, at which stage she picked it up and examined the photo carefully.

It was a dramatic sunset over a beautiful lagoon and the colours made Rachel gasp with wonder. As usual, Bridie had crammed the back of the card with her small, tidy script. Rachel settled down to enjoy her mother's latest missive.

My darling Rachel, We are in the most beautiful place called Comacchio on the East coast of Italy and no, that picture isn't touched up, the sunsets really are that magnificent!! This stop wasn't on our original itinerary but we heard that the beaches over here were beautiful and we fancied a paddle. And they are beautiful, although we've spent as much time on bicycles in the pinewoods as we have on the beach. Yes, your mam and dad on bicycles – are you shocked or what??!! – but you can see so much more from the bike than the car and they have cycle tracks everywhere. Last night we ate at the most wonderful seafood restaurant down at the port and your father had the local speciality – eels!! I couldn't even look but he said they were lovely. Today we are going to sail through the canals of the Po Delta – the waiter told us about it last night and said we'd be mad not to do it before we left. Friday, we head up to the place I've dreamed about visiting for years – Venice – so you can probably expect half a dozen postcards from there!! Love to Gary and a big kiss and hug to Alex from his crazy granny. Take care of yourself, darling, I'll talk to you soon, x, Mam

Rachel loved reading her mother's postcards, although they also made her realize how much she missed Bridie. She tried to imagine her parents on bicycles and giggled at the thought. It was amazing that they were doing all of these things and being so adventurous. A couple of years ago her father wouldn't have tried a different brand of coffee, never mind eaten eels!

Rachel pinned the postcard on the noticeboard with the others and then took her tea into the dining room and sat down at the computer in the corner. It was the old machine Gary had used before he got his laptop and he'd rigged it up so that Alex could play games and they could log onto the internet. Rachel hadn't been all that interested to begin with until she discovered a website that grabbed her attention.

MumSpeak was dedicated to maternity and parenting problems, and Rachel had found it a couple of weeks ago when she'd been searching the web for natural remedies to her sleep problems. Each night she went to bed exhausted and was asleep within minutes, but come two o'clock every morning, she would wake and toss and turn for hours. She had often suffered from bouts of insomnia over the years and in the past had resorted to strong sleeping tablets that would send her into a deep sleep, leaving her drowsy for most of the next day. But now that she was pregnant, drugs were out and the usual remedies of hot baths and milky drinks weren't working.

She hadn't found any answers to her problem on *MumSpeak* so she decided to go into the chatroom and ask other mums if they had any ideas. The almost instantaneous flood of replies had amazed and touched her. Fliss from Carlisle was very sympathetic and told her to try meditation. GroovyBabe from Blackpool told her to drink camomile tea and Vanessa from Cork suggested lavender-scented candles. Rachel immediately wrote back, thanking them for their sympathy and suggestions, and after that she signed in at least once a day to talk to her new friends.

How's the indigestion, BabyJ? she keyed in now on one thread about tummy troubles, and, *Anyone know where I can find maternity trousers that don't make me look like a whale?* she entered on the thread about clothes. After browsing through some other threads, Rachel reluctantly signed off and went into the kitchen.

She was just loading the washing-machine when she heard Alex call out. Abandoning the washing, she hurried upstairs. 'What is it, sweetheart? Are you going to be sick again?' When she pushed open the door, Alex was hopping up and down on the bed and using his teddy as a football. 'Can I have something to eat, Mum?'

Rachel smiled with relief. 'How about some toast?'

'Great. I don't have to go to school, do I?'

'No, not today.'

'So can I come downstairs and play?' He looked at her hopefully.

'Oh, I suppose so.' She laughed as he jumped into her arms.

'Thanks, Mum, you're cool!'

When Gary walked in the door later that evening, Alex was sitting on the floor eating Rice Crispies and playing with his Yu-Gi-Oh cards and Rachel was asleep on the sofa. 'What's going on? Alex, why are you in your pyjamas?'

'I'm sick.' Alex grinned at him.

Rachel opened her eyes and went to sit up but was hit by a wave of nausea. 'Oh God.'

Gary frowned. 'Have you been drinking?'

Rachel glared at him. 'Of course I haven't!' She stood up slowly and went out to the kitchen to get a drink of water, with Gary hot on her heels.

'What's going on?' he asked, looking at the pile of dishes in the sink, cereal spilled all over the counter and the washing hanging out of the machine.

Rachel stood at the sink, sipping water and counting to ten. 'Alex was sick this morning so I kept him home.'

'And then aliens attacked and threw stuff all over the kitchen?'

'Oh, fuck the kitchen, Gary!'

'Rachel! What if Alex heard you?'

'I don't care!' Rachel snapped but she checked the doorway and was happy to see that Alex was still engrossed in his game and oblivious to his parents bickering.

Gary made a big production of cleaning down the worktop. 'This house is in a right state and you don't look too good yourself.' He shot a disgusted look at her stained old tracksuit.

Rachel gasped, hot tears pricking at her eyes. 'How can you talk to me like that?'

'Well, it's true,' Gary said, but he did look a bit shamefaced. 'You seem to do nothing but sit around the house all day and I can't believe you kept Alex home. What's wrong? Was it too much of an effort to get him dressed?'

'I told you, he was sick!'

'Yeah, right, he looks it!'

'He puked all over the place,' Rachel protested. 'Check the laundry basket if you don't believe me.'

Gary wrinkled his nose. 'You've left clothes covered with vomit in the laundry basket?'

It was her turn to look shamefaced. 'I meant to wash them, I just forgot.'

'For God's sake, woman!' Gary turned on his heel. 'I don't know what's got into you.'

'A baby, Gary,' Rachel called after him. 'That's what's got into me!'

Gary stopped in the doorway and turned. 'What did you say?'

Rachel flopped into a chair, the tears running down her cheeks unchecked. 'I'm pregnant.'

Gary came over and sat down opposite her. 'Are you sure?'

'Of course.'

'How far along are you?'

Rachel couldn't meet his eyes. 'Nearly ten weeks, I think.'

'What? But how come you didn't know? You must have felt something.' Then realization dawned. 'You've known about this for ages, haven't you?'

'Not that long.'

'But you kept it from me.'

'I just wanted to get used to the idea. It's a bit of a shock, that's all. And I've been feeling so awful.'

Gary's expression softened and he put a hand out to squeeze hers. 'Morning sickness?'

'All day, more like,' Rachel exaggerated, desperate for sympathy.

'Poor you. Have you been to the doctor?'

Rachel shook her head.

'I'll make an appointment for you. You have to get checked out and anyway, shouldn't there be a heartbeat by now? Wouldn't you like to hear it? I remember with Alex you'd be counting the days between visits to the hospital.'

Rachel managed a weak smile. 'I'm just feeling so lousy it's hard to associate it with a baby. It doesn't seem very real.'

'It will seem real enough in a few months when we're up all night every night,' Gary told her.

Rachel resisted the temptation to remind him that she had been the only one whose nights were disrupted when Alex came along.

'I don't suppose you've done anything about dinner,' he was saying.

Rachel shook her head.

'No problem. I'll go and get us a takeaway. What about Alex?'

'He's okay. He's been eating toast and cereal all day and I think that's enough for him.'

'Great, then let's pack him off to bed and we'll have a nice quiet evening together.'

Rachel began to feel the tension ease away. 'I wouldn't mind a bath.'

'No problem. You go and have a nice long soak. I'll tidy up here and get Alex to bed. And Rachel?'

'Yes?' She looked up at him.

'Sorry for being so hard on you.'

'You weren't to know.' Rachel smiled gratefully.

Gary came over and kissed her lightly on the lips. 'You go on up and I'll bring you a nice mug of tea.'

Rachel left him whistling to himself as he loaded the dishwasher. Well, at least now he knew. She hadn't meant to tell him quite like that, of course, but – oh well, it was done now. Going into the bathroom she turned the hot tap on full and added lavender bath oil. As she undressed she wondered at Gary's reaction. He hadn't seemed bothered or fazed at the idea of becoming a father again, but then why would he? She was the one who had to carry the child for nine months and she'd be the one doing all the work after it was born.

Gloom descended on her once more as she lowered herself carefully into the bath. The prospect of maternity jeans and no drink filled her with dread, not to mention the thought of pendulous boobs and varicose veins. Was it any wonder if Gary got turned off? How could she blame him if he looked at other women? She should have worked harder to get her figure back after Alex was born. Now it was too late; she'd be even bigger after a second baby and her boobs would never be quite right again. Rachel took a deep breath and ducked her head under the water. The silence enveloped and cushioned her, completely blocking out the outside world. If only she could stay here.

Chapter 10

Anna swallowed hard as she stood in the doorway of the second bedroom of number 8, Talbot Road. The duvet was in a pile in the centre of the bed, a pizza box of dubious age sat on the pillow, empty beer cans rolled on the floor leaving a trail of drops on the once cream carpet and there were piles of dirty laundry everywhere. Anna held up the tape measure against the wall and then picked her way gingerly through the mess.

'Teenagers, eh?' the mother giggled. 'Carlton won't let me come near it although he said it was okay for you to come in and measure up today.'

'Very kind,' Anna murmured, writing the measurements down and hurrying out of the room. 'And this is the box room?' She followed the woman through the next doorway and found herself in a tiny room decorated in suffocating shades of pink.

'My daughter's room,' the lady explained unnecessarily, straightening the My Little Pony collection on the shelf. 'Cute, isn't it?'

'Lovely.' Anna decided if she ever had a daughter

she wouldn't so much as put a pink ribbon in her hair.

Hurrying through the remainder of the house, Anna promised she'd be in touch the next day with her valuation and escaped to her relatively clean and sweet-smelling car. Finishing her notes, she switched on the engine and drove back out on to the airport road. Glancing at the clock she decided to visit the Kenny place before she took a break for lunch. She was feeling a bit nostalgic about returning to Riverside Court, the tiny cul de sac in the old Malahide estate where her family had lived for more than twenty years.

When her parents had sold up their small terrace house just over a year ago, she had been quite sad. The place was full of happy memories of her childhood, and Anna felt strange at the idea that someone else was now going to live in their comfortable little home. The new owner would probably pull down the ancient tin hut at the end of the garden that they'd used as a playhouse. Some other kids would sleep in the front bedroom that she and Rachel had shared until Anna turned fifteen. Then she'd decided that she couldn't stand her sister another minute and moved lock, stock and barrel into the tiny box room. That was the room where she'd lain in the single bed, dreaming of her latest boyfriend or writing in her diary. It seemed like a lifetime ago now.

The Kenny home was straight across the road and

when Anna pulled up outside she sat for a few moments staring at her old home. The new owners hadn't changed much on the face of it and she could almost believe that if she went up the path and rang the doorbell, her dad would answer and wrap her in his arms in one of his bear hugs.

Sighing, Anna picked up her clipboard and climbed out of the car. As she walked up the drive-way the door opened and Clive Kenny stood waiting for her. 'Hi, Anna, how's it going?'

Anna held out her hand. 'Hi, Clive, good to see you again,' she lied.

She and Rachel had always kept well out of the way of Clive and his brother Rory. The brothers had delighted in tormenting and bullying the girls and then there had been the episode with the bike. It had been Anna's tenth birthday and to her delight, her parents had bought her a beautiful bike, painted mint green and with a pretty white basket on the back. Anna and Rachel had sped up and down the cul de sac all day, Anna kindly letting her little sister take turns. The Kenny brothers waited until Anna's parents had gone out to the shops to fetch the birthday cake before pushing Anna off the bike and then racing it in and out of the thorny bushes at the end of the road, scraping all the lovely new paint. In tears, Anna had begged them to stop but it was only when her dad's car turned back into the road that Clive had shoved the bike at her and run back across the street. 'Don't tell or it'll go missing tomorrow and you'll never see it again,' he'd threatened and so Anna and Rachel had dried their tears, cleaned up the bike and told no one.

'It's been a long time, Anna,' Clive was saying now, leading her through to the kitchen. 'Of course I don't get home as much these days.'

Anna nodded. Bridie had often raged about how the Kenny boys had left their aging father to his own devices after their mother had died. 'I was surprised to hear that your dad wanted to sell up. I thought he loved this house.'

Clive looked sorrowful. 'Yes, well I'm afraid he's not able to manage on his own any more. He's in St Joseph's at the moment.'

'Oh, I'm sorry, I didn't know he was sick.'

'He's having some problems with his legs – doesn't get about too well,' Clive told her. 'We can't possibly let him go on living here on his own.'

'I understand.' Anna tried not to show her astonishment at his sensitivity.

'And the Blossom Hill Retirement Home is really very comfortable. He'll only have to share his room with two other old lads – the company will do him good.'

Anna's mouth settled into a grim line. Blossom Hill had a reputation for being a badly run tip that was full to overflowing because it was the least expensive residential care home on the north side of Dublin. The Kenny brothers, it seemed, hadn't changed.

'Let's get started then.' As she went through the

old-fashioned rooms, filled with the memorabilia of forty years of family life, Anna wondered how Clive and Rory could so easily pluck their father from his home and toss him into an anonymous institution. He'd be heartbroken, she was sure of it. He had been very upset when her parents had moved out, and had told her then that the only way he'd leave Riverside Court was in a box. It seemed, however, that Mr Kenny was destined to spend his last days playing bingo in the afternoons and wondering what was for tea.

Clive wrinkled his nose at the dusty, cluttered rooms. 'I told Dad he should get rid of some of this stuff, but of course he wouldn't listen. You know, my mother's clothes are still up in the wardrobe! Rory and I are going to have some job clearing the place out.'

'It must be hard to let go,' Anna murmured.

'Yes, well, life goes on.' Clive smiled broadly. 'So, how much do you think we'll get for the old place?'

'Asshole,' Anna muttered later as she sat at her desk munching an apple.

'What's that, dear?' Val looked over her specs.

Anna told her about her neighbour's plight and his hard-hearted sons.

'I'm afraid it's all too common, dear,' Val said sorrowfully. 'Some children can't wait to lock up their parents.'

'I could understand it if they'd been horrible, but

Mr and Mrs Kenny were lovely. In fact, it's hard to know how they managed to produce two such terrible children. They made Rachel's and my life miserable. We never played out the front unless we knew they weren't around.'

'The little gurriers! Did you not get your dad to sort them out?'

Anna shrugged. 'It would never have occurred to us. They were the days before bullying was talked about so we just kept quiet and got on with it.'

'I was bullied when I was young,' Val said suddenly. 'By my sister.'

Anna's eyes widened. 'Edna?'

Val nodded. 'I was eleven and there was this beautiful blue hair-band in the window of our local drapery that I wanted so badly. Mother said it was too expensive and that if I wanted it, I'd have to save up for it. Well, I knew that by the time I had enough money the hair-band would probably be gone. So,' Val put a self-conscious hand to her greying bob, 'I took the money from my father's jacket pocket. I'm no thief,' she hastily assured Anna. 'I've never done anything like that before or since.'

'Of course not.'

'Anyway, Edna saw me and she said that unless I did whatever she asked for a month and gave her the hair-band whenever she wanted, she'd tell our mother.'

'What a bitch!' Anna exploded before she could stop herself.

Val gave a sad smile. 'Ah, sure, she was young and children can be cruel. She doesn't even remember it now.'

'But you do.'

'Every problem is always a huge crisis to a child. I'm sure I exaggerated it all in my head.'

Judging by the way Edna still treated her younger sister, Anna doubted it. Maybe Rachel wasn't that bad after all.

'Anyway, what about the house?'

Anna looked blank.

'The Kenny place,' Val reminded her. 'Is it in good condition?'

'It could do with a new kitchen, bathroom suite and I'd say it needs rewiring, but the rooms are a wonderful size and it has an enormous garden that's not overlooked.'

'So we should have no trouble selling it.'

'No. Poor Mr Kenny. Do you think he even knows what Clive is up to?'

'Probably not, dear, but you're not going to be the one to tell him.'

'You can't tell him, Anna,' Liam told her later after she'd retold the whole sorry saga. 'It's none of your business.'

Anna sighed. 'I know, but I just feel so sorry for the poor man.'

'You're such a softie, you know that? I know it's

hard, love, but this is business and Mark would kill you if you got involved.'

'You're right.'

Liam folded her in his arms. 'Come on, sweetheart, I'm sure Mr Kenny will be well looked after. The nursing home might not be the best but I'm sure the staff are fine. In fact, I think my mother knows one of the nurses. Speaking of Mum, we'd better get a move on. She said dinner would be ready at seven.'

Anna obediently went to fetch her shoes and bag and tried to work up some enthusiasm for the night ahead. It wasn't easy as her mother-in-law didn't like her and she didn't try very hard to hide the fact.

Josie Harrison was a lonely and dissatisfied woman who had never really forgiven Anna for coming from a council estate. She made no secret of the fact that she believed her son could have done much better for himself and that Anna had fallen on her feet the day she met him. It hadn't been so bad when her husband, Arthur, had been alive. He and Anna had liked each other from the start and Arthur had made sure his wife behaved herself, at least when he was around. Shortly after Anna and Liam had married, however, Arthur had suffered a massive heart attack and died the next day. Liam had been devastated but Josie had been inconsolable. She clung to her son for support and Anna knew that she had pressured Liam to move back into the family home. Thankfully, Liam had resisted and

Anna didn't have to get involved. He assured his mother that he would be there for her and she would always be welcome in his home, but that he and Anna had their own life too.

Anna knew that it would be a completely different story if, God forbid, Bridie was in the same situation. Anna would move her mother in without hesitation. In fact, she and Rachel would probably come to blows over who she should live with. But then Bridie was a very different woman to Josie. She believed in the old adage, live and let live. Josie, on the other hand, had an acid tongue and was a terrible gossip. Anna did her best to ignore any jibes or insults – after all, Josie was Liam's mother and he loved her – but it wasn't always easy. Limiting her exposure to Josie seemed the best course of action; she could deal with the woman in small doses.

Dinner once a week in Josie's wasn't too much of a sacrifice as whatever her other faults, Josie was a great cook. She took every opportunity to force food into her son as she believed Anna completely neglected him. When she first found out that Anna refused point blank to cook red meat, she nearly had a fit.

'How can he possibly do a hard day's work without some proper food inside him? He must be anaemic – in fact, I'd swear on it! Look at the colour of him.'

Anna had obediently studied her husband, who was positively glowing with health, and told Josie that if he fancied some meat, he could always cook it himself.

Josie wasn't impressed. She had very old-fashioned ideas about a lot of things and she didn't keep them to herself. Anna would try and suppress a grin when, over their weekly dinners, her mother-in-law would hold forth on some of the things she didn't agree with. Married women working (they shouldn't), jeans (only sluts wore them), and the evils of make-up (I never needed any when I was young).

'If your mother had her way, I'd be barefoot and chained to the kitchen sink,' she'd joked with Liam after the last dinner.

'Now there's a thought,' he'd laughed. 'You know, she'll be scandalized if you keep working when we have a baby.'

'Ah, it'll give her something new to moan about. Anyway, she'll forgive me everything once I've finally produced her first grandchild.'

'True,' Liam agreed. 'I can just imagine her face when we tell her.'

'We're not going to tell her we're trying, are we?'

'God, no, she'd expect a weekly report on our progress – way too weird!'

Tonight, Anna was pleasantly surprised to smell the delicious aroma of roast chicken when they arrived at the old house in Glasnevin. Josie rarely cooked white meat, taking every opportunity to give her son the red meat that his wife denied him.

'I didn't like the look of the beef,' Josie said grudgingly, 'and the lamb looked more like mutton.'

'It smells great, Mum.' Liam bent to kiss her cheek.

'Well, I've done a nice piece of ham to go with it, love. Chicken on its own is no dinner for a man.' She shot her daughter-in-law a look.

Anna thought of the spaghetti hoops that Liam had eaten in front of the television last night and suppressed a giggle. Josie had no concept of how they lived. It was a rare occasion when Liam and Anna sat down to a home-cooked meal. Liam would have left her long ago if it wasn't for the takeaways and TV dinners!

Of course, she would probably have to learn to cook once a baby came along. She remembered watching Rachel cooking potloads of vegetables, puréeing them and painstakingly transferring them into tiny pots to be frozen. 'Why don't you just use the jars?' Anna had asked. Even she knew of the vast selection of baby food now available.

Rachel had shot her a look of pure horror. 'Don't you know how much salt and sugar are in those things?'

Anna didn't, and had almost nodded off as her sister instructed her on the evils of processed food. Anna thought she was overreacting. After all, it was probably what most kids were brought up on and they'd survived.

But Rachel had very rigid ideas on stuff like this.

She'd spent most of her pregnancy researching car seats to make sure that Alex had the safest and most comfortable model. She could talk for hours on the pros and cons of soothers and knew everything there was to know about lactose intolerance. How could Anna go wrong? Rachel would soon tell her when she went astray. Oh, there was a thought to put you off having kids!

'Finish the meat, love,' Josie was saying. 'There's no one for it. And have some more potatoes.'

'This is gorgeous, Mum.'

Josie gave her daughter-in-law a triumphant look. 'It's wonderful to cook for someone who appreciates it. Your dad, God rest him, loved my cooking. He had no interest in going to fancy restaurants. He said, "Why would I go out to eat when I eat like a king at home?"'

'But he loved his fish and chips, didn't he?' Anna couldn't help herself. 'He always said that chipper up at the corner was fantastic.'

Josie sniffed. 'He only ever had that for supper occasionally.'

'That chipper makes the best burgers in Dublin,' Liam told his wife.

His mother looked aghast. 'Don't tell me you've eaten their burgers, Liam! My God, sure you could get BSE or God knows what from them.'

Liam laughed. 'Well, I've been eating them since I was about fourteen and I'm not dead yet.'

*

'I don't think Mum looked well tonight, Anna, what do you think?' Liam said, putting his hand on her knee when they were in the car on their way home.

'She's fine,' Anna assured him. 'She was probably just tired after all that cooking. She must have started at daybreak, the spread she put up.'

'True,' Liam laughed. 'You know, at her age she should be taking it easy. Maybe we should start having her round to our place for dinner instead.'

'And feed her what, exactly?' Anna enquired. 'Fish fingers and pizza?'

'It can't be that difficult to do meat and two veg. I'm sure we could manage it between us.'

Anna raised an eyebrow. 'You think?'

Chapter 11

'It was nice of you to meet me,' Rachel said to Jill. 'You must be so busy.'

Jill laughed. 'We're all entitled to a lunch break, Rache. And now we can have lunch together every time you come in to see your obstetrician. It will be fun.'

'I'd like that.' Rachel had always been jealous of Jill and Anna's weekly lunch dates. She'd imagined them talking about important things in very glamorous cafés.

'What time is your appointment?' Jill asked.

'Two.'

'Good, we won't be too rushed.'

A sullen-looking waiter, chewing gum, leaned across her to clear the table. 'What can I get ya?'

'A tuna salad and a mineral water, please,' Rachel said.

Jill ran her eye down the menu and then shut it with a snap. 'Chicken curry and grapefruit juice, please.'

'Grapefruit juice?' Rachel stared at her.

'It's my new diet. You have grapefruit with every meal. It burns off all the fat in the food and you lose weight.'

'Then why not have egg and chips and grapefruit juice?'

Jill made a face. 'Don't be smart. This one's going to work, you mark my words.'

Rachel shook her head. Being thin wouldn't suit her voluptuous, attractive cousin. Her ample curves suited her wide smile, dark flashing eyes and mane of black hair. She had a presence and a style that most women would kill for, but Jill still wanted to be thin. Or maybe she was just addicted to diets. 'What happened to the Neander-Thin diet?'

Jill waved a dismissive hand. 'Impossible with my lifestyle. You weren't allowed any processed foods and, like, I live on the stuff! Show me the woman who goes home after a long day at the office and eats fresh pasta and vegetables and I'll show you a liar.'

'Or someone with their own private chef,' Rachel commented.

'That's it, you know!' Jill nodded enthusiastically. 'I need to get rich to get thin. If I had someone to prepare tasty, low-calorie dishes for me, I'd be a size ten in no time.'

'Is Andy a good cook?'

Jill grinned. 'No idea. We don't usually have time to eat.'

'He's still around then?'

'He's still around – for the moment.'

'Oh Jill, you're a terrible woman.'

'Why?'

'You just don't give men a chance.'

'Rubbish!'

'It's true. I mean, what about Dermot? He was lovely.'

'He was a mummy's boy.'

'Okay, then – Ollie. What was wrong with him?'

'Golf bore.'

Rachel shook her head. 'You know you're looking for a man that doesn't exist, don't you? Nobody's perfect.'

'I'm not looking for perfection,' Jill said, her eyes lighting up as the waiter approached with their lunch. 'Just a good body, white teeth, a decent line in conversation and a big bank balance.'

'As if you need a man with money, with your high-powered job and flashy car.' Rachel scoffed.

'I don't, but I don't want a sponger either.'

'Like I say, you're impossible to please.'

Jill tucked cheerfully into her curry. 'Choosy maybe, impossible no. Anyway, enough about me. How far along are you now?'

'Twelve weeks.'

'Wow, that's a milestone, isn't it?'

'Yes. The chances of miscarriage are much lower once you get past the first trimester.'

'That's wonderful. Rache, you must be delighted.'

Rachel nodded as she picked the diced cucumber from her salad.

'And what about Gary – is he all excited?'

'He's happy.' Rachel didn't look at her cousin. After his initial excitement wore off, Gary's reaction had been rather disappointing. He wasn't as sympathetic as he'd been when she was pregnant with Alex and he was still working ridiculously long hours even though she'd complained of tiredness and asked him for more help with their son.

'And?'

Rachel looked up to see Jill studying her. 'And nothing. I'm just a bit fed up. I feel so fat and frumpy.'

'You don't look it.'

'Yes, I do, don't lie to me. Have you seen Anna at all?' She decided it was best to change the subject before she told Jill to feck off and stop patronizing her.

'No, she seems to be very busy in work.'

'Isn't she always? She was supposed to have Alex over to stay one night, but of course it didn't happen.'

Jill frowned. 'You know she'd never let Alex down without a very good reason.'

'I suppose.' Rachel pushed away her salad and looked longingly at Jill's curry.

'Any word from your folks?'

Rachel brightened. 'I got a postcard yesterday from Venice. They were planning to move on today but Mam's feeling a bit under the weather so they're going to stay on for a few days.'

Jill rolled her eyes dramatically. 'Oh God, imagine being stuck in Venice! Wouldn't your heart go out to them?'

Rachel laughed. 'Mam doesn't seem that keen on the place. She says it's smelly.'

'I think I could live with it. Have you thought any more about going out to see them with Alex when school breaks up?'

'Yes, but he's got such a busy summer lined up, what with soccer camp and everything, I'm not sure when I could organize it.'

'Try,' Jill urged her. 'It would do you the world of good and your mam and dad would love to see you.'

'I suppose.' Rachel's smile was vacant. She'd lost interest in the idea of going abroad. The thought of travelling with a young child and a large bump wasn't very appealing. And she was nervous about leaving Gary – God only knew what he'd get up to in her absence. She'd love to talk to Jill about Gary but if she put it into words, said it out loud – well, then it would be real. Much better to say nothing and get on with it. Things would work out, especially when the baby arrived. She was not going to mention any of her suspicions to Jill; she was probably blowing things out of proportion, just the way she always did. To make sure her resolve didn't weaken – Jill was so kind and such a good listener – Rachel changed the subject yet again.

'How's the job going?'

Jill looked faintly surprised. 'Fine.'

'Did you sort out that fella who's after your job? Vinny, wasn't it?'

'Yeah, Vinny Gray.'

'He sounds like that gangster.'

'The Kray twins.' Jill winced. 'God, I don't think the world could handle it if Vinny had a twin brother. He's a right little shit but clever with it, unfortunately.'

'Still, once you do your job well that's all that matters.'

'Maybe,' Jill nodded, thinking how naïve her cousin was. Rachel had no idea how cut-throat office life could be. 'At least Sue, that's my boss, is no fool. I'm sure she sees right through him.'

'There you go then. You've nothing to worry about.'

'No,' Jill agreed, although she didn't believe it.

She had always felt so confident, so sure of her ability, but lately she was beginning to doubt herself and it was all because of Vinny Gray. Not because of the sponsorship deal he'd come up with for the lingerie company – anyone could get lucky – but because she'd just found out that Sue Boyle had head-hunted him from their biggest competitor and that had made her nervous.

When Jill first started in this business, she knew that she'd found the perfect job. It was immediately obvious to her and everyone else that she had a knack for it. She was usually able to come up with quirky ideas and, where possible, she tried to incorporate humour. Sue Boyle had recognized and nurtured Jill's talent, and her rise through the company's ranks had been meteoric. Now, Jill had some competition in the shape of Vinny Gray, and she'd have to really pull the stops out if she didn't want to see him being promoted above her. The thought made her feel slightly ill.

'Are you having dessert?' Rachel had snatched the menu that the waiter had handed her when he returned for their plates.

Feeling decidedly depressed now, Jill nodded. 'I'll have the tiramisu with some ice-cream.'

Rachel beamed. 'And I'll have the chocolate cheesecake.' She called the waiter and they gave their order. 'And a latte, please.'

He turned to Jill. 'Tea or coffee?'

'Another grapefruit juice,' Jill told him. 'Make it a large one.'

As her sister and cousin indulged themselves, Anna was making her way home. Val had taken a message from Liam asking her to meet him there. The dirty devil! It was a while since they'd nipped home at lunchtime for a bit of rumpy-pumpy. Anna stopped off at the deli in the village for some sandwiches and a punnet of strawberries – had to keep their strength up, after all!

'I'm home,' she called as she breezed in and dumped the bags in the kitchen. 'Yoo-hoo, Liam.' She headed for the stairs, unbuttoning her shirt as she went.

'In here,' Liam called from the sitting room and she turned to come back down, a smile on her face.

'So this is where you are.' She posed in the doorway and smiled seductively. 'I hope you're feeling peckish.'

'Sit down,' Liam said, his voice faint.

Anna dropped the pose and noticed for the first time that her husband's eyes were red and swollen and his face ashen. 'Liam, what is it?' She hurried to his side. 'Is it your mother?'

He shook his head.

'Then what? For God's sake, tell me what's happened!'

Liam gulped and grasped her hands in his. 'I've lost my job.'

It took nearly an hour for Anna to get the full story out of him. All the clandestine meetings that Liam had assumed were a prerequisite to his promotion had actually been to discuss how they were going to rescue the company, for Patterson's was suddenly in a lot of trouble.

'They lost the Drayson order and another customer is going into receivership. Patterson's would have gone to the wall too unless they took radical action.'

'So they fired you?' Anna exploded. 'But they need you! If they're going to ride this out, they need strong management.'

Liam's smile was resigned. 'Apparently I'm too

expensive. Frank Boylan has taken early retirement, Greg Dunne and I have been made redundant and Ted is going to run things.'

'What about Phil?'

Liam's eyes hardened. 'He's staying. You know he knew all about it? I can't believe the bastard didn't warn me. And I thought he was a mate.'

'They can't do this, Liam, they just can't!'

'They've done it, Anna. That old bastard has been stringing me along. He must have been thinking about this for a while. Bloody Sarah probably knew too – she does all his typing.'

'It's unfair dismissal, we'll sue them.'

Liam shook his head, his eyes weary. 'It's not dismissal, it's redundancy. I would only have a case if they replaced me.'

'Ted can't possibly run it on his own.'

Liam closed his eyes and said nothing.

Anna took a deep breath, forcing herself to calm down. He was in a bad enough state without her losing it. 'It's going to be okay, darling, I promise. You'll walk into another job. With your qualifications and experience, companies will be queuing up to hire you. You'll probably get an even better job.'

Anna sat for ages, clinging to his hand and comforting him, but she felt as if someone had kicked her in the stomach. If one thing in their life had seemed secure, it was Liam's career. He had known from an early age that he'd wanted to go on to college and study engineering – Josie told everyone how hard he'd worked and how he'd always been at the top of his class. After college, he'd worked as a supervisor in a small company before securing a job as Line Manager in Ted Patterson's company, specialists in switches and connectors. He was only twenty-three and Josie had been delirious.

After a while, Anna rang the office and told Val she wouldn't be back in that afternoon. 'Bit of a family crisis.'

'Oh, I'm sorry, love. Nobody's sick, I hope?'

'No, Val. I'll fill you in tomorrow,' Anna promised and rang off. Then she dragged Liam down to the pub and poured several pints into him. As the alcohol started to take effect, Liam came out of his stunned stupor and began to talk about their future. As he went on about the possibilities and the types of business he'd like to get into, Anna felt herself relax. This was more like it. This was the Liam she knew. Not the devastated tearstained man that she'd walked in on at lunchtime. Liam would very quickly find himself a new job, a better job. They would get through this; she would do everything she could to help him. And then when they came out the other side, they could concentrate on starting their family.

Chapter 12

'I won't be home for dinner,' Gary said over his shoulder as he wrestled with his tie in front of the mirror.

From her position in the bed, Rachel barely reacted. Gary was rarely home for dinner. 'Fine. I'll have something with Alex.' Rachel thought she'd pick up a pizza for them both. She didn't have the energy to even consider cooking.

'It's an important meeting, I can't get out of it.'

'It's okay, Gary, I understand.' She managed a smile.

'Good.' He bent to kiss her forehead and was gone.

Rachel lay back on the pillows and tried to remember when Gary had last kissed her on the lips, properly, deeply, passionately. She gave up, pulling the sheet up to her chin and closing her eyes. Now that Alex was going to school with his friend, Rachel could go back to bed in the mornings. She hadn't felt this weary on her first pregnancy, but then when she was expecting Alex she'd been excited at the thought of becoming a mother. This time there was no excitement. Rachel felt riddled with guilt as she stroked her small bump. God only knew how this poor child would turn out. Before it was even born, it had a lousy mother. Rachel felt the tears well up but swallowed hard and sat up. Crying wasn't going to do her or her baby any good. And she'd felt awful the other day when Alex caught her at it.

He'd wandered into the kitchen looking for a snack and discovered her weeping over the potato peelings. Running to her, he'd wrapped his skinny little arms around her. 'Please don't cry, Mummy, I hate it when you cry.'

Rachel got up, put on her dressing-gown and went down to the computer. Once she'd signed in to *MumSpeak*, she went to the mums-to-be section on the discussion board and started to type, not giving herself time to think about what she was doing or why. The anonymity of the service allowed her to be a lot more forthcoming than she would ever be with Jill, and it seemed to be the same for many of the other mothers. There were topics on this website that you'd never hear discussed at a mother and baby session, that's for sure. She typed quickly and when she was finished, read it back once.

'I know there are lots of you out there with much bigger problems than me, but can anyone tell me why I'm so miserable? I'm pregnant with my second child and I just don't want to get out of bed in the morning. While my husband seems pleased about the baby, he doesn't show

much interest in me or it and I feel very lonely. I hate to admit this but I'm not sure I want this baby at all. Is this all down to hormones? Does anyone else feel this way? Am I a horrible person? Al'sMum

She'd chosen to call herself Al'sMum because she felt that's all she was. She had decided against using Alex's full name in case someone recognized her. Well, you never knew. This was an Irish website and Ireland could be a bloody small place when you least needed it.

She quickly posted the question before she could change her mind, switched off the screen and went out to the kitchen to make some camomile tea. She'd actually kill for a really strong coffee but knew that if she started drinking the stuff again she wouldn't be able to stop. When the tea was made, she carried it back to the computer. Flicking the screen on she realized she was holding her breath as she checked for a reply. Nothing.

As she sipped her tea, Rachel browsed through the other topics. Many queries related to maternity hospitals and the cost of going private, and there were lots of threads about the various symptoms women were experiencing. Rachel read eagerly in the hope of finding someone else who was feeling the same way, but though many were going through rough pregnancies, they all sounded bright and breezy and seemed to agree that it would all be worth it in the end.

Rachel finished her tea and signed off. She really

had to stop thinking about it so much and just get on with life. Fine, she hadn't wanted this pregnancy but there was nothing she could do about that now. While lack of sleep was still a big problem, she was having a reasonably good pregnancy. On top of that, she had a wonderful son and although her marriage might not be ideal, Gary wasn't the worst. Her granny would have told her that she didn't know she was born and that she should count her blessings.

What would her mother say? Rachel wished her parents had invested in a mobile phone so that she could at least keep in touch. Rachel didn't begrudge her parents some fun in their golden years but it would be nice if they came home occasionally.

Rachel didn't know any other pensioners who'd sold their home and gone off to travel the world. Gary's parents rarely left Dublin, never mind Ireland, and Josie, Liam's mother, never went further than Cork, although Anna would probably throw a party if her mother-in-law decided to travel the world. Rachel smiled as she thought about the stories her sister told of Josie's meddling ways. Kathleen, Gary's mother, was a kind but distant mother-in-law who wouldn't dream of interfering in her son's life.

Rachel put on her jogging pants with a white polo shirt and pulled her hair back into a ponytail. 'You'll do,' she told her reflection in the bathroom mirror. A bit of make-up wouldn't go amiss, but she didn't have the energy. Anyway, there was no one to doll herself up for. Apart from the other mothers picking up their kids she wouldn't see another soul today. She'd probably be back in bed by the time Gary got home.

Going back downstairs, Rachel paused en route to the kitchen to check her screen for replies. Her heart flipped when she saw there were two new messages against her entry. She sank into the chair as she pressed Enter on the first.

*No, you're not horrible!! Don't even think that!! And yes, it is probably hormones, they do terrible things to you. What you need is a good night out with your man – does the trick for me every time. I feel so ugly and fat when I'm pregnant (blooming my ar**!!) but a bit of loving from my fella makes me feel a lot better. Good luck! GalwayGal*

Rachel smiled. It was a lovely reply and it did make her feel better, until she got to the 'bit of loving' part. There seemed little chance of that at the moment. Rachel clicked on the second reply.

You're very brave, Al'sMum, good on ya! Not many of us will admit that we're not very happy about being pregnant but lots of us feel it from time to time – yes, I've been there too. My third wasn't planned and I had set my heart on getting this new kitchen – God, sounds pathetic, doesn't it? Anyway, once we knew Baby was on the way, that was the end of my kitchen. I was really fed up. Actually, if I'm honest, I was annoyed. Took it out on Him, of course. I'd begged him to have the snip but he wouldn't, told me it was too final and that I might change my mind. Well, my baby son is now eight months old and yes, he's better than a kitchen any day! Keep your heart up, Al'sMum, it will get better. Good luck, MaryK

By the time she finished reading the message, tears were flowing down Rachel's cheeks. Quickly she typed in a response.

Thanks, GalwayGal, thanks, MaryK, I feel better already!

She paused for a moment and then, wiping at her tears with the back of her hand, continued typing.

No chance of any loving, tho. He doesn't fancy me pregnant. He says he doesn't want to hurt the baby but I can tell that he's lying. I think there might be someone else. Anyway, thanks for replying, I feel much better. Al's Mum

This time Rachel posted the message without reading it, signed out of the website and closed down the machine. God, what had she done that for? Going into the downstairs loo, she splashed water on her face, grabbed her bag and keys and went out for a walk. Normally she'd wander around the shops in the village and then go down along the seafront, but today she didn't want to meet anyone, didn't want to listen to excited congratulations, didn't want people asking her if she wanted a boy or a girl, didn't want to have to pretend to be happy.

Rachel turned instead towards the path along the estuary. On a grey and windy weekday morning she was less likely to meet one of the busy mums down here. They'd all be in the gym, at aqua-aerobics or in the many coffee-shops, discussing the price of school-books, the latest fake tan and what wife was doing what with which husband. A faint drizzle started to fall and Rachel held her face up to the grey sky, welcoming the miserable weather that matched her mood.

Anna was sitting in her car staring out at the rain falling on the estuary when she saw her sister walking along the path, her shirt sticking to her body and her hair in rat's tails around her face. Anna's initial response was to drive off – she was in no mood for dealing with Rachel's moods today. But her poor pregnant sister was a good ten minutes' walk from home with no coat on, and the rain looked like it was down for the day. Pressing hard on the horn, Anna got out of the car and waved at her sister.

'Rachel! Over here!'

Rachel raised her head and just looked at her.

'For God's sake, hurry up and get in.'

Rachel approached the car. 'I'm fine, it's only a bit of rain.'

'Rubbish. You're soaked through – now come on.'

Without another word, Rachel went around to the passenger door and climbed in.

'Are you okay?' Anna glanced at her as she turned the car.

'Yeah.'

'Are you sure?'

'Yes! I said, didn't I?'

'I was just asking, there's no need to bite my head off. What the hell are you doing out in this weather?'

'What the hell are *you* doing sitting staring at the water in the middle of the day?' Rachel shot back.

'Liam's been made redundant,' Anna replied, too miserable to lie.

Rachel immediately reached out a hand to her sister. 'Oh God, Anna, I'm sorry.'

'Yeah, me too.'

'But I thought Liam had it made at Patterson's? Wasn't there talk that one day he'd be the boss?'

Anna's smile was bitter. 'Oh, there was lots of talk. Unfortunately, that's all it was. Patterson's is going through a rough patch so Ted's decided to get rid of the senior management and run things himself.'

'That's terrible. Poor Liam. How's he taking it?'

'Not great.'

'Still, I'm sure he will walk into another job.'

'Yeah, he should be fine.' Anna tried to smile. 'He's doing a tour of the employment agencies today.'

'He'll probably have found himself a new job by the time you get home.'

'Probably.' Anna turned into the pretty cul de sac of neat, modern semi-detached houses where Rachel and Gary lived. 'How's Alex?'

'Fine.'

'I probably won't be able to have him over this weekend—'

'Of course not,' Rachel interrupted. 'Don't worry about it.'

Anna nodded and smiled. 'Thanks, Rache.'

'Yeah, right. Look, if there's anything I can do . . .'

'I'll call you,' Anna promised and drove off.

When she got into the office, Val looked up at her, a frown on her face. 'Shouldn't you be out with Charlie Coleman?'

'Shit!' Anna exploded and turned on her heel. 'Would you phone him, Val, and tell him I'm on my way?' She ran back to her car and drove the short distance along the coast road to Portmarnock.

'I'm so sorry,' she said breathlessly, hurrying over to his car.

'No problem,' Charlie said with a grin. 'At least I wasn't on the bike!'

Anna smoothed back her wet hair and looked at the sky. 'It looks as if it's clearing up. Anyway, come on, let me show you the house.'

'So was there a major crisis at the office?' he asked as she struggled with the key.

'Sorry?'

'Did Mark forget to order enough paperclips or something serious like that?'

'Oh no, nothing like that.'

They stepped into the hallway and Charlie touched her cheek. 'You look a bit peaky. Are you sick?'

'No, just a bit of a problem at home.'

'Want to talk about it?'

Anna shook her head, embarrassed. 'Oh no, really, there's nothing to talk about. Now let's have a look around. I feel terrible for keeping you waiting.'

Charlie allowed her to guide him around the house and he listened carefully while she told him about the different features in each room.

'You don't like it, do you?' she said with a small sigh.

'Not particularly,' he admitted. 'The location is great.' He waved a hand towards the large bay window that looked out on the seafront. 'And there's plenty of land. But as for the house . . .' He paused and looked around him. 'It's just a bit . . .'

'Dead?' Anna suggested.

'That's it exactly. The place has no soul, no character.'

'Maybe it needs someone to give it character?'

Charlie nodded. 'Yes, a big family, some kids, a few dogs, but a guy like me with a part-time daughter isn't going to do it.'

Anna heard the sadness in his voice. 'Would you like a big family some day?'

He looked at her in surprise. 'I think it's a bit late for that.'

'Why? You're not that old. Anyway, all you need is a younger woman.'

'Is that an offer?' he murmured, moving closer.

'I'm afraid I'm spoken for,' she joked, thinking how nice his aftershave was.

'Ah yes, to Mr Liam Harrison. I hope he knows how lucky he is.'

'Not at the moment,' Anna found herself saying.

'Oh?'

'He was made redundant last week.'

'Ah. That was the family crisis, I take it?'

'Yes – well, no – well, I suppose I'm just a bit distracted at the moment and I completely forgot our appointment.'

'I'll try not to take that personally.'

'I'm sorry.'

'Just joking, Anna.' He led her to the love-seat by the window. 'So what happened?'

Anna sat at his side, staring out at the view. If she turned to face him she'd be way too close for comfort. 'Apparently the business is in trouble and the boss decided to get rid of the senior management and run things himself.'

'That's rough. So how's your Liam taking it?'

'Up and down. At first I think he was in shock and then he started to worry. Now, thankfully, he's feeling a bit more optimistic.'

'So the redundancy was out of the blue?'

Anna's eyes narrowed. 'Totally. He was expecting promotion, had been told that it was in the bag. Everyone thought he'd take over the business when Patterson retired!'

'Ted Patterson?'

Anna turned her head to look at him. 'You know him?'

Charlie shrugged. 'Not personally, but I've heard all about him and his electronics company. He's a fairly tough customer, I believe.' He took her hand in his. 'Look, try not to worry. Liam will probably end up better off in the end.'

Anna smiled. 'I think so, too. He's very clever and gets on so well with people and he's such a hard grafter.'

Charlie's eyes were thoughtful as they met hers. 'He has something else going for him, too.'

'What's that?'

'A wonderful wife.'

Anna blushed and stood up. 'You've no idea – I'm terribly hard to live with.'

'I think I'd take a chance.'

Anna felt her cheeks grow hot. 'My God, look at the time. We'd better get a move on. I told the owners we'd be out by three.'

Charlie got slowly to his feet and walked over to her. 'Don't worry about them, are you okay?'

She nodded. 'Sorry for offloading all of this stuff on you – it's not very professional of me.'

'Don't be ridiculous,' he said, looking annoyed. 'I would hope at this stage you'd see me as a friend as well as a client.'

'Of course. Thank you, Charlie. You've made me feel a lot better.'

Immediately, his smile returned. 'Good. Now let's get out of this mausoleum.'

Chapter 13

Liam heard the post thud on to the mat and abandoned his cornflakes to go and check it. There were three envelopes: one of them a gas bill, one a credit-card bill and the other an invitation to a conference in Cork. He was staring at the credit-card bill, his cornflakes forgotten, when Anna walked in pulling her jacket on. 'Anything interesting?' she asked as she spooned coffee into a mug and poured water from the kettle.

'This has to stop,' Liam replied.

'What has?' Anna asked. 'Ugh, this water's cold! Liam, I asked you to put on the kettle.'

'You have got to stop spending, Anna. There's a balance of nearly two grand on this card and I hate to think what you owe on your Visa.'

Anna turned her back on him as she filled the kettle with fresh water. 'It's fine, really. Please stop worrying.'

'Stop worrying! Jesus, Anna, what cloud are you living on? We can't spend like this any more! At least, not until I find work. You have to cut back.'

'We don't owe anyone that much. My biggest expenditure at the moment is the supermarket shop.'

'And what about the mortgage and the electricity and the gas?' He flung the other bill across the table. 'I used to pay these directly from my account but you're going to have to take them on for the moment.'

Anna turned to face him. 'We'll cope, Liam. It won't be for long, I'm sure it won't. Please try not to worry so much.'

He sighed. 'Okay, but will you in turn please try and go easy on the credit cards?'

'I promise.' Putting down her coffee, she dropped a kiss on his forehead, picked up her bag and headed for the door. 'I've got to go.'

'What time will you be home?'

'It'll be late this evening, I have a few appointments. Bye, sweetheart.'

'Bye.'

Liam went into the sitting room and switched on the television. The prospect of another day alone stretched out in front of him, and he dreaded it. He hated the boredom, he hated having nowhere to go, he hated having no meetings to hurry to, and he hated watching Anna carry on as normal. He knew she had to and he knew he should be grateful that she had a good job, but he wasn't. If anyone should be at home it should be her. She wouldn't mind. She could have babies and that would more than make up for losing her job. But what was he supposed to do? How was he supposed to stay sane?

It was nearly four weeks now and there was still no sign of a suitable job. An old mate from his college days had offered him a temporary position working on the factory floor but Liam had no intention of taking a step backwards. Something suitable had to come up soon; he just hoped he didn't go quietly mad while he was waiting. Flicking off the TV he stood up and went upstairs. He'd throw on some clothes and take his toolbox over to his mother's. There were a few jobs needed doing around the house that he hadn't had a chance to tackle when he was at Patterson's. She'd be delighted with the company and it would mean he'd get a decent lunch too, which would make a nice change.

Feeling slightly better, Liam splashed water on his face, brushed his teeth and pulled on jeans and a clean white T-shirt. He could do with a shave but he wasn't in the mood and it wasn't as though there was anyone to impress. His mother wouldn't approve but she'd be afraid to say anything. She'd been shocked when he'd told her he was out of a job and had spent most days since on her knees praying for him. Liam had been very blasé with her, assuring her that the right job would come along in no time but he was finding it hard lately to keep up the bravado.

He secured the toolbox on the back carrier of his mountain bike and cycled to Josie's house. He had thought he'd really miss his company car but now he actually enjoyed going out on the bike. The physical exercise felt good and it was a great place to do some uninterrupted thinking. It was also a damn sight better than sitting in bloody traffic jams. Less than twenty minutes later he had turned into his mother's drive and was chuffed that he wasn't even that much out of breath.

'Finally getting a bit of exercise, Harrison?' a voice jeered at him as he bent to lock the bike to the gate.

He looked up and smiled at the woman leaning over the wall. 'No, Tara, I just don't have a car any more.'

Tara looked at him, horrified, her hand going to her short blonde bob. 'Oh Liam, I'm sorry. God, that was tactless. Still, I always had a knack for putting my foot in it, didn't I?'

'You did,' he laughed.

'Any luck with the job-hunting yet?'

He shook his head. 'Nobody seems to be hiring at the moment.'

'I need a manicurist if you're interested,' she joked, her pretty eyes twinkling. 'The pay isn't great but I'd throw in a free massage once in a while.'

'I'm tempted,' he told her, 'but I'm not sure my mother would approve.'

'Rubbish, your mum loves me,' Tara said confidently.

'That's because you give her a discount.'

'Well, she is my neighbour,' Tara pointed out and then added with a wink, 'and we were almost related.'

Liam brandished his toolbox. 'I'd better go on in. She has a few jobs lined up for me.'

'If you've got a moment later, you could do a few jobs around the salon for me.'

'What's it worth?' he challenged.

'Well, I wouldn't dream of offending you by offering money, but like I say, I do a very good body massage.' Tara's eyes roamed appreciatively over his torso.

'I'll keep it in mind,' he promised. 'Seeya, Tara.'

Liam and Tara had started dating when they were sixteen, and it was only when Tara decided to drop out of college three years later and run off to England to seek her fortune, that their relationship came to an end. Her fortune had turned out to be sweeping up and washing hair in a backstreet salon in Liverpool, but Tara wasn't afraid of hard work and it wasn't long before she found a better job in more salubrious surroundings. Her boss quickly spotted the potential in this beautiful, feisty blonde and trained her as a beautician, sending her on all the latest courses in skincare and massage.

Tara had just been thinking of branching out on her own when she'd got the call that her mother was sick. As the only child, Tara felt she had no choice but to come home and take care of her mother, and when she died ten months later, Tara realized that she didn't want to leave Dublin again. With her modest savings, she turned the downstairs of her family home into a salon and upstairs into an apartment for herself. She was confident that as the house was around the corner from the shops and the church, which had a large car park, the location was perfect for women who didn't want to travel into town every time they needed a facial.

Now, three years later, Tara had a regular clientèle, a steady, healthy income and the total admiration of Liam's mother. Josie had always hoped that Liam and Tara would get back together. She was perfect wife material. From a good family, she had attended the local Loretto convent school and was very pretty too. But by the time Tara had come home, Liam and Anna were already married and Josie had to settle for having Tara as a neighbour rather than a daughter-in-law.

'Mum, it's me,' Liam called, letting himself in with his key.

Josie appeared at the top of the stairs with a pillowcase in her hand. 'Hello, son, what are you doing here?'

'I thought I'd come around and do a few jobs for you.' He held up the toolbox. 'I'll start with the lamp in your bedroom, shall I?'

'Just let me make you a cup of tea first.'

'It's okay, Mum, I don't want tea. I'd prefer to get started.'

'Then you must stay for a bit of lunch. I'll slip around to the butcher's and get a nice few chops.'

'Okay, thanks.' Liam went straight up to her

bedroom and got started. Physical work was the best way to take his mind off his troubles and by the time lunch was ready, Liam had fixed the dodgy switch on the lamp, sorted out the strange noise in the cistern of the loo and put a new cable on the lawnmower.

'Thanks, love, that's wonderful,' Josie told him as she loaded his plate with carrots and parsnip.

'No problem,' Liam told her. 'I quite enjoyed myself.'

'No word on the job front, I suppose?' his mother asked, unable to keep quiet any longer.

'No.'

'Maybe you should think about taking something else,' she suggested. She knew that her son had turned down a couple of jobs already that only paid half the money he'd been getting, but surely any work was better than no work?

Liam tensed. 'I know what I'm doing, Mum.'

'Sorry, love, of course you do.' Josie patted his shoulder.

Liam left as soon as he'd finished lunch, wanting to escape before she started asking him more questions. He knew she meant well but she didn't understand how things worked at this level, and that if he ever wanted to work as a senior manager again, the last thing he should do was accept a low-level, hands-on job.

Tara was walking round the corner laden with shopping as he cycled down the road. 'Need a hand?' he asked, pulling in beside her.

'Only if you'll come in for a coffee,' she told him.

'Haven't you got any clients?' he hedged.

'I don't open on Mondays,' Tara reminded him. 'Besides, I have a dripping tap in my bathroom you could have a look at.'

'Okay then,' Liam agreed, taking her bags and hanging them from his handlebars. 'But don't tell my mother. I told her I had to rush off.'

Tara looked at her watch. 'She'll be having her nap by now and you'll be gone by the time she wakes up.'

Liam looked anxiously at his mother's house as he waited for Tara to open her hall door.

'Bring the bike in and leave it in the hall,' she told him and then led him upstairs to her flat.

'This is nice,' Liam said, wandering around her small cosy living room as she made the coffee.

'I like it. The bathroom's through the door to the right. The cold tap in the bath is the one giving the problem.'

Taking a spanner from his toolbox, Liam went through the door and found himself in Tara's bedroom. Averting his eyes from the purple satin-covered bed, he went on through another door into a surprisingly large bathroom with a double power shower and a large Jacuzzi bath. 'Very nice,' he called back to her as he admired the midnight-blue marble tiles that covered the floor and walls. The suite was in white and there was a shelf with an abundance of white, fluffy towels. White candles of varying sizes were arranged around the room in wrought-iron holders and a large mirror covered the top half of the wall over the bath. He went to work on the faulty tap and was still crouched by the bath when he felt her hand on his shoulder.

'It has underfloor heating,' Tara said at his shoulder. 'Great when you step out of the bath.'

'Oh, really?' Liam cleared his throat and thought that the room didn't feel so big all of a sudden. 'I think I've sorted your problem. Any chance of that coffee?'

Tara laughed and led the way back to the living room. 'Don't worry, Liam, I'm not going to jump on you.'

'I know that.' Liam laughed too but he still sat in the armchair rather than beside her on the large sofa.

'You must be cracking up, hanging around the house all day,' Tara said, pushing a plate of biscuits towards him.

'I am,' he agreed. Most people pussy-footed around him these days, but not Tara.

'You should do something.'

He bristled. 'I've been to all the recruitment agencies and I go through the papers every day, but—'

'No, that's not what I mean.' She waved a dismissive hand. 'I mean do something completely different to keep you occupied until the right job comes along.'

'Like what?'

'Travel?'

'Travelling costs money,' he reminded her.

'Then odd jobs,' she continued, undeterred. 'Do what you just did for your mum and me. You could advertise in the local supermarket.'

Liam shook his head. 'No, I'd prefer to concentrate on finding the right job. I'm a good engineer, Tara, with years of experience and I'm still relatively young. They should be queuing up to get me.'

'And I'm sure they will. Give it time, Liam. Now, tell me, how's Anna doing?'

'Great, really great.'

'Good, that's good.'

'Yeah.'

'You must be proud of her.'

'Sure I am.'

Tara's eyes were speculative as she watched him. 'It must be hard watching her go off to work every morning.'

'It is,' Liam admitted, 'although we'd be in a right mess if she didn't have such a good job.'

'But it makes you feel dispensable.'

Liam stared at her. 'How did you know?'

Tara shrugged her slim shoulders. 'You're an old-fashioned kind of guy, Liam, just like your dad was.'

Liam smiled at the mention of his father. Arthur Harrison had insisted that Josie give up work as soon as she'd agreed to marry him. He'd worked in the same job for forty years and Josie had never seen a household bill, let alone paid one. Liam had taken over the running of the house when his father had died as he knew Josie wouldn't even know where to begin.

'Anna's not an old-fashioned girl and I wouldn't want her to be,' he added quickly.

'Of course not.' Tara's voice was soothing. 'But you don't want to be a kept man either.'

Liam looked bleak. 'Isn't that a bit pathetic?'

'It's perfectly natural, any decent man would feel the same. Anna's a very lucky woman.'

Liam's eyes met hers and he quickly looked away again, swallowed the dregs of his coffee and stood up. 'I'd better be going. Thanks for the coffee.'

'Thanks for fixing my tap,' Tara said, walking with him to the door. 'And don't be a stranger. If you need someone to talk to, I'm always here.'

Liam quickly planted a kiss on her cheek. 'Thanks, Tara, I appreciate that. Bye.'

'Bye.' She stood watching as he wheeled his bike out onto the path.

He turned to close the gate. 'Bye, then.'

'Bye, Liam.'

Tara shut the door and went through to her bedroom, pulling off her clothes. As she ran the bath, she hummed to herself, a smile playing around her lips. It had taken longer than she'd hoped, but not only had she finally got Liam into her flat, he'd actually been in her bedroom and bathroom too. Next time he was here, she vowed as she lowered herself into the scented water, it wouldn't be to fix a tap.

Chapter 14

Anna was in a very bad humour by the time she got home that evening. One of the house sales she'd secured last month had fallen through and the vendor had called this morning to say she was taking her business to a different agent. Also, a couple that she'd spent the last two days driving around half the properties on their books had decided that maybe they weren't ready to move after all.

Anna was absolutely exhausted and yet she had nothing to show for it. Also, she admitted to herself as she sat in the car in the driveway, she dreaded going inside. She never knew what kind of humour Liam would be in these days, but it was a fairly safe bet it wouldn't be good. When she finally dragged herself out of the car and went inside she was cheered by the sight of the toolbox in the hall. The noise from the television drew her towards the sitting room and she forced a smile to her lips as she opened the door. 'Hi, sweetheart, I'm home.'

'Hey.' Liam was stretched out on the sofa, a can

of beer in his hand, the newspaper at his feet and the remote control on the seat beside him.

'How are things?'

'Okay.'

Anna moved the remote and sat down. 'Any news?'

'No.' He didn't take his eyes off the television.

'I see you had the toolbox out – what were you doing?'

'I just went around to do a few jobs for Mum.'

'See, you did have news,' she teased him. No response. Anna stood up again. 'I'm starving. Is there anything for dinner?'

'I'm not hungry. I ate in Mum's.'

Anna went out to the kitchen. 'I'll get myself something then, shall I?' she muttered as she went to the cupboard. She didn't have the energy to make anything so she just grabbed the box of cornflakes and fetched a bowl, but when she went to get the milk, the only carton in the fridge was almost empty. 'Oh, for God's sake, Liam, couldn't you at least have brought some milk?' she said, carrying the empty carton back into the sitting room.

Liam looked up. 'Sorry?'

'There's no milk, Liam, and there's no dinner, because *you're* not hungry.'

'But I never make dinner,' he retorted. 'That's always been your job.'

'Yes, well – that was when we were both working.

Now I think that, just occasionally, it could be your job and the very least you could do is make sure that we don't run out of bread or milk.'

'All right, all right, keep your hair on!'

Anna took a deep breath. 'Look, I don't expect you to turn into a househusband, you know? I realize you're busy chasing up jobs. I'm just asking you to help out with the shopping. With my weird hours, getting to the supermarket isn't always easy.'

'I said I would, didn't I? Stop nagging.'

'I am not nagging!' Anna marched back out to the kitchen in disgust and got herself a beer from the fridge, her appetite now completely gone. She was sitting on the kitchen step watching next door's cat preening itself in the last of the evening sun when Liam came out and sat down beside her.

'Sorry,' he said, leaning his head against hers.

'Yeah, me too.' She turned her head and kissed him. 'You know, now that you've got that tool box out you could fix the garden gate and stop that bloody dog getting in and doing his business on my roses.' Anna's rose garden had always been a joke between them. They only had a tiny yard with a few pot plants, but most of her attempts to grow anything had failed dismally.

'Oh, for God's sake, can't you just leave me alone?' Liam stood up and stormed back inside.

Anna stared after him. 'I'm not having a go! It was just a joke. Liam?' But he had closed the door behind him and she was talking to herself.

Wearily, Anna got to her feet and went upstairs to have a bath. She turned the hot tap on full and added a generous helping of bath oil. Leaving it to run, she went into the bedroom and took off her clothes. She felt really upset at Liam's overreaction. She didn't expect him to don a pinny and do the ironing and wash floors – in fact, she'd hate that – but it would be nice if he helped a bit more without her having to ask.

She was trying so hard to cheer him up but nothing worked. She'd even paid off her credit card and then cut it up into tiny pieces so that she wouldn't be tempted again. Now they had one card between them and Anna was careful to discuss any major purchases with Liam first. She'd also offered to write letters or update his CV for him because she knew how much he hated doing that sort of thing, but lately he'd told her that he didn't need her help.

In fact, he'd changed so much in the last few weeks that Anna hardly recognized him. When he'd first lost his job, he'd discussed all the possibilities with her and they'd pored over the employment notices together, discussing what he should apply for and what wasn't suitable for him. But now she didn't have a clue what jobs he was applying for because he didn't tell her. Anytime she asked, he answered in monosyllables and changed the subject or left the room.

With a heavy heart, Anna turned off the water which had long ago gone cold and slid into the bath.

She was at the end of her tether. She wanted so much to help Liam through this, but they seemed to be growing further and further apart. Maybe if she asked Mark for a raise it would cheer Liam up. Then, at least, he wouldn't have to worry so much about money.

Mark could hardly refuse her. She'd had so many sales in the last month she definitely deserved it. And when Charlie Coleman finally bought a house it would mean a large commission for Mark and major kudos for her. Thinking of Charlie made her smile. She'd miss him when he finally found the right place – if he ever *did* find the right place. Sometimes Anna thought that it was unlikely.

Charlie's heart wasn't in the search and his daughter didn't seem to care as long as her pony was catered for and she was near a bus route or train station. For all his charisma and confidence, Charlie seemed a lonely figure to Anna, and vulnerable in a way. He obviously craved companionship and yet she couldn't understand why he was alone. He was good-looking, great company and he was obviously loaded – surely every woman's dream man. But Anna got the feeling that despite all his flirting, Charlie didn't like to get involved. In fact, he probably just flirted with her because she was married and he didn't have to worry about her taking him seriously.

On that day when she'd told him about Liam's redundancy, he'd been kind and considerate and, she thought, quite annoyed with her when she'd tried to treat him as a client. 'I hope you see me as a friend,' he'd said. And Anna did in a way. When they went to view houses she found herself commenting on décor and offering opinions, something she would never do with other clients. And yet, she felt Mark would approve. Charlie wasn't like other clients and Mark had wanted her to give him the red-carpet treatment. She figured the best way of doing that was to be brutally honest with him, and so far it seemed to have worked.

Tomorrow she was going to take him to see a much smaller property, but it was nestled in a quiet spot by the estuary and had a large field to the side and back of the house. Anna thought it would suit him much better than all the ostentatious show homes they'd viewed so far. It was an old cottage with just three bedrooms and one bathroom, but they were big rooms and there was plenty of scope for adding en-suites to at least two of the rooms. The kitchen needed to be gutted but it was a good size with a small, tiled fireplace and a large window overlooking the back field. The living room though, was Anna's favourite. Two sides were practically all window, giving breathtaking views of the estuary, and there was another large stone fireplace that Anna could imagine sitting beside on a cold winter's evening with a cup of hot chocolate in her hands.

She sighed, thinking how perfect a house it would be for her and Liam if they started a family. Part of the back field could be sectioned off to make a safe little garden, and Anna could imagine herself barbecuing on warm summer evenings while Liam played with the kids. With a sigh, she eased herself out of the now tepid water. There was no point in this kind of dreaming. The way things were at the moment, they'd be lucky to hold on to the house they had, never mind buy a bigger one.

And as for kids, Liam had made it very clear that starting a family was definitely on the back burner for the moment. But of course she understood that; he was quite right. She mustn't get downhearted. She was only thirty-one and there was plenty of time for kids. Liam would get a job, it was only a matter of time, and then life would go on as before. They would be close again and the silly rows would stop. Liam would go back to being the confident, fun-loving man she'd married. And then she would be able to slow down a little and focus on becoming a mother.

Chapter 15

'I don't know about this diet,' Karen complained as they sat in the canteen. 'I never really liked cabbage.'

'It's not *just* cabbage,' Jill said, stirring the murky green mixture. 'It's onions, peppers, tomatoes, celery—'

'And cabbage.'

Jill sighed. 'And cabbage. Still, it's less than three hundred calories.'

'It feels like it – I'm starving.' Karen spooned the soup into her mouth, her nose wrinkling in disgust.

'I'm more worried about the side-effects,' Jill confided. 'I have a presentation this afternoon.'

Karen giggled. 'That could be fun.'

Jill rolled her eyes. 'Sound-effects are the last thing I need!'

'Vinny would be thrilled.'

Jill's head snapped up. 'What do you mean by that?'

'Oh, come on.' Karen lowered her voice. 'It's obvious he's out to get you.'

'Out to get me?'

'Well, your job anyway.'

'Has someone said something to you? Has Vinny?'

It was Karen's turn to roll her eyes. 'Of course not. Vinny's way too smooth for that, but it's obvious that he's not happy being number two.'

'So you think he's after my job?'

'Everyone does, although he'd probably be happier with Sue's.'

'There's nothing wrong with ambition.' Jill pushed her bowl away. 'He wouldn't be a good adman if he wasn't ambitious.'

Karen shot her a knowing look. 'Right.'

Jill smiled brightly. 'Got to go and make myself beautiful before the presentation. If my lipstick is loud enough it might distract them from any strange noises.'

As she redid her make-up in the ladies loo, Jill thought about what Karen had said. It was no surprise really. She had spotted Vinny's naked ambition – why wouldn't the others? And, no doubt, Sue was thrilled by the new competitive edge in the company; it could only mean good things for ADLI. But Jill didn't feel turned on by the idea of a fight, as she once might have been. Lately she'd found it hard to concentrate on projects. Getting excited about a new kitchen cleaner or dental-hygiene product didn't come naturally any more and she often wondered what she was doing and where she was going.

It didn't help that she'd had a bust-up with Andy. She had initiated it. He'd been crowding her and getting very heavy, and she hadn't liked it. Now that he'd taken the hint and backed off, however, she found she was missing him. Wasn't that just typical of her? Jill ran her hands through her hair, made a face at herself and went back to her office. She was just sitting down at her desk when the phone rang.

'ADLI, Jill Clarke speaking.'

'Hi, Jill.'

'Rachel?'

'No! It's Anna!'

'Oh sorry, Anna, sometimes you sound alike.' Usually when Anna was on a downer. 'What's wrong?'

'Why do you think something's wrong?'

Jill sighed. 'Isn't there?'

'Well, yes, there is.'

'Liam?'

'Oh Jill, I'm at my wit's end. I've done everything I can think of to help him, to distract him, to cheer him up, but nothing works. He's so depressed. He hangs around the house all day doing nothing. Either that or he's round at his mother's.'

'He must find the day very long.'

'Yeah, he does. Oh Jill, I can't stand it. I feel so helpless. There must be something I can do to help him through all this.'

'All you can do is hold his hand and listen,' Jill consoled her.

'I don't even get to do that any more. If I ask him

how he's feeling or make any suggestions, he bites my head off. He never used to be like this. We could always talk about everything.'

'I suppose he's not in the mood for talking.'

'He's happy enough to talk to his mother. He spends so much time over there, Jill, he might as well move back in.'

'Josie must be pleased.'

Anna's laugh was bitter. 'She's delighted. Waiting on him hand and foot, making all his favourite meals.'

'Well, I suppose he needs a bit of cosseting at the moment.'

'Yes – I just wish he'd let me be the one to do it. I feel so lonely, Jill, and I hate to admit it, but I'm actually jealous of Josie. Why does he want to spend time with her and talk to her, and yet he hardly opens his mouth to me?'

Jill wondered if she should point out to Anna that her husband probably resented her but decided against it. The poor girl was upset enough. 'Give him time and space, Anna. He's going through one of the hardest things a man can experience.'

'I know, Jill. Oh, I'm sorry for being such a moan.'

'You're not. But I'm afraid I have to go now. I have to do a presentation on a new haemorrhoid cream.'

Anna giggled. 'What a glamorous life you advertising people lead.'

'You'd better believe it! Take care, babes.'

*

The presentation went without a hitch and Jill was feeling quite proud of herself as she packed up her briefcase.

'Can I have a quick word?' Sue put her head around the door.

'Sure.' Jill smiled at her boss and gestured to a chair.

'It's about Ideal Interiors.'

Jill racked her brain. 'Oh, you mean the Gordon account.'

'That's right, although I do like their new name, don't you?'

'Yes, it's very catchy.'

'Vinny came up with it, you know.'

'Good for him.' Jill's expression didn't change.

'You'll remember he took over the account when you were away last month?'

'At the conference,' Jill said, making sure Sue remembered that she'd been away on business.

'Yes. Well, anyway, he seemed to get on very well with Gordon's marketing team so I thought it might be better if we left him on the case.'

Jill stared at her. 'You're taking the Gordon account away from me?'

'No, I'm just talking about this particular campaign.'

'And if it goes well and they like working with him?'

'We'll talk about it then. Don't look on this as something negative. You have more than enough on your plate at the moment.'

'You think I'm not coping?'

Sue stood up. 'I'm not saying that at all, but if Vinny takes over the Gordon account you'll have more time and energy to invest in your other accounts.' She looked at her watch. 'Now, I really must fly. We'll talk more tomorrow. Goodnight, Jill.'

'Goodnight.'

Jill sat staring into space for a long time after she'd left. It looked like Vinny had won. One of her major accounts was being taken away from her – she didn't buy the 'just this campaign' line – and it was only a matter of time before other accounts would follow. On impulse, she picked up the phone and dialled Andy's work number. She got his voicemail saying he was out of the office until the following Thursday. Frowning, she tried his mobile but it was obviously switched off. Either Andy was out of the country or he just didn't want to be contacted.

She couldn't blame him. She'd made it perfectly clear that she didn't want him around. That had probably been a mistake – one of the many she seemed to be making at the moment. Feeling restless and not wanting to go home alone, Jill dialled Rachel's number. Some home cooking and a dose of Alex's exuberant personality would cheer her up. Yet again, she just got an answering machine. Without thinking, she dialled Gary's mobile. This time she was in luck.

'Hello, Gary Hanlon?'

'Hey, Gary, it's Jill.'

'Jill!' Gary sounded surprised. 'Is everything okay?'

'Yeah, fine. I was just going to drop over and see Rachel but she isn't there.'

'She isn't? Oh well, she's probably just gone down to the shops. Come on over anyway. I'm on my way home, should be there in ten minutes.'

'Okay then,' Jill agreed. 'I'll stop off for a bottle of wine.'

'Great, see you soon.'

Jill bought two bottles, one non-alcoholic rosé that Rachel liked and a bottle of the Australian Shiraz that Gary enjoyed. A box of sweets for Alex and she was in her Audi, top down and cruising over to Rachel's house.

Gary was standing at the door when she pulled up outside the house and he came to meet her. 'No sign of Rachel yet, don't know where she could have got to.'

'Is Alex with her?'

'No, he's at a sleepover tonight. Let's go and check the kitchen and see if there's any sign of dinner. If not, I can go and get us a curry.'

The kitchen was devoid of any enticing cooking aromas and, on inspection, the fridge was quite bare. It was a beautiful, balmy June evening so Gary poured them both some of the wine Jill had brought and they took their glasses out to the garden to enjoy the last of the sunshine.

'I think I'll be going for a takeaway,' Gary said, stretching out his legs. 'Even if Rachel has gone to the supermarket it would take ages to cook something and I don't think I can last that long.'

Jill thought about her cabbage-soup diet, about the Gordon account and about Vinny. 'Me neither. Anyway, Rachel wasn't expecting me. Did she know you were coming home early?'

Gary closed his eyes and held his face up to the sun. 'I think I mentioned it.'

'Her pregnancy seems to be going well this time – apart from the tiredness.'

He opened one eye. 'You think?'

'You don't?' Jill countered.

'She seems so down, Jill. You must have noticed.'

'It's just the tiredness.'

'I'm not so sure. She doesn't seem very interested in the baby. I remember the last time, the house was full of pregnancy and baby magazines and she spent months planning the nursery.'

Jill smiled. 'I remember. Still, it's always different with a second child and she's probably a bit scared of being a mother again.'

'Scared?' He looked bemused.

'It's a big responsibility, not to mention hard work.'

'I suppose.'

'Give her some time and space.' Sounds familiar, she realized, having said the same words to Anna earlier about Liam.

Before Gary could reply, Rachel appeared in the doorway. 'Jill! Hi, what are you doing here?'

'Just called in for a chat.'

'That's nice.'

Gary stood up. 'Will I bring in the shopping?'

'What shopping?' Rachel looked vague.

'Weren't you at the supermarket?'

She shook her head.

'So where have you been?'

'I went for a walk.' She sat down on his vacated deckchair.

'Oh, right. Looks like it's takeaway, Jill.' Gary shot Rachel a bemused look before going inside to find a menu.

'Are you okay, Rachel?'

'Yeah, fine.'

'You look tired.'

'Nothing new there then,' Rachel said, with a wry smile.

Jill looked at her cousin, a worried frown knitting her brows. With the exception of her bump, Rachel was beginning to look quite gaunt. Ironic really, considering that one of the reasons she didn't want to get pregnant again was because she didn't want to put on even more weight. 'You know, once you've had this baby you're going to be really skinny.'

Rachel looked down at her body. 'Do you think so?'

'Definitely! We'll have to go out and get you a whole new wardrobe.'

Rachel laughed but her eyes were sad. 'I don't

think I'm going to have time for shopping when this little person comes along.'

'Sure you will. Gary will babysit.'

'What's that?' Gary said, as he returned with two menus.

'I was just saying that Rachel would have to go on a few shopping trips for new clothes when the baby is born and she says that she won't have time. But that's what dads are for, isn't it, Gary?'

He shrugged. 'Yeah, sure.'

Rachel shot him a look of pure disbelief.' So you're going to miss out on your golf so that I can go shopping?'

'No problem.'

'That's what he says now,' Rachel told Jill, 'but he'll come up with some excuse when the time comes.'

Gary shook his head. 'There's no pleasing you, is there? Now, will we have Indian or Chinese?'

'I'm not hungry,' Rachel said, not looking at him.

Gary sighed and turned to Jill. 'What about you, Jill, what would you like?'

Jill shook her head and stood up. 'You know what? I don't think I'll stay for food, if you don't mind, guys. Rachel could do with an early night and I have a healthy bowl of soup waiting in my fridge. I'll hate myself in the morning if I have a three-thousand-calorie curry.'

Gary looked from his wife to her cousin and

turned away, shaking his head. 'Oh, please yourselves.'

Rachel walked her cousin to the door. 'Sorry, Jill, I wish I was better company.'

'Hey, it's not your fault! You've got a hungry little munchkin in there, sapping all of your strength. You go to bed and rest.'

Rachel hugged her and smiled. 'Thanks.'

Gary appeared and offered to walk Jill to the car. 'Sorry about that,' he said. 'I thought Rachel would enjoy the company.'

She reached up to kiss his cheek. 'Hey, there's no need to apologise. The poor girl is obviously exhausted.' She started the car and waved her hand as she pulled away. 'Take care, and have a lovely weekend!'

As soon as she'd got around the corner; her smile disappeared. Poor Rachel. She was so miserable, and Gary didn't seem to know what to do to help. What with Anna's problems with Liam and her own break-up with Andy, they weren't having a lot of luck with relationships at the moment. Mentally, Jill tipped her soup down the drain and stopped off on the way home for a pizza and another bottle of wine. Sod the diet.

Chapter 16

Rachel pounced on the postcard in the hall and carried it into the kitchen. It had been ages since she'd got one and the last phone call had been a disaster, with a horrible echo on the line. She hadn't realized how much she looked forward to hearing from her mother. If it wasn't for her and the girls on *MumSpeak*, Rachel thought she'd go crazy. The long summer days were dragging and Alex got bored very easily. He hated being holed up in the house and garden all of the time but Rachel was usually too tired to take him to the park or the beach.

Pouring herself a large glass of water, Rachel sat down to read her postcard.

Hello, my darling, how are you keeping? I would so love to see you – are you getting big now? I make it that you're now about halfway through – is that right? Maybe you could come out to meet us now that Alex has finished school, although July can be very hot down here. It might be best to wait until the end of August and we could meet up in a nice beachside resort so that Alex could build sandcastles. Talk it over with Gary and let me know. As you can see, we are now in Milan. It's big and noisy – aren't all cities – and we're only going to stay a couple of days before moving on into France. Your father is trying to get seats for a matinée in La Scala for some obscure opera we've never heard of. He says it would be sacrilege to visit Milan without going to the opera. I'm just praying the seats are comfortable and I can have a nice snooze! I'll call you in a few days, darling. Give Alex the biggest kiss from his granny and grandad. Love, Mam

Rachel turned over the card and studied the photo of the Via Montenapoleone, the famous street where all the main fashion-design houses were located. Wouldn't it be nice to be there right now? It was clear from her mother's card that she had been talking to Anna, who had been talking to Jill. They were all dying to pack her off to the continent. And it wasn't such a bad idea, she supposed, although the heat would be a problem. Her feet were starting to swell already and hot weather was bound to exacerbate the problem.

After pinning up the postcard, Rachel went over to the computer and signed into *MumSpeak*. The thread that she'd started when she'd come out about her ambivalence towards the new baby had grown and grown, and she'd been touched at the warm replies she'd received. Her suggestion that Gary might be playing around had resulted in a flood of replies, most telling her that she was imagining things and her paranoia was a side-effect of pregnancy. Flojo said: *I'm sure he loves you, honey, it's just your hormones getting the better of you. And let's face it, none of us are feeling very attractive right now!* And Funnybun said: *Maybe he really is working late, having a new baby is an expensive business after all.* Though she wasn't entirely convinced, the thoughtfulness and kindness of the comments made her feel better and she found, as she read, that her hand kept gravitating towards her bump.

She decided not to contribute to the board today but instead browsed through other threads and read about other mothers' problems. One girl, RuthieB, was asking for prayers because her three-month-old was having surgery today for a heart defect. Tears filled Rachel's eyes as she thought about what that poor mother was going through, and she thanked God that Alex had always been so fit and healthy.

God, Alex! She looked at her watch and saw it was nearly one o'clock and she was supposed to be picking him up from his arts and crafts class in fifteen minutes. She'd have to run all the way to the school if she was to make it on time. She hated the thought of Alex's anxious face and his teacher's disapproving one if she was late again. Being pregnant only won you so much sympathy. She arrived as the children were emerging and she leaned heavily against the gate to catch her breath.

'Rachel? Are you okay?' Gretta Mullins, pristine in a grey trouser suit and perfectly coiffed hair, was watching her, a frown wrinkling her perfectly made-up face.

Rachel, conscious of the perspiration on her brow, shook her head at the other mother. 'I'm fine, just fine.'

'Can I drop you and Alex home? I have to go into the village anyway. Marianna has a dance class.'

The thought of being cooped up in Gretta's sporty little Mini, with Alex and Marianna tearing each other's hair out in the back was enough to make Rachel straighten up and take a deep breath. 'Oh no, it's too nice a day. We're going to go for a good long walk.'

Gretta shot a confused look at the darkening sky above. 'Well, if you're sure . . .'

Rachel smiled brightly. 'Sure, thanks, Gretta. Alex? Come on, sweetheart, let's go.' Quickly propelling him back down the path, Rachel kept the pace up until she'd left the other mothers far behind.

'Are we really going for a long walk?' Alex asked, skipping ahead.

'No.'

'But you said—'

'I'm tired now, Alex. I need to go home and have a rest.'

The little boy scowled. 'You're always resting.'

'Don't be so cheeky, young man!'

Alex looked mutinous but wisely said no more

and the remainder of the walk home was in silence.

'Would you like a snack?' Rachel asked, kicking off her sandals when they got inside.

'No.'

'No, thank you,' Rachel corrected him.

'No, thank you,' Alex muttered. 'Can I watch television?'

'No, go outside and play.'

'But it's starting to rain,' Alex told her, pointing to the fat drops that were starting to fall on the patio outside.

Rachel sighed. 'Then play inside with one of your toys – you have enough of them.'

With much moaning, Alex started to root through his toybox in the corner, finally pulling out a noisy remote-control car. After five minutes of him racing the screeching toy up and down her hall, Rachel gave in. 'Okay, you can watch television for a little while,' she told a triumphant Alex, and after settling him in front of *Pokémon*, went out to the kitchen to make some camomile tea. She was sitting at the kitchen table when the phone rang.

'Hello, Rachel, love.'

'Mum? Mum, is that you?'

'And who else would it be? How are you?'

'Fine – well, tired, but I'm okay. How's Milan?'

'Oh, that was last week! Now we're in Nice. Oh Rache, it's so lovely here. Really nice. Nice, get it? Ha-ha.'

Rachel smiled. 'Very funny, Mam. So where are you heading next?'

'Oh, we're going to tour around here for a while and then we'll head off to Barcelona.'

'Oh, I didn't know Barcelona was on your itinerary.'

'It wasn't, but Patricia and Matt are coming out to meet us in Benalmadena and you know how glam Patricia always is, so I thought I'd stop off and do a spot of shopping first.'

Patricia and Matt Quinlan were old friends of her parents and had already met up with them twice since they'd started their travels. 'So you're going to stay in Benalmadena for a while then?'

'Yes, that's the plan. We're going to rent an apartment there.'

'An apartment? But why?'

'Oh, we just thought we'd push the boat out and treat ourselves. We need somewhere decent to entertain Patricia and Matt.'

'Well, excuse me!'

'Now, you don't begrudge your old parents a bit of comfort in their dotage, do you?' Bridie Gallagher retorted. 'We went without for long enough to make sure that you pair had everything.'

'Yes, Mam, you've told us often enough.'

'Cheeky!' Bridie said, laughing. 'Anyway, tell me about you. How are you feeling, love?'

'Grand,' Rachel lied.

'I hope you're taking care of yourself and eating well. This is no time for diets, you know.'

'I'm not dieting, Mam.'

'Good, you need all your strength now.'

'So, how's Dad?'

'Red and fat,' her mother laughed. 'He won't wear suncream and he drinks far too much beer, but he's having the time of his life.'

'Good, I'm glad. Give him my love.'

'I will. How's my favourite grandson?'

'He's wonderful. Oh, that reminds me, Mam. You wouldn't mind getting me some shoes for him, would you?'

'Of course not. Just tell me what size and style.'

Rachel quickly gave her the details and her mother scribbled them down.

'Right, darling, I'd better go. Your dad is going mad for a cup of tea. Now you take care of yourself.'

'I will. Bye, Mam.' Rachel replaced the receiver with a sigh.

Phone conversations like that were so frustrating. Nothing really said, just pleasantries, time-of-day stuff. Rachel needed more than that. Bridie mightn't be the most conventional mother in the world but she usually had a commonsense solution for most problems. Rachel wondered what she'd have to say if she confided her fears about Gary or told her how ambivalent she felt about the new baby.

Alex stuck his head through the doorway. 'I'm hungry, Mum.'

Rachel waved him in and gave him a hug. 'I'll make you a sandwich.'

'And a bun?' Alex's eyes twinkled up at her.

Rachel smiled. 'And a bun.'

Chapter 17

Liam heard the door bang and swore softly. Another day and yet another row. He didn't mean to bite Anna's head off but she just seemed to say all the wrong things. As soon as she got in the door in the evening she wanted to talk about jobs and what the latest news was, whereas all he wanted to do was forget about it. He spent all day thinking about his unemployed status and what he needed from Anna was diversion.

He realized, of course, that she was just worried about him but he was finding it hard to keep his patience with her. Didn't she have any idea how terrified he was? Didn't she know how much of a failure he felt? And every time she quizzed him about what steps he was taking or how he'd worded a particular letter of application, he felt more inadequate.

To avoid confrontation, Liam stayed out of her way as much as possible. Sometimes he went to his mother's, sometimes he went to the cinema. Occasionally he went to the pub although he had never liked drinking alone. And sometimes, sometimes he dropped in to see Tara.

He never went upstairs to her apartment – the image of her bedroom was still fresh in his mind and made him uncomfortable – but he had a cup of coffee with her in the small kitchen at the back of her salon. Occasionally a client would be there having a body wrap or a facial and Tara would throw him out when her timer went off. 'Sorry, my lady is cooked, time to get back to work!'

He enjoyed their time together. Tara was fun and clever and he was able to talk to her about subjects other than his unemployed status. That made a nice change. Though it was all completely innocent, he hadn't mentioned his visits to Anna. He knew she'd get the wrong idea and he couldn't deal with yet another argument. His mother didn't know either.

Though she loved Tara, Josie wouldn't approve of a married man, especially her son, spending time with another woman. So to avoid any nagging from that quarter, he timed his visits for when he knew she'd be out. If Tara was aware of this, she didn't say anything but by unspoken agreement, she hadn't mentioned his visits to Josie either.

He was also considering Tara's suggestion of advertising himself as a handyman and enjoyed tossing this idea around with her. She had a lot of potential clients for him. It made more sense than what Anna wanted him to do. She seemed to spend all of her spare time finding him positions in large local companies doing work that required few, if any, of his skills.

'You must be joking!' he'd exploded last night when she'd shoved the Vacancies section of the newspaper under his nose and pointed to the ad that she'd ringed. 'Customer Service Operator in Dixons? Have you completely lost your mind?'

'Why? You'd be fixing stuff, using your knowledge, and it would be a step on the ladder of a very large and successful company,' she'd protested. 'And it's better than doing nothing.'

'No, Anna, trust me, it would not be better than doing nothing.'

'God, you're as big a snob as your bloody mother! It's a job, for God's sake, and the way things are going, you can't afford to be so damn picky!'

Liam had glared at her, his eyes like ice. 'Firstly, leave my mother out of this. Secondly, if you think I'm still unemployed because I like doing nothing all day then you don't know me at all.'

And Anna had gone to bed and then left the house this morning without opening her mouth to him. Liam couldn't remember a row ever having lasted this long before, but then nothing was the same these days.

Mark had just given Anna a salary increase and she was on an all-time high as a result. There was no doubt that Anna had found her niche and although he was pleased for her, Liam couldn't help feeling envious. He wasn't proud of himself for being that way and he knew Anna was disappointed in the lack of interest he showed in her work, but he just couldn't help it. He found the fact that she was the main breadwinner very hard to handle and the thought of accepting a job with a salary much lower than hers was completely abhorrent to him.

Which is when he'd started to seriously consider the handyman idea. He had enough experience to run his own business and he quite liked the idea of being hands-on again, too. Once things were up and running, he could take on one or two guys but he wouldn't make the mistake of expanding too quickly. The only fly in the ointment, however, was finance. He and Anna had few savings and to set up a proper business he'd need the right tools.

He hadn't checked out financing but he couldn't imagine a bank wanting to take a chance on him. It was embarrassing to admit that at thirty-three he had sod-all savings! He hadn't planned for this to happen, had been smug in his cosy little job at Patterson's. Bloody idiot! He had paid into a pension plan and life assurance, so Anna would be fine if he popped his clogs, but it had never occurred to him that he would ever be out of a job. What the hell had been the point of all those years in college, for God's sake? Unemployment only happened to unskilled people, or so he'd thought. So, given his naivety, he was hardly great loan material.

Tara had hinted that she would loan him the money he needed to get up and running, but Liam would die rather than take it. He could ask his mother, as he knew she had a few bob tucked away, but that went against the grain too. God, he was surrounded by women with money and it didn't half make him feel inadequate. Feeling very sorry for himself, Liam turned over in the bed and closed his eyes. Doing nothing was a very tiring business.

In the office of Donnelly's Real Estate, Anna tried to concentrate on what Mark was saying but kept reliving the horrible row she'd had with Liam last night. She couldn't believe that he hadn't tried to make it up. She knew that he was awake when she'd left this morning, although he'd stayed well buried under the covers.

'So, have you had any luck with Charlie? *Anna?'*

'Sorry, what was that?' Anna pushed her hair back off her face and looked at her boss.

'What's wrong?' he asked bluntly. 'You're in another world this morning and you look terrible.'

'Thanks.'

'Oh, come on, love, you can tell me. Is it Liam?' Mark settled his ample figure back in the chair and waited.

'We had a row last night.'

'Ah. Well, that's marriage for you, darling. We all have little disagreements from time to time.'

'I suppose, but we seem to be having more than our fair share these days. I can't say or do anything right. The least thing and he jumps down my throat.

I saw a vacancy in Dixon's that I thought would suit him and he threw a complete wobbler.'

'A management job?'

She shook her head. 'No, but you've got to start somewhere, haven't you?'

Mark chuckled. 'No, Anna, I don't agree with that.'

'Neither does he, but he's so miserable at home. Surely any job is better than nothing?'

'Not really. You see, at the moment, the last job on his CV is a very senior one. If he were to take a lower-paid job, companies would see it on his CV and be less likely to offer him a management role.'

'But the longer he's at home, the bigger the gap on his CV. Surely that's worse?'

'Not necessarily. He can always say that he decided to take a sabbatical, that he could afford to take a break and wait for the right job to come along.'

'But we can't!' Anna cried in frustration.

Mark looked at her. 'They don't know that, do they? It's really a game of chicken, Anna. If Liam keeps his head, looks the part and plays the game, he may well ride this out.'

Anna absorbed this. 'So you think I'm wrong to push him into just any job?'

'In a word, my love, yes.'

Anna sighed. 'Shit. I'm just trying to help, Mark.'

'Just hang in there, love. He'll get through this and no doubt come out much better off at the other end.'

'Everyone says that, but I'm beginning to wonder.'

Anna blinked back the tears. 'I feel so completely helpless, Mark. I just wish I could do something to help. I hate to see him so miserable.'

'All you can do is stand by him,' Mark said softly. 'That's all he wants from you right now.'

Anna blew her nose. 'You're right, Mark, thanks.'

'That's fine. Now, is there any chance we could get a bit of work done?'

'Your boss makes a lot of sense,' Jill said when Anna relayed the conversation over their lunch later that day in a pub in Clontarf. This was their usual lunchtime haunt as it meant they were both only twenty minutes' drive from their offices. Jill tucked into a chicken salsa wrap, pausing to dab at the sauce running down her chin.

'Aren't you on a diet?' Anna said.

'Nah, I'm on a break. So what are you going to do now?'

'Try harder, I suppose. I was thinking on my way over here that I'm complaining about Liam not talking to me, but I suppose he hasn't had that much opportunity. I've been so busy and a bit preoccupied.' Anna paused and with a groan, dropped her face in her hands. 'Oh God.'

'What?'

'I just remembered I had a go at his mother last night too.'

'Oh.'

'No wonder he wouldn't talk to me this morning.'

'I think you could both do with some cooling-off time. Why don't we go out tonight?'

'Oh, I don't know.'

'It would give him time to think and it would do you good to have a night out.'

'Yes, okay then. Where will we go – into town?'

'No, let's stay in Malahide. We could try out the new wine bar and then go to Gibneys.'

'Sounds good.' Anna checked her watch. 'I'd better go, I've an appointment at two. What time will I see you?'

'About seven?' Jill suggested.

'Great, see you then.' When Anna was back in her car, she noticed the postcard that she'd snatched off the postman this morning and hadn't had a chance to read yet. She smiled at the photo of the Promenade in Nice. Oh, to be walking along that right now! Turning over the card, she started to read.

Hello, my darling Anna! Sorry we missed you when we phoned the other night but it was nice (no pun intended!) to talk to Liam. He does sound a bit down, the poor man. Please God he'll get something soon. I light a candle in every church we visit – your father thinks I've lost my mind because I'm lighting candles for Rachel too. She doesn't say much, Anna, but I don't think she's very well at the moment. Please keep an eye on her. I rely on you, you know, to look after your little sister.

Anna paused. Jill was also worried about Rachel but she'd been so preoccupied with her own problems at the moment she had little time to think about her sister. She'd call her tomorrow, she promised herself guiltily. Bending her head, she went back to the postcard.

I've asked her to come for a visit before Alex goes back to school: maybe you could try and persuade her. It would put my mind at rest if I could see her. I seem to be running out of space, my darling, so I'll go now and call you soon. Hugs and kisses to you and Liam.x, Mam

Anna put down the card with a sigh, turned the key in the ignition and headed back to work. If her mother was so worried about Rache, why didn't she just come home? She could fly from Nice to Dublin, dead easy. Anna immediately felt bad at the way her mind was working. She was turning into a right misery-guts altogether, and it was all because of Liam. She wasn't the same person these days. She didn't laugh as much and it was all down to the constant bickering and nitpicking that seemed to fill their time when they were together.

She missed curling up with him on the sofa in the evenings and discussing their days, laughing, making plans and eventually making love in front of the fire because they hadn't the patience to wait until they got upstairs. She would have to try harder to keep the peace. They needed each other now more than ever. She would go out tonight with Jill, let off some steam and then tomorrow, she would start again.

Anna was the last in the office that evening and once she'd locked up and put on the answering machine, she went out to the tiny loo to freshen up. She decided to let her hair down from its tight knot and leave her jacket at the office. She was wearing a cropped black T-shirt that was too informal on its own for the office but perfect for a girls' night out. When she walked into the small restaurant, Jill was already at a table in the corner.

'You're looking very sexy,' she said as Anna sat down opposite her.

'You can talk!' Anna admired Jill's low-cut, green top and black gypsy skirt. 'I feel positively formal.'

'You look gorgeous,' Jill assured her.

Anna made a face. 'I wish I felt it.'

'A couple of glasses of wine and you will.'

'I'm driving,' Anna reminded her.

'Leave your car here and we'll take a taxi. I came out on the train so that I could have a couple of bevvies. You can't let me drink alone.'

'I suppose not,' Anna agreed with a grin. 'But don't blame me if I get all maudlin and cranky and cry on your shoulder.'

'I'll risk it.' Jill called the waiter and ordered a bottle of the house white wine. 'Did you tell Liam you were going out?'

'I sent him a text message, saying sorry and telling him I was meeting you. He didn't reply.'

'Oh, poor you.'

Anna shook her head. 'Forget it. We are *not* talking about Liam tonight. I came out for a break.'

'Fair enough. Tell me about work then.'

Anna's eyes lit up. 'Oh Jill, I love it so much – although I'm working all hours, which doesn't impress Liam.'

'I thought we weren't going to talk about him?' Jill teased as the waiter poured their wine.

Anna groaned. 'No, we're not, sorry.'

They quickly gave the waiter their order, Jill ordering two starters instead of a main course – one meat and one fish. 'Atkins Diet, no carbs,' she explained and then settled back with her wine.

'So what do you think is going on with Rachel?' Anna asked. 'I got a card from Mam today and she's worried about her too.'

'Oh, I'm sure it's just her pregnancy getting to her but I do worry about how isolated she's become. She's not telling you or me her problems and your mother's miles away, so who does she talk to?'

'Gary?' Anna suggested with a shrug.

Jill shook her head. 'I don't think so. Maybe you should ask Bridie to come home for a visit.'

'Maybe,' Anna said. 'Let me drop in and see Rache at the weekend first and I'll see if I can find out what's going on.'

'Oh, okay.' Jill looked mildly surprised.

Anna rolled her eyes. 'Don't look so bloody shocked. I'm not that heartless, you know!'

'Never said a word.' Jill laughed.

The subject was dropped as their food arrived and instead Jill entertained Anna with stories of her and Karen's diets and the antics of the staff in ADLI.

'What about the guy who's after your job?' Anna asked.

'Vinnie? Oh, he's as big a pain in the ass as usual but I can handle him.'

'Good woman. You'll have to show me how it's done. I should stand up to Mark more.'

'He does seem to work you quite hard.'

'He's just a natural skinflint and refuses to hire anyone else even though we've got at least thirty per cent more business now than we did six months ago. But I'm saying nothing. It's enough that Liam's out of work, I don't want to join him.'

'But your job's safe, surely?'

Anna shrugged. 'It probably is, but after what happened to Liam, I wonder if anyone's job is really safe any more.'

Jill shivered as an image of Vinny Gray sitting behind her desk flashed through her mind. 'You could always apply for a job at a different estate agency,' she said, forcing her mind back to her cousin's situation.

'Oh no, I don't think so. I know I complain about Mark but he's not the worst. Better the devil you know and all that.'

'He's a lecherous sod, though.'

'He is, but not with me. He knows that Liam would throttle him if he tried it on!' Anna smiled as the waiter handed her the dessert menu. 'Are you allowed dessert on the Atkins Diet?'

'No idea, but I'm having the chocolate fudge cake. Chocolate's protein, isn't it?'

'I doubt it,' Anna laughed. 'I'll have the apple pie. Maybe I'll sneak it home to Liam – he loves the stuff. It could be a little peace-offering.'

'You know, Anna, I'm sure it will all work out fine. I know that's hard to believe right now, but we both know that Liam would be an asset to any company. It's only a matter of time before the right job comes along.'

Anna nodded. 'You're probably right, Jill, it's just such lousy timing. Our life should be going in a completely different direction right now.'

'What do you mean?'

'We had just decided to start a family.'

Jill's eyes widened. 'I had no idea! Congratulations!'

Anna sighed. 'Don't congratulate me, it's not going to happen now. Liam won't even talk about it.'

Jill squeezed her hand. 'Well, that's understandable. He has enough on his plate at the moment.'

Anna nodded. 'I expect so. But you know, I was showing a beautiful little cottage a couple of weeks ago and I fell in love with it as soon as I walked into the place. It was too small for the client but it would be just perfect for us – Liam, me and our little baby.'

Jill saw the wistful look on Anna's face. 'There will be other cottages even more perfect.'

Anna looked at her cousin and nodded. 'Of course there will.' She glanced down as her apple pie was placed in front of her. 'This is way too delicious for Liam. Oh Jill, I said I wasn't going to talk about him and I haven't shut up all night. No more, I promise. Tell me about Handy Andy instead.'

'Nothing to tell,' Jill said, tucking into her cake.

'Oh, don't be so coy. Come on, you haven't mentioned the guy in weeks.'

Jill finished her dessert and then turned to signal the waiter for the bill. 'That's because I finished with him.'

'Oh no! He seemed perfect for you.'

'How can you say that? You never even met him.'

Anna shrugged. 'Well, no, but from what you told me it was obvious that you were happy.'

'Was it? Yes, well, it's too late now.'

'You could always do something really strange. You could always try to get him back.'

'Who says I want him back?'

'Okay, okay, if you don't want to talk about it, you just have to say.'

'I don't want to talk about it.'

'Fine. Let's go to the pub.'

'I shouldn't have any more to drink,' Anna was saying as they pushed their way through Gibneys.

'Don't worry, darling, I'll carry you home,' Jill promised.

'I'd be glad to offer my services too,' a voice said from behind them.

Anna whirled around. 'Charlie!'

'Hello, Anna.' Charlie smiled down at her. 'Mark and I are sitting down at the end of the bar. Will you ladies join us?'

'Do we have to?' Jill murmured.

'Sure, why not?' Anna said, ignoring her cousin and following Charlie. 'Hi, Mark.'

Her boss swivelled around on his stool. 'Anna, what are you doing here? And Jill! What a pleasant surprise!'

'Is it?' Jill climbed up on a stool, aware of his eyes on her legs.

'What can I get you, my darling?' His eyes had moved up to her chest.

'Oh, to hell with it, I'll have a gin and tonic.'

'And you, Anna?'

'White wine, please.' Anna took the other stool and Charlie leaned against the pillar beside her. 'So, how's it going?' she asked.

'Fine, thanks. Are you going to introduce me?' He nodded towards Jill.

'Oh, sorry. Charlie, this is my Cousin Jill. Jill, this is Charlie Coleman, a client of ours.'

Jill watched with interest as Charlie frowned. He quite obviously saw himself as more than a customer and she wasn't sure she liked the way he was leaning on the back of Anna's stool, his bare tanned arm touching Anna's. 'Pleased to meet you,' she said. 'Is Mark trying to squeeze a larger commission out of you then?'

He laughed. 'He can try but I wouldn't rate his chances.'

Mark groaned as he paid for the drinks. 'I work for a pittance, you know that?'

'You work?' Anna retorted. 'Charlie's *my* client.'

'I thought estate agents represented the vendor, not the buyer,' Jill said.

Mark puffed out his chest. 'At Donnelly's Real Estate we offer a better class of service, especially to valued clients such as Mr Coleman here.'

'Oh, cut the bull, Mark, it's me you're talking to.' Charlie turned to Jill. 'I'm an old friend and I asked him to help me find a place in Malahide.'

'I wouldn't have, if I'd known you'd be so difficult to please,' Mark complained. 'How many houses have you shown him, Anna?'

'Seven.'

'Seven! Seven of the best properties on this side of Dublin and they're not good enough for you.'

Charlie shrugged. 'I just haven't seen anything that suits.'

'Charlie's changing his mind about what he wants,' Anna told her boss.

'I am?' said Charlie.

She nodded. 'Yes, for a start I think big houses scare you off. What you really want is something warm and homely. That cottage would have been perfect.'

'Too small.'

'There was plenty of room to extend,' she pointed out.

'It just wasn't right,' he told her. 'And what about the animal?'

'Animal?' Jill asked.

'My daughter has a pony,' he explained.

Mark turned to Anna, his eyes speculative. 'What about the Brennans' place?'

She nodded thoughtfully. 'You know, that might well fit the bill. I'll set up an appointment, Charlie. When would suit you?'

He shrugged. 'Whenever, sweetheart. You know I'm always available for you.'

Anna giggled. 'I bet you say that to all the girls.'

Jill groaned inwardly. The fourth glass of wine was obviously beginning to take effect. She'd better get Anna out of here before she got silly. There was way too much flirting going on for her liking.

'So, Jill, how are things? I haven't seen you in a long time.' Mark leaned closer. 'Any man on the scene?'

'Several.' Jill sat back on her stool.

'Excellent. A girl like you should play the field.'

'A girl like me?'

'You know – successful, sexy, mature.'

'You were doing fine until you said mature,' she said dryly.

'Hey, that was a compliment. You're in your prime.'

'Thanks,' Jill replied, trying to listen in on what Charlie and Anna were talking about.

'Any man would be glad to have a woman like you,' Mark continued, licking his lips.

'You have a very interesting way with words, Mark, you know that?' She finished her drink and shot her cousin a meaningful look. 'Hey, Anna, let's get going.'

'But it's early,' Anna protested.

'It's a work day tomorrow,' Jill reminded her.

'But I'm with my boss,' Anna beamed, waving her glass precariously. 'You won't mind if I'm a teensy bit late tomorrow, Mark, will you?'

'I suppose we could call this business,' he agreed with a knowing wink at Charlie.

'Come on, Anna, I'm tired and we're sharing a taxi, remember?'

'I could drop her home,' Charlie interrupted. 'I've only had one pint.'

'There you go.' Anna smiled at her cousin. 'Problem solved. You go on home, Jill, I'll call you tomorrow.'

'Oh well, maybe I'll stay for a bit longer,' Jill said, loath to leave her cousin alone with Charlie and Mark.

'That's more like it,' Mark said, squeezing her knee. 'Have another drink. The night is young.'

Chapter 18

'Did you have a good night?' Liam asked, as Anna wandered into the kitchen the next morning looking pasty and red-eyed.

'Yeah, not bad.'

'I didn't know you were planning such a late one.'

'We weren't.'

'Where did you end up?'

Anna poured herself a cup of stewed tea from the pot and wondered if a slice of toast would help or finish her off altogether. 'Tamango's.'

'Just you and Jill?'

Liam's voice sounded normal enough but Anna knew he was annoyed. 'No. Mark and one of his friends were with us.'

'I see.'

Anna groaned inwardly as Liam's mouth set in a grim line. 'We were just having a laugh, Liam, no big deal.'

'Right.'

'I'd better get a move on or I'll be late.' Suddenly neither the tea nor the toast held any appeal and

Anna knew if she didn't get out quick, there'd be another row.

'Well, the boss won't mind, will he? You and he are obviously close.'

'Oh, for God's sake, Liam. I just bumped into him! Stop being so ridiculous.'

'Sorry, I didn't think I was being ridiculous, just curious. Any man would be if his wife didn't get in until three in the morning.'

Anna winced. She didn't think he'd heard her coming in but then she probably hadn't been as quiet as she'd thought. 'It was just a bit of fun. Remember what that is, Liam?' Guilt made Anna's tone sharper than she'd intended.

'Vaguely.' Liam's voice was calm but his eyes were cold. 'But then I haven't had much of it lately,' he said and brushed past her.

'Liam, wait a minute—' But he was already on the stairs and moments later, Anna heard the door of the bedroom slam behind him. 'Shit.'

'That was a good night, eh?' Mark winked at her when he breezed in the door at half past ten.

'I don't know, was it?' Anna managed a weak smile.

'Indeed it was. Where did you and Charlie get to? One minute you were dancing beside us and the next you were gone.'

Anna felt her face grow hot as Val eyed her curiously. 'Oh, you know me, Mark. I got a bit wobbly and Charlie offered to drop me home.'

'Wobbly? You were plastered!' Mark's grin broadened as he sat down on the corner of her desk. 'Bring him in for coffee, did you?'

'No, I did not.' Anna buried her head in a file and prayed that he would go away or the phone would ring or the ceiling would fall in.

'Probably just as well. Liam wouldn't have been impressed.'

'Don't be silly, Liam wouldn't mind. He'd be delighted that someone had seen me home safe and sound.'

'Ha!' Mark laughed as he stood up and went into his office. 'Of course he would.'

'I need a cup of coffee,' Anna said and hurried out of the room before Val could say anything.

'Jill's on hold,' Val told her when she returned.

Anna set down the coffee with an unsteady hand and picked up the phone. 'Jill?'

'Hi, Anna. How are you?'

'Lousy. You?'

'Fine. You got home okay, then?'

'Yeah, sorry about that. I'm afraid I forgot all about you. Bloody wine, I really should give up the stuff.'

'Maybe you should.' Jill sounded very unimpressed. 'I take it you were with Charlie?'

Anna glanced at Val. 'I can't really talk right now, Jill.'

'No, I don't suppose you can. Meet me for lunch at one.'

Anna groaned as she put the phone down.

'Problem?' Val asked.

'I think Jill's annoyed with me. We were supposed to share a taxi home but I forgot.'

Val's eyes narrowed. 'Forgot?'

'Yes, Val, I forgot! What are you trying to say?'

Val held up her hands. 'Nothing! Sorry I spoke.'

'No, *I'm* sorry, Val. It's just my head is hopping and I do feel awful about last night. I should never have left Jill and I should never have accepted a lift from Charlie. Mark's right, Liam would go mad if he knew. He was furious as it was because I was home so late.'

'But you only got a lift, didn't you?'

'Yes! Oh, we had a laugh and a dance but it was all very innocent. And maybe it's a crime, Val, but I enjoyed myself.' Anna rested her head in her hands. 'It was nice to have a bit of fun for a change.'

'Well, I'm glad you enjoyed yourself, dear, and I'd love to hear all about it sometime but,' Val glanced at the clock, 'if you don't get moving you're going to be late for your first viewing.'

Anna sprang to her feet and then clutched her head. 'Shit, damn, I completely forgot. Oh God, I really shouldn't drink midweek. I really shouldn't drink full stop,' she corrected herself as she picked up her bag and keys and headed for the door.

'Don't forget you're meeting Jill for lunch,' Val called after her.

*

'I hope you're feeling as bad as you look,' Jill remarked later when Anna slumped into the seat beside her.

'My stomach's sick, my head's throbbing and I've spent the last hour with a woman who has a voice like a pneumatic drill.'

'Have some soup,' Jill suggested. They quickly gave their order and then Jill turned questioning eyes on her cousin.

'Nothing happened,' Anna told her, sipping iced water.

Jill arched an eyebrow. 'You sound almost disappointed.'

Anna glared at her. 'Don't be silly, of course I'm not. Charlie's a nice guy, we were having a laugh. Oh, come on, Jill, you know what I'm like when I have a few drinks.'

'I've seen you make an eejit of yourself plenty of times,' Jill agreed, 'but I've never seen you leave with a man before.'

'It wasn't as if I picked him up,' Anna protested. 'He's a friend.'

'I thought he was a client.'

'Oh, for God's sake, stop trying to trip me up. I've done nothing to be ashamed of – except forgetting about you, of course.'

'Did you really forget me?' Jill shot her a look of pure disbelief.

'Yeah, sorry,' Anna said, not quite meeting her eyes. 'Oh, good, here's my soup.' She turned her attention to her lunch while Jill picked at her roast chicken. 'I thought you were on a diet?'

'I am. No chips, just chicken.'

Anna decided she was in enough trouble with her cousin without pointing out that you probably weren't supposed to have your chicken soaked in fat and breadcrumbs. 'So how's your head?'

'Fine. I had a glass of water between each round.'

Anna made a face. 'Aren't you the sensible one? You and Mark seemed to be getting on well.'

'Please.' Jill rolled her eyes. 'That man's unbelievable. His hands were everywhere and his eyes were practically glued to my chest!'

Anna giggled. 'He does seem to like you.'

'Lucky old me. So, what did Liam say?'

'He had a go at me for getting home so late.'

'Did he see Charlie?'

'No.' Anna hesitated. 'At least I don't think he did.'

Jill watched her cousin as she ate her soup. 'Are you sure that Charlie is just a friend? Are you sure that that's all you want him to be? You did seem very close.'

Anna paused, the spoon halfway to her mouth. 'Jill, you know I love Liam,' she said very quietly.

'That doesn't stop you fancying someone else, though, does it? It happens all the time.'

'Not to me,' Anna told her, putting down her spoon and pushing away her soup. 'I would never cheat on Liam.'

'Hey, I'm sorry, okay? I didn't mean to upset you.'

'Yeah, I know. Look, would you mind very much if I headed off now? If I'm quick I could go by the house and make my peace with him. I'm fed up with all of this bickering, it's such a waste of time.'

Jill smiled. 'You go for it, cuz. Good luck.'

As Anna drove, she felt guilt eating her up inside as she thought about what Jill had said. As usual, her cousin was spot on. She *was* attracted to Charlie, and when he'd bent his head to kiss her last night she'd very nearly let him. 'But I didn't,' she reminded herself. She'd been aware of Charlie's interest in her and enjoyed the attention and the flattery, but she wasn't prepared to take it any further. She'd never do that to Liam.

As she turned the car into her estate, she promised herself that she'd be a more tolerant and understanding wife. It wasn't Liam's fault that he was grumpy, it was only natural given what he was going through. This was the first real crisis they'd had to face as a married couple and she should be handling it a lot better than this. That's what marriage was about, wasn't it, for better, for worse, in good times and in bad?

As she parked, she noticed Liam's bike leaning against the wall. Good, he was home. She hurried up the path and opened the door with her key. 'Liam? Liam, where are you?' She poked her head into the sitting room but it was empty and the TV was off.

'Liam?' She carried on into the kitchen, stopping dead at the sight of Tara Brady lounging against the counter, the kettle in her hand.

'Oh hi, Anna. He's in the shower. Would you like some tea while you're waiting?'

Anna dashed the tears from her eyes as she drove back to the office, still not able to believe the evidence of her own eyes. She had been standing staring at Liam's ex-girlfriend when he'd appeared at her side – in a towel.

'Anna! I didn't know you were coming home for lunch.'

'That's pretty obvious,' she'd replied, looking him up and down in disgust. Ignoring his protests, she turned on her heel, went out to the car and pulled away from the kerb, the engine roaring.

God, how could he? And in their own home, their own bed! She shook her head, as if by doing so, it would banish the image of Tara standing in her kitchen. And here she was, feeling guilty about a kiss that hadn't even happened! Liam and Tara! Suddenly, Anna understood her husband's odd behaviour over the last few weeks. She, naively, had put it down to the redundancy but it was obvious now that the reason was Tara Brady. The woman had been after him for years and it looked as if he'd finally capitulated. Anna let out an involuntary sob. But why now? Had she driven him away? Had he turned to Tara because she had been more understanding?

Anna drove round and round the village looking for a parking spot. 'Damn, shit, damn,' she cursed as she got caught in the yellow box and a bus driver blasted her out of it. 'Okay, okay.' She nudged the car up as far as she could, but she was still blocking the road. Tears ran down her cheeks as she waited for the lights to change, and when she finally rounded the corner and a car pulled out of a parking spot, the relief unleashed another flood of tears.

Anna finally managed to park without crashing into anything, and after taking a few deep breaths, she wiped her face on her sleeve and got out of the car. As she was attempting to lock it with shaking fingers she became aware of someone watching her. Looking up, she saw Charlie standing across the road. Oh no, that's all she needed. She tried to smile but felt the tears welling up again. Turning her back to him, Anna quickly buried her face in a tissue.

'Are you okay?' Charlie had crossed and was standing at her side now, his eyes concerned.

'I've got something in my eye,' Anna told him, aware that her voice was wobbly.

Charlie steered her towards the pub.

'What are you doing?' Anna asked shakily. 'I've got to get back to work.'

'In that state? I don't think so.'

Anna let him lead her inside and went to sit at a table in a dark corner while Charlie walked up to the bar.

'I wasn't sure what to get you.'

Anna looked up to see him balancing tea, water and brandy. She laughed. 'Looks like you covered all eventualities.'

'It's my Boy Scout training.'

Anna was tempted to drink the brandy but settled for the tea instead. After she'd taken a couple of sips she looked up at Charlie and managed a smile. 'Thanks.'

'Want to tell me what's wrong?'

She shook her head.

'Is it my fault?'

Anna frowned. 'No, of course not, why would you say that?'

'I thought maybe you got into trouble over last night.'

'Oh no, nothing like that.'

'Oh right, that puts *me* in my place.'

'Look, Charlie, I didn't mean—'

He chuckled. 'It's okay, Anna.'

She finished her tea. 'I'd better go.'

He stood up. 'You sure you're up to it?'

'Yes, I'm fine, thanks.'

'Not a problem.'

'I was going to call you this afternoon actually,' she said as they went outside.

'Oh, yes?'

'Yes. I can show you the Brennan house tomorrow evening if you're free.'

'Right. I'll call you and let you know. See you, Anna.'

She watched as he strode away, wondering why he'd suddenly become so abrupt. But as she turned to walk towards her office, thoughts of Charlie Coleman were quickly replaced by images of Tara in her kitchen and Liam in a towel. How in God's name was her marriage supposed to recover from this? And suddenly it occurred to Anna that maybe Liam didn't want it to. Maybe he'd wanted her to find him and Tara together. Maybe after all these years he'd decided that his first love was, in fact, the deepest.

Chapter 19

'Anna, love, what's wrong?' Val asked when a puffy-eyed Anna sat down at her desk.

'Nothing, I'm fine.'

'Liam called.' When Anna didn't answer, Val sighed, shook her head and went back to her typing. Moments later, the phone rang again. 'Donnelly's Real Estate, can I help you? Oh, hello again, Liam.' She listened, then said: 'Could you hold on for a moment? Thanks.'

'Please, Val, I don't want to talk to him,' Anna mumbled.

Val hesitated but when Anna's eyes filled up, she quickly nodded. 'Liam? Sorry about that. I'm on my own here so it's a bit mad. I'm afraid Anna's in a meeting. Well, yes, of course but I expect she'll be tied up for the afternoon. Right, so, Liam. Bye now.' She hung up and looked at Anna.

'Thanks, Val.'

'No problem, love, but you can't avoid him for ever.'

'I know.'

'If you've had a row it's best to sort it.'

Anna's grip tightened on her pen and she forced a smile. 'I will, but it's better to do it face to face when I get home, don't you think?'

'Well, yes,' Val admitted. 'Not a good idea to bring your personal problems to work.'

'Exactly – and I've got such a lot to do.' Anna bent her head over a file and was relieved when Val left it at that.

The phones hopped all afternoon and Anna didn't have a chance to dwell on her problems. She buried herself in her work, returning calls that she'd been putting off and writing up flowery prose about houses that were dull or downright ugly. Heartache was obviously good for productivity, she mused. Mark would certainly get his money's worth out of her if her marriage fell apart. She gasped at the thought and quickly disguised it as a cough when Val's head jerked up. Life without Liam was something she'd never considered. Life without Liam was unimaginable. She quickly ducked out to the loo, splashing cold water on her face in an effort to avoid more tears. She had a meeting with Mark in half an hour and he would be very unimpressed if she started to cry. She couldn't expect him to tolerate yet more of her marital problems. If she kept arriving into his office in tears, he'd begin to ask himself what he was employing her for and he'd be right. Anna patted her face dry, took a few deep breaths and returned to her desk.

'I've made you a nice cup of tea,' Val said.

'Thanks, you're very kind.'

'Are you okay, love?'

'I'm fine.' Anna smiled and immediately picked up the phone. When she had finished the long and difficult call with a client it was time for her meeting with Mark.

'How's it going?' he said with a wide smile.

'Great,' she replied, setting down a pile of files on the edge of his desk. 'At least it would be if Mr Delaney were to fall off the face of the earth.'

'Delaney?' Mark frowned. 'The old lad in Marlboro Road?'

'The very same.'

'But that's all settled. He agreed to accept four hundred.'

'Ah yes, but then he was on the phone to his daughter in Australia and she told him that he was being robbed.'

'Oh, for pity's sake!'

'I know, I know. It's the McHughs I feel sorry for. It was such a stretch for them to go to four hundred and they have to move out of the place they're renting by the end of the month, but now Delaney's adamant he won't sell.'

'He'll sell all right.' The veins stood out on Mark's temples and his eyes bulged. 'I'll soon sort him out, leave it to me.'

Anna was happy to and they moved on to the next client. It was almost seven o'clock when they finally finished. Though Anna was tired, she was sorry the day was over and that it was time to go home and confront her husband.

'I'd better get my skates on, I've a viewing in ten minutes.' Mark stood up and pulled on the jacket of his suit.

'I'll do it if you like,' she offered.

Mark eyed her curiously. 'No, that's okay. Tell me, what's the story with Charlie Coleman? Have you arranged to show him the Brennan house?'

Anna shook her head. 'I offered to take him over there tomorrow but he said he'd let me know.'

Mark frowned. 'You call him, Anna. Paul Brennan is getting impatient. His house has been on the market for months now. And as for Charlie, he's dragging his heels too much for my liking.'

'He just hasn't found the right place.'

Mark's look was speculative. 'Or maybe it's not a house he's after.'

'I don't know what you're implying, Mark—'

'Oh, don't play the innocent with me, Anna. You know the man likes you and,' he held up his hand as she went to protest, 'I couldn't give a monkey's what's going on between you two. Just sell him a bloody house and fast, okay?'

'Okay,' Anna muttered.

He grinned at her. 'And I won't even charge a matchmaking fee.'

'I think you're forgetting that I'm married!' Anna stood up and gathered her files.

Mark picked up his phone and keys and headed for the door. 'What's that got to do with anything?' he asked, getting the last word in as usual.

Feeling slightly sick, Anna went back to her desk and stared at the phone. The last person she wanted to talk to now was Charlie, especially after the way she'd made a show of herself earlier, but she knew she had to do it.

'Charlie, hi, it's Anna Gallagher,' she said in a brisk, businesslike tone when he answered.

'Hi, Anna. Are you feeling better?'

'Oh yes, thanks,' she stammered, his gentle tone putting her offguard.

'So, what can I do for you? Brandy, tea or some sympathy?'

She forced a laugh. 'I just wanted to arrange a time to show you the house Mark was telling you about.'

'Oh, I see.'

'Would tomorrow evening suit?'

'I'm free right now, as it happens.'

'Now?'

'Is that a problem?'

'Er, no. The owner's moved out and I have the keys.'

'Excellent. I'll be right over.'

'Okay.' Anna hung up with a sigh. Well, she hadn't wanted to go home and face Liam, and the sooner she showed Charlie the house, the sooner she could make a sale. The more she thought about it, the more she was sure that the Brennan house was right for him. Knowing Mark, he would probably claim the commission for himself as it had been his idea. Not that she really cared any more. If Charlie did decide to put in an offer and it was accepted, it would be over to the lawyers and there would be no reason for them to meet again.

That would definitely be for the best all round although Anna knew she was going to miss him. The thought made her feel guilty even though she had no reason to be, she reminded herself, pulling out her make-up bag and mirror. Liam was the one who should be feeling guilty. He had been messing about with Tara while all she'd done was a little harmless flirting. And what woman would be able to resist Charlie Coleman? Looking in the mirror, she saw the tears fill her eyes and she closed them, swallowing hard. 'You are not going to cry all over this man again!' she told her reflection. 'You are going to behave like a professional.' There would be plenty of time for her to fall apart later when Liam told her that their marriage was over.

Putting her make-up away, her fingers closed around her mobile phone and she drew it out. She had left it switched off all afternoon and knew that there were probably dozens of messages for her by now. But if she switched it on, Liam might call and she couldn't talk to him now. Resolutely, she put the phone back in her bag and went to lock up the office.

By the time she'd set the alarm and switched off the lights, she could see Charlie's silhouette at the door. Pulling her shoulders back and fixing a smile on her face, she went out to meet him. 'Charlie, perfect timing.'

'Well?' Anna stood in the hall looking up at him. He'd been wandering around for a good ten minutes now but still hadn't uttered a single word.

Charlie slowly walked down the stairs towards her. 'It's perfect.' He strolled through the downstairs rooms again, pausing in front of the huge bay window that looked out over a large field, with the sea twinkling blue in the distance.

Anna smiled. 'Oh, good. Do you think Sophie will like it?'

He laughed. 'She'll nab that attic room for herself straight away!'

'It's cool, isn't it? I'd have loved a room like that when I was a teenager. Want to have a look at the outbuildings? I'm sure one of them could easily be converted into a stable. Not that I know anything about horses.'

'I'm sure it's fine.' Charlie followed her out to the back of the house.

'The fencing seems secure but I can check that for you.'

'Anna?'

'Yes?'

'Are you okay?'

Anna nodded and looked quickly away from the concern in his eyes. 'Fine.'

'You don't look fine.' He moved closer.

'Thanks a lot!' She rolled her eyes in mock disgust.

'Don't do this.'

'Sorry?'

'Don't push me away.'

She turned to face him. 'Look, Charlie, I'm here to sell you a house, nothing else.'

'What's that supposed to mean?'

'You know what it means.' She turned on her heel and headed back to the house and when he finally followed her, she was standing in the hall, ready to go. 'So, would you like to put in an offer? It's been on the market for a while so they'll probably be happy to negotiate.'

'I'll pay the asking price.' He went through the door without looking at her.

'Are you sure—'

'I'm sure.' He got into his car and switched on the engine, pulling away as soon as she'd climbed in beside him.

They travelled back to the office in silence. 'I'll phone Mr Brennan first thing in the morning,' Anna said when he screeched to a halt outside the building.

'Fine,' he replied without looking at her.

'Bye, then.'

'Goodbye, Anna,' Charlie said, and was gone in a puff of exhaust.

Anna watched him leave, her eyes sad.

'I've been waiting for you.'

She whirled around to see her husband standing in the entrance to the agency. 'Liam!'

'I've been trying to call you all evening.'

'Yeah, well, I didn't want to talk to you.'

'It's your dad, Anna. He's in hospital.'

Chapter 20

'Will you please calm down, Rachel, you'll make yourself sick,' Gary begged his wife.

'How can I calm down?' she said, pacing the living room. 'My dad's in some crummy hospital halfway across the world and God knows what state he's in!'

'It's not halfway across the world and the French healthcare system is a damn sight better than ours.'

'How would *you* know?' she said rudely. 'Oh, why the hell hasn't Mam phoned? I'm going to ring the hospital again.'

'There's no point,' Gary said, pulling her down on to the sofa. 'You know they won't tell you anything.'

Rachel turned frightened eyes to him. 'Oh Gary, he will be okay, won't he?'

'Of course he will. Your dad is as strong as an ox.'

'An ox that eats all the wrong food and smokes forty a day,' she said miserably. 'And you can bet he's been lowering back the San Miguel – oh, why didn't they stay in Ireland? What the hell was Mam thinking of, dragging him all over Europe in a bloody caravan at his age?'

'He's only sixty-four, Rachel, and I don't think your mam had to do much dragging. Look, carrying on like this won't do you or the baby any good.'

Rachel's hand moved to her bump. 'I'm sorry, it's just I'm so worried.'

'I know.' He put an arm around her shoulders and hugged her to him.

The phone rang and Rachel jumped. 'You answer it,' she said.

Gary picked up the phone. 'Hello? Oh hi, Anna. Hang on, I'll put her on.' He handed the phone to his wife.

'Anna? Have you heard anything?'

'No, Rachel, Liam just told me what's happened. I was hoping you'd have heard something.'

Rachel sighed. 'No, nothing.'

'Tell me exactly what Mam said.'

'Well, they had just come back from the beach when he complained of a pain in his chest. Mam went to get him some Alka-Seltzer and when she came back, he was rolling about the place.' Rachel's voice shook as she talked and Gary's hand tightened around hers. 'Mum called the ambulance and now he's in Casualty.'

'Is he conscious? Are they operating? What the hell's happening, Rache?'

'They were running some tests when Mam phoned. She had to go because there was a queue for the phone. I don't know if he's conscious or not, she didn't say and I was too flustered to ask. Sorry.'

'Hey, that's okay. Don't mind me, it's just all been a bit of a shock.'

'I know. I tell you, I don't care what they say, I'm buying them a bloody mobile phone after this!'

'Damn right,' Anna agreed. 'Will I come over?'

'Please.'

'Hi, Anna.' Gary opened the door and kissed his sister-in-law's cheek.

'Is she okay?'

'A bit upset but not too bad. How about you?'

'I'm fine.'

'Go on in, she's in the living room.'

'Hiya.' Rachel stood up to hug her sister. 'Sorry for dragging you over here.'

'I'd prefer to be here worrying with you than at home on my own,' Anna told her sister.

'Why, where's Liam?'

'Oh, nowhere.'

'Glass of wine?' Gary appeared brandishing a bottle and two glasses.

'Oh yes, please.'

'I have the kettle on for you, Rachel.'

'Thanks.'

'So did she say when she'd call again?' Anna asked.

'When she had some more news. Do you think we should go over there?' Rachel looked to her big sister for guidance.

'I don't know. I suppose if it's serious . . .' They

stared at each other, afraid to think of what might lie ahead.

'It won't be, don't worry,' Gary told them.

'Maybe we should check out flights, just in case,' Anna said.

'Already done,' he said quietly. 'There's an Aer Lingus flight every morning and there are seats available on tomorrow's flight.'

'Should we book it?' Rachel asked.

Gary shook his head. 'There's no point in doing anything until you talk to your mother.'

'But either way she'd probably like one of us to be there,' Rachel murmured.

'I can't just fly out there in the morning, Mark would go spare.' Anna fretted, taking a gulp of wine.

'You may not have a choice.' Rachel's voice was sharp.

'This is a pointless conversation,' Gary said, frowning at his wife.

'Oh, I don't know. I think it's a very interesting conversation. Anna's job is obviously more important than our dad's life!'

'Rachel!' Gary looked from one sister to the other.

'That's not fair,' Anna defended herself. 'That's not what I said. I just need to give Mark some notice, that's all.'

'And what if it's serious? Really serious?' Rachel's eyes challenged hers.

'Then of course I'll go.' Anna stood up and walked to the window.

'I'm going up to check on Alex.' Rachel stormed out of the room.

'Take no notice – she's just upset,' Gary said apologetically.

'I know.'

'Listen, Anna, I don't mean to pressurize you, but if you don't go . . .'

'Yeah, I know, I might live to regret it. Don't worry, Gary, I'm not going to let anyone down.'

Gary checked his watch. 'Like I said, there's no point in making any decisions right now. We're probably worrying about nothing.' He was topping up Anna's glass when Rachel returned, her hand massaging the small of her back. 'Is he okay?' he asked.

'Fast asleep.'

The phone rang again and Gary jumped on it. 'Hello? Oh hi, Jill. No, no news yet, we're waiting for Bridie to call. Yes, I will. Thanks. Bye.' He hung up. 'Jill sends her best.'

'Oh God, I wish Mam would just phone, I can't stand this.' Rachel slumped on to the sofa and closed her eyes.

'Maybe you should go to bed,' Anna said, noting her sister's pale face and the dark circles under her eyes.

'I couldn't possibly sleep.'

'But you could rest,' Gary replied.

'Can you both just leave me alone, please?' Rachel hissed.

'Okay, okay. I'll go and make some more tea.' Gary stood up and went out of the room, closing the door.

Immediately, Rachel turned to her sister, her eyes flashing. 'How can you even think of not going? He's our dad, he's sick, he might be dying, for God's sake, and you're more worried about your job!'

'I'm not! I just want to be fair to Mark. It's a small company, Rachel, and we're very busy at the moment.' Anna took another swig of wine.

'Of course, silly me. They couldn't possibly do without *you*. No doubt the business would fall apart if you went away for a few days.'

'Don't be such a cow, Rache. Anyway, it's not as if Mam's some feeble little old lady. She's well able to look after Dad and herself.'

'God, Anna, how can you be so hard?' Rachel's eyes widened.

Anna looked away. 'I'm not. I'm just reminding you that we have very independent parents.'

'And what the hell does that mean? Are you saying that now they've left the country we shouldn't care about them any more?'

'All I'm saying is that if they needed us, they wouldn't have left the country in the first place.'

'My God! You resent them for leaving Ireland, don't you?' Rachel breathed.

Anna whirled around to face her. 'Of course not!'

'Yes, you do!'

Anna flopped into a chair, her hair falling forward to hide her face. 'I just miss them, that's all.'

Rachel shrugged. 'Well, so do I, but they have their own life to live.'

'I know that. I suppose I just miss having our home to run to when the going gets tough. Does that sound silly, coming from a thirty-one-year-old woman?'

Rachel relaxed a little. 'It doesn't matter what age you are,' she agreed, 'you still need your parents. Well, maybe not need them, but you don't expect them to just walk out of your life. That's supposed to be our job. We're the ones who are supposed to flee the nest. *We* should have been off touring Europe or emigrating to Australia, or, or something.'

Anna stared at her little sister. 'I didn't know you wanted to travel.'

'I didn't, I don't. Oh, I don't know what I want.'

Anna moved to sit beside her and squeezed her hand. 'For once I think I know exactly what you mean.'

'Tea, anyone?' Gary hovered uncertainly in the doorway.

Rachel managed a wobbly smile. 'I think my sister needs it.'

'And what's that supposed to mean?' Anna objected, pushing her away.

'You never could hold your drink,' Rachel retorted. 'Dad always knew when you'd been on a bender.'

'Did he?' Anna looked surprised.

Gary laughed as he set a tray down on the table in front of them. 'Yeah, he said whenever you arrived home at one in the morning all ready for a heart-to-heart he knew you were drunk.'

'Rubbish,' Anna said, but accepted the tea. The last thing she needed was another hangover.

Rachel sighed. 'I can't remember the last time I was drunk.'

'Well, we'll remedy that as soon as the sprog comes out,' Anna told her.

Rachel's expression clouded. 'I won't have the time or energy for socializing when I've two children to look after.'

'That's what babysitters are for,' Gary replied.

'Oh well, that's easy for you to say.' Rachel retorted, two angry red spots on her cheeks.

'Why are you attacking me?' Gary stared at her, mystified.

'Because you don't understand. You don't know what it's like.'

Anna put down her cup. 'Maybe I should go.'

'You can't drive after all that wine,' Rachel snapped.

Gary stood up. 'I'll take her home.'

'No, really—' The phone rang and the three of them froze.

Rachel turned to her husband. 'Oh Gary, you answer it. Please?'

Gary grabbed the phone and said, 'Hello?'

'Hello, Gary love, it's me.'

'Bridie? How is he?'

'Well, love—'

'What's she saying? Let me talk to her.' Rachel snatched the phone off him. 'Mam, it's me. How's Dad?'

'Oh, he's fine, love. Bloody silly man. I told him often enough, but would he listen?'

'Mam, what is it? What's wrong with him?'

'He's got an ulcer.'

Rachel looked at Gary and Anna's expectant faces. 'An ulcer?'

'Yes, so they say, and I don't doubt it, the way your father eats.'

Anna and Gary looked at each other and then back at Rachel.

'But what about the chest pain?' she asked her mother.

'Chest pain? No, love, he had a pain in his stomach.'

Rachel gritted her teeth. 'You said it was his chest, Mam.'

'Did I? I was sure I said stomach. Oh well, never mind. Sure, I didn't know whether I was coming or going. Well, that's it now, I've told him. He'll have to stop eating all those fry-ups – and as for that beer, I'm going to pour every last drop down the sink!'

'An ulcer?' Anna was saying. 'Is that all?'

Rachel nodded. 'So what happens now, Mam? Are they going to operate?'

'Operate? No, not at all, love. They've just given him a few tablets and a diet sheet.'

'That's it?'

'Yes, though looking at this diet, I'll have my work cut out for me, keeping him to it.'

Anna took the phone from her sister. 'Mam? It's Anna.'

'Oh, hello Anna, love! Isn't it lucky that I should ring when you're there too.'

'Yes, Mam, very lucky. Look, are you sure that Dad's okay? I mean, with the language difference and all that . . .'

'Oh, there's no problem with language. Everyone speaks English and they're all very nice.'

'And what medicine have they put him on?'

'They're big white things,' Bridie said helpfully. 'He's going to have great fun swallowing them.'

Anna suppressed a sigh. 'And has he to go back and see them again?'

'No, no, they just told him to go to his doctor if he has any problems.'

'But he doesn't have a doctor, does he?'

'No, of course not, love. We'll find someone when we get down to Benalmadena.'

'You're still going?'

'Well, of course we are! We won't stop off in Barcelona, though. I think that might be too much for him. Now listen, love, I'd better go. There's a poor man here waiting to use the phone, his wife is having a terrible time with her bowels. I'll call you tomorrow. Bye, love. Bye.'

'So what's happening?' Rachel demanded. 'Are we flying out there in the morning?'

Anna shook her head and handed the phone back to Gary. 'I don't know about you, but the only place I'm going is home to bed.'

'How's your dad?' Liam asked, switching on the lamp as she walked into the bedroom.

Anna jumped. She hadn't expected him to be still awake. 'He's got an ulcer but they're just going to treat it with medication and they've put him on a diet.'

'I thought it was his chest?'

Anna sighed. 'So did we.' She looked around her, wondering what to do next. She couldn't bear the thought of getting into *that* bed but the spare room wasn't made up. It would have to be the sofa. She fetched her dressing-gown, picked up a pillow and turned to leave.

'Where are you going?'

'Downstairs.'

'No, wait, we need to talk. You've completely jumped to the wrong conclusion. Tara just dropped in.'

'Oh, please.'

'It's true! I was just getting into the shower and the doorbell went. I let her in and she said she'd make herself some tea while I had my shower. It was completely innocent. God, Anna, how could you think anything else?'

'Maybe it was the guilty look on your face,' Anna shot back. 'And what the hell were you doing, coming downstairs in a towel?'

'I didn't think—'

'You certainly didn't. God, she loved every second of it.'

'Oh Anna, you're exaggerating.'

'Don't tell me I'm exaggerating! That woman deliberately led me to believe there was something going on.'

Liam looked away. 'Well, there wasn't.'

Anna looked at his downcast expression and felt her heart sink. 'But if I'd been just a little bit later there could have been.'

'I love *you*,' he insisted.

'A denial would have been so much better,' Anna said with a sad smile and walked out.

Downstairs she twisted and turned on the small sofa, wishing he'd come down and tell her she was being silly and that it was all a misunderstanding. He didn't.

Chapter 21

Jill sat doodling her name around the edge of the page and wondering what she'd eat for lunch. She'd finally found a diet to suit her and her mouth watered at the thought of having something interesting to eat for a change. Lettuce leaves and celery sticks had never done it for her – she was a meat and potatoes kind of girl and this diet allowed – no, insisted – on plenty of carbohydrates. Yahoo!

'Jill?'

She looked up to see Sue's questioning gaze on her. 'Oh sorry, what was that?'

Her boss sighed irritably. 'I was asking about the radio advertising schedule for the Mitchell campaign.'

'Oh.' Jill flicked through the pages in front of her. 'They're here somewhere.'

'Have my copy.' Vinny produced an A4 page with a flourish and handed it to Sue.

'Thank you, Vinny.'

Jill glowered at him. She was sure that he'd taken those figures from her file – they couldn't just have disappeared.

'You seem to have concentrated times around mid-morning and afternoon,' Sue was saying with a puzzled expression.

'Have I?' As she didn't have a copy of the schedule in front of her and she couldn't recall it off the top of her head, Jill was completely at sea.

'But this is a product targeted at young women,' Sue reminded her impatiently. 'You're putting this ad out when they're at work or college.'

'That can't be right,' Jill said, ignoring the smirk on Vinny's face. 'Leave it with me and I'll check it out, Sue.'

'Do it now, please,' the woman told her. 'We can't afford to screw this up.'

'Sure.' Mortified, Jill rose to her feet and walked to the door. Flying down the corridor to her office, Jill shrieked at Karen to bring in the Mitchell file. As she waited, she looked back at the email correspondence from her team about the advertising schedule but could find no copies of the times.

'What's up?' Karen appeared in the doorway with the thick green folder.

Jill took it from her and started to flick frantically through the pages. 'There's some mix-up over the radio schedule. Dammit, where the hell is it?'

'What?'

'The original document that RTE sent over.'

'Well, it's not going to be there, is it? Vinny took it yesterday.'

Jill stopped in her tracks and stared at her secretary. '*Vinny* took it?'

'Yeah, he was dealing with a query from the customer.'

'But why was he involved? I handle the Mitchell account.'

Karen reddened. 'Well, you weren't around and Vinny was here at the time so he offered to look after it.'

'I'll bet he did,' Jill muttered.

'Well, what was I supposed to do?' Karen demanded.

'Nothing, Karen, it's okay,' Jill soothed. 'You did exactly the right thing.'

Mollified, Karen turned to go. 'Do you want me to print off a copy of the schedule you put together?'

'Not much point as it's completely wrong,' Jill told her. 'Although would you check the Word file and see when it was last updated and by whom?'

'Sure.'

As Jill waited for Karen to return, she sat drumming her fingers on her desk, her mind working overtime. There was no way she'd make such an obvious, stupid mistake with those times so either the radio station had screwed up and she hadn't noticed – still, not a good thing – or someone had changed the times in order to make her look bad. No prizes for guessing who would do something like that.

Karen returned with the printed history of the file. 'Ollie changed the document yesterday.'

Jill stared at her. 'Ollie? Weird.' Taking the sheets she made her way back to the meeting room.

Sue smiled at her as she rejoined them. 'Oh Jill, there you are. Mystery solved. Vinny spotted the problem. Ollie was updating the schedule for the Michaels account and went into the Mitchell's document by mistake.'

'Sorry,' Ollie said, red-faced.

'I've called RTE and asked them to fax over a new copy of the schedule,' Vinny told her.

'Haven't you got the old one?' Jill asked, watching him carefully. 'Karen said you took it out of the file yesterday.'

Vinny rolled his eyes. 'And I gave it straight back to her. Sometimes I wonder about that girl!'

'Let's move on,' Sue said impatiently. 'We've wasted enough time.'

'Jill, I'm really sorry about that,' Ollie hurried after her as the meeting broke up. 'I don't know how it happened.'

Jill turned to face him. 'Tell me, Ollie, were you called away at all when you were working on the Michaels schedule?'

'No. I had to nip out for a jimmy riddle, but that's all.'

'I see. Well, don't worry about it, Ollie, these things happen.' Heading back to her office, Jill was more convinced than ever that Vinny had deliberately tampered with the Mitchell schedule just to make her look bad. And it had worked. Despite Ollie's admission, Sue had obviously been unimpressed with her input at the meeting. Or lack of it.

Jill had to admit that she wasn't performing very well lately. She just couldn't get excited about her job the way she once had, and she knew that it was all because of Vinny Gray. Competition was supposed to be healthy but she hated the atmosphere that he created, and there were days when she'd even been tempted to phone in sick, something she would never have dreamed of doing in the past.

Glancing at her watch she realized she'd be late for her lunch with Anna if she didn't get her skates on. Imagining a steaming plate of pasta or shepherd's pie, Jill's spirits lifted as she left her office. And Anna should be in good form too, now that she knew her dad was okay. Jill chuckled as she imagined Shay's reaction to being put on a diet. Most of his favourite foods came out of a deep-fat fryer.

'Hi, Jill. Going out for a nice long lunch, are we?'

Jill stopped in her tracks at the sight of a very smug Vinny, leaning against the reception desk.

'No, actually, I'm off to the gym.' She reached out and squeezed his large paunch. 'You should try it.' And without a backward glance, she went out to her car and drove over to the pub in Clontarf.

She had read the menu through three times and changed her mind twice before Anna finally arrived. 'About time, I'm wasting away to nothing here! Quick, look at the menu and I'll nab a waiter.'

'Just coffee for me,' Anna said, slipping into the seat opposite.

Jill lowered her hand as she took in her cousin's dishevelled appearance. Anna's hair was scraped back into a ponytail and her pale face was devoid of make-up. 'God, what's wrong with you? You look terrible. Oh Jesus, it's not your dad—'

Anna shook her head. 'No, no, he's fine.'

'Then what? Anna?'

Anna raised red-rimmed eyes to hers. 'It's Liam. And Tara.'

Jill's eyes widened. 'What?'

'What can I get you?' The waiter stood over them, pad and pen in hand.

'Two coffees and a cheese sandwich,' Jill told him, closing the menu with a snap and turning her attention back to her cousin. 'They're having an affair?'

Anna shrugged. 'If they're not then they're thinking about it.'

Jill shook her head. 'No way! You've got it wrong.'

'I walked in on them yesterday, Jill. In my house. Tara was making tea and Liam was wearing a towel.'

Jill was silent for a moment as she digested this piece of information. 'Well, it could have been innocent,' she ventured.

'He said nothing happened but I think that was just because I interrupted them.' Anna broke off and buried her face in a tissue.

'Oh, love!' Jill shifted position so that she could put an arm around her cousin.

'I couldn't sleep with him last night,' Anna said, her voice shaking. 'The thought that they might have done it there, in our bed – oh, God! What am I going to do?'

'For now, absolutely nothing,' Jill told her. 'Let me think for a minute.'

The coffee arrived and Anna took a small sip and then pushed it away. 'She was so pleased with herself, Jill. You know, I think she was delighted that I walked in on them.'

'She's always had her eye on him,' Jill agreed. 'Bitch! What did you say? Did you hit her?'

Anna shook her head. 'I just left.'

'And what did Liam do?'

'Well, he couldn't exactly follow me – not in a towel. He tried to call me but I left the phone off and then he came to the office last night to tell me about Dad. I went straight over to Rachel's. He wanted to come with me but, to be honest, I couldn't bear to look at him. Then he waited up for me but though he denied it, I just couldn't quite believe that it was all as innocent as he makes out.'

'I blame Tara Brady, the conniving little cow. What man is going to refuse when it's handed to him on a plate? Think about it, Anna. He has all this time on his hands, he's feeling very low and you are out at work all day. If she's dropping by from time to time offering a shoulder to cry on, well, he'd be a saint not to be tempted. But I'm sure he'd never actually do it,' Jill added hurriedly.

'But what if he fancies her? If he does, then he can't really love me any more.'

Jill hugged her. 'Don't be silly, Anna, couples have come through worse than this. I'm sure this has nothing to do with Tara and everything to do with how crap Liam is feeling at the moment.'

'You think?' Anna dabbed her eyes as she looked at her cousin.

'I do. But maybe you need some time apart. You could move in with me for a while or . . .'

'Or?'

'You could go and stay with your folks.'

Anna shuddered. 'I'm not sure that'd be a good idea. Three of us cooped up in that camper van? Mam would know something was wrong and she's got enough problems at the moment.'

'Didn't you say that they'd rented an apartment in Benalmadena?'

'Oh yeah, you're right.'

'And you could take Rachel along. Your folks would be thrilled to see her. It would cheer them both up.'

'Oh, I don't know.' Anna shook her head wearily.

'I'm sure you'd like to see for yourself if your dad's okay,' Jill continued, 'and a change of scene would do Rachel the world of good. I was talking to Gary earlier, and he was saying that she would love to go and see her parents but would be nervous travelling alone.'

'Then why doesn't *he* take her?' Anna retorted.

'Someone has to look after Alex.'

'They could both go and take Alex with them.'

'The point, Anna, is that you and Rachel are the ones that need the break.'

Anna sighed. 'Mark would go mad. We're very busy.'

'I bet if you put in a few extra hours this week he could spare you for one week. Gary says there's a cheap flight out on Sunday.'

'Sunday? What – this Sunday?'

'Do it, Anna,' Jill urged. 'It will give you and Liam time to think. It will be good for Rachel and it would make Bridie and Shay very happy.'

Anna thought about it. 'I'll talk to Mark.'

'Excellent!'

'Don't you say a word to Rachel until I know for sure,' Anna warned.

'My lips are sealed,' Jill promised. 'Oh, it's going to be great. Sun, sea, sangria. I almost wish I was coming with you.'

Anna looked at her. 'Then why don't you?'

Jill laughed. 'Oh, I couldn't.'

'Why not?'

Jill thought about it. She was due some time off. She was totally fed up with ADLI, and Vinny and Sue in particular. There was no attentive lover to leave behind and last, but by no means least, Anna and Rachel would probably need a referee. She smiled slowly. 'Why not indeed?'

Anna squealed. 'Oh Jill, that would be fantastic!'

Jill's face clouded. 'But would there be enough room?'

'Sure. There's the apartment *and* the camper van, remember?'

'Gosh, I haven't slept in a caravan since we went on holidays to Tramore when I was twelve.'

'And it rained and rained and rained,' Anna reminded her. 'But you can't really compare the camper van to the little tin cans we used to stay in.'

'It is quite luxurious, isn't it?'

'Microwave, fridge-freezer, fantastic shower, the works,' Anna said.

Jill looked at her watch. 'I need clothes! If I head back to the office now, I can get a bit of shopping in later.'

Anna made a face. 'I won't have any time for that. Mark will make me work my butt off this week.'

'What will Liam say?' Jill asked, suddenly remembering the reason for the trip.

Anna's smile disappeared. 'I don't know. Maybe he'll be delighted. He'll be able to get on with his new romance without interruption.'

'Anna.'

'Oh, who knows, Jill. I certainly don't. But you're right, I could do with a break from him. I just hope I manage to get through a week with my sister without killing her.'

'I'll make sure you do,' Jill promised. 'And you never know, you might even enjoy yourself.'

'Next week?' Mark looked at her as if she'd lost her mind.

'I'm sorry for the short notice but it's just with Dad being sick.'

'It's only an ulcer, Anna.'

'Yes, I know that but, well, Rachel and I would still like to see him and make sure he's getting the right treatment.'

Mark snorted. 'And maybe get in a bit of sunbathing too.'

'I haven't had any time off since March,' Anna said firmly. 'I'll work late every night this week. And Val said she'd do some viewings for you while I'm away.'

'Oh, okay, go if you must,' he capitulated. 'Only a week, mind.'

'Only a week,' Anna promised with a smile.

'What does your husband think of you sodding off to Spain without him?' he called after her as she went back out to her desk.

'I don't know and I don't care,' Anna retorted, earning herself a worried look from Val.

'And Jill's going too?' Mark followed her out. 'Maybe I should come along to look after you girls.'

'We're going to see my folks,' Anna reminded him.

'And if *you* were with them, they'd really need looking after,' Val said in an uncharacteristic outburst.

Mark looked at her, amazed. 'Val, I don't know what you mean!'

The older woman reddened and turned her attention back to her work. 'I'm sure.'

'I just hope Rachel doesn't go into labour while we're away,' Anna said.

'How far is she gone?' Val asked.

'Thirty-four weeks, I think.'

'Another six to go, then. I'm sure she'll be fine.'

Anna shuddered. 'She'd better be. I don't see myself as a midwife.'

'Just tell her to keep her legs crossed. In fact, same advice to you and Jill!' Mark went back into his office, laughing uproariously.

'One of these days I'm going to wash that man's mouth out with carbolic soap.' Val tutted.

'He's a lost cause,' Anna told her. 'I don't know how Jan puts up with him.'

'Oh, it's all front,' Val assured her. 'He's actually a very good husband.'

Anna shot her a look of pure disbelief. 'He hides it well. Anyway, I'd better get going. I've got four houses to visit before lunch.'

'And another five this afternoon.'

'And a viewing at six-thirty.' Anna groaned. 'By the end of this week I'm going to need a holiday.'

'I'm going to Spain.' Rachel put down the phone and stared at herself in the hall mirror. 'What clothes do I bring? God, what about Alex? I'll need to fill the freezer or Gary will just take him to McDonald's every night. And then there's his lunch – I wonder is it okay to freeze ham sandwiches? Maybe I'll post the question on *MumSpeak*.'

Rachel continued to mutter to herself as she went through her wardrobe and gazed at the awful baggy clothes that hung there. Given the lousy weather this summer all the tops were long-sleeved and way too warm for the hot weather her parents were enjoying in Spain. She'd have to find time to drop into Mothercare and see if she could pick up something more suitable.

She closed the wardrobe, went down to her desk and flicked on the computer. As she waited for it to come on, she started a 'to-do' list. It would be the first of several if Gary was to survive without her for a full week. She couldn't believe that not only was Gary encouraging her to go, but he was taking a week off work to mind Alex. She wondered what he'd do if Alex woke during the night. Gary loved his sleep and was very grumpy when he didn't get it. She chuckled as she signed on to *MumSpeak*. Maybe a week without her was exactly what he needed. As she entered the chatroom, she scanned the latest messages, coming up short when she saw *Message for Al'sMum*.

Quickly she tabbed down to the message and pressed Enter. She groaned at the question and began to wish she'd never opened her heart to these people.

Hey, Al'sMum. Haven't heard from you for a while. Is

everything okay? Have you talked to your husband? How do you feel now about the baby? You're in my thoughts and just wondered if you're okay. Galway Gal

'Oh no.' Rachel hadn't tackled Gary, of course she hadn't. The last thing she needed was to hear her worst fears confirmed. Rachel winced as the baby gave a particularly violent kick. 'Hey, you, stop that.' She caressed her bump. 'Mummy does love you, you know that.'

Forgetting about her questions for the other mothers, Rachel closed the *MumSpeak* window and switched off the machine. She'd have to cope on her own from now on. The last thing she needed was well-meaning strangers telling her what she should do. With a bit of luck, she might get to spend some time alone with her mother during this holiday. If anyone would understand what she was going through, it would be Bridie.

Chapter 22

'Oh, look. They have that wonderful concealer, Touche Éclat. I think I'll get that.' Jill eagerly checked out the duty-free magazine as the last of the passengers finished boarding.

'I can't get this bloody belt around me,' Rachel complained, pulling in her tummy and trying unsuccessfully to close it.

'They have extensions for fat people,' Anna told her. 'Ring for an air hostess.'

'Flight attendant,' Jill corrected, leaning across Rachel and loosening the belt. 'You don't need an extension. There.'

'Thanks, Jill.' Rachel looked across her cousin and scowled at her sister. 'And thanks for your sensitivity, Anna.'

'Oh, for heaven's sake!' Anna turned away and looked out of the window. It was only half six on a cold Sunday morning and Liam was probably still snoring his brains out.

She'd said goodbye to him last night and even put their differences to one side to wish him well in the interview he had later that week. The job would be perfect for him and Anna knew he was excited about it. 'The taxi's picking me up at four so I don't suppose you'll want me to wake you,' she'd joked feebly as she was going to bed, but she'd been very hurt when Liam had just shrugged and wished her a pleasant holiday. God, he was like a stranger. He hadn't even attempted to kiss her. Anna's eyes filled as she watched the baggage handlers dumping cases into the hold. He was probably glad she was going. Maybe he wouldn't be there when she got back. He could easily move into Tara's place, there was plenty of room and then he'd have his beloved mother next door. What more could he want? He'd never have to work again with those two clucking over him.

'Here we go,' Jill said as the plane pushed back and the flight attendants started their spiel on safety.

Rachel fiddled nervously with her belt as she watched the lifebelt demonstration. This was the first time she'd been away without Alex and she had found it very hard to leave him. She had wanted to hug him before she left but Gary had nearly had a fit. 'It's the middle of the night, Rachel, would you leave the kid alone. You said goodbye to him already.'

'Do you think he'll be okay without me, Gary?'

'He'll be fine as long as you bring back lots of presents,' Gary had assured her.

But Rachel knew that Alex would miss her; it was his father she wasn't so sure about. Gary had been very enthusiastic about this trip – too enthusiastic. Still, he wouldn't be able to get up to much while she was away, what with Alex to look after. And maybe, just maybe, he'd appreciate her more when she got back.

Jill's mind was also wandering as the attendants moved down the aisle, checking seatbelts were fastened and tables were up. As soon as she'd returned from her lunch with Anna, Jill had gone straight in to see her boss. Sue hadn't been too pleased about her taking time off at such short notice but, as Jill hadn't had a summer holiday, she reluctantly agreed. Jill got no more work done that day, spending her time on the internet and the phone arranging flights and checking with Gary that Rachel's passport was current. After work she'd headed down to Grafton Street. The shops were already full of the new styles for autumn but luckily, skimpy tops were all the fashion and you could always rely on Brown Thomas when it came to swimwear. She'd gone home that evening exhausted, with a boot full of bags, including a large box of shortbread for Bridie. She had ended up buying Shay an opera CD. She usually bought him chocolate, booze or fags, but her life wouldn't be worth living if she brought him anything remotely unhealthy.

'I think I need a drink,' Rachel said, her hands digging into Jill's arm as the plane turned on to the runway.

'You'll be fine.' Jill patted her hand. 'It's a very

short journey; it will be over before you know it.'

Rachel squeezed her eyes shut and offered up a silent prayer. *'I know I don't talk to You as often as I should but please, please, please keep me and my baby safe and bring us back in one piece. And keep Alex safe too. And I promise I'll take him to Mass more often.'* Surreptitiously she crossed herself and clung on to Jill's arm. Once they were up she'd be fine. It was just that horrible feeling when the plane first took off that got her. And the turbulence, of course. And she wasn't so keen on the landing. 'I definitely think I'll have a drink. One won't do any harm. What do you think, Jill?'

'Oh for God's sake, will you shut up?' Anna snapped at her sister. 'A plane crash will be the least of your worries if you keep rabbiting on like this!'

'She's nervous,' Jill hissed in her ear. 'Give her a break.'

'I'm sorry.' Anna turned mournful eyes on her cousin. 'I'm just a bit down.'

Jill patted Anna's arm with her free hand. 'We'll talk about it when Rachel falls asleep,' she whispered.

'How do you know she's going to fall asleep?'

'Take a look.'

Anna leaned forward to get a better look at her sister and suppressed a giggle as she saw that Rachel's head was already lolling on Jill's shoulder.

'Gary told me she didn't go to bed at all last night so she's knackered. Five minutes tops and she'll be gone.'

Anna leaned across to say gently, 'Don't worry, Sis, we'll be there in no time.'

Rachel sleepily smiled her thanks and closed her eyes.

'Can I get you ladies a drink?' A pleasant-looking attendant stood over them.

'Three white wines,' Jill told her, rummaging for her purse.

'Here, I'll get them.' Anna pulled out 20 Euros and handed it over.

'Thanks.' Jill took her drink and Rachel's.

'Do you think she'll actually get to drink that?' Anna asked.

'No, but I'm sure you and I will manage it between us. Happy holiday!'

'Cheers!' Anna raised her plastic glass. 'God, what are we like, boozing at this hour of the morning.' Most of the people around them were drinking tea, coffee or juice.

'They're just cheapskates,' her cousin told her. 'I've noticed that a lot of people don't drink on planes when they have to pay for it themselves.'

Anna took another sip. 'Miserable sods.'

Jill grinned as Rachel let out a small snore. 'I think it's safe to talk now. So, how are things?'

'Terrible. Liam didn't even get up to say goodbye to me.'

'Well, it was the middle of the night,' Jill said reasonably. 'Has he said any more about Tara?'

'He's tried,' Anna admitted, 'but I don't want to

hear it. You know, I just don't trust myself. I feel so angry I'm afraid of what I might say.'

'Anger's good,' Jill assured her.

'It is?'

'Yes. Much better than being sad or defeatist.'

'Oh, I feel all that too but at the moment I feel mad more than anything. You know that day that I walked in on them, I had been feeling so guilty over Charlie?'

Jill's eyes widened. 'You didn't!'

'No! That's just it, Jill, I didn't do a damn thing! My biggest crime is that when Charlie tried to kiss me, I thought about letting him.'

'You didn't?' Jill said again.

'I didn't. But I felt guilty because I was kind of sorry I didn't. I wondered what it would be like.' She sighed. 'And because I felt like that, I went rushing home to Liam and look what I found.'

'It will all work out in the end. You two are made for each other.'

Anna stared into her drink. 'I'm not so sure.'

'One word of advice,' Jill added.

'What's that?'

'Keep away from Charlie Coleman. It's harder to resist temptation when you're vulnerable.'

'You don't have to worry about him, I won't be seeing him any more. He's put in an offer on a house and I'm pretty sure it will be accepted.'

'That's good. Isn't it?'

'I suppose it is, but to be honest, he's the only

thing that's kept me going these last few weeks. You know I've deliberately been taking on extra work because it's preferable to going home?'

'I didn't know things were that bad.'

'They've never been worse.'

'Rachel, Anna, cooee!' Bridie Gallagher bounced up and down on her tiptoes trying to attract her daughters' attention.

'Bridie!' It was Jill who was the first to spot her aunt as they came through Arrivals. 'Come on, girls.'

'Howaya, Da.' Anna hugged her father. 'You're still alive then?'

'Hard to kill a bad thing,' Shay said, swinging her off her feet.

'I'd like to see you try that with me,' Rachel joked as she kissed her mother.

'No bother, you're only a slip of a thing.' Shay pulled her gently into his arms and patted her bump. 'How's my little grandchild doing then?'

'Kicking like hell. How are you?' She studied her father's tanned face and bright eyes. He certainly didn't look very sick.

'I'd be fine if your mother fed me occasionally.'

'Just ignore him.' Bridie released Anna and turned to hug Jill. 'Hello, love. You look a bit tired.'

'Oh, I'm grand, Aunty.'

'A bit of sun and sleep will do you the world of good.' Bridie winked at her. 'And I might even have a Señor for you.'

Anna rolled her eyes. 'The last thing Jill needs is one of your lame dogs.'

'What's that supposed to mean?'

'It means you attract every loser for miles around,' her husband said, taking Rachel's case. 'And then you swan off leaving me wondering how to get rid of them.'

Bridie laughed. 'Ah, will you stop! Sure I'm just doing my Christian duty. Love thy neighbour, and so on.'

'Charity begins at home,' Shay told her. 'And you're supposed to be looking after *me* at the moment.'

'Ah, will you go away out of that! I'm fed up trying to look after you.'

'How's the diet going, Dad?' Anna asked, falling into step beside her father.

'Bloody rabbit food, fish and chicken, that's all she's feeding me. And one flamin' glass of wine a night! I ask you!'

'I'm sure you can have more than that once the ulcer is under control.' As they emerged into brilliant sunshine, Anna looked around for the camper van. 'Where's the passion wagon?'

'Matt lent me his car,' her father explained, leading the way to the car park. 'Him and Trish are spending the day at the beach.'

'So where are we sleeping, Mam?' Rachel asked, praying she wouldn't have to share with her sister.

'Your father and I are going to sleep in the van and

you three can have the apartment all to yourselves.'

'Oh no, Bridie,' Jill protested. 'That's not fair at all.'

'You haven't been in our van, have you, Jill?' Shay remarked.

'No, but—'

Bridie waved away her protests. 'Trust me, love, it's more than comfortable. We only took the apartment so we could entertain while we were here and that's off now that Shay has to behave himself.'

'She'll be making me go to bed at eight, next,' Shay complained.

'Are you sure about this, Mam?' Anna asked.

'Of course, love. You three will be able to roll in at whatever time you like without fear of disturbing us.'

Rachel looked down at her bump. 'I may well come rolling in, but probably before teatime.'

'Poor Rache.' Jill hugged her cousin. 'You could always have a siesta and that way you might last a bit longer.'

'That's not a bad idea.' Rachel brightened as they climbed into the car and set off for the resort. With Alex around she rarely got to take a nap in the afternoon. 'I don't know what's going on. I can't sleep at night and I can't stay awake during the day.'

'Your body goes through changes when you're pregnant,' her mother said wisely.

'And so does your mind,' Shay added. 'And if

you're anything like your mother, it won't change back.'

Bridie took a swipe at him. 'It's a wonder I still have a mind at all, married to you!'

Rachel and Anna exchanged smiles as they listened to their parents' affectionate bickering.

'I'm so glad we came.' Rachel settled in against her mother's ample figure.

Bridie patted her face. 'And we're happy to have you, love.'

The pretty one-bedroom apartment was like every other Spanish apartment Jill had stayed in, with the exception of the view. 'Wow!' She stood on the balcony drinking in the scene. 'This is incredible.' Though the complex was close to the heart of Benalmadena, it was set out on a headland and all you could see for miles was sea and sand.

'It is nice here, isn't it?' Bridie sighed happily. 'If we were going to settle anywhere I think this might be the place.'

Anna looked at her in surprise. 'After all the places you've been? I mean, don't get me wrong, it's very nice but isn't it a bit commercial?'

'It's rather like home,' her father told her, coming out to join them. 'There are a lot of Irish and English people living out here, it's cheap, the food is good and look at this weather! Your mother hasn't complained once of her back since we got here.'

'Really, Mam?' Rachel asked.

Bridie nodded. 'It's the first time in years that I've had some relief from the arthritis.'

'The swimming helps,' Shay added.

'It does,' Bridie agreed. 'I swim in the pool every morning without fail.'

'I would too if I had a pool like that.' Jill eyed the kidney-shaped pool with the waterfall at one end and hot tub at the other. There was a plentiful supply of sunbeds and brightly coloured parasols, and a white-coated waiter weaved his way between the tourists, bringing drinks, ice-cream and fresh towels.

'This place must be costing you a fortune,' Rachel remarked.

Her father grinned. 'We booked it in a travel agent in France a couple of days before we came out and got it for half-price.'

'So what would you like to do first?' Bridie asked as she served up tea, coffee and fresh croissants and cakes. 'You can have a slice of wholemeal toast,' she told her husband.

'I'd be quite happy to just lie by the pool,' Rachel admitted.

'I think that's a good idea,' Jill agreed. 'And then when it gets too hot we could go and see the sights.'

'All the shops will be closed from twelve till about four,' Shay warned.

'We can go to Kitty's for lunch,' Bridie announced. 'You'll love it, girls and you'll get to meet all the locals. Well, the ex-pat locals anyway. Everyone's very friendly.'

'Sounds good,' Anna said, 'although I'd like to go into Marbella at some stage.'

'Do Marbella at night,' her mother advised. 'There are wonderful shops, great restaurants and everyone dresses up just to parade up and down looking at each other.'

Anna nodded. 'I know, Mam, I have been here before, remember?'

'Oh, that's right! I'd forgotten. That was your first holiday with Liam, wasn't it?'

'Yeah,' Anna murmured, regretting she'd brought the subject up.

'How is he, love?' Shay asked.

'Oh, he's okay.'

'Pity he couldn't come down with you.' Bridie had a soft spot for her first son-in-law.

'He has an interview this week.'

'Oh, that's great, love! We'll go down to the church and light a candle for him. And how's Gary and young Alex, Rachel?'

'Fine, though I'm not sure how they'll survive on their own.'

Shay laughed. 'Ah, once they've a good chipper and video shop near them, they'll be grand.'

'Probably,' Rachel agreed.

'They'll be counting the days till your return,' her mother assured her. 'There's a great shoe shop up the road I must take you to, love. They have a wonderful range for kids.'

'That would be great, Mam. The ones you sent him are already scuffed.'

'Are there any decent beauty salons around, Bridie?' Jill asked. 'I'd love to have a pedicure and a manicure while I'm here.'

'There's one here in the complex, they do a lovely facial.'

'You went for a facial?' Anna raised an eyebrow at her sister. The most their mother had ever indulged in at home was a shampoo and set.

Bridie reddened. 'It was Patricia's idea. I went along for the laugh but I must say it was very relaxing.'

'I told her she should go back for a massage,' Shay chipped in. 'Keep those aches and pains at bay.'

'We should *all* go,' Jill announced. 'This is supposed to be a holiday. We deserve some pampering.'

'I don't think so,' Rachel looked down at her bump. 'Even if I managed to climb on to a table, I doubt I'd get back down again.'

'Maria has a lovely comfortable reclining chair,' her mother said. 'That's what she uses for doing reflexology and pedicures. I'm sure she could do a facial for you in that.'

Rachel brightened immediately. 'Ooh, reflexology! I've always wanted to try that.'

'I tried that in Powerscourt Springs,' Jill told her. 'It was cool.'

'Well, I'm up for anything,' Anna said. She couldn't really afford to be indulging in such pampering but she didn't give a damn any more and she certainly didn't have to worry about saving for a baby now. 'I think I'll go and unpack.'

'I've cleared out the wardrobes for you,' Bridie said, following her out to where their cases lined the hallway. 'Do you think Jill will mind sleeping on the cot-bed in the living room?' she whispered to her eldest daughter.

'I'll take the cot-bed,' Anna told her. 'Jill can go in with Rachel.'

'Whatever you want, love. There's a small closet behind the door you could use if you don't want to traipse back and forward to the bedroom.'

'That's grand.'

Bridie hugged her. 'It's so good to have you here, love.'

Anna held her mother close and breathed in the familiar perfume. 'It's good to be here, Mam.'

Rachel lay dozing in the shade of a palm tree while Anna, Jill and Bridie stretched out by the pool and chatted. 'Where's Dad gone?' Anna asked as she rubbed cream into her mother's shoulders.

'He's gone for his daily constitutional and his sneaky beer.'

Jill laughed. 'Does he know you know?'

'Thanks, love.' As Anna finished, Bridie settled down on her tummy. 'No, he thinks he's fooling me but sure you've got to let them have their little vices.'

'How is he doing, Mam?' Anna asked, stretching out on the sunbed between her mother and her cousin.

'He's fine. We've found a lovely doctor just up the road and he's keeping an eye on him.'

'Any more pain?' Jill asked.

'No, unless he eats anything fatty, then he pays for it.'

'He seems fed up with the diet,' Anna remarked.

'Not at all, he just enjoys moaning. We get lovely fish out here and he likes that, and he can still have his spuds, as long as they're boiled. It's just the fry-ups that he misses. Sometimes I grill him a little bit of bacon,' Bridie admitted, 'because, as my mam always said, "a little of what you fancy does you good".'

'Well, I think he looks great. You both do,' Jill said. 'This Romany life must be agreeing with you.'

'It's been wonderful,' Bridie admitted. 'We're closer now than we've been in years. You know what we used to be like, Anna. Propped up in front of the telly every night, hardly saying a word to each other. Selling up was the best thing we could have done and has given us a whole new lease of life.'

'What made you do it?' Jill asked her aunt curiously. 'It was very spur of the moment. My mother thought you'd both lost your reason.'

Bridie laughed. One night since then, after a couple of sherries, her sister had admitted to her that she had been a little bit envious. 'It all came about when the car-insurance renewal arrived.'

Anna propped herself up on her elbow and took off her shades. 'What do you mean?'

'Well, your father was giving out about all the bills coming in and how were we going to manage on just our pensions. Then the car-insurance renewal came in and he said that maybe we should just sell the car because it wasn't as if we ever went anywhere.'

'You came to see me and Rachel and you went on holidays every year.'

'Malahide, Courtown and Tramore.' Bridie ticked them off on her fingers. 'Yes, we lived in the fast lane, didn't we? So we decided it was high time we made the most of the life we had left together. And after the scare he gave me last week, I'm more convinced than ever that we did the right thing.'

'I'm glad, Mam, but it was awful getting that phone call from you and knowing that we couldn't just hop in a car and come and see you both.'

'Yes, I do realize that.' Bridie took Anna's hand. 'And there are times when I miss you both terribly, but I still think it was the right thing to do. And flights are so cheap now you can come and visit us any time you like. Rachel will be able to send Alex out to us when he gets a bit older. Think of what a wonderful experience that will be for him!'

'Are you planning to continue to travel?' Jill asked. 'Or are you going to settle somewhere?'

Bridie shrugged. 'Well, we can't travel for ever.'

'Would you come home?' Anna looked at her hopefully.

Bridie met her daughter's eyes. 'Honestly, love? No, I don't think so.' She gazed out at the twinkling blue water, dotted with swimmers and windsurfers. 'Why would we?'

Anna sat up, swung her legs off the sunbed and shoved her feet into her sandals. 'I'm going to get a drink, do you want anything?'

'No, thanks,' Jill said.

'No, thanks, love.' Bridie sighed as her daughter stalked off. 'I don't think I said what she wanted to hear.'

'Don't worry about it,' Jill consoled her aunt. 'She just got a bit of a fright when Shay got sick – they both did.'

Bridie nodded. 'So did I. I always thought he'd go on for ever. He's always been so healthy, so strong. But he won't. Neither of us will.'

'Oh, I think there's plenty of life left in you yet.'

'There's a bit, love, and I plan to make the most of it. Is that so wrong?'

Jill patted her hand. 'No, of course it isn't.'

Chapter 23

'Have you bought me any presents, Mum?' Alex asked when Gary put him on.

'I'm fine, thanks, Alex, how are you?'

'Uh, sorry, Mum. Are you having a nice time?'

'Lovely.'

'And have you got me anything?'

'Alex!'

Rachel smiled as she heard Gary's voice. 'I might have. Are you being good for Daddy?'

'Yes. Mum, there's this new beyblade . . .'

'Alex!'

'I'm just telling her about it!' Alex protested.

'Say goodbye to Mummy.'

'Bye, Mummy.'

'Bye, sweetheart, I miss you.'

'Materialistic little sod, isn't he?' Gary said after Alex had handed over the phone.

'Nice to know he's missing me.'

'He is,' Gary assured her. 'He's quite clingy and it takes a lot longer to get him asleep.'

'Is he waking during the night at all?'

'No, he's slept straight through every night.'

Typical, Rachel thought. 'That's good.'

'How are you? Are you sleeping any better?'

Rachel was warmed by the concern in his voice. 'Not really, but I'm having a siesta every day which is nice.'

'Good, I'm glad. How's your dad doing?'

'Not a bother on him and he looks great.'

'Alex is screaming for his dinner, I'd better go.'

'Make sure that he eats some vegetables.'

'I will.'

'And cut any fat or gristle off the meat or he won't eat it.'

'Will do.'

'And—'

'Rachel!'

'Okay, okay. Bye.'

'Bye, sweetheart, take care of yourself.'

'I will, Gary, I promise.'

Rachel switched off her mobile phone and went back into Kitty's Café where her family were sitting relaxing after a late lunch.

'How's Alex?' her mother asked, patting the seat next to her.

'Doing fine.' Rachel sat down heavily, fanning her face.

'Are you all right, love?' Bridie asked with a worried frown.

'Just finding it a bit warm today.' She was feeling hot and sweaty, and being around her sister and cousin didn't help. Anna was looking cool and sexy in a black mini-dress and Jill – sitting up at the bar deep in conversation with Kitty – was looking equally gorgeous in a flamboyant red sarong. In her white, drawstring trousers and multi-coloured top, Rachel felt like an oversized clown. And with her flushed face and swollen ankles she knew that she was looking her worst.

'Would you like to go back and have a lie-down, love?' her father asked.

'Yes, I think I will,' she agreed.

'I'll walk with you.' He stood up and pulled her to her feet. 'You girls stay here and have a chat.'

'Are you sure?' Bridie looked at Rachel.

'Yes, really, Mam. You stay here and enjoy yourself. I'll be fine once I've had my siesta.'

'We'll pick you up in a couple of hours for your pedicure,' Anna said, settling back with her glass of wine.

'Okay, see you later.'

'Am I going too fast for you, love?' Shay asked.

'Dad, I'm pregnant not sick,' Rachel protested, laughing.

'Sorry, love, it's just your feet look so sore.'

Rachel sighed. Her ankles had swollen up even more since they'd got here and she had been reduced to wearing a pair of her mother's flat sandals. 'They look worse than they feel. What about you, Dad, how are you?'

'Ah, sure I'm grand, love.'

'You gave us an awful fright, you know. I know this diet lark is a bit of a pain but please try and stick to it. Not just because of the ulcer. Carrying all of that extra weight isn't doing your heart any good either and you're not getting any younger.'

'Dear God, are you trying to cheer me up or what?'

'I'm serious, Dad. You need to take care of yourself and Mam too.'

'Well, to be honest, love, that's the main reason I'm going along with this bloody diet. She's keeping to it as well and with her blood pressure and cholesterol, the doctor says it's important that she loses weight and cuts down on her fat intake.'

Rachel stopped in her tracks. 'Mam has problems with her cholesterol and blood pressure? I didn't know that.'

Shay groaned. 'Oh, now don't say that I told you or she'll murder me.'

'But how long has she known? Was it before you left Ireland?'

Shay nodded, as he propelled his daughter on towards the apartment complex. 'Yes, it was. And before you have a go, Dr Mulvany gave us his blessing when we told him we were leaving. He said the Mediterranean weather and diet would do us both the world of good.'

'That's all well and good, but who is there here to look after you if you get sick?'

'That's what health insurance is for, Rachel. I would never expect you or Anna to look after us, no matter what happened.'

'Oh Dad, you know that we'd want to!'

'Well, we're not going to need looking after so enough of this depressing talk. I'm going to get skinny and fit so that I can bounce this new little lad on my knee.'

Rachel smiled. 'Who says it's a boy?'

'Do you know?'

She shook her head.

'I suppose every woman wants a little girl.'

'I don't care, once it's healthy, but a boy might be safer. I've a feeling Gary would spoil a girl and make Alex green with jealousy.'

'Gary must be delighted, is he?'

'Yeah, he's pretty chuffed.'

'And what about you?'

Rachel looked up to see her father studying her carefully. 'What do you mean?'

'I'm not as green as I'm cabbage-looking, love. You're not yourself at the moment. Is it just the pregnancy or is there something else?'

'I'm fine, don't worry.'

'I'll always worry – you're still my little girl. You can always come to me, you know that?'

'Yes, Dad, but it's not that easy with you all the way out here,' Rachel pointed out.

He stopped and turned her to face him. 'If you needed me I'd be there in a heartbeat. I swear it.'

Rachel stepped into his hug. 'I know, Dad, I know.'

Jill's mobile rang again and she ignored it.

'Is that work bothering you again?' Anna asked.

'Yeah, but they can get lost,' Jill said, switching it off.

'You're quite right, love,' Bridie said. 'You're entitled to your holiday. Those bloody mobile phones are a curse.'

'Although you're getting one,' Anna told her. 'Think how much easier it would have been if you'd had one last week when Dad got sick.'

'I didn't need it at all,' her mother argued. 'I called for an ambulance from the phone on the campsite and it came.'

'But look at the hassle you had, keeping in touch with us.' Anna shot her cousin a look of total frustration.

'I'm sorry I called you at all now. There was no need to worry you both. What could you do from Ireland other than worry?'

'Mam! You can't keep something like that from us! Promise me now that you'll always call us if anything happens.'

Bridie rolled her eyes. 'Oh, for heaven's sake, Anna, stop fussing. We're not children. We're more than capable of looking after ourselves.'

Deciding that mother and daughter needed some time to themselves, Jill stood up. 'I think I'll head back to the apartment. I'd like to have a shower before my massage.'

'Right, love, see you later.' Bridie smiled at her niece before turning back to face her daughter. 'What's wrong?' she asked without preamble.

'Nothing.'

'Are you sure?'

Anna sighed. 'I got such a fright, Mam. You know, Rachel and I thought we might be coming out here for Dad's funeral.'

Bridie crossed herself. 'Well, thank God he's fine. We both are.'

'Would you not come home, now, Mam? You've had a nice time, you've seen so much – aren't you ready to come back so that Rachel and I can look after you and Dad?'

'But we don't *need* looking after!'

'Mam, you know what I'm saying.'

'I do and it's a load of rubbish.'

'Mam!'

'Will you stop saying "Mam"?' Bridie tutted in frustration. 'I think you should tell me what's wrong.'

'What do you mean?'

'I'm your mother, Anna, and I'm not stupid. This isn't about me or your father. There's something else going on. Is it Liam?'

Anna didn't answer.

Bridie sat forward and took her hand. 'Look, love, I'm here now. Talk to me.'

'There is something. Liam's been spending a lot of time with Tara Brady, the girl he used to go out with.'

'The one who lives next door to his mother?'

Anna nodded.

'The bastard!'

'Mam!'

'Your father will kill him when he hears this. And what has that stuck-up mother of his got to say about it?'

'I don't think she knows and, Mam, I'm not sure there is anything to know.'

Bridie looked her in the eye. 'Aren't you?'

Anna gave a sob. 'Oh Mam.'

'Come here to me, you poor child.' Bridie gathered her elder daughter into her arms as if she were a three-year-old.

'Liam says nothing's happened and I believe him, but I think he wants it to. I think he fancies her.'

'It's taken him long enough to realize that, hasn't it?'

'He's been spending more time around at his mother's so I suppose he just kept running into her.'

Bridie snorted. 'I'm sure. It sounds to me like he's got too much time on his hands.'

'Or he realizes that he married the wrong woman,' Anna wept.

Bridie hugged her fiercely. 'Don't be silly, love, the lad is mad about you!'

'Not any more, Mam. You haven't seen him in ages. He's changed completely. He hardly opens his mouth to me from one end of the day to the other.'

'He's just having a rough time and doesn't know whether he's coming or going.'

'That's what Jill says. She says that the way he's behaving has nothing to do with me or Tara but with what's going on in his own head.'

'Your cousin's got her head screwed on the right way. She must have got that from me because her mother was the thick one of the family.'

Anna laughed through her tears. 'Oh Mam, I've missed you.'

'I'm sure everything will work out with Liam, love. He's a good man. Maybe he's done something silly – let's face it, most men do – but I'm sure he loves you. You just have to decide whether or not you can forgive him and put this all behind you.' Bridie stood up and pulled Anna to her feet. 'Come on, my darling. Let's go and get Jill and Rachel. We're due at the salon in half an hour. A nice massage will do you the world of good.'

'But it won't solve my problems, Mam, will it?'

Bridie hugged her close. 'No, it won't, my darling, but it might help you to calm down and do some thinking.'

Back at the apartment, Jill was sitting on the balcony checking her phone messages. There were three from Karen, one from Ollie and another from Rebecca, all relating to Vinny and his handling of some of her accounts. A month ago, Jill would have been on the first plane home but suddenly, it didn't seem that important any more. She found it hard to get excited about a department-store sale or a new type of contact lens or a hand cream that could get rid of liver spots (she must get some free samples for her mother and Bridie). The world of advertising had lost its appeal and Jill felt completely switched off. She was also still missing Andy, which came as something of a shock, as she usually had no trouble walking away from men. It must be her age. That damned body-clock was probably ticking and any day now she'd start to look longingly at babies.

Having said that, she wasn't the slightest bit envious of her cousin. Though she'd obediently put her hand on the bump to feel the baby kick, Jill had felt no answering kick at her heartstrings. Thank God! Baby blues when you didn't even have a man would be too complicated even for her. And things were complicated enough at the minute. She was beginning to wonder whether she'd been right to come to Spain in the first place. Rachel was obviously not herself and Jill was hoping that Bridie had noticed this. As for Anna, well, the poor girl was falling apart in front of her eyes and Jill wasn't sure what she could say or do to help. There wasn't much time to wonder or worry about her own problems, which was probably just as well.

For the first time in years, her confidence in her own ability was faltering. Was she a wimp who just couldn't handle the competition? Was she past it?

Had she had her day and now it was Vinny Gray's turn? It was depressing to think that she might have reached her peak and already be on the way down before she'd even hit thirty. What the hell was she supposed to do now? Stay in ADLI and watch younger, smarter people overtake her? Go to another company and start the whole dog-eat-dog process again? Or drop out and do something completely different? At the moment working at a checkout in Tesco's seemed very attractive, and certainly preferable to returning to ADLI.

'Jill, Rache? Are you ready? Mam's waiting downstairs.'

Jill stood up at the sound of Anna's voice. 'Coming.'

Chapter 24

Liam poured cornflakes into a bowl, slopped milk in on top of them and carried his breakfast into the sitting room. Switching on the TV he tuned into the Discovery Channel and found himself watching a documentary about battles through the ages. Finishing the cereal, he moved some plates on the coffee-table to make room for his bowl and flopped back in the chair, flicking impatiently through the channels. When the doorbell went he ignored it. He was used by now to the interruptions that peppered the day. The collectors for charity, schoolkids selling lines and salesmen selling crap that even they didn't want. He'd answered the door the first week and been polite to them all but now he'd learned that it was easier not to answer the door at all. When the bell went for the third time, he stood up and stormed out, ready to snap the head off whoever had disturbed him.

'Well, about time. I hope you weren't still in bed at this hour.'

'Mum!'

Josie pushed past him and made her way into the kitchen. 'Dear God, would you look at the state of this place! Really, Liam, I thought I'd brought you up better than that.'

'Leave it, Mum,' Liam snapped as she took off her coat, rolled up her sleeves and started to clear the piles of crockery strewn across every surface.

'I certainly will not! I'm not having Anna coming home to this mess. What would she think?'

'What the hell has it got to do with you?'

'Don't take that tone with me.' Josie paused in her work to wag a finger at him. 'I don't know what your father would say, God rest him.'

'Sorry,' Liam muttered.

'That's okay, son. I know it's not easy for you at the moment. Why don't you go up and have a shower, and when you come down we'll have a nice cup of tea and a chat.'

The last thing Liam wanted was a 'chat' but it was easier to go along with her. 'Right so.'

'Good boy.' Josie turned back to her work.

Liam listened to her humming happily as he went upstairs. She was always happiest when she was doing something for him, he realized. She had called him every day since he'd lost his job and frequently she announced that she'd made him lunch and it would only go to waste if he didn't come straight over. As he had little else to do, Liam usually went. He told himself it had nothing to do with the fact that his mother lived next door to Tara Brady although he had to admit to a certain buzz when his ex appeared at the window or in the doorway.

But he'd been really pissed off at her turning up here unannounced like that, although how was she to know that Anna would come home for lunch? Still, she'd seemed to enjoy the whole sorry episode and that irritated him. Flirting was one thing but trying to screw up his marriage was another matter entirely. Not that he and Anna needed any help at screwing things up at the moment, he thought as he stepped from the shower. No matter how hard they tried, they seemed to be constantly treading on each other's toes. Anna always wanted to talk his problems through when all he wanted to do was forget about them. The last thing he needed was reminding of his abject failure as soon as she walked through the door every night. She had solved the problem by coming home later and later, and he couldn't really blame her. Liam put on a clean shirt and jeans, combed his hair and went downstairs.

'You could have shaved,' his mother said, eyeing his rough stubble disapprovingly as she set the teapot on the table. Still, he was a good-looking man and the green shirt emphasized his tanned skin and the wonderful eyes he'd inherited from his father. But he was getting thin, despite her efforts to feed him at every opportunity, and the light had gone out of his eyes. 'There's nothing but rubbish in your cupboards,' she complained. 'Not even bread to make a piece of toast.'

'There's Mars bars,' Liam told her, taking the pack out of the cupboard.

'You can't live on that stuff!'

He grinned. 'I don't. I go round to my dear mother and she makes me wonderful dinners.'

Josie smiled reluctantly. 'Well, someone has to look after you.'

'So, any news?' he asked.

'Tara was asking after you.'

'Oh yes?' He kept his voice casual, aware of the curious glint in her eye. 'How's she doing?'

'Well, you should know. She was saying she dropped in to see you last week.'

Liam's tea went down the wrong way and he coughed and spluttered.

'Are you okay, love?'

'Yeah, fine.'

'So, what did she want?'

'Sorry?'

'Tara?' Josie said impatiently.

'Oh, she was just dropping off some cream for Anna.'

Josie's eyes widened in disbelief. 'Anna's buying Tara's products?'

'Well, no – I am. It's a surprise for her birthday.'

Josie seemed to accept this. 'I see. So tell me, are you all set for this interview?'

He shrugged. 'I suppose.'

She tut-tutted. 'You suppose? What suit are you wearing? Does it need dry-cleaning? And what about a shirt? Have you got a clean one? Do you want me to iron one?'

Liam shook his head. 'All under control,' he lied.

Josie shot him a look. 'I'll be the judge of that. You need a nice white shirt, not one of your weird ones.' Liam often wore dark-coloured shirts that she didn't approve of at all. Anna's taste, obviously. 'And a nice tie. When we've finished our tea you can show me what you've got.'

Liam sat eating his Mars bar and felt like a schoolboy again. 'Actually I've got to go out in a minute.'

Josie raised an eyebrow. 'Oh? Where?'

'I need to get some references photocopied for the interview,' Liam said, impressed with himself for thinking on his feet.

'Oh, I see. Where do you get that done – in the village? I'll drop you.'

'No, that's okay, Mum, I'll go on the bike. I need the exercise.'

'Rubbish.'

'Still, the cycling helps me think. I can go over my interview technique in my head.'

'Well, be careful,' Josie told him as she stood up to go. 'And if you decide you want anything washed or ironed, drop it over later. In fact,' she brightened, 'why don't you come over for tea?'

'I can't today, Mum.'

'Why not?'

'I just can't. Will you stop with the inquisition?' he snapped.

'Well, I'm sorry I spoke.' Josie picked up her handbag and with a sniff, stalked into the hall.

'Sorry, Mum,' he said, following her. 'I'm just a bit nervous about tomorrow.'

'That's okay, dear, I understand completely.' She held up her cheek for his kiss. 'Now call me as soon as you get back tomorrow, won't you?'

'I will,' Liam promised and stood in the doorway until she'd climbed into her little Fiat and driven away.

The one plus about his mother's unexpected visit was the reminder about clothes, because he would never have given any thought to what he should wear for the interview until it was time to walk out of the door. Anna usually left something out for him and he wore it without question. Going up to his wardrobe, he took out his best suit, examined and sniffed it. It looked okay but there was a faint whiff of smoke. If he hung it on the line for an hour it should be fine. Next, he flicked through his shirts. Despite his mother's advice, he pulled out a pale grey one, with a grey and green silk tie that Anna had bought to match it. She'd always said the colours suited him and he looked like Managing Director material when he wore it. Well, he'd settle for Factory Manager.

Leaving the shirt and tie hanging on the wardrobe door, Liam carried the suit downstairs and hung it out on the clothesline in the back garden. It was a cool day and there were some dark clouds in the distance but the rain should hold off for a while.

Going back inside, Liam noticed for the first time that not only had his mother done all the washing up, she'd tidied as well and the house was looking almost presentable. Anna would be very impressed if she came home and it was like this, although she'd guess that his mother had had a hand in it.

He toyed with the idea of phoning Anna, but what was the point? It would be another disaster with silences punctuated by monosyllables. If he could only get a job, he knew that everything would be all right again. Feeling optimistic and determined, Liam went to the desk in the corner of their kitchen and started to put together the file that he would bring with him tomorrow. Maybe this was the one. He must be due a break by now.

Tara watched Josie getting out of the car. No prizes for guessing where she'd been. Tara didn't know how Liam put up with the old bat – she seemed to live in his pocket. The young woman felt an uncharacteristic pang of sympathy for Anna; having a mother-in-law like that couldn't be easy. Having said that, Tara was able to handle Josie and women like her without batting an eyelid. Working in this business you learned how to deal with people and you learned how to tell them what they wanted to hear. Josie positively lapped it up when Tara praised her mothering skills, her fabulous garden and her amazing chocolate cheesecake. She eagerly agreed when Tara ventured the opinion that married women were better in the home looking after their husbands, and how it was best to have children young. At this point, Tara would add how it was a great sorrow to her that she herself didn't have any children yet, and with tears in her eyes, Josie would comfort her that she was still young. Tara could imagine Josie dreaming of what it would have been like if Liam had married her instead of Anna, sure that they would have given her a grandchild within the year.

And what beautiful children they'd have produced, Tara thought, closing her eyes. Boys, tall and green-eyed like their father. Girls, blonde and blue-eyed like her. Tara opened her eyes and shook her head. This was a dream she often had. Letting Liam Harrison go had been the biggest mistake of her life but now she had a second chance. She'd settle for being the mistress, although playing second fiddle to Anna Gallagher didn't really appeal to her. It would be much better if they split up and eventually got a divorce. Then, not only would she get her man, she'd get a wedding day too.

As Tara daydreamed, Josie came back outside and started picking up the stray litter that had blown into her garden. Checking the appointments book, Tara saw that she didn't have an appointment for another hour. Just enough time to give her dear neighbour a free manicure. After all, she knew only too well that the way to any man's heart was through his mother!

Chapter 25

Rachel sat in the shallow end of the pool, grateful that there were no little monsters around to disrupt her peace as she enjoyed the feeling of the water supporting her bump. It had been the beauty therapist's suggestion when Rachel told her of the problems she was having with her pregnancy. The water would help with her swollen ankles, Maria said, and also give her a rest from carrying so much weight around. Rachel was not only enjoying the rest but the time alone too. Anna had gone shopping, Jill had disappeared off somewhere soon after breakfast, her dad was snoozing on a sunlounger and Bridie was curled up in a chair beside him engrossed in a paperback. As it was still early, the complex was quiet and Rachel had the pool all to herself.

Splashing water up on her neck and face, she rested her head against the side of the pool and closed her eyes. Although she was too hot most of the time, Rachel was still enjoying her holiday much more than she'd expected. She missed Alex, of course, but from the conversations she'd had with him, he was doing okay without her. While she was glad that he was happy, it hurt a little that she could be so easily done without. Gary seemed to be managing very well and there had been none of the panicky phone calls she'd been expecting.

Every night when he called she drilled him about what Alex had eaten, worn, whether he was brushing his teeth properly. Gary answered her questions the first couple of nights but then just told her that everything was fine and she should stop worrying. As if that was possible, married to him, Rachel thought, slapping at a fly on her arm.

'Ooh, this is lovely!'

Rachel opened her eyes to see her mother lowering herself into the water beside her. 'Finished the book?'

'Yes, it was marvellous. I do love a good thriller. So, how are your ankles this morning?'

Rachel lifted one foot out of the water for inspection. 'Fine. They always are until I try walking anywhere.'

'Not long now,' her mother comforted her. 'By Christmas you'll be back in your high-heels.'

Rachel laughed but her eyes were sad. 'Where would I be going in high-heels? Out to the washing-line or down to the supermarket?'

Bridie sighed. 'You're not looking forward to this baby, are you, love?'

Rachel opened her mouth to protest and then closed it again.

'Don't beat yourself up about it, Rache, you wouldn't be the first woman to feel that way. You know, your Aunty Pat went through a very tough time when she was expecting Jill.'

'I didn't know that.' Rachel was immediately diverted. 'What happened?'

'Oh, God love her, she got sick all day every day for the first four months – or at least it seemed that way – and then they said there was something wrong with her womb and she'd have to stay in bed until the baby was born.'

'She must have had pre-eclampsia,' Rachel surmised.

'It was a terrible time and the maternity hospitals weren't very nice places in those days. She was totally miserable and decided there and then that she'd never have another child.'

'Poor Aunty Pat.'

'So you see, you're not alone.' Bridie shot her a knowing look. 'Although I think your situation is a bit different, isn't it?'

'What do you mean?' Rachel hedged.

'It's not your feet or your back or the insomnia that's really bothering you, is it? Come on, love, what's going on? You know you can tell me.'

There was a lump in Rachel's throat at her mother's gentle, loving tone. 'Oh Mam, I don't know what to do.'

'About what, love?' Bridie moved closer.

'About my life. I'm so unhappy and I don't know

what's going to happen when the baby comes. I mean, how can I look after two children if I can't even sort myself out?'

Bridie patted her hand. 'You have Anna, Jill and of course Gary to help you. And I'll come home and stay with you for a while if you like.'

'Oh, would you, Mam?'

'Of course, love. You just let me know when you need me. I don't want to get in the way though. You and Gary will want some time alone with the children. How much leave will he take?'

Rachel shrugged. 'As little as possible, probably.'

Bridie frowned. 'Don't be silly, love. Sure, didn't he take time off to mind Alex while you came out here?'

'Yes, but that's because I wasn't going to be there. Gary does everything to avoid me. He goes out early, comes home late and when he is home, he's working on that bloody laptop.'

'Everyone works so hard these days,' Bridie sighed. 'But then again your father was the same. That's why I'm so glad he took the early retirement.'

Rachel glanced over at her father's sleeping form. 'He played hard too though, Mam, didn't he?'

'What do you mean?'

'You know what I mean.'

'That was all over a long time ago. Why are you bringing it up now?' Bridie's voice was reproachful.

Rachel held her gaze. 'Because I think I might finally understand what you went through.'

Bridie's puzzled frown disappeared as realization dawned. 'Gary? Gary's having an affair?'

'I think so.'

'Dear God, what a family,' Bridie muttered.

'Pardon?'

'Never mind, just tell me everything.'

'Not here.' Two toddlers were now playing by the pool and their mother was hovering nearby.

'Let's go for a coffee,' Bridie said, helping her daughter out of the pool.

Shay was still snoring peacefully as they donned sarongs and went up the steps to the poolside bar.

'Orange juice, please,' Rachel told the waiter.

'And a cappuccino for me.' Bridie smiled at him and then turned concerned eyes on her daughter. 'So?'

Rachel sighed. 'I'm not sure where to begin.'

'When you first suspected there was someone else.'

'That was the night Alex got his appendix out.'

'But that was over a year ago!'

Rachel nodded. 'That's right.'

'And you've kept it to yourself all this time. Oh, you poor girl!'

'He told me that I was wrong and he'd just been out with a colleague from work and some clients. I accepted his explanation and left it at that.'

'Did you really?'

'No. I have never been able to get past it and I'm suspicious whenever he's late or he gets strange phone calls. God, I even go through his pockets.'

'Perfectly natural,' her mother assured her. 'Have you ever followed him?'

'No!'

'I followed your father on a regular basis,' Bridie said quietly. 'It was after he had finally admitted everything. He told me it was all over and I forgave him, as you know, but I just had to be sure. I wanted to know I could trust him again.'

Rachel nodded. 'Trust. That's what it comes down to. I suppose I just don't feel I can trust Gary.'

'Have you had it out with him?'

'No.'

'In case you're right and he admits there's someone else? In case he decides to leave?'

Rachel looked up in surprise.

Bridie smiled. 'Been there and got the T-shirt, as they say. Oh love, what can I tell you? Yes, it would be terrible if that happened, but would it be any worse than what you're going through now? This must be eating you up inside.'

'It is,' Rachel admitted.

'Then it's time to have it out with him.'

'I can't.'

'You can and you must, Rache. Sure, the poor lad might be completely innocent. But you won't know one way or the other unless you tackle him.'

Rachel stared into her juice. 'It's not supposed to be like this. This wasn't in my plan.'

Bridie's smile was sad. 'It's never in anyone's plan,

my darling, but you just have to handle what life throws at you. Dear Lord, it's no wonder you haven't been sleeping with all this rattling around inside your head. Promise me you'll talk to him as soon as you get home.'

'I'll think about it, Mam, but if I decide not to, you have to promise me you won't interfere.'

'I promise, love. Whatever you decide to do, I'll stand by you.' Bridie's eyes were full of pride at the look of determination on her daughter's face.

Rachel excused herself and went up to the apartment, leaving her mother sitting at the table staring into her cold coffee. It was heartbreaking that both her daughters were in these terrible situations, but it was even worse that she wasn't able to comfort Rachel the way she'd comforted Anna. She couldn't tell Rachel that it would be okay and that Gary loved her, because she wasn't convinced that he did.

She had been horrified at the haste in which they'd married but had said nothing. Bridie, unlike her sister Pat, didn't believe in meddling in her daughters' lives. And if she'd said anything negative about Gary, Rachel would have ignored her anyway. She'd convinced herself, as the years went by, that her worries had been unfounded. Gary and Rachel were never exactly love's young dream but they seemed to be getting along all right. Until now. Bridie felt sick at the thought of what Rachel had been going through for more than a year. She knew first-hand how suspicion could devour you and colour everything you did. And now there was a new baby on the way and Rachel might well have to raise it alone. But Rachel would never be alone as long as she and Shay were alive, Bridie promised herself fiercely. Those children would have all the love they needed and deserved, whatever happened.

Anna had enjoyed the morning, rambling around the shops and selecting some small gifts for Val and Mark and a tablecloth for Josie. She was damned if she was bringing anything home for Liam but she couldn't ignore her mother-in-law or the old bat would guess something was up. Anna wondered what she'd think if she knew about Liam and Tara. God, maybe she already did! After all, the girl did live next door. Anna felt sick at the thought of Liam slipping across the back fence for a quick massage with his mother's blessing. It would be too weird if she was in on the whole sordid business.

Anna glanced at her watch. 'Damn.' She was supposed to have met Jill in Kitty's for lunch at noon. Hurrying down the road, she waved as she saw her cousin sitting on a chair outside the café, soaking up the sun.

'Sorry I'm late, Jill,' she panted.

'No problem, I've been enjoying sitting here watching the world go by. You know I never get time to do that at home?'

'Our weather doesn't exactly lend itself to that kind of pastime, now does it?'

Jill laughed. 'True. Now, are we having lunch or would you prefer to get back?'

'Oh, let's have lunch.'

'Hello, you two,' Kitty said as they came in. 'Where's the rest of the gang?'

'Probably still sleeping by the pool,' Anna told her, climbing up on to a bar stool.

'What will it be?' Kitty asked.

Jill looked at her cousin. 'Beer, wine or are we being good?'

'Good? Don't be silly, we're on our holidays. A bottle of house rosé, I think,' Anna suggested.

'Mmnn, yes, sounds good,' Jill agreed.

'And are you having some lunch?'

'Definitely,' Jill said, eyeing the Specials on the blackboard. 'That tuna salad sounds good.'

'It's lovely and fresh,' Kitty promised.

'And I'll have a Spanish omelette,' Anna said hungrily.

'That's your third this week,' Jill remarked. 'Are you supposed to eat that many eggs?'

'I don't care, they're gorgeous. Anyway, I never eat eggs at home.'

Kitty cut some bread and put it, along with some olive oil flavoured with garlic and herbs, in front of them to nibble at. 'Coming right up.' She turned to the fridge and took out the eggs and milk and carried them to the work area.

'I just love that you can see all the food being

prepared,' Anna whispered to Jill. 'She is such a great cook.'

Jill nodded as she too watched Kitty. 'This place must be a goldmine.'

'In the summer months yes, but it's probably quiet the rest of the year.'

'With the size of the Irish and English community living around here? I doubt it.'

'I suppose.'

'It's not a bad life, is it? Imagine working in this climate and being your own boss.'

'It's hard work though.'

'Yes, but if you're working for yourself then the money's going straight into your pocket.'

Kitty moved back over to the worktop in front of them to prepare the salad.

'Have you been here long, Kitty?' Anna asked.

'Nearly four years.'

'What made you leave Ireland?'

Kitty made a face. 'It was my husband's idea. He'd been made redundant and was finding it hard to get work. We'd visited the area a couple of times and he had a friend who was already working out here as a builder so he knew the score. This place came up for sale and within two months I'd chucked my job and we'd moved, lock, stock and barrel.'

'Were you working as a chef in Dublin?' Anna asked.

'Lord, no.' Kitty laughed. 'I worked in the accounts

department of a travel agent. Ben was the cook – we'd never have made such a move otherwise.'

'You're a quick learner then,' Jill said finally. 'The food here is great.'

'Thanks.' Kitty flashed her a smile. 'Much as I hate to admit it, that's thanks to my husband. He was a good teacher. Just as well, really, or I'd have been rightly stuck when he ran off with one of our customers.'

'Oh, I'm sorry, Kitty. That's awful,' Anna said with feeling.

'Don't worry about it, I'm over it now. And to his credit, he let me keep everything.'

Anna snorted. 'Big deal.'

'Well, technically, he could have made me sell up and claimed half of everything,' Kitty told her. 'But the woman he ran off with was loaded and has set him up in his own restaurant in Madrid.'

'And have you been running the place single-handed ever since?'

Kitty shook her head. 'I had a Manager up until a couple of months ago, but she married a guy from Barcelona and has moved up there with him. I've been meaning to replace her but I haven't had time.'

'How do you keep going?' Anna marvelled.

'Well, Juan and Pepe are great.' She gestured at the two waiters who were busy cleaning down tables and setting out cutlery. 'And when it's quiet I nip upstairs for a break.'

'Is that where you live?'

'No, I have an apartment outside town. Jeanette, my Manager, lived upstairs. It's quite a nice apartment although a bit small. I thought about moving in but I like having some time away from the business and I was hoping that whoever eventually took the Manager's job would live there.' She looked up and smiled at Jill. 'It would be nice to have someone on the premises all the time, just in case. Now, ladies, I hope you enjoy your meals,' she said, setting their food in front of them and topping up their wine glasses. 'Shall I get Pepe to carry them over to a table for you?'

Anna shook her head. 'No, we're fine here. Thanks, Kitty, this looks delicious.'

Jill was already forking tuna into her mouth. 'Mmm – nothing like the stuff out of a tin. If I could have this sort of food every day, I'd be so thin.'

Kitty smiled and then went back to the preparation area at the back of the kitchen.

'She's a very impressive woman – isn't she?' Jill murmured to her cousin.

'She's certainly got a head for business – and she's very attractive,' Anna said. 'It's a shame that she's on her own.'

'She's probably better off. I mean, who wants a man if all he's going to do is betray you at the first possible opportunity?' Jill was stopped by the grief-stricken look on her cousin's face. 'Oh God, Anna, I'm sorry! What a bloody stupid thing to say. You know I didn't mean Liam.'

'Why not? If the cap fits . . .'

Jill sighed 'Has he been in touch?'

'Only once, and that was just to tell me that my motor-tax renewal had arrived.'

'That's a good sign.'

'It is?'

'Yes. Think about it. You don't have to pay that for a couple of weeks at least so it could have waited until you got home. He just used it as an excuse to call you.'

Anna brightened. 'Oh! I hadn't thought of that.'

Jill smiled. 'There, you see? Sometimes I do have my uses.'

'Occasionally,' Anna allowed. Her gaze drifted to where Kitty worked, her hands moving deftly across the chopping board as she hummed along to the background music. 'I don't know if I could do what she's done.'

Jill followed her gaze. 'Not everyone's cut out to run their own business.'

'No, I just mean carrying on without him,' Anna explained. 'Any plans I've made, I've made with Liam. And all those plans are based on us being together.'

'Then you need to fight to make sure that they still happen. Go home and sort it out, Anna.'

Anna glanced at her watch. 'He's got an interview this afternoon. It's for a job as Factory Manager, and from what he's told me, it's exactly what he's looking for and it would be more money than he got in Patterson's.'

Jill pushed the mobile phone towards her cousin. 'Call him. Wish him luck.'

Anna picked up the mobile and took it outside. She held her breath as she waited for Liam to answer, but after the tenth ring, she gave up. 'There's no reply – he must have already left,' she told Jill when she went back inside.

'Want to drop into the church on the way back and light a candle?'

Anna nodded. 'Yes, please.'

Chapter 26

When the phone rang, Liam ignored it, concentrating instead on shaving without cutting himself to ribbons. His mother had been on twice already. Had he remembered to iron his shirt? And then, a few minutes later, had he polished his shoes?

'For God's sake, Mum, will you please stop calling me? I'm not a child.'

'Shoes say a lot about a person,' his mother went on, undeterred. 'Now don't forget, call me as soon as you get out, won't you? Better still, drop over and I'll make us a nice bit of dinner.'

'I don't know, Mum—'

'Oh, do. Sure, where else have you to go?'

Liam had smiled at his mother's tactlessness. 'Okay, then. See you later.'

Now, as he splashed his face with water and patted it dry, his thoughts turned to the interview ahead. He was perfect for the job, he knew that, but what he didn't know was what his competition was like. How many other guys out there fancied themselves as the future Factory Manager of Elektrix

Ireland? It was a wonderful position in a great company that had been expanding steadily since it came to Ireland five years ago. Liam had done his homework and knew that this was a company that was going places. Unlike Patterson's, it was more innovative and used the latest technology, something that made the job even more attractive. For years, Liam had had to work with ancient computer systems and meagre budgets, and it would be refreshing to be able to concentrate on the job at hand rather than worry about whether the payroll system would screw up the salary slips this month or the thirty-year-old forklift would break down.

He showered and dressed quickly, his fingers trembling slightly as he knotted his tie. 'You'll do,' he said, eyeing his reflection and splashing on some of the Boss aftershave Anna had bought him. For a moment, he thought about calling her but if he did that, they'd probably end up rowing and that was the last thing he needed right now. He felt a bit hurt that Anna hadn't called to wish him luck. Maybe she'd forgotten all about it. Maybe she didn't give a damn one way or the other. Banishing her from his head, Liam shrugged into his jacket and went downstairs to collect his briefcase. He was early but he wasn't quite sure where the Elektrix premises were so he didn't want to take any chances. He found his keys, locked up the house and went out to Anna's car.

It felt cold and damp inside and there was a faint smell of Anna's perfume. Liam closed his eyes briefly and inhaled. When he opened them again, he looked around him, smiling at the uncharacteristic tidiness. Since she occasionally had to ferry clients around, Anna had been forced to change her ways. Before she went to work for Mark, her car had been like a travelling wardrobe, with make-up and hair products crammed in the glove compartment, and spare jackets and tights tossed on the back seat. Today, some lip balm and a hairbrush were the only personal items in evidence. As Liam guided the car out of the estate, he sighed heavily, aware of an aching loneliness inside that had nothing to do with the fact that Anna was in Spain. He had been alone for a lot longer than that.

He and Anna had really drifted apart and neither of them had made much effort to pull things together again. The episode with Tara had been the final straw; although Liam thought it had just brought things to a head sooner rather than later. He wondered sometimes if Anna secretly despised him for losing his job. Perhaps she thought he was to blame and was disappointed in him . . . He jumped as the car behind him blasted its horn because the traffic-light had changed. 'Okay, okay, I'm going.' He waved a hand at the irate driver and forced himself to take deep breaths and focus all his concentration on the interview ahead. This was the first chance he'd had to put things right and he wasn't going to screw it up.

*

'Alex! I'm warning you. Pick up those toys or there'll be no treats for you today.'

'Don't care, don't want any treats.'

'Don't be so cheeky. What would your mum say?'

Alex shrugged. 'Don't care.'

Gary sighed and counted to ten. Volunteering to mind Alex during the summer holidays had been madness. Work was easy compared to keeping a five-year-old occupied and happy, twelve hours a day. Of course, Alex was never like this with Rachel. She knew exactly what to say when he was acting up. Gary racked his brains. What would she do in this situation? An idea suddenly came to him. 'Come on, if we clear this mess up we'll be able to set up your racing track.'

Alex's head whipped around, his eyes lighting up. 'Really?'

'Sure, but I warn you, I'm going to win.'

'No chance,' Alex told him, bending to pick up toys. 'I'm Michael Schumacher!'

'Are you indeed? Well, even he loses sometimes.'

'Hardly ever,' his son assured him.

The two of them tidied away the toys and Gary fetched the racing track down from the attic.

'Daddy, when is Mummy coming home?'

'Sunday, sweetheart – the day after tomorrow.'

Alex bent his head over his car, pushing it backwards and forwards on the ground next to his father's knee.

Gary looked down at the small blond head. 'Do you miss her, mate?'

Alex nodded.

Gary hugged him briefly. 'She'll be back before you know it. Now come on, get your car ready for defeat.'

Alex frowned. 'What's defeat mean?'

His father grinned. 'It means I'm going to beat you.'

'No way!'

Gary had managed, with great effort, to lose for the third time when the phone rang.

'Hello?'

'Hi, Gary.'

'Rachel! How are you?'

'Fine, thanks.'

'That's good. Weather nice?'

'Lovely.'

'Want to talk to your son and heir?'

'Yes, please.'

'Alex, it's Mum.' Gary held out the phone.

Alex, now absorbed in his racing, turned impatient eyes on his father. 'I'm busy.'

'Don't be cheeky, say hello to your mum.'

Alex took the phone. 'Hi, Mum,' he mumbled.

'Hello, darling. How are you?'

'Okay.'

'And what are you doing now?'

'Playing with my racing track.' Alex brightened. 'I keep beating Daddy. I'm Michael Schumacher!'

'Oh, really. That's great, darling.'

'Bye, Mum.' Alex shoved the phone into his father's hand and went back to his cars.

'Alex? Alex?'

'He's gone,' Gary told her. 'Sorry about that but we are in the middle of a game.'

'Oh!'

'No need to sound so surprised,' Gary muttered.

'No, I'm not. Sorry, darling. Look, I'll leave you to it.'

Gary immediately felt bad for snapping at her. 'We'll pick you up from the airport on Sunday.'

'Oh, are you sure? It's very early.'

'Yeah, well our son doesn't exactly sleep late, does he?'

Rachel laughed. 'No, he doesn't, does he? That would be great, thanks, Gary.'

'No problem. See you then. Bye, sweetheart.' Gary hung up and returned to Alex's side but his mind was on his wife.

She didn't sound quite as hostile as she usually did. Maybe this break had been exactly what she needed. Being at home with Alex all the time wasn't as easy as he had thought it would be. Though he'd enjoyed these few days with his son, there had been times when he'd been ready to throttle him, and as for the cleaning, dressing and feeding . . . the routine was mind-numbingly boring.

Maybe he'd been unfair to Rachel, leaving her to do all the work around the house and disappearing to the golf course most weekends. His guilt grew as he thought of her swollen ankles and the way he often woke in the night to find her sitting up reading or pacing the floor. She had been having a rough time and he had been so caught up in his own life that he hadn't really noticed. Alex's delighted surprise this week when Gary had offered to play with him or take him somewhere had made him feel very small indeed. And as he'd listened to his son's excited chatter each day, he'd come to realize how little he knew about what went on in Alex's life.

Now with a baby on the way, Alex would inevitably be side-lined while they came to grips with the new routine. He would have to talk to Rachel about that. They'd have to make a special effort not to exclude their elder son, and make sure he knew that he was still loved.

'Daddy, come on! It's your turn.'

Gary laughed at his son's impatience. 'Okay, okay, I'm coming – and this time I'm going to beat you!'

'What is going on with those two?' Shay nodded his head towards his daughters as he followed his wife into the kitchen.

'What do you mean?'

'Oh, come on, Bridie, they're always at each other. I thought we'd have some fun this week but all they do is mope around or snap at each other. It's a good job Jill's here. Mind you, even she seems to be in a world of her own sometimes.'

Bridie's smile was tolerant as she made the tea. 'Don't be so hard on them. Anna is worried about Liam and Rachel isn't well and she's probably missing Alex.'

Shay shot her a knowing look. 'There's more to it than that.'

Bridie turned away to take the cups down. 'I don't know what you're on about.'

'All right, keep me in the dark – sure, I'm used to it. You girls never tell me anything.'

Bridie turned back to him and patted his cheek. 'You concentrate on your diet and let me worry about the girls.'

'They are okay though, aren't they?' He glanced up at her, his eyes filled with concern.

'They are, love, they are.'

Chapter 27

'I'm going for a walk,' Anna announced as they were sitting around the apartment later that afternoon.

Rachel got slowly to her feet. 'I'll come with you.'

'Actually, I'd rather go alone, if you don't mind.'

'Anna!' Bridie glared at her elder daughter.

Rachel shrugged. 'It's okay. She walks too fast for me anyway.'

'I wouldn't mind going for a paddle, Rache,' Jill said.

'Ooh, yes, good idea.' Bridie clapped her hands.

'Okay then.' Rachel shook her head as the door banged after Anna. 'What's eating her?'

'I think she wants to phone Liam,' Jill confided. 'He had an interview today.'

'Oh, so he did.' Bridie crossed herself. 'Please God he'll get it.'

'I hope he does,' Rachel said with feeling. 'Maybe she'll be easier to live with.'

Shay was settling down for a snooze as the three women finally left the apartment.

'I can't believe tomorrow's our last day,' Jill said as they made their way down to the golden beach.

'We must do something special,' Bridie announced. 'We could take a run over to Granada if you like.'

'Isn't that very far?' Rachel looked doubtful.

'No, not at all and it's very pretty.'

'Oh, I don't know, Mam. You know I get tired easily and the heat is bound to be worse inland.' Rachel leaned on her mother for support as she bent to take off her sandals.

'Okay then, why don't we make a nice picnic and take it down to one of the lovely little beaches along the coast?'

Rachel wrinkled her nose. 'I'm not that keen on eating outside, not with all the flies.'

'I'd quite like a lazy day, hanging around the pool,' Jill said, bending to scoop the cool seawater on to her arms and chest. 'It's going to be hectic in work next week and I want to make the most of my last day and really relax.'

Bridie's eyes lit up. 'I know – we could book another session with Maria!'

Rachel finally looked enthusiastic. 'Oh yes, I wouldn't mind another go at that reflexology.'

'I'll treat you,' Bridie told her.

'Thanks, Mam.'

'And what about you, Jill? What do you fancy?'

'One of those wonderful head and neck massages. I nearly fell asleep the last time.'

'That Swedish girl, Steffi, does a great massage,'

Bridie told her. 'I'll drop into Maria's later and arrange it.'

'What about Anna?' Jill asked. 'Should we book something for her?'

'A facial to get rid of some of those frownlines,' Rachel said bitchily.

Bridie gave her younger daughter a gentle push. 'Don't be horrible.'

'Well, she deserves it,' Rachel retorted. 'She's so caught up in her own little world. She has a face on her a mile long because Liam lost his job, but she's not worried about *him*. She's just afraid that there won't be enough money for socializing with all her fancy friends.'

'That's enough, Rachel.' Bridie's smile had disappeared.

'Oh, that's right, I'm not allowed to say anything about darling Anna. She can do no wrong in your eyes, can she, Mam?'

'Ah, Rache.' Jill put a hand on her cousin's arm. 'Leave it.'

Tears sprang to Rachel's eyes. 'Oh, I'm the villain, am I? Just because I say what you're all thinking.'

'I think you should go back to the apartment and have a lie-down,' Bridie replied. 'Maybe when you wake up you'll be able to talk some sense.'

With an angry snort, Rachel turned awkwardly on her heel and lumbered away.

'She doesn't mean it.' Jill linked an arm through her aunt's.

'I don't know about that, love. Those two are always at each other's throats when they used to be thick as thieves.'

'People change and they are both stressed out at the moment.'

Bridie stopped and turned to face her niece. 'You've been a good friend to them, Jill. I'm glad they have you.'

'They're good to me too.'

'I'm not so sure about that,' Bridie said as they continued their walk. 'I never hear them asking you about what's going on in your life at all.'

'Oh, they do of course.'

'So tell me.'

'Sorry?'

'What is going on in your life?' Bridie prompted.

Jill smiled. 'Not a lot.'

'Oh, go away out of that! Anna tells me you're a real career woman.'

Jill laughed. 'I was, but I'm not so sure any more.'

Bridie frowned. 'Why, love, what's wrong?'

'Oh, there's a guy snapping at my heels at the moment and he's doing a very good job of making me look bad.'

'That's terrible! But you're such a clever girl, I'm sure you'll see him off, no problem.'

'You know, Aunty, I'm not sure I want to? I think I'm ready for a change.'

'Well, whatever you turn your hand to, you'll be great.'

'Thanks for the vote of confidence.'

'Any ideas on what you'd like to do?'

Jill smiled slowly. 'Maybe.'

Bridie patted her arm. 'You tell me when you're ready, and in the meantime don't let those daughters of mine lean too heavily on you. They've got me too, you know.'

'I'm glad we came. I think they needed to see you both.'

'Do you think we were wrong to leave Ireland, Jill?' Bridie said suddenly, her voice tinged with worry and guilt.

'No, of course not.'

'Anna and Rachel do. I didn't realize how much they resented it until this week.'

'No, you're wrong,' Jill argued.

'Okay, maybe resent is too strong a word but they obviously weren't happy about it. But it's not like they were teenagers, Jill! We waited until they were both settled and happy before we did anything. And I had to think of what was best for me and Shay. I'm not sure our marriage would have survived if we'd stayed in Dublin. They wouldn't have wanted that, would they?'

'No.'

'But now I feel awful. They're both going through such a difficult time.' She shot Jill a knowing look. 'You don't have to break any confidences, love, we both know what I'm talking about. But maybe if I was in Dublin I could have helped.'

Jill shook her head. 'You can't live their lives for them, Aunty.'

'More's the pity,' Bridie muttered. 'Right now I'd like to take my two sons-in-law and bang their heads together. If Shay knew . . .' She broke off. 'God, I feel so helpless. Maybe we should come home with you.'

Jill stared at her in alarm. 'I'm not sure that's a good idea. They've had a week away to think about things – maybe that's all they needed.'

Bridie looked unconvinced. 'Do either of them look any happier to you?'

'No, but that's because they haven't tackled their problems yet,' Jill said sensibly. 'At least give it a few weeks and then decide. You'll be coming over for the birth, won't you?'

Bridie nodded. 'That's the plan. And I told Rachel we'd stay on if she needed us.'

'Then that's all you can really do for the moment.'

Bridie shot her niece a curious look. 'You're a deep one, aren't you, Jill?'

'What do you mean?'

'You play your cards very close to your chest. Tell me, do Anna and Rachel have any idea what's going on in each other's lives?'

Jill sighed. 'Not a clue.'

Anna dialled the house again but with no luck. Liam still wasn't home and he hadn't left the answering machine on. She couldn't phone him on his mobile because he didn't have one. Patterson's had taken the company one back and Liam had refused to pay out for another. Dammit, where was he? The interview should have been over hours ago. Maybe he was in Josie's. She could, of course, call Josie, but she dreaded the prospect of talking to her mother-in-law and she didn't know exactly how much or how little Liam had told the woman. Anna wandered through the town. It was still quiet, as the shopkeepers were only just opening up again after siesta-time and the tourists hadn't returned from the beach or left the poolside yet.

Fed up with her own company, Anna decided to go back to Kitty's for another coffee. Pepe looked up and smiled as she walked into the gloom of the café. '*Hola!*'

'Hi, Pepe. Are you on your own?'

He nodded. 'They have all deserted me. But now I have beautiful company.' He smiled, his teeth gleaming. 'What can I get you?'

'Just a latte, thanks.' Anna climbed up on a bar stool. 'Have you worked here long?' she asked.

'Since Kitty bought the place.'

'Oh, so you knew her husband?'

'Ben? Yes, I knew him. A great guy.'

Anna stared at him. 'Really?'

Pepe slid her coffee in front of her. 'Really. Some marriages just aren't meant to be. It's no one's fault. If you make each other miserable, then you are better apart.'

'I suppose.'

Pepe went out front to set up tables while Anna sat staring into her coffee and wondering if she and Liam would be better off apart. If they weren't talking and he was messing around with Tara then maybe it was over between them. And then there was Charlie. Surely she wouldn't have flirted with him the way she had if she was still in love with Liam? Her thoughts turned again to the interview and she checked her phone to make sure the signal was strong. How could he do this to her? He must know she'd be wondering how he'd gotten on! Or maybe he was too busy telling Tara all about it. Maybe he was sitting in her kitchen at this very moment going through the interview blow-by-blow, with her hanging on to his every word. Or maybe they'd progressed to the bedroom. Anna closed her eyes and tried to block out the image.

'Anna!'

She turned on her seat to see Jill standing in the doorway. 'Hi. Were you sent to find me?'

'Er, no. Your dad's still asleep and your mam and Rachel were having a chat so I thought I'd make myself scarce.' Jill glanced around the empty bar. 'It's quiet, isn't it? Where's Kitty?'

'Dunno. Pepe's the only one here. Do you want a coffee?'

Jill climbed up beside her. 'Yeah, okay.'

Pepe came back into the café and went behind the counter. 'Hello, Jill, how are you today?'

'Fine, thanks, Pepe.'

'Coffee?'

'Yes, a cappuccino, please.'

'So is Mam annoyed with me?' Anna asked.

'No, but it would have saved a lot of hassle if you'd just told them you wanted to call Liam. So, how did it go?'

'I don't know, there's no answer.'

'Maybe it went really well and he's gone for a drink to celebrate.'

Anna's expression remained glum. 'Yeah, but who with?'

Jill smiled her thanks as Pepe put her coffee in front of her. 'Don't think the worst, Anna. You've no reason to think he's with Tara.'

'I've no reason not to.'

'Have you called Josie?'

Anna shook her head.

'Do you think she has any idea what's going on?'

'So you agree now that something's going on?'

'I meant between you and Liam. Anna, stop being so prickly, you're not with Rachel now.'

Anna dropped her head into her hands. 'God, I'm sorry, Jill, I shouldn't be taking this out on you. I'm turning into a right witch, aren't I? It's just I'm so scared.'

'I know.' Jill took a sip from her coffee. 'So like I said, do you think Josie knows?'

'I doubt it.'

'So you could phone and ask quite innocently if she'd heard from him? What could be more natural.'

Anna looked at her phone. 'Maybe . . .'

'You want to know how he got on, don't you?'

Anna picked up the phone and dialled before she could change her mind. 'Hello, Josie? It's Anna.'

'Anna?' Josie sounded as if she were trying to place her. 'Oh hello, how are you?'

'Fine, thanks. I was wondering, is Liam there?'

'No, no he's not.'

'Oh.' Anna felt suddenly deflated. 'I was just wondering how he got on. He had an interview today.'

'Well, of course I knew that! He thinks he did very well.'

'Oh, you were talking to him then?'

'He came straight here afterwards.' Josie's tone implied, where else would he go?

Relief flooded over Anna. He hadn't been with Tara. 'I'll wait for a while and ring him at home then.'

'Oh, he won't be there. He had somewhere else to go first.'

'Oh, I see. Any idea where?' Anna forced herself to keep her voice light.

'I'm sure I didn't ask.'

'Oh, okay then. Well, I'll keep trying. Maybe if you're talking to him before I am, you'd ask him to call me?'

'Of course.'

'Okay, then. Well, goodbye, Josie.'

'Goodbye.'

'So, he got on well then?' Jill enquired, having heard one half of the conversation.

Anna shrugged, distracted. 'She says so. I wonder where he is.'

'Well, it can't be next door or Josie would know all about it.'

'Yes, but would she tell me?'

'I can't see Josie approving of Liam carrying on, no matter how much she adores Tara Brady.'

'I wouldn't bet on it. Tara went to the right school, lived in the right street, has the right accent. Josie would kill to have someone like her in the family. I think she'd be delighted if Liam and I broke up.'

'That's awful.' Jill stared at her, her nose wrinkled in disgust.

'That's Josie.'

'Try the house again,' Jill prompted.

Anna dialled the number and listened while it rang out. 'He obviously doesn't want to talk to me.'

'You don't know that,' Jill said. 'He could be anywhere. It could be to do with the job, did you think of that?'

Anna stood up. 'I know you're trying to make me feel better, Jill . . .'

'But you're determined to think the worst.'

'Can you blame me? Are you coming?'

As Jill went to get up, Kitty walked in the door and Jill settled herself back on her stool. 'I'll catch up on you after I've finished my coffee.'

'Oh, sorry! God, what am I like?' Anna went to sit down again.

Jill waved her away. 'No, you go on. I'll take my time and chat to Kitty.'

Anna turned and smiled at Kitty. 'Oh, hi!'

'Hello, ladies. I hope Pepe's been looking after you.'

'He's been great.' Anna shot the Spaniard a wide smile.

'Hey, you, stop flirting with the staff,' Jill warned.

Laughing, Anna picked up her bag and turned to leave. 'See you later.'

'Bye,' Kitty called, as she slipped behind the bar and pulled on an apron. 'So, Jill, how are you?'

'I am just fine, Kitty. Sitting here, contemplating my future.'

'Glad to hear it.' Kitty glanced at the clock and then poured herself a coffee. 'I've got about thirty minutes before the rush starts. Tell me more.'

Rachel was alone on the balcony when Anna returned to the apartment. 'Where's Mam and Dad?'

'They're out in the camper van.' Rachel kept her head in her book.

Anna sat down opposite her. 'Any good?'

Rachel shrugged. 'It's okay.'

'Look, I'm sorry about earlier.'

'Don't worry about it.'

'It's just I wanted to call Liam.'

'Yeah, Jill said. So how did it go?'

'He wasn't there.' Anna gazed out at the beach where a young couple were messing about in the surf.

The girl splashed him and he lunged at her, grabbing her around the waist and pulling her down into the water. Her screams were mixed with delighted giggles that stopped abruptly when he turned her face to his and kissed her.

'I can't remember the last time Gary and I fooled around like that,' Rachel said wistfully.

Anna looked at her in surprise and Rachel gave an embarrassed smile. 'I suppose that's what happens when you get married and have kids.'

'Surely you can still have fun? Just you've got Alex too. Doesn't that make it even better?'

'Oh, well, yes, of course,' Rachel sat up and nodded politely. 'We have wonderful times with Alex.'

But not with Gary, Anna was going to say, but decided against it. Rachel would probably jump down her throat. Anna pulled out her phone and checked the signal. Full strength. He could call her any time he wanted.

'Everything okay?' Rachel was watching her curiously.

'Sure. Why wouldn't it be?'

'Oh, forgive me for asking!' Rachel rolled her eyes and heaved herself out of the chair. 'I'm off for a bath.'

As soon as she was alone, Anna snatched up the phone and dialled again. She was just about to hang up when a breathless Liam answered.

'Hello?'

'Hi, it's me.'

'Anna!'

'I just called to see how the interview went.'

'It went really well.'

'Oh good, I'm so happy for you.'

Liam laughed. 'Me too. You know, I really think this could be it.'

'And about time too. You deserve a break,' Anna told him.

'Thanks, sweetheart.'

'I called you earlier to wish you good luck but I must have missed you.'

'I left early, I was terrified I wouldn't be able to find the place.'

'Oh, right. And then I tried to get you at your mother's but you had left.' She waited.

'Oh, yeah? I was going to call.'

'Were you?' *Not before you visited your beloved Tara.* Anna felt misery engulf her. *Ask him*, she urged herself. *Ask him where he's been.*

'Yeah, of course.'

Anna waited but he still didn't offer any explanation as to where he'd been. 'Look, I'd better go. My battery's low.' *Ask me not to hang up. Tell me where you've been. Tell me you love me.*

'Anna?'

'Yes?' *Maybe . . .*

'Thanks for calling.'

She closed her eyes, as she held the phone tight against her ear. 'No problem. Bye.'

'Anna?'

'Yes?' *Please, oh, please . . .* She realized she was holding her breath.

'Would you like me to pick you up from the airport on Sunday?'

Tears rolled unchecked down Anna's face. 'No, that's okay. We're getting in really early. Gary's going to be there so he can drop me.'

'Well, if you're sure.'

'I'm sure.'

'Then I'll have breakfast waiting for you.'

'That would be nice. Bye, Liam.'

'Bye, sweetheart.'

'Yoo-hoo, I'm home!'

'Shit!' Anna charged out to the kitchen as she heard Jill let herself into the hall.

'Anna? Rachel?'

'I'm in the bath,' Rachel called back.

Anna was just wiping her eyes with a teacloth when her cousin walked in. She quickly turned away and buried her head in a cupboard. 'Oh hi, I didn't hear you.'

'What on earth are you up to?' Jill put down her bag and flopped into a chair.

'Just looking for the chocolate biscuits.'

'We finished them last night when we came in from the pub.'

'Oh, right.' Anna didn't move.

'Let me guess. You've been talking to Liam.'

Anna turned slowly to face her, her eyes red, and nodded.

'So what happened? What did he say?'

'The interview went very well.'

Jill arched an eyebrow. 'And that made you cry?'

Anna wrung her hands together as she paced the tiny kitchen. 'I told him I'd called his mother's but that he'd already left and he said nothing.'

Jill frowned. 'I don't follow?'

'He didn't tell me where he'd been!'

'Why didn't you just ask him?' Jill followed her cousin with her eyes. 'Oh, please sit down, you're making me seasick.'

Anna sank on to a chair and buried her face in her hands. 'If it was innocent he would have told me, wouldn't he?'

Jill sighed. 'You really have a way of complicating things, Anna. Why don't you ring him back and ask him?'

Anna took her hands away and looked at her. 'Just like that?'

'Just like that.'

'But then he'd know—'

'That you cared?' Jill interrupted. 'That you were jealous? Maybe he needs to know that.'

Anna pulled her phone out of her jeans pocket and plonked it on the table.

'Go on. What have you got to lose?'

Anna looked at her and then looked back at the

phone. 'But what if he tells me he was with her?' she said in a small voice.

Jill's heart went out to her cousin. She looked so small and frightened, almost childlike. 'Then at least you'll know for sure. You're going to drive yourself mad if you carry on like this.' She ruffled her cousin's hair and stood up. 'I'm going to read my book until it's my turn for the bathroom. With Rachel in there, I'll probably get to finish it!'

Left alone, Anna considered her cousin's advice. Jill, as usual, was right. She was behaving like a lovesick teenager. Liam wasn't a mindreader. 'If you want something, Anna, please just tell me,' he'd begged her many times. 'You know I'm lousy at picking up on subtleties.'

Before she could change her mind, she picked up the phone and dialled again.

'Hello?'

'Liam, it's me again.'

'Is there something wrong?'

'Yes, yes, there is.'

'Your dad—'

'No, nothing like that,' she assured him. 'I just want to know where you've been.'

'Sorry?'

Anna took a deep breath. 'Where did you go after you left your mother's?'

'The supermarket, why?'

'Nowhere else?'

'No.'

'You weren't with Tara?' She could hear Liam sigh at the other end of the phone.

'No, love, I wasn't with Tara.'

'Oh, okay.'

'I'm sorry.'

'For what?' Anna asked.

'Everything.'

Anna swallowed hard. 'We need to talk, Liam.'

'Yes.'

'I mean it, Liam. We need to really talk.'

'I'll pick you up on Sunday, okay? And we'll come home and talk.'

'Promise?'

'I promise.'

She closed her eyes and pressed her lips to the mouthpiece. 'See you Sunday.'

Chapter 28

Jill didn't get an opportunity to ask Anna if she'd talked to Liam, but it was pretty clear that she had. The girl was positively glowing and she was even being nice to Rachel! Saturday turned out to be a lovely day. After breakfast on the balcony, they'd lazed around the pool, gone to Kitty's for lunch and then while Shay went for his snooze, the women made their way to the beauty salon for a final pampering.

Anna giggled as Steffi applied a fluorescent green face mask to her sister. 'If Alex saw you now, he'd run a mile.'

'You can talk.' Rachel retorted. Anna's mask was equally colourful.

'You're both gorgeous, nearly as beautiful as your mother.' Bridie winked at Maria who was giving her a manicure.

'Yeah, after this session, Mam, you'll have Matt all over you.' Anna laughed.

'Oh, go away out of that.' Bridie blushed.

'He's always fancied you, Mam.'

'Hardly surprising, married to that old bag,' Rachel pointed out.

'Patricia's not so bad,' Bridie protested half-heartedly.

'She's a loud-mouthed gossip,' Anna retorted.

'A right pain,' Rachel agreed.

Jill smiled, thinking how much fun her cousins were when they were getting on.

'Now we're not spending the whole evening with them, Mam,' Anna warned. 'This is our last night.'

'I told them we'd meet up for a drink after dinner,' Bridie promised her. 'Then you three could go dancing if you want.'

Anna glanced over at her sister. 'What about it, Rache?'

'I don't know about dancing but I suppose I could sway a little.'

Jill clapped her hands together. 'Good woman.'

'That's settled then.' Bridie sat back in her chair and closed her eyes.

'I wish we weren't going home tomorrow,' Rachel said with a wistful sigh.

Anna looked over at her sister. 'I thought you'd be dying to see Alex.'

'Of course I am, but I'll miss this wonderful weather.'

'And what about me?' Bridie asked.

'Ah, we'll miss you a bit too.' Anna reached over to squeeze her mother's hand.

'So, Mam, when are you coming home?' Rachel asked.

Bridie opened her eyes. 'I told you, love, as soon as you need me. We're moving back up into France in a couple of weeks and I thought we'd visit Lourdes.'

Rachel's eyes widened. 'Lourdes?'

Bridie flushed. 'Well, I'm not the most religious person in the world but I would like to give thanks for your father's recovery. And I've always wanted to see the place. We'll keep heading north and as soon as you call, we'll be on the next boat home!'

'But how can I call you?' Rachel asked.

Bridie glanced at the clock on the wall. 'You can reach us on the mobile that your dad is buying right about now.'

Anna grinned delightedly. 'Oh, good on you, Mam!'

'Yes, well, I want Rachel to be able to reach us when this baby decides to make an appearance.'

'You'll have to remember to charge it, Mam,' Anna told her.

'Now, isn't it well you told me that?' Bridie's voice was loaded with sarcasm.

'Sorry.'

'You won't know yourselves,' Jill told her aunt. 'Once you get a mobile phone you wonder how on earth you ever managed without it.'

Bridie wrinkled her nose. 'I've never liked the things but I suppose it's a necessary evil.'

Rachel smiled. 'Thanks, Mam, it means a lot to me.'

'That's okay, love.'

'We'll have to teach you to send text messages.' Jill winked at Anna.

'There's a challenge,' Anna laughed.

'Carrier pigeon might be quicker,' Rachel added.

'I hope you lot aren't making a laugh of me.'

'Wouldn't dream of it, Mam!'

Jill groaned and held her stomach as the plane hit some turbulence and the seatbelt sign came on. Maybe that last gin and tonic hadn't been such a good idea. It had turned into a very late night and they'd only had three hours' sleep before it was time to go to the airport. Jill was dreaming of bed and planned to crawl in as soon as she got home. The unpacking and laundry could wait. The plane lurched again and Rachel gripped her arm. 'It's okay, Rache, don't worry.'

'Why the hell doesn't he fly above it?' Rachel muttered. 'I feel sick.'

'Me too,' Anna said as she gazed out at the grey skies.

Jill pressed the button for the flight attendant. 'Three brandies, please.'

'I can't drink brandy!' Rachel protested as the attendant went off to fetch their drinks.

'One won't do you any harm. It will settle your stomach and help you doze off.'

'Great idea,' Anna agreed.

'Well, if you're sure.' Rachel still looked doubtful as the drinks were set in front of them. 'You take half of mine, Jill.'

'No problem.' Jill lowered half of Rachel's glass in one go. 'Ooh, that's better!'

Rachel took a tentative sip and wrinkled her nose. 'Ugh, it's like medicine.'

Anna laughed. 'My kind of medicine.'

Rachel shifted in her seat, trying to get comfortable. 'Maybe I will try and doze for a while.'

'You do that, chicken.' Jill patted her arm and settled back to enjoy her drink and ponder her next move.

Excitement bubbled up inside her but she kept her feelings to herself. It was too soon to tell her cousins her plans and she wasn't quite sure what their reaction would be. Or maybe she was, she admitted to herself, and that's why she hadn't said anything. Still, it was early days and there was a lot to sort out before she'd be in a position to do anything. The thought of all the work ahead was both exciting and scary. It would be very hard to knuckle down and concentrate at the office tomorrow. She took another sip of brandy as she imagined the chaos that would greet her. But it didn't matter any more, she realized serenely. At the beginning of the holiday she'd been confused and depressed as to what her future held. Now she had a new goal, a new challenge, and she couldn't wait to get her teeth into it.

Anna was relieved that Rachel was asleep and Jill was nursing her hangover. She didn't feel much like talking. She was getting more and more nervous as they got nearer to Dublin. She had pestered Liam to talk to her for weeks, but now the prospect of a frank conversation scared the wits out of her. What if she didn't like what she was going to hear? Maybe she'd imagined the softening in his tone. Maybe he was feeling guilty because he didn't love her any more. God, she put a hand to her mouth, maybe he was going to sit her down and tell her their marriage was over. Anna took a gulp of brandy and flinched as it scorched her throat and burned its way down to her stomach. Well, she told herself, there was no point in worrying about it. In less than two hours she'd be sitting next to Liam in the car on the way home to a conversation that could very well change her future for ever.

Rachel kept her eyes shut tight. She didn't feel like talking. Her tongue felt thick and dry in her mouth. Her stomach was fluttering with nerves that weren't entirely due to the turbulence and the baby was kicking her ribs impatiently, as if aware that it was going home to Daddy. Rachel knew her mother was right and that she should talk to Gary, but the prospect still frightened her. What if he went straight up and packed his bags? Or what if he told her she was right, confirmed her suspicions and told her that the late nights at the office had actually been spent in the arms of another woman? Rachel bit her lip hard to stop a sob escaping. God, she'd have to stop all of this bloody crying. How would she get through this if she was an emotional wreck to begin with? She clutched her glass and forced herself to breathe slowly and evenly. If she was going to do this, and she was, she had to do it when Alex was out of the house. Then she had to make sure Gary came home from work early. That wouldn't be easy. She'd have to come up with some reason for him to be home that he couldn't wriggle out of. Because if he did, she'd lose her courage and probably let things continue as before. Quite apart from the fact that Bridie would kill her if she didn't sort this out, Rachel knew she'd go quietly mad if her life continued like this for much longer.

This week had taught her a lot about how much she'd changed over the last year. She was well aware that she hadn't been the best of company, Anna didn't hide the fact, and being away from home had seemed to highlight her sadness. Rachel opened her eyes with a start. That was it. That summed it all up. She was sad. She was grieving for her dead marriage. Closing her eyes again, Rachel kept her lips clamped firmly together and swallowed her tears. Though she was dying inside, there was a certain relief that she had finally come to this point. Things couldn't really get worse now. And no matter what happened, she realized as she cradled her bump with her hands, she still had Alex and her baby.

*

Bridie sat on the balcony wondering what to do. Both her daughters were in crisis and on their way home to God knows what and she was here, miles away, unable to help. When she had left Ireland she had believed it to be the right decision. Now she thought that maybe it had been a selfish one.

Shay ambled out to join her. 'Stop it,' he said, lowering himself into a seat.

'Stop what?'

'Torturing yourself.'

Bridie blew her nose. 'I don't know what you're on about.'

'I'm not completely thick, Bridie. I don't know what the crisis is this time,' he held up a hand, 'and I don't want to know, but it's not your problem.'

'Shay!'

'No, love, I mean it. They're big girls and it's about time they sorted out their own problems. They shouldn't be even bothering you with them.'

'Of course they should – aren't I their mother? Anyway, it's not their fault that I worry about them. That's just the way I am.'

He smiled. 'Don't I know it. But, Bridie, we thought long and hard about leaving Ireland. We weighed up all the pros and cons then, and you know that we did the right thing.'

Bridie's eyes met his. 'I'm not sure we'd still be together if we'd stayed in Dublin.'

'Don't you think I know that? So how can you have any regrets?'

She sighed. 'I suppose I'm feeling a bit selfish, putting us before them.'

'You've put them first for thirty years,' he reminded her. 'Don't you get time off for good behaviour? If they need you, you're at the end of a phone,' he nodded at the mobile on the table, 'twenty-four hours a day now, thanks to that bloody thing. And they have Jill. She's a great girl.'

Bridie nodded. 'I think I would have been on the plane back with them if it wasn't for her.'

Shay frowned. 'You're worrying me now. What is it, Bridie? What's going on?'

She looked at him. 'I'll tell you if you promise not to interfere.'

'I won't.'

'And don't get all worked up, as that won't do your ulcer any good.'

'Just tell me, Bridie.'

'Anna thinks Liam might be seeing someone else.'

'No!'

'And so does Rachel.'

'Rachel thinks Liam is seeing someone else?'

'No, Gary.'

He shook his head. 'You're confusing me now.'

'Rachel thinks Gary might be messing about too.'

'Gary *and* Liam? Jesus! I'll kill the pair of them.'

'You'll do no such thing, Shay! You'll say nothing because you don't know anything about it. And besides, you promised you wouldn't interfere.'

'Shag that! What the hell do they think they're playing at?'

Bridie looked him straight in the eye. 'You should know better than anyone.'

'Ah, now, Bridie, you promised you wouldn't throw it back in my face.'

'And I won't, but don't go casting the first stone,' she warned.

He sat back in the chair, his hands in his lap, looking at her as if she were mad. 'I can't believe I'm hearing this. Are you defending them now?'

'Of course I'm not! It's just that Anna and Rachel don't have any real proof yet.'

Shay shook his head. 'I can't believe it. They're both lovely girls, pretty girls. Why would the lads want anything more?'

Bridie glared at him. 'You're really not helping yourself here.'

'Sorry, sorry, it's just I feel so helpless.'

Bridie nodded. 'I know.'

'So what did you say to them?'

'I told them both to go home and talk to their husbands.'

'Oh.'

'Well, what else could I say?'

'Nothing, I suppose. At least they can comfort each other, being in the same boat like.'

'Ah, Shay, would you listen to yourself? They hardly talk to each other, never mind confide in each other.'

'And what's that about?' Shay was bewildered. 'I mean, you and Pat were like chalk and cheese but you were still friends.'

Bridie nodded. 'We used to kill each other but it didn't really mean anything. Anna and Rachel used to be like that too.'

'So what happened?'

'Who knows?' Bridie said thoughtfully. 'Like you said though, at least they have Jill.'

'Come on, you two,' Jill urged as she hurried towards the baggage carousel. Now that she was back in Dublin her tiredness had disappeared and she couldn't wait to get home. There was so much to think about, so much to work out. She wanted to make a huge pot of coffee, grab a pad and pen and spend the rest of the day alone with her thoughts.

'The bags haven't even started to come out yet,' Anna pointed out. She was in no hurry to walk into Arrivals. Coming face to face with Liam, the thought of looking into his eyes filled her with excitement and fear. What would she see there?

Rachel was the last to reach the carousel. Like Anna, she was a bit nervous about seeing her husband again, but apart from that, her feet were killing her and she was feeling slightly nauseous. 'Are we at the right one?' she asked, peering at the tiny monitor above them.

'Yeah, this is it,' Jill said.

'It's always the bloody same,' one woman said

loudly. 'You'd be quicker going out and getting them yourself!' There was a chuckle from her fellow passengers and she flashed a rueful smile. 'Ah, lousy weather and crap service, isn't it great to be home?'

'Hoorah!' her son shouted as the carousel started up. 'They're coming, Ma, they're coming!'

'Don't hold your breath, love,' his mother warned him.

As the woman predicted, it was a good ten minutes later before the cases finally appeared.

'If ours are last I'm going to cry,' Rachel said, leaning heavily against a nearby pillar.

'You go and sit down and I'll get your case,' Jill told her.

'Thanks, Jill.'

'She's very pale,' Jill said to Anna as Rachel went in search of a seat.

'It's fright,' Anna assured her. 'She's always been terrified on planes. When she was small she used to throw up before the plane had even taken off! Oh look, there's my case, and isn't that yours behind it?'

'Thank God for that,' Jill pushed her way into the carousel, grabbed the two bags and handed them to Anna. 'Now all we need is Rachel's.'

It was another ten minutes before Rachel's bag appeared. 'About bloody time!' Anna snatched it up and carried it over to where Jill and Rachel were sitting. 'Let's get out of this place.'

Rachel rose slowly to her feet and swayed slightly.

'Are you okay?' Jill took her arm.

'Yeah, just a bit tired.'

'You'll be home in no time,' Anna promised. 'Come on.'

As they walked out into the Arrivals area, Rachel forgot her tiredness and aching feet as a small figure hurtled towards her.

'Mummy!'

Rachel bent and pressed her son close to her chest. 'Hello, darling, how are you? Oh, it's so wonderful to see you. Have you missed me?'

'Yeah, what did you bring me?' Alex's eyes went to her case.

'All in good time.' Gary had joined them. He bent and kissed Rachel's cheek. 'Welcome home, Rache.'

'Thanks.'

'I don't see Liam.' Anna looked around her.

'He's not coming,' Gary told her as he led them towards the exit. 'He got a call just before he was about to leave for the airport. His mother's been taken ill.'

Anna stared at her brother-in-law in disbelief. 'And of course he went running!'

Gary shot her a strange look. 'Well, he is the next-of-kin.'

Anna stopped. 'What do you mean? What's wrong with her?'

'All I know is that she's in hospital.'

'Oh, my God!'

'That's terrible!' Jill put a comforting hand on Anna's arm.

'I'd better get over there.'

'We'll drop you,' Gary said.

'No, that's okay—'

'We'll drop you,' he insisted.

Rachel shot him a grateful look. 'Would you like me to come in with you?' she asked her sister.

'No, there's no need. Anyway, you're exhausted.'

'I'll come with you,' Jill told her. 'I can get a taxi home from the hospital.'

'Thanks, Jill.'

They reached the car and Gary loaded their luggage into the boot.

'Can I have my present now, Mum?' Alex ventured, oblivious to the mood.

'No, darling, you'll have to wait until we get home.'

The little boy's smile disappeared. 'Ah, Mum!'

'Another word from you, young man, and there won't be any presents at all,' Gary said quietly but firmly.

'Sorry, Daddy,' Alex said and hopped into the back seat, clambering into the middle so he could have Anna on one side and Jill on the other.

Rachel stared at Gary in amazement. What on earth had been going on in her absence? On the rare occasion that Gary corrected his son, Alex usually ignored him. But not only had Alex listened this time, he'd obeyed Gary without question. Rachel got into the passenger seat, closed her belt and then stared out of the window as Gary guided the car out of the car park. She should be thrilled at this new development but it actually made her feel surplus to requirements. Alex was more excited about his present than seeing her, and Gary's kiss had been almost brotherly. Rachel's resolve to tackle her husband started to falter. She had a horrible image of a look of total relief crossing Gary's face and him asking her for an amicable break-up.

'Are you okay, love?' Gary was looking at her, a frown on his face.

'Fine.' She smiled weakly. She twisted in her seat so that she could see her sister. 'Had Josie been sick?'

Anna shook her head. 'No. She's always complaining about something or other but she's basically quite healthy.'

'Is she going to die?' Alex chipped in.

'No, of course not!' Rachel rolled her eyes at her sister.

'But she's very old, isn't she?' he persisted.

Anna smiled and ruffled his hair. 'Only about sixty.'

He wrinkled his nose. 'That's ancient!'

Gary laughed. 'You'd better not say that to either of your grannies or you'll be in big trouble.'

'Why?' Alex asked.

'Ladies don't like getting older,' Jill told him.

'I do, I love it. I'm five and three-quarters, nearly six, isn't that right, Mum?'

'Yes, sweetheart, you're getting very old,' Rachel agreed as Gary turned into the hospital grounds and drove around to the Accident & Emergency entrance.

'Thanks, Gary,' Anna said as he stopped the car.

'No problem. Would you like me to drop your case off at the house?'

'Oh, would you? That would be great.'

'Sure.'

'Call us when you have some news, won't you?' Rachel said as Anna and Jill climbed out.

As Gary went to the boot to get Jill's bag, she bent her head to smile at Rachel. 'I'll give you a call later, Rache. Thanks for a great week.'

Rachel smiled back at her cousin. 'Thank *you*. It wouldn't have been the same without you.'

'Bye!' Anna called.

'Bye, good luck. Give Liam our love.'

'Will do.'

'So, how was the holiday?' Gary asked as they drove away.

'Yeah, it was fine.'

'And your dad?'

'He's great but giving out like hell about his diet.'

'He must be missing his pint.'

'He still has the odd one, not that we're supposed to know that.'

'And what about the cigarettes?'

'He's given them up.'

'You're kidding?' Since Gary had first dated Rachel he'd been amazed at the number of cigarettes Shay got through in a day.

'Well, apparently he'd already cut down to five a day so it hasn't been too hard.'

'I'm impressed.'

'Yes, I was too.'

'I thought maybe we could order in tonight,' Gary told her. 'I knew you'd probably be too tired to cook and I didn't want to inflict my cooking on you.'

'Sounds good,' Rachel agreed, amazed that Gary had even thought about dinner. 'We probably should do a shop on the way home,' she added, stifling a yawn.

'Alex and I did one yesterday.'

'Oh!'

'I'm sure we forgot lots of stuff,' he laughed, 'but we got the basics. There should be enough food to keep us going for a couple of days.'

'Great, thanks.' God, she was definitely redundant. What had prompted this New Man act – a guilty conscience, maybe? Or maybe he'd also decided it was time to talk and he was preparing the ground.

'Aren't you visiting the obstetrician this week?' Gary was saying.

'Yes, Thursday.'

'If you like, I could come with you.'

Rachel stared at him. 'Why?'

He looked slightly embarrassed. 'It's just an idea.'

'Yeah, that would be great, thanks.' Now Rachel was completely confused. But she didn't have time to think about it as Gary had turned into the driveway and Alex was bouncing up and down.

'Presents time, presents time. Come on, Mummy, hurry up!' He opened the door and jumped out, hopping impatiently from foot to foot as his father fetched the case and Rachel levered herself out of the car. Gary opened the front door and carried the case into the living room. 'Are you okay?' he asked, all concerned as Rachel gasped when she went to sit down.

She made a face. 'Fine, just Baby is doing somersaults and giving me sore ribs.'

Gary crouched down beside her and put a hand on her stomach. 'Not long now, Baby, hang in there.'

Rachel gulped at his tender expression.

'Come on, Mummy,' Alex pleaded. 'Pleaaaaase!'

'Okay, darling, okay.' She laughed as she unzipped the case and handed him out his toys. 'I'm afraid I went a little bit overboard,' she told Gary, as Alex yelped with delight at the jeep, the Yu-Gi-Oh cards, a *Dr Seuss* book and a *Pokémon* DVD. She'd also bought a model of a 737 in the plane on the way home.

'It's like Christmas,' Gary said, smiling at his son. 'Have you anything to say to Mummy, Alex?'

Alex ran to hug her. 'Thanks, Mummy, you're the best mummy in the world!'

Chapter 29

Rachel sat in an armchair sipping her camomile tea and not watching *Coronation Street*. Gary had insisted she put her feet up while he put Alex to bed and read him his new *Dr Seuss* book but she couldn't concentrate on the soap. All she could think about was this dramatic change in Gary and what it meant. He had been very attentive all evening and when he hadn't been checking on her, he'd been on the floor playing with Alex. There was a change in Alex too, she'd realized as she watched them. He was more relaxed and there had been no tantrums or sulking. At one stage when he didn't win a Yu-Gi-Oh game, he'd started to moan but Gary had distracted him and defused the situation. Rachel had looked on in amazement.

Her thoughts were interrupted as Gary stuck his head round the door. 'Why don't you order our dinner? I'll only be ten minutes or so. He's asleep on his feet.'

Rachel smiled. 'The usual?'

He nodded. 'Please.'

Rachel picked up the phone, dialled the number of their local Chinese takeaway and ordered the same food that they'd been ordering for years. Beef and green pepper stir-fry for Gary and Satay chicken for her.

She sighed as she went to set the table. Neither of them had hit middle age yet and they lived such a boring, predictable life. It was no wonder Gary stayed out late. It was no wonder that she was feeling restless. While she had grown to love the baby growing inside her and was feeling excited as her due date grew nearer and nearer, she still dreaded the humdrum, boring life that bringing up a baby entailed. Every day the same – no adult conversation, no job satisfaction – God, how she envied women who worked!

Sometimes, when she was in the supermarket in her tracksuit and trainers and a woman passed her in a suit and high-heels, she felt like crying. How wonderful to dress up and wear make-up every day! How nice it would be to feel proud of your appearance and get appreciative stares from men again. How lovely to go to fancy restaurants for lunch or drop into the pub after work without feeling guilty.

Since Alex had started school she got out more, sometimes even going out for lunch. But the difference was that the conversation always revolved around children. It was as if *she* didn't exist as a woman in her own right any more. That her sole reason for being was motherhood.

Rachel leaned heavily against the worktop and wiped a tear from her eye. The few days in Spain hadn't really helped. Being surrounded by beautiful women in tiny bikinis had made her feel like a monster, especially when she was lying beside her skinny sister. Listening to the conversations she and Jill had didn't help either. They discussed everything from books and clothes to famine in Sudan and the state of the Irish economy. Rachel didn't really have opinions on anything other than education, healthcare and child-friendly restaurants.

Still, it had been nice to see her parents again. Gossiping with her mam made her feel almost normal and when her dad hugged her, she actually felt small! But leaving them had been hard. The holiday had made Rachel realize exactly how much she missed them, and she knew it was the same for Anna. She wondered if her sister had tackled them about leaving. She'd said nothing in front of her although there had been a few smart comments that Bridie and Shay either didn't notice or chose to ignore.

Whatever had been said or not said, Mam and Dad were going ahead with their travels and though they were coming home for the birth, Rachel knew that it would only be a visit. She felt slightly jealous of the deep and private relationship they shared. They seemed closer now than they had been when she and Anna lived at home. Maybe kids were just bad news for relationships. Her mam had concentrated on them while Shay went off and found company elsewhere. Just like Gary. Maybe that meant they'd end up together in their old age.

The doorbell went and she found her purse and went to answer it. After she'd paid the delivery man and closed the door she called up the stairs, 'Gary? Dinner.'

Gary emerged from his son's bedroom. 'Alex would like to say goodnight.'

Rachel put down the bag and went upstairs. 'How was your new book?' she asked, sitting down on the edge of Alex's bed.

'Deadly!' Alex's eyes sparkled up at her. 'Thanks, Mummy, for all my presents.'

'You're welcome, sweetheart.' She leaned over to hug him.

'Will you play Yu-Gi-Oh with me tomorrow?'

Rachel was about to refuse but the look on his face went straight to her heart. 'Sure.'

'Yes! Thanks, Mum.'

'Now, sleep, young man. You've got summer camp in the morning. Goodnight.'

''Night, Mummy. Love you.'

Rachel paused in the doorway. 'I love you too.'

Gary was standing on the landing waiting for her. 'He really missed you,' he murmured as they went downstairs together.

'I doubt that,' she laughed.

'It's true.' Gary carried the food out to the kitchen and fetched himself a beer. 'What would you like to drink?'

'Just some water, please,' Rachel said, as she opened the cartons.

'I did too,' Gary said as he took his seat beside her.

'Did what?'

'Miss you. I missed you.'

'Oh!'

'Look, darling, I want to say sorry.'

Rachel closed her eyes briefly, and gripped the edge of the table. 'Sorry? For what?'

'Not being here, really. Being at home with Alex this week has given me a taste of what your life's like. Just a taste,' he added hurriedly as she went to interrupt. 'I know you left food in the freezer and clothes ironed and all of that, but I suppose I got a feel for the day-to-day . . .' He searched for a word.

'Monotony?' Rachel offered.

'Yes, that fits.'

'If you think it's monotonous now, try taking a week off after the baby arrives. At least Alex is capable of conversation, even if it is only about Beyblades, Scooby-Doo and Yu-Gi-Oh.'

'Are you sorry you got pregnant?' Gary asked as he forked beef and rice into his mouth.

Rachel put down her knife and fork and met his eyes: 'Yes, I am.'

Gary nearly choked on his food and he hastily reached for his beer.

'Sorry. Are you okay?'

He nodded, staring at her. 'Why didn't you say something?'

She shrugged. 'What difference would it have made? It's not as if we'd have got rid of it.'

'No,' Gary agreed, 'but you still could have talked to me.'

'Too late for that now.'

'But it's not too late for me to help out more,' Gary told her. 'And I will. Rache, you just tell me what you want done and I'll do it.'

'Even the bins?' Rachel's eyes twinkled.

'Even the bins. You know, I learned a lot this week, mainly about how little I know my son and, to be honest, that hurt. And I realized how great a mother you are because he is a great kid, Rache, and that's all down to you. And I now know that I don't want to be a stranger to my kids. Lately, I've only seen Alex for an hour in the morning and maybe a few minutes at bedtime. That's got to change. I want to do things with him, with both of them. And you too, of course.'

'Of course.'

He sat back and watched her, wiping his mouth with a piece of kitchen towel. 'You don't believe me, do you?'

Rachel shrugged. 'Anytime I complain about the long hours you work, you tell me there's nothing you can do about it, that that's the job.'

'Maybe it's time to change jobs.'

Now Rachel shot him a look of pure disbelief. 'You're going to walk away from your big salary, your BMW and your shares?' Gary had dreamed of making it to the top of his company for years. There was no way he'd give that up. Unless . . . 'You've been offered another job, haven't you?'

'Not exactly.'

'Then what, Gary? What's going on?' Rachel pushed her plate away and leaned forward.

'Well, I've been talking to a few contacts and I'm thinking of going out on my own.'

Rachel stared at him. 'You want to set up your own windows company?'

He nodded enthusiastically. 'Yeah, I think I could do really well. I've made a lot of contacts in the industry and Jack Brennan would come with me, and he's the best fitter we've got.'

'But where would you get the money?'

'I've saved a few thousand and the bank would give me a loan, no problem.'

'Let me get this straight,' Rachel said, her voice dangerously quiet. 'We're about to have a baby and you want to risk our life savings and put our whole world at risk? Have you taken leave of your senses?'

Gary scowled. 'It's nice to know you have such faith in me.'

'Oh come on, Gary,' Rachel exploded. 'Get real! We have a young family and I'm not working. We can't afford to take risks like this! And anyway, what about what you were saying earlier, about spending more time with the children? If you were running your own business, we'd never see you.'

'That would just be for the first few years until I got established.'

'Oh well, that's fine, so. When I'm forty and the kids are practically raised, we'll have plenty of time together.'

'Okay, enough! Forget I mentioned it.' Gary banged the table and stood up.

Rachel stood up too, her hands shaking as she pushed the chair in. 'I'm going to bed. Now that you're the soul of domesticity, you won't mind cleaning up, will you?'

Gary said nothing as she walked past him and went upstairs. God, what was he up to, she thought as she closed the bedroom door and slumped on to the bed. First all this New Man crap and now this bombshell. Had that been what all today's performance was about? Had he just been buttering her up? And where did his girlfriend or girlfriends fit into this picture? Rachel shook her head in confusion. He was too young for a midlife crisis but something had to be going on. Getting to her feet, Rachel moved to Gary's wardrobe and opened it. She hesitated for only a second and had just slipped her hand into the inside pocket of his favourite suit when the phone rang. She quickly closed the wardrobe and was just sitting back down on the bed when Gary walked in.

'It's Jill.'

Rachel took the phone and watched him leave. 'Jill? What's happening, how's Josie?'

'She's a bit shaken but she's going to be fine,' Jill

told her. 'Apparently she tripped on the steps on the way into Mass and broke her ankle.'

'The poor woman. So she's still in there, is she?'

'Yes. I'm just on my way home.'

Rachel gasped. 'You're only leaving the hospital now?'

'Yeah. While we were in Casualty, only Liam was allowed to stay with Josie and Anna had to wait outside. I didn't like to leave her on her own.'

'So when will they let her out?'

'Tomorrow, I think. The place is a bit chaotic and Josie was still on one of those bloody trolleys when I left.'

'Still, Liam must be relieved. It could have been a lot worse.'

'Yeah, well, I didn't get much of a chance to talk to him but I'm sure he is.'

'So is Anna still with them?'

'I'm not sure. I think Liam was trying to persuade her to go home without him.'

'I can't believe she didn't call me,' Rachel complained.

'Sorry, but we weren't allowed to use the phones in the hospital and it was pissing with rain outside.'

'Oh, right. Blimey, Jill, you must be exhausted. After the night we had last night!'

Jill laughed. 'I'm ready for a nice warm bath, that's for sure. Can you believe how cold it is?'

'Freezing.'

'Ah, it's great to be home! Bye, Rachel.'

'Goodnight, Jill.'

Rachel hung up and wondered if she should call Anna. But why bother her? Jill had filled her in, Anna was probably tired and Liam might be trying to get through. And, Rachel admitted, she didn't feel up to talking to her sister right now. Going out on to the landing, she left the phone on the top stair and went back inside, closing her door firmly. If Gary didn't get that hint then he was totally thick.

As quickly as her bulk allowed, she crossed back over to his wardrobe and resumed her search. There was the usual mix of parking vouchers, receipts – which she scrutinized carefully – and mints. Other than the fact that he seemed to be spending a lot of money on books, Rachel didn't make any discoveries. Her husband was either very clever or he was innocent. Rachel wished she could believe the latter. Surely he wouldn't be buttering her up and talking about their future if he had another woman? Maybe he really had been putting in long hours at the job. Or maybe he'd been meeting all of these so-called contacts who were going to help him start his own business. She could almost hear Bridie say, 'Well, you won't know until you ask him.'

Rachel sighed as she undressed, turning away from the reflection of her swollen body in the mirror. She knew she'd have to do it sooner or later, but there had been enough excitement for today. She needed to sleep.

Chapter 30

Anna turned over, opening one eye to look at the clock. Eleven-thirty and still no sign of Liam. Where the hell was he? Josie was probably sleeping her brains out now after all the excitement of the day and there was no need for him to be at the hospital. Anna could have cheerfully throttled the woman when she finally got in to see her. Josie was sitting up in bed looking the picture of health and enjoying all of the attention whereas Liam was at her side looking white-faced and haggard. Anna's heart had gone out to him and for a moment the misery of the last couple of weeks was forgotten. After kissing Josie's cheek she'd moved to his side, taken his hand and squeezed it tightly. Liam had shot her a grateful look before turning his attention back to his mother.

'It seems to be a straightforward enough break so that's a good thing,' he'd informed Anna, 'but I've been telling Mum she's going to have to take it easy for a while.'

Anna nodded. 'He's right, Josie.'

Josie regarded her plastered foot. 'I don't have

much choice, do I? But who'll clean the house, and make the dinner and keep the garden tidy? Houses don't run themselves, you know, and I couldn't live in a messy house.' The last comment was delivered with a pointed look at Anna.

'You won't have to lift a finger, Mum, will she, Anna?'

Anna looked at him in alarm. 'Er, well, of course we'll help as much as we can . . .'

'No, you have your job to worry about. I'll look after Mum, I have the time, after all. I never thought there'd be an up-side to being unemployed. It would probably be best if I moved in with you for a few days, Mum. At least until you get used to using the crutches.'

Anna stared at him.

'It won't be for long,' he said, his eyes pleading for understanding. 'She needs me.'

Josie was trying to hide her delight and failing badly. 'Well, I suppose I should have someone there in case I took another tumble.'

'Then it's settled.'

'Right.' Anna forced a smile. 'We'd better get home and pack a bag for you.'

Liam looked slightly shocked. 'Oh no, I'd prefer to stay here for a bit longer. I can throw a few things together in the morning before I come to get Mum.'

'Aren't you lucky having such a good son?' A nurse had bustled in to check Josie's blood pressure.

'I am,' Josie agreed with a proud smile.

Liam and Anna had moved away to let her do her job. 'You go on home, Anna. You look tired.' He handed her the keys of her car.

'Not half as tired as you. You look awful. Come home with me. There's nothing else you can do here and I'm sure sleep is the best thing for Josie now.'

'I was hoping to have a word with one of the doctors.'

'You can do that tomorrow.'

'Well, I'll just stay with her until she drops off.'

And reluctantly, Anna had left him there. God knows what Josie had done now to keep him by her side. But then, it wouldn't take much to persuade Liam. Irritating, frustrating and annoying as Josie was, Liam loved her and would be devastated if anything happened to her. Thank goodness it was only a broken ankle. He'd be in a right state if it had been anything serious. Anna turned over her pillow and thumped it in an effort to get more comfortable. Josie's timing could have been better, she thought as she pulled the duvet up under her chin. She had been very anxious about seeing Liam again and thrashing things out. Now that would have to wait. She'd be lucky if he ever came home again. She'd seen the way Josie's eyes had lit up at the idea of having him staying with her. And then there was Tara.

The thought of Liam staying next door to that bitch made Anna sick with jealousy. She could just imagine Tara popping in and out to 'help'. And what would Liam do? Would he weaken? Had he already?

Anna buried her face in her pillow and groaned. If they managed to come through this then they could come through anything. 'Sleep,' she muttered to herself. She had to go to work in the morning and could imagine the state her desk would be in. It didn't help matters that she wouldn't have the car. Liam would need it to collect his mother. If she had to do any visits, she'd have to borrow Mark's car.

Anna glanced again at the alarm clock. It was just coming up to midnight. Liam had probably decided to stay the night. That was their last chance of talking out the window and God only knew when they'd get another one. Maybe that conversation was destined never to happen. It was nearly an hour later before Anna finally fell asleep. By which time, the pillow was soggy with her tears.

A few hours later, Anna slipped out of the house and closed the hall door as quietly as she could. Liam had finally climbed into bed beside her at one o'clock and immediately fallen into a heavy sleep. Anna had crept around the place this morning, trying not to disturb him. She would call him in a couple of hours. He'd told her, before conking out, that he had to pick Josie up at about eleven. Anna walked past her car and began the ten-minute walk to work. At least the rain had stopped and it wasn't quite as cold as yesterday.

As she walked, she tried to switch into work mode, mentally going through her current list of clients and thinking who she should call first. An image of Charlie Coleman flitted into her head but she swatted it out again. She had no reason to call him any more, unless something went wrong with the sale. Guilt flickered through her at the disappointment she felt. How could she accuse Liam of harbouring feelings for Tara when she was daydreaming about another man? Even when she'd been in Spain, crying to her mother about Liam's supposed infidelity, she'd still found time to think of Charlie. Oh God! There was no point in torturing herself. She wouldn't be seeing Charlie again anyway, and whatever thoughts or feelings she'd had, she hadn't actually done anything to be ashamed of. But would Liam be able to say the same – if they ever got to discuss it? And how would he handle staying next door to Her?

As Anna arrived at the office, she thought that it would almost be a relief to go back to work and get wrapped up in other people's problems. She'd go nuts if she thought about the mess that was her own life any longer.

'So, had you a nice holiday? How's your father?'

'The holiday was lovely, we had a fabulous apartment with an amazing view. Dad is wonderful although ready to throttle Mam if she forces any more salad down his throat.'

Val chuckled. 'If he's well enough to complain it's a good sign. I always worry when Edna goes quiet. She never stops moaning, you see, so it wouldn't be natural if she was quiet.' She stopped and put her hands to her cheeks. 'Oh, what a terrible thing to say!'

'You're human, Val, and she's lucky to have you.'

'She's my sister,' Val said simply. 'If I didn't look after her, who would?'

Anna wondered guiltily if she'd be as caring if Rachel ever needed her, or vice versa for that matter.

'You have a lovely colour, but you look a bit tired for someone who's just come back from a holiday,' Val observed.

The phone rang, preventing Anna from replying and she hopped on it gratefully. 'No rest for the wicked, eh? Hello, Donnelly's Real Estate, Anna Gallagher speaking.'

The morning flew from then on and Anna was grateful that she and Val had little opportunity to chat. Predictably, Mark was annoyed when she told him she didn't have her car with her.

'Bloody inconvenient,' he grumbled. 'I told Val to line up three appointments for you this afternoon. And what about the apartments? There's a viewing tonight and you're supposed to be doing it.'

'I'll still be able to show the apartments,' she told him calmly, 'and if you lend me your car I can keep all of my appointments.'

'I suppose so,' he grunted, 'but put a mark on that BMW and it'll come out of your salary.'

'Speaking of salary, when am I getting my commission on the Brennan sale?'

'When it goes through and not before. Actually, give Charlie a call and hurry him along, will you? Paul Brennan says his lawyer is an idiot and he's dragging everything out.'

'Wouldn't it be better if you had a word?' This was the last thing Anna needed.

Mark smiled for the first time. 'Ah no, I think he'd prefer to talk to you.'

'Stop messing about, Mark.' Anna glared at him. 'Charlie's a client and no more than that.'

'Did I say a word?' He held up his hands and tried to look wide-eyed and innocent. 'Look, Anna, just deal with it, will you?' He threw her his car keys. 'I need you back here by five.'

'I'll be here,' Anna said and went back out to her desk.

Val stood up and put on her coat. 'I'll just pop out and get a sandwich. Would you like something?'

'No, that's okay, I'm not hungry.'

Val shook her head. 'It's not good to go all day without food, Anna.'

'I'll get something later, okay?' Anna was sharper than she'd intended and she sighed as Val walked out of the office without another word. She'd have to apologize when she got back. Val was only being kind and she didn't deserve to be snapped at. Particularly considering the extra workload she'd shouldered so that Anna could go on holiday. Anna promised herself she'd make it up to her. Before she had time to figure out how, the phone rang again and she was forced to put Val to the back of her mind as she focused on the caller.

Later, when Val returned and Anna had made her a cup of tea and grovelled a bit, she took Mark's car keys and headed off to her first appointment. It was a viewing of Beech Wood, an old house in its own grounds about a mile outside the village, and Val said the man who'd made the appointment, Mr Grainger, sounded very keen. 'Apparently his wife used to live near there,' Val had briefed her, 'and she wants to move back into the area.'

'I hope they're serious,' Anna had said with a shudder. 'I hate going to that house, it gives me the creeps.'

Now, as she drove up the long driveway, she was relieved to see that the clients had already arrived. 'Mr Grainger?' she said, getting out of the car.

'That's right.' The heavyset man came over to shake hands.

'Anna Gallagher.' Anna forced herself not to pull her hand away from his sweaty grip. She looked around him. 'Isn't your wife with you?'

'She couldn't make it, I'm afraid, but she's happy for me to check the place out. If I like it, we'll come back for a second viewing. Could we get on? Only I'm in a bit of a hurry.'

'Of course.' Anna went back to the car to get the house keys and brochure and then led the way across the gravel to the front door. 'The property is a wonderful example of Edwardian architecture but it is in need of attention,' she told him as she unlocked the door.

'You're not kidding,' he said as she turned on the light to reveal an imposing hallway with flaking paintwork and peeling wallpaper.

'It's in a bit of a state,' Anna acknowledged, 'but I think that's reflected in the price.'

'Well, show me the rest of the place and I'll tell you if I agree.'

'Fine, let's start with the drawing room.'

Anna led him from room to room, speeding up as she began to sense that he wasn't really that interested. Apart from which, she didn't like the way he was looking at her. Maybe she was overreacting, this house had that effect on her, but she would be a lot happier when she was back in the safety of Mark's car. 'And this is the family bathroom,' she said, throwing open the door and walking into the room. 'There's an excellent view of the garden from here.' She went over to the window and peered out.

'I *do* love the view.'

She jumped as she realized he was standing right behind her, his mouth close to her ear.

'I wonder if the shower works.' He ran his fingers up and down her arm. 'Maybe we should try it out.'

Anna turned, finding his face only inches from hers. 'I don't think so,' she said, forcing a smile. 'I'm afraid I have another appointment to go to.'

'Ah, there's no hurry,' he said, manhandling her back against the wall. 'You must have a great time bringing men to all these empty houses.' He licked his lips and the excitement dancing in his eyes scared Anna more than the feel of his groin pushing against her.

'Let me go,' she murmured, trying desperately to keep calm. He was probably just chancing his arm and would back off when she made it clear that she wasn't interested.

His eyes stared into hers as his hands moved to the neck of her blouse. 'I will, of course I will. Anna, isn't it?'

She nodded.

'We'll just have a little fun first.' He fiddled clumsily with her buttons and Anna bit back a scream.

'Wait,' she told him, giving him a coy smile. 'You'll tear it. Let me.' And pushing his hands away, she started to open the buttons. When he stood back to watch, she seized her opportunity and with every ounce of strength she possessed, she kneed him in the groin. As he screamed and crumpled to the floor in front of her, she stepped around him and started to run, not stopping until she got to the car.

Getting in, she fumbled with trembling fingers for the door lock – damn car, where the hell was it? Turning on the engine, she swung the car round, spraying gravel everywhere, and drove back down the driveway at speed. When she was out on the main road, she drove until she reached a petrol station, pulled in and phoned the office.

'Put Mark on,' she told Val. 'Now.'

'You've crashed the bloody car, haven't you?' Mark said as soon as Val had put her through.

'No, I've been attacked.'

'Jesus! Oh my God, Anna, are you okay?'

'Yes, I got away before he did anything. But I'm afraid I just ran out of the house and left him there.'

'Don't worry about that, you did exactly the right thing. What house?'

'Beech Wood on the back road.'

'Right. You come back here, or go home, whichever you like. I'll get a taxi and go out there.'

'But what are you going to do? What if he has a knife or something?'

'If he had a knife he would have produced it. Don't worry I won't take any chances. I'll get the police to meet me at the house.'

'I still have the house keys and what about your car—'

'Will you stop worrying, Anna? I can pick the car up later. Are you sure you're okay?'

'A bit shaky but otherwise I'm fine. I gave him a knee in the balls.'

Mark roared with laughter. 'Good woman! We can certainly let you out on your own.'

'Will you call me and let me know what happens?'

'Sure. Now go home and drive carefully. I don't want you pranging my car.'

'I won't.'

Anna put her phone down on the passenger seat with a shaking hand. A car pulled into the forecourt beside her and she jumped, letting out a yelp. A little old lady got out and proceeded to fill her tank. Anna laughed. She was as jumpy as a cat, probably with delayed shock. She decided to sit there for a while before driving anywhere. The last thing she wanted to do now was crash poor Mark's car. A gentle knock on the window made her jump again.

'Anna, what's wrong? It's just me, Charlie. Are you okay?'

Anna's mouth opened and closed like a goldfish but she couldn't seem to get the words out.

'I'm coming in, okay?' He waited until she nodded before going around to the passenger door and climbing in beside her. He took her hands in his. 'God, you're freezing.'

Anna nodded. 'Yes, I do feel a bit cold.'

'What's wrong?'

She quickly explained what had happened, ending with: 'I'm fine, really I am. I just can't seem to stop shaking. I'm not sure I should drive – certainly not this thing.'

'Leave it to me,' Charlie said, pulling out his phone and dialling. 'Hello, Mark? It's Charlie. Yes, I know, I won't keep you. I ran into Anna in the filling station outside the village. She's not really up to driving so I think we should leave your car here and I'll take her home. Right, then. Be careful. Bye.' Charlie hung up and reached out a hand to smooth Anna's hair. 'Come on, you get into my car and I'll take you home.'

'But what about Mark's car?'

'We'll leave it here and he can pick it up later. It's all arranged.'

Anna obediently opened the door and swung her legs out. When she went to stand, however, she felt a bit wobbly and clutched on to the door.

'Hang on there.' Charlie hurried across, put an arm around her waist and practically carried her over to his car. 'I'll just park Mark's car and drop the keys inside. I'll be back in a minute. Will you be okay?'

'I'm fine, honestly! I don't know why I'm shaking so much, it's ridiculous.'

'You've had a shock, that's all. Don't worry about a thing. I'll have you home with a nice cuppa in your hand in no time at all.'

Chapter 31

'Is Liam home?' Charlie asked, as he pulled up outside her house.

'Yes – oh, no. He's staying with his mother. She broke her ankle yesterday.'

Charlie switched off the engine. 'Where are your house keys?'

Anna fumbled in her bag for a few seconds until finally Charlie took the bag from her. 'May I?'

She nodded and he quickly found her keys, helped her out of the car and led her inside. Sitting her down at the kitchen table, he put the kettle on and started to ransack the cupboards. 'Have you any brandy?'

Anna shook her head. 'There's some saké in the fridge.'

His eyes widened as he turned to face her. 'Saké?'

'Liam's going through a Japanese phase.'

Anna watched as Charlie took out the saké, poured some into a jug and put it into the microwave. 'What are you doing?'

'It will be more comforting warm. It's nicer too.'

When Anna took a sip, she nodded. 'It is nicer. Won't you have one?'

'I think I'd better stick to coffee. It's strong stuff and one glass never seems to be enough.'

It wasn't long before Anna felt the alcohol warm her and the shaking finally stopped. Charlie carried his coffee over and sat down.

'I'd love to know what's happening,' Anna said, shooting an anxious look at the clock. 'I wonder if Mark got there before Mr Grainger left? I'm not sure how much I hurt him.'

'I'd say you've left him with a few bruises. Would you like me to phone Mark and find out what's going on?'

'Yes, he'll probably tell you more than he will me. The phone's in the hall.'

Charlie went outside and she listened to him murmuring and then the ring as he put the phone down. 'Well?' she asked.

'There was no one in the house when Mark got there.'

Anna made a face. 'I didn't hurt him too much, then.'

'I don't suppose you could give a description of the car?'

'It was green and it was a four-door saloon – apart from that, I've no idea. I'm not really good on cars.'

'Did you notice the registration?'

She shook her head. 'God, I'm pathetic, aren't I?'

'No, of course not. Though, in the future, it might

be a good idea to take a note of details like that.'

'Val must have an address for him – well, at least a contact number. I should call her.'

Charlie shook his head. 'Mark already checked. They have no address and he gave a false number and presumably a false name too.'

Anna's face paled. 'So he planned this? He set me up?'

Charlie shrugged. 'He's just a sleazebag who was trying his luck. Forget about him, he's a loser. You handled yourself brilliantly, and hopefully he'll think twice before he tries it on with any other woman.'

'I hope you're right.'

'Why don't you call Liam? I'm sure he'd want to be here with you.'

Anna thought about it and then shook her head. 'He has enough on his plate at the moment. Anyway, I'm okay – why worry him?' She held up her glass. 'This is helping. Thanks, Charlie. If you hadn't come along I think I'd still be sitting on that forecourt.'

He reached out a finger and ran it down her cheek, his eyes tender. 'I quite like being your knight in shining armour.'

'Or jeans,' Anna joked, pulling back slightly. Charlie's touch aroused all sorts of feelings in her that she knew she shouldn't be having. 'It's funny, but you were top of my "to do" list. I was going to call you as soon as I got back to the office. After I'd done my other calls – oh, my God, I never contacted those poor people!'

'Relax, Mark is on top of it. He said you were to forget about work and even take a couple of days off if you want.'

'Crikey! Is he feeling all right? You know, he can be the most sexist, difficult, annoying boss and then he can be so sweet like he was today.'

'Sweet? Mark?' Charlie guffawed. 'Oh, he'd love that!'

Anna laughed too. 'Yeah, I suppose it's not the image he'd like to project.'

'So, you mentioned you were going to call me.' Charlie's voice was light, but his eyes bored into hers.

Anna looked away. 'Yeah, Mark asked me to. Apparently your lawyer isn't moving fast enough for Paul Brennan.'

'Oh.'

'So if you could hurry him along, that would be great. Or if there's a problem . . .'

'There's no problem.'

'Oh well, that's good. You must be looking forward to moving in. Have you shown Sophie the house yet?'

'Yes.'

'And she liked it?' Anna struggled on, trying to ignore his clipped tone and the sudden change in atmosphere.

'Yeah.'

'Look, Charlie—'

'Hey, it's okay, I get the message loud and clear.'

'You're a wonderful guy, Charlie.'

He stood up, pushed the chair in and leaned heavily on it. 'I'm feeling a bit foolish so I'd be grateful if you spared me the "sod off" speech.'

'I wasn't going to make a speech.'

His eyes met hers. 'But you were going to tell me that our relationship had to remain purely professional, weren't you?'

She sighed. 'Yes, I was.'

'Then there's nothing more to say.' He turned to leave.

'Please don't go,' Anna begged. The saké had given her a warm, fuzzy feeling and she didn't want to fight. Nor did she want him to go.

Charlie turned to face her. 'Give me a reason to stay.'

Anna grinned. 'I make a great chicken curry.'

'Really?'

'No,' she admitted. 'But I'm a dab hand with a microwave.'

'Are you inviting me to stay for dinner?'

'Yes, Charlie. Look, you're a friend, a good one. I don't want to lose you.'

Charlie's mouth twisted into a wry smile. 'I'm not that good at being friends with women, especially when I fancy them.'

Anna reddened. 'Well, if I wear a bag over my head, will that help?'

Charlie laughed. 'Okay, I'll have dinner with you but I'm afraid frozen curry won't do the trick for me. Let's go out.'

'Oh!'

'What? Will you be in trouble if you're seen eating with a strange man?' he taunted.

'No, of course not. And you're not strange – well, only a bit.'

'So, shall we go?'

At Anna's suggestion, they went to a busy Italian restaurant in the heart of Malahide. Charlie joked as they were handed their menus, 'Either this is all above board or we're very indiscreet lovers!'

'Charlie!' Anna hissed, with an anxious look at the neighbouring tables which were much too close for comfort.

Charlie smiled warmly at the waitress who'd brought their wine. 'Thank you, that's lovely. Relax,' he told Anna when she'd left. 'We know that we're just friends, and that's what matters, isn't it? If Liam walked through that door right now, you'd be able to look him in the eye and tell him this is a perfectly innocent dinner, wouldn't you?'

Anna's eyes dropped to her menu. 'Sure. Gosh, I didn't realize how hungry I was.'

Charlie's lips twitched. 'Pizza for me, I think.'

'Me too.' She closed her menu and took a sip of her wine. 'Thanks again for today.'

'You're welcome. I hope Mark has learned something from this. He really needs to put some security measures in place.'

Anna didn't reply as the waitress arrived to take their order but when they were alone again, she resumed the conversation. 'You were talking about safety measures. Like what?'

He shrugged. 'You should always call back viewers before a viewing, that way you know the phone number is legitimate.'

'Good idea.'

'And you should always make sure that the office knows where you are. Maybe you could call them after each viewing so that if they don't hear from you, they'll know something's wrong.'

She shook her head. 'It gets way too busy in our office for that and there's only Mark, Val and me. Half the time, Val's there alone.'

'Then send her a text.'

'You're full of good ideas, aren't you? Anyway, here's to you, Charlie, my knight in faded denim. I don't know what I'd have done without you.'

'Hey, you're making me blush. I'm sure if Liam had been at home you would have been fine.'

'If,' Anna said with feeling, and instantly regretted it. Bloody booze, it always loosened her tongue and got her saying things she shouldn't.

'I take it you're not impressed that he's gone home to Mummy.'

Anna scowled. 'It's not like that. She's sick, she needs him.'

'Of course.'

'Charlie, stop trying to wind me up.'

'Hey, what did I say now?' He stared at her, all innocence.

'Nothing. I suppose I'm a bit sensitive at the moment. And no, I'm not happy about Liam going to his mother's.' There, she'd done it again. 'But she needs help and he's the only one she's got. It's just until she gets used to the crutches, anyway, so it's no big deal.'

'He's still out of work, I take it.'

Anna nodded. 'Although he had an interview on Friday and apparently it went very well.'

'Good. These past few months can't have been easy for you both.'

Anna took another drink. 'They haven't.'

'Want to talk about it?'

'No, Charlie, I don't. Now stop fishing.'

'Just making conversation.'

'No, you're not. You're trying to find out how strong my marriage is.'

Charlie raised an eyebrow. 'And why would I want to know that?'

Anna looked away. Those dark, gorgeous eyes always seemed to be able to see right inside her.

'Oh, I don't know.'

'Yes, you do,' he murmured, resting his chin on his palms and looking into her eyes. 'You know exactly why I want to know. You know that I fancy you, can't stop thinking about you and, right now, I'd really love to kiss you.'

Anna sat mesmerized, her eyes moving from his eyes to his mouth and back again. 'You can't say things like that.'

'I just did.'

'Margarita?'

Anna jerked back and stared at the bored waiter. 'Oh yes, that's me.'

'And pepperoni?'

Charlie nodded, not taking his eyes off Anna.

'This looks nice,' she said, when the waiter had topped up their wine glasses and left.

'So what would you do, Anna?'

'Pardon?'

'If I kissed you, what would you do?'

Anna laughed nervously. 'I'd kill you. I mean, how public can you get?'

'Ah, so you don't object to the kiss, just the location.'

'No! That's not what I meant! You're twisting things.'

'Am I?' Charlie bit into a slice of pizza with perfect white teeth.

Anna bent her head over her dinner. 'You've had too much wine.'

'Actually, I've only had about half a glass. I'm driving, remember?'

Anna looked in dismay from her glass to the half-empty bottle. No wonder she was feeling woozy.

'So, where shall we do it?' Charlie continued.

'Do what?'

'Kiss. I suppose we could go back to your place . . .'

'Are you mad?'

'Then it will have to be my place.' Charlie produced a key from his pocket. 'Paul Brennan has been very helpful. He even gave me a key in case I needed to measure up for curtains.' He winked at her. 'You could hold my tape measure.'

'Charlie!'

'It's the perfect answer if you think about it. If anyone sees you there they'll just think you're on business.'

'I am not coming back to your house,' Anna hissed.

'But you do want me to kiss you.'

'I do not!'

'You disappoint me, Anna. I always thought you were such an honest woman.'

'I am!'

'Then look me in the eye and tell me that you don't want to kiss me.'

Anna's eyes met his. 'It's never going to happen.'

'Ah ha!' Charlie grinned delightedly. 'You couldn't say it!'

Anna put down her knife and fork and raised her eyes to his. 'No, I couldn't. And maybe I do fancy you, Charlie, but I'm married and I don't play around.'

'And yet you'd like me to kiss you. What a wonderful compliment.'

'Charlie, stop,' she begged, throwing down her napkin. 'This was a bad idea. I should never have suggested dinner. I'm obviously sending out the wrong signals.'

'Or the right ones.'

'Charlie—'

'Come back to the house with me,' he urged, reaching across to take her hand.

His touch was electric and Anna stared at the dark hairs on the back of his hand, as his fingers stroked the inside of her palm. It was so innocent and yet it was turning her insides to liquid. She looked up into his face and nodded.

Charlie's eyes lit up and immediately he signalled to the waiter for the bill.

They drove to the house in silence, Charlie keeping a tight hold of her hand, even when he was changing gear. Anna felt as if she was in the middle of a dream and she didn't particularly want to wake up. This was wrong, she knew that, but she couldn't help the excitement she felt at the thought of being alone with Charlie in a deserted house with no one to disturb them.

Charlie turned into the driveway and parked to one side, where the car wouldn't be visible from the road. Turning off the engine he turned to face her. 'Last chance.'

Anna looked at him and said nothing.

Charlie groaned and brought his lips down on hers in a hungry, probing kiss. Anna felt herself melt against him and before she realized what she was doing, her hands were tangled in his hair, pulling him closer.

Charlie pulled away, his breath ragged. 'Let's go inside.'

Looking into his eyes, Anna knew she was agreeing to a lot more than a kiss. With a barely imperceptible nod, she picked up her bag, got out of the car and stood waiting for Charlie to unlock the house. She noticed that his hands were trembling, too.

'Oh! The alarm isn't on. I'll have to make a complaint. Anyone could just wander in here and do what they like.' With a slow smile, he pulled her towards him and kissed the tip of her nose. 'You are gorgeous.'

'Who's that? Who's there?' Anna and Charlie sprang apart as the light went on and Paul Brennan emerged from the kitchen. 'Charlie! Anna! Jesus, you put the heart crossways on me!'

Charlie laughed. 'Sorry about that, Paul. I bumped into Anna in the village and persuaded her to come and give me her opinion on my ideas for the kitchen.'

'Oh, right.'

'But you're busy, so we'll come back some other time,' Charlie continued.

'No problem. The removal van is coming tomorrow but I wanted to collect some of the more fragile pieces myself.'

'You're right, those guys aren't exactly careful, are they?'

As the two men chatted, Anna moved back towards the door, wishing the ground would open up and swallow her.

'Anna's been telling me that my lawyer is playing silly beggars and holding things up.'

'Yes, well, he seems a bit hung up on paperwork,' Paul grunted.

'I'll talk to him first thing,' Charlie promised.

'Right.' Paul looked from him to Anna. 'So, are you going to take a look at the kitchen?'

Anna glanced at her watch. 'You know, Charlie, it's really late. Would you mind if we did this some other time?'

'No, of course not, Anna. I'm sorry if I've delayed you.'

'That's okay. Nice to see you again, Paul. Good luck with the move.'

'Thanks, Anna, bye-bye.'

Charlie stretched out his hand to shake Paul's. 'You should be hearing from my lawyer tomorrow. If there are any more problems, just give me a call.'

'Appreciate that. Good night, now, safe home.'

'Jesus.' Anna breathed when they were back in the car. 'I have never been so humiliated in my life. What must he think of me?'

'What's the problem?'

Anna stared at him. 'What's the problem? Are you kidding me? Do you honestly think he believed that we went there to look at the kitchen?'

Charlie grinned. 'Probably not.'

'How can you be so blasé?' she exploded. 'What if he says something to Mark?'

'What if he does? Mark's a friend. He's not going to tell anyone, certainly not your husband.'

'Oh right, so it's all boys together, is it? Tell me, do

you cover for each other often? How many other married women have you brought to your new house?'

Charlie pulled into the side of the road and turned to face her. 'Now you're just being silly.'

'Well, it's okay for you—' But she didn't get any further because Charlie was kissing her again.

Anna gave herself up to his kiss, thinking how soft his lips were for a man and what a damn good kisser he was. 'No, no,' she said, finally pulling back. 'Not here, not like this.'

Charlie took her hand and kissed her palm. 'Then where and when? Can I come back with you now?'

'No!'

'Don't make me wait, Anna, I don't think I can.' He dropped her hand and bent his head to kiss the side of her neck.

Anna gasped and closed her eyes. 'Oh, please stop, Charlie. Anyone could come along.'

'Let's go to a hotel. No one will know. Liam's not going to miss you.'

'He'll be phoning and wondering where I am.' Anna glanced at the clock; to her dismay, it was nearly ten o'clock. 'Shit, I've got to go.'

'Call him on your mobile. Tell him you're just about to go to bed.' Charlie's eyes twinkled wickedly as he pushed her shirt back and began to kiss her shoulder.

Anna pulled back, horrified. 'I couldn't do something like that!'

'Hey, I'm sorry, it was just a joke.'

Anna straightened her clothes and turned away from him. 'Please take me home.'

'Only if you promise to meet me tomorrow.'

'I'll get out and walk,' she threatened, her hand on the door handle.

'Okay, okay.' He turned on the engine and drove back on to the road. 'I'm sorry, I didn't mean to upset you.' He put his hand on her thigh and squeezed it. 'It's just I'm so crazy about you.'

Anna closed her eyes. Her head was beginning to throb and she felt a bit sick. 'I just want to go home.'

Charlie turned up the radio and said no more until he'd stopped the car outside her house. 'Will you meet me tomorrow?'

'I don't know.' She had already opened the door and was stepping out of the car.

'I'll phone you.'

'No. No, I'll phone you.'

Charlie leaned across so that he could look up at her. 'Promise?'

She nodded and hurried inside. As he drove away, Anna flopped on to the bottom of the stairs and closed her eyes.

'Anna?'

Her eyes flew open again and she looked up to see Liam's silhouette in the sitting-room doorway. 'Liam!'

Chapter 32

'What are you doing here?'

'I thought you'd need the car tomorrow and that maybe we could talk. Where have you been? Who was that dropping you off?'

Anna couldn't believe that she hadn't even noticed her car outside. She'd really have to give up alcohol.

'Anna?' Liam's face was pale, his lips in a thin line.

'That was Charlie Coleman, a client and a good friend of Mark's. There was a bit of trouble today and I didn't want to come home to an empty house so he took me out for a pizza.' Pizza sounded much more respectable than dinner, she thought.

'What kind of trouble?' Liam was still looking suspicious.

'I was showing Beech Wood to a couple. You know the old house out on the back road?'

Liam nodded.

'But only the husband turned up. When we got as far as the bathroom he pinned me against the wall and started groping me.'

'Oh Anna!' Liam was on his knees at her side, his eyes now full of concern, and his fingers stroking her cheek.

'It's okay. I managed to get away. When I got into the car I phoned Mark and he came over with the police. He told me to go home but I was shaking so much I was afraid of crashing. I pulled into the filling station and just sat there. The next thing I knew, Charlie was hammering on my window.'

'Oh love, why didn't you call me?' Liam pulled her into his arms and cradled her like a baby.

'You had enough on your plate,' she said weakly. 'I didn't want to give you anything else to worry about.'

'Did the police catch the bastard?'

She shook her head. 'No, he was gone by the time they got there and it turned out he'd given a fake contact number.'

'You should never have been put in that position. Mark is going to have to take steps to make sure this doesn't happen again.'

'That's what Charlie says.'

'So you went out with this Charlie guy?'

She nodded. 'Like I said, I couldn't face coming home.'

Liam pulled back to look at her face. 'So who drank the saké?'

'Oh, I did, I forgot. Sorry, it must be the wine. Charlie brought me home, but I'd forgotten you weren't going to be here. When Charlie went to leave, I realized I couldn't stay here alone so we went back into the village.'

'You could have asked him to drop you over to me,' he pointed out.

'Like I said, I didn't want to worry you.'

'I called your mobile a few times.'

'I switched it off. I wasn't exactly in any condition to talk.'

He hugged her to him and kissed the top of her head. 'I don't suppose this is the best time for a chat either. And I really should be getting back to Mum.'

'Oh, of course, she'll probably be nervous on her own.' Anna stopped at the guilty look on Liam's face. 'Ah, she's not alone, is she?'

'Tara dropped in to see how Mum was and she offered to stay with her until I got back.'

'That was nice of her.'

'Anna—'

She stood up. 'It's okay, Liam. Look, I'm exhausted. You get home to your mum and we'll talk tomorrow.'

'I hate leaving you. Are you sure you're all right?'

'Fine.'

'Okay, then. Lock up when I'm gone, will you?'

'I will, stop worrying.'

After the door had shut behind him, Anna collapsed back on to the stairs and buried her head in her hands. That had been so close! What if she'd gone to a hotel with Charlie? Or worse, what if they'd kissed again outside the house or she'd brought him inside? Not that she would have, of course. She dragged a hand through her hair and groaned. As if going to an empty house with him was any better, she thought, knowing full well what would have happened if Paul Brennan hadn't appeared. She and Charlie would have had sex, and even though the fact riddled her with guilt, she knew that she'd really wanted it.

As she moved around the house, locking doors and turning off lights before carrying a large glass of water to bed, she relived the moment when Liam had appeared in the sitting-room doorway. She'd felt physically sick, thinking she'd been discovered. If she hadn't been attacked today, it would have been very hard to come up with a plausible reason for Charlie's presence. She shuddered, thinking how strange it was to be grateful to a terrifying pervert who'd tried to rape her.

Anna undressed and climbed under the covers, aghast at how easily she'd lied to Liam and how readily he'd believed her. How could she even think of starting a family with him if she went to bed with the first man who asked her?

Anna closed her eyes tight and tried to banish the image of Paul Brennan's knowing look. God, he probably thought she did this on a regular basis. His image was replaced by that of Liam, and how his closed, guarded expression had melted into one of tender concern when she'd told him about the attack.

Well, that was it, she certainly wouldn't see Charlie again, but what about Liam? If she truly loved him, surely she'd never have gone with Charlie in the first place? And yet, if she didn't love Liam, why was she so jealous of Tara? The questions ran round and round in her head until she finally fell into a troubled sleep where strange men lurked in shadows and she was chased by Charlie while Liam watched.

Liam was glad he'd put the bike in the boot rather than taking a taxi home. While he cycled through the clear night air he was able to think, and the physical exercise helped to keep his increasing panic at bay. Between his mother's accident and Anna's attack there was plenty going on to distract him. But still, at the back of his mind there was a little voice reminding him that he hadn't got a phone call. The interview had only been on Friday and, for all he knew, they could be doing more interviews this week but that didn't matter. He'd expected a call. He knew in his heart that he'd done an excellent interview and he knew they'd been impressed. He should have heard something by now. He'd called the recruitment company first thing this morning to give them his mother's phone number, and any time he'd left the house, he'd placed the phone by Josie's bed. He was beginning to wish he'd taken Anna's advice and bought a cheap mobile phone. It would be much better to be contactable wherever he was. Maybe tomorrow he could slip out and get one – there was a good place in the village where Tara had bought her latest snazzy new phone.

He turned on to Ballymun Avenue and into a freezing cold wind. Crouching lower over the handlebars, Liam pushed himself even harder, almost enjoying the pain in his calf muscles. Physical pain was a lot easier to deal with than the emotional stuff. On one side, he had Anna who seemed to be moving further away from him, and he wasn't sure how to get her back or even if he should. On the other, he had Tara, gorgeous, sexy and funny, but she was beginning to suffocate him.

They'd fallen into the habit of having the odd cuppa together but recently, Tara had started wearing fewer clothes when he was around and making some very suggestive comments. Liam, who had been enjoying the mild flirting, had gotten the fright of his life. Tara had practically offered herself on a plate, making it clear that while she'd accept the post of mistress in the short term, she'd expect a bit more at a later stage. Liam had immediately pulled back and tried to visit his mother only when Tara was busy with clients, but Josie's accident had put paid to that strategy. Tara had been on the doorstep within seconds of them arriving home from the hospital today, and while she'd said all the right things and sympathized with Josie, she couldn't hide her delight when Josie had told her that he was moving in for a few days. When Josie had added that Liam had to drop back to his house later, Tara had immediately offered her services. When Liam had thanked her, she'd winked at him and said that he could make it up to her later. Liam groaned at the memory.

As he got nearer to his childhood home, he wondered how he'd get it through to her that he wasn't interested. She would be upset because, in a way, he had led her on. He'd given her the whole 'my wife doesn't understand me' spiel and lapped up the sympathy she'd given in return. And while he hadn't made any moves on her, he hadn't pulled away when she'd put a hand on his thigh or leaned up against him or bent over him in a low top showing off small but exquisite breasts. It would be a lot easier to go to bed with her and have done with it, but the thought of being unfaithful to Anna sickened him.

When she'd arrived home tonight in another man's car, he couldn't believe the wave of jealousy that had engulfed him. It had been like a slap in the face. It was a relief of course to know that the man had only been a friend in need, but Liam still couldn't help feeling that she should have called him. In the old days she would have. He had always been the one she turned to first when she was upset or in trouble. But she obviously didn't see him in that way any more. Now he was an unemployed, broke loser who spent his days wallowing in self-pity.

After his interview on Friday, Liam had been in buoyant form and when Anna had called, it felt like fate, and he was convinced that they could get back on track. But today he hadn't heard about the job and when his wife had been in trouble she'd turned to someone else. He was surplus to requirements, he thought miserably as he turned into the driveway and got off his bike. Tara and his mother were the only ones who wanted him. Somehow that thought depressed him even more.

Chapter 33

Jill's first day back at work had been as frenetic as she'd expected and more. Vinny had been lighting a few fires in her absence and ruffling a lot of feathers. Many of those who had supported him in the past were beginning to see him as a threat, and even Sue had upbraided him on one occasion.

'He's inclined to take too much on himself,' she'd told Jill, 'and though I'm the first to encourage independence and ambition, he needs reminding that he's part of a team.'

Jill should have been overjoyed at this little titbit of information but in her head she'd already moved on and Vinny Gray's machinations no longer interested her. She had sat in the large boardroom today watching her colleagues bicker, debate, nitpick and backbite and she'd felt like a scientist studying a swarm of angry, demented ants.

Whatever had attracted her to this job, she'd wondered, recalling how she used to be in the thick of these sessions. How could anyone get so worked up over an advertisement for crisps? When she thought of the money she earned, the car she drove, the generous bonuses that she got paid and the relative pittance that teachers, nurses, or firemen received, she felt humble and somehow ashamed.

As she finished tidying her desk and rose to leave, Jill chuckled at the way her mind was working. Next thing, she'd find God and go off and join a cult in the middle of nowhere! She could see herself now – hair tied back, no make-up, making sandals and growing vegetables, living on home-made soups and rough bread. Not!

Jill called an immediate halt to her fantasy. Wherever she ended up and whatever she ended up doing, she was determined there would be no more dieting. She loved her food and that was that; so what if she was a little on the curvy side? It hadn't stopped her attracting some seriously fine-looking men.

She sighed as she remembered Andy and his gorgeous, sexy smile. There had been no one else since they'd broken up. Somehow, Jill hadn't been able to get him out of her head. She'd thought of calling him a couple of times but she always chickened out, too proud to go crawling back. What if he turned her down flat, how embarrassing would that be? It would be so much better, she thought, as she picked up her briefcase and headed for the door, if they just ran into each other in a pub or restaurant. Then she could check out the lie of the land without making an idiot of herself.

Not that she was going to have much time for socializing now, she reminded herself as she breezed through Reception giving the security man a friendly wave. She had to sell her car, her apartment – oh yes, and hand in her notice. Strangely, the only thing that she had doubts about was giving up her beloved car. She patted the glossy hood lovingly before slipping behind the wheel. Her apartment had always been more of a statement than a home, and as for her job, well, it had been fun but now it was time to go.

Jill had promised Kitty that she'd be over in time to help out with the Christmas rush. They had agreed on a six-month contract to allow them both a chance to see if they could work well together. Then, Jill would either buy into the business or move on to pastures new. The latter, Jill believed, was unlikely. Kitty O'Driscoll seemed to be a woman after her own heart. Kitty's plans to expand the bar into a full apartment complex were comprehensive and well thought out. She had a good head for business but, at the moment, she didn't have the time or the cash to implement her plans. If things worked out and Jill came on board, she would have both.

This was a big move for Jill and she could imagine her parents' reaction when she told them, but she knew it was something she had to do. For the first time in months she felt adrenaline course through her veins, as she contemplated the challenges ahead. To finance the project she would need every penny she had. To cut costs she would live over the bar and buy a moped or use Kitty's van to get around. It was going to be a far cry from the level of luxury she was currently used to, but Jill didn't care. It would all be worth it in the end. A new country, a new lifestyle and hopefully, less stress, although Kitty had warned her that running a restaurant was a very stressful business indeed.

Jill didn't doubt it but she was used to pressure and hard work. In ADLI, she'd often worked round the clock to impossible deadlines and limited budgets. In Spain she might have to work equally hard but it would be for her and she wouldn't have any office politics to contend with.

As Jill drove to her parents' house, she pondered when to tell everyone her plans. Being her usual independent self, she didn't feel the need to consult her parents or friends about her decision and she didn't want advice. But she would like their blessing. After the initial shock, she felt sure that she would get that from her cousins. As for Mam and Dad . . . ah well, they'd come around eventually. After all, they'd have somewhere new to go on their holidays. The flat over the restaurant was small but it had a second bedroom so she would be able to have family and friends to stay. No, she was completely confident that she was doing the right thing and had no regrets about what she was leaving behind – with the possible exception of Andy.

Jill couldn't help but feel that she'd made a big

mistake ending it with him. They'd enjoyed an easy-going, relaxed relationship that she'd never found with a man before. Andy had not only made her pulse quicken; he'd made her laugh as well. She'd be very lucky indeed if she found another man like him. Still; he was gone now and there was no point in dwelling on it.

Her mother was cleaning the front window when she pulled up outside the house.

'Shouldn't Dad be doing that?' Jill called as she got out of the car.

Pat looked around at her daughter and smiled. 'I won't hold my breath.'

'Good to see you, Ma,' Jill said, kissing her cheek.

'Nice holiday?' Pat asked, leading her daughter inside.

'It was great. Bridie and Shay send their love.'

'How is he?'

'Not a bother.'

'He had it coming, you know, although I blame Bridie. She feeds him all the wrong food.'

'Not any more,' Jill assured her, taking off her jacket. 'They've gone all Mediterranean.'

Pat sniffed. 'Boiled potatoes, poached fish and plenty of greens, they're what the man needs. Look at your father, almost five years older than Shay and in the whole of his health.'

'Thank God,' Jill said automatically. 'Where is he?'

'At a Neighbourhood Watch meeting in the community centre.'

'Telling the Gardaí what they should be doing, no doubt.' Jill laughed.

'Someone has to,' Pat told her. 'So what's the news? Are they coming home?'

'They'll come back for the birth.' Jill watched as her mother made a pot of tea and took some buns out of a cake tin.

'Are they going to stay?' Pat quizzed.

'I don't think so.'

Pat shook her head. 'I don't know what they think they're doing. They're behaving like a couple of teenagers.'

'Would you not be tempted, Ma?'

'Indeed I would not,' Pat scoffed. 'Why would I leave my own lovely home?'

'You don't have to do anything as drastic as selling up,' Jill pointed out. 'Just take a couple of holidays abroad now and then. You must know every last inch of Enniscrone and Wexford at this stage. Aren't there countries or cities you've always wanted to visit? Rome? Naples? My God, you haven't even seen London, have you?'

'And what would I do in London?' Pat said. 'One city is no different to another. I'm quite happy to stay in my own country, thank you very much. Although your father was saying that maybe we would go up to Donegal next year,' she confided. 'Wouldn't that be lovely?'

'Lovely.' Jill smiled. Her mother was nothing like her sister Bridie and she'd never change. It was funny, Anna and Rachel wanted their parents to be conventional and traditional and to stay at home, while she was trying to persuade hers to be more adventurous.

'So.' Pat sat down opposite her daughter and lifted her cup to her lips. 'Any news?'

'News' was Pat's coded way of asking Jill if there was a man in her life. She wasn't interested in her daughter's successful career. She wanted to see her march up the aisle and have lots of babies, preferably in that order. That was real success as far as Pat was concerned.

'None,' she told her mother.

Pat sighed. 'How's Rachel coping? Is she huge?'

'Not really. She found the heat a bit much in Spain and her feet swelled up like balloons in the evening.'

'I was just the same when I had you,' Pat told her. 'The poor love, I must give her a ring.'

'She'd like that. I think she's missing Bridie.'

'Well, of course she is. She needs her now more than ever. And little Alex could do with his grand-parents too. It's hard for little ones when a new baby comes along. They need to be pampered and reassured.'

'Well, like I said, they are coming home for the birth,' Jill reminded her.

'Yes, but for how long? They really should be a bit more responsible at their age,' Pat tut-tutted. 'And now that Shay's health is failing he'd be better off settling down.'

'His health is not failing,' Jill protested. 'He just has a bloody ulcer.'

'No need for that language,' Pat retorted.

'Sorry.'

'Has Liam found himself a job yet?' Pat asked as she poured herself more tea and pushed the cakes towards her daughter.

Jill shook her head and helped herself to one.

'I don't know what his problem is. There's plenty of work out there for those willing to do it,' Pat said self-righteously. He's too picky, that's all. It's that mother of his and her airs and graces. Josie Harrison always thought she was better than the rest of us. She certainly thought Liam was too good for our Anna and now look at them. He's idling at home and she's the breadwinner.'

'Liam hates being unemployed,' Jill said, sneaking a look at her watch and standing up.

'Are you going already?' Pat said, disappointed.

'Yeah, sorry, I've got to meet someone.'

'A man?' Pat's eyes lit up.

'Yes,' Jill confirmed with a wink. 'He's tall, dark and about Dad's age.'

'Jill!' Pat's eyes were like saucers.

'Don't worry, Ma, it's business.'

'Huh, aren't you very funny?' Pat started to clear away the dishes. 'You and your work! Don't you think it's time you concentrated a bit more on your own life and forgot about that company for a while?'

Jill nodded. 'Yes, Ma, as it happens, I do.' Planting a quick kiss on her mother's cheek, she made a quick exit before Pat could question her further. 'I'll see you at the weekend,' she called as she headed for the door, grabbing her jacket off the banister in the hall. 'Tell Dad I said hi.'

'Will you be here for dinner on Sunday?' Pat hurried after her. 'I was going to do a nice pork roast.'

'I'll be here,' Jill promised, getting into her car. 'See you, Ma.'

As Jill drove away she could imagine the conversation at her parents' table that evening. 'That daughter of yours still doesn't have a man,' her mother would start. Her father would grunt and keep eating while her mother would remind him that both Anna and Rachel were settled, Rachel with her second child on the way, and yet 'his daughter' was only married to her job.

Well, Jill didn't think that was such a bad way to be. Look at Kitty O'Driscoll. There was an advertisement for living alone if ever there was one. According to Pepe, the business was more successful now than it had been when her husband ran it, and Kitty had every single male in the area queuing up to take her out. Jill grinned to herself. A queue of men would be very nice. If she ever got the time off to go out, that is. Kitty had warned her that the hours would be unsocial but given that they were in the centre of town, there was nearly always something to do or somewhere to go. Still, she'd miss meeting Anna for lunch and having girly nights out.

But tonight she had to see if she could get a good price for her car. There was a dealer coming over to see it and Jill was hoping he'd make her a reasonable offer. Then she could concentrate on selling the apartment. She was confident that she would sell it easily as it was in an excellent and tranquil location, surprisingly spacious, and it came with its own parking spot, something very coveted in this area. She would ask Anna to handle the sale, of course, but not just yet.

First, she wanted to hand in her notice and she couldn't do that until she'd had a quiet word with Karen and her team. She might be walking away from her career but she was still very aware of the responsibility she had to them, especially with a shark like Vinny around. She had allowed herself a week to do this and then she would talk to Sue. She was curious as to how her resignation would be received. Sue was a pragmatist and would probably wish her well and turn her mind towards the matter of a replacement. Vinny would be positively triumphant and the others would no doubt see it as an opportunity. And if they didn't, she'd tell them in no uncertain terms that it was time to reconsider their positions. This was a competitive business and no place for people who wanted a quiet life with a generous salary at the end of every month.

Jill drove into her apartment complex and parked the car in its designated spot. It was amazing that she could feel so happy about leaving all this, she marvelled as she watched the electric gates close behind her. She'd come a long way from her childhood in a three-bedroom council house in Malahide. And though her mother didn't understand why her daughter was so driven, she knew that both of her parents were proud of her and boasted of her success to anyone who'd listen. What they would make of her leaving it all behind to go and work her butt off in a restaurant in Spain she could only imagine. She laughed at her own stupidity. She wouldn't have to imagine at all. Her ma and dad wouldn't think twice about telling her exactly what they thought!

Chapter 34

Anna dragged herself into the office, thanking God it was Friday. Since that dreadful day of her attack, she had avoided Charlie like the plague. He had got more persistent as time went on and she'd resorted to erasing his texts without even reading them. She didn't trust herself with him and if she read his messages or took his calls, she knew that she'd probably end up agreeing to see him. That would be disastrous. She and Liam talked briefly every day, but any time he'd suggested having 'that chat' she'd fobbed him off. Ironic, really. She'd tried to get him talking for months and now when he was ready to do just that, she couldn't handle it. Feelings of guilt consumed her and she didn't think she could even look him in the eye.

She had, of course, had to call over to see Josie but she managed to spend the evening concentrating all her attention on her mother-in-law. When it was time for her to go, she hurried out to the car, imagining Tara Brady's eyes on her. Of course, for her benefit, Anna should have kissed Liam long and hard at the garden gate but she couldn't bring herself to do it. She felt dirty, sick and cheap.

The only consolation was that she hadn't actually had sex with Charlie. But she couldn't take any credit for that. If Paul Brennan hadn't appeared on the scene she would have gone the whole way, without even a thought for Liam. And the reason she was avoiding Charlie was because she still wasn't sure she could trust herself alone with him. The attraction between them was palpable. How that left her marriage or her commitment to Liam was another matter. She just knew she couldn't cope with either man at the moment.

Today she was going to do her first viewing since her attack and she had to psych herself up for that. Val had begged her to leave it for another few days but Anna knew that Mark's patience was wearing thin and she was afraid he'd start thinking she wasn't up to the job any more.

'I'll come with you,' he'd offered when she'd told him that she was going out today, but she refused with what she hoped was a confident smile.

'There's no need, Mark. Val has called this couple a few times and they are genuine buyers. I'll be fine.'

'Bring your mobile and call us if you have any problems, any problems at all,' he'd said, patting her arm awkwardly.

'I will, thanks.' But Anna was determined to stand on her own two feet.

She was just getting ready to leave when the phone rang and Val held it out to her. 'It's your sister.'

'Oh.' Anna sat back down to take the call. She hadn't talked to Rachel all week although her sister had called a few times. 'Hi, Rache.'

'Anna, hi, is everything okay? Haven't you got my messages?'

'Yeah, sorry, Rache, it's just been a bit mad here.'

'How's Josie?'

'Getting around a lot better now.'

'So is Liam coming home?'

'Er, probably not. Look, Rache, I'm late for an appointment.'

'Okay, okay.' Rachel sounded irritable. 'I was just calling to invite you to tea tomorrow – and Liam too of course if he's home.'

'I'm not sure . . .'

'Alex has been asking for you. I thought it would be a nice surprise for him.'

'Okay, then, Rache, I'll be there.'

'About five, okay?'

'Yes, five is fine, see you then.'

Anna hung up with a sigh. She would much prefer to spend tomorrow in bed but she had promised Alex at the airport that she would see him soon. Anyway, playing Power Rangers or cards with her nephew might be the very distraction she needed at the moment.

Val walked back into the room as she was pulling

her jacket on. 'Will you be okay, love?' she asked, her eyes full of concern.

'I'll be fine,' Anna assured her. 'I should be back in an hour or so.'

'Call me when you're on your way,' Val urged.

'I will.'

Anna hurried out to her car and drove the short distance to the new estate by the sea. The property for sale was in a busy road, littered with bikes, prams and skateboards, and there were two mums having a chat at a gate nearby. Anna started to relax. It was a total contrast to the afternoon at Beech Wood and she felt her confidence returning. She wouldn't let that animal stop her doing the job she loved. She glanced up as a red Opel Corsa rounded the corner and pulled up across the road. A young girl got out from behind the wheel and waved to her before going to help an older woman from the passenger seat.

'Anna?' she asked as they crossed the road.

Anna held out her hand and smiled. 'That's right. You must be Delia Cross?'

Delia nodded. 'Yes, and this is my mum, Celia. Tommy couldn't come so I roped Mum in instead.'

Anna suppressed a smile as she shook the other woman's hand. Celia and Delia! 'Let's go in.'

Delia fell in love with the property almost immediately, and though Celia was more cautious, she agreed that the house had a lot of promise. 'You'd need to change the bathroom suite,' she told her daughter.

'And the kitchen,' Delia said. 'But this house is way under our budget so we could afford to.'

Anna led them out into the back garden. 'If you wanted to extend at any stage, planning permission shouldn't be a problem.' She pointed at two other houses further down that had extensions. 'They've set a precedent so it should be easy for you to do the same.'

'Oh, we could have a conservatory.' Delia rubbed her hands together, her eyes twinkling.

Celia rolled her eyes. 'Don't get too carried away, love. We still have some other properties to look at.' She directed this at Anna.

'No problem,' Anna assured her.

'Could I bring Tommy back to see it over the weekend?' Delia asked, ignoring her mother's disapproving look.

'I'd have to check with the vendors but we could probably set something up for tomorrow. I would have to give them some notice,' she warned.

'I'll talk to Tommy this afternoon and call you then.'

'That's fine.' Anna led them back outside and locked the hall door.

'It's a lovely area, isn't it, Mum?'

'Very nice,' Celia agreed, 'but I still think you should see the other properties.'

'Okay, Mum, come on. But I'm telling you this is the one. I'll call you later, Anna.'

Anna smiled at them both. 'I'll look forward to it.'

Back in her car, she heaved a sigh of relief. The viewing couldn't have gone better. As soon as she'd got into her spiel, she'd felt fine. She called Val and told her the good news.

'Oh, I'm so glad, Anna. I was worried about you.'

'No need, and as I'm ahead of schedule and it's such a nice day, I'm going to drop over to the property on Redfern Road and take the outside photos.'

'Shall I call them and let them know you're coming? If they're in, you could get the measurements done at the same time?'

'Good idea.'

'Right, I'll call you back in a minute.'

Anna drove out of the estate, down through the village and out the other side. She was only a minute's drive from Redfern Road and Val hadn't called back. Glancing at the fuel gauge, Anna decided to get petrol while she was waiting. She was just twisting the petrol cap back on when her mobile rang. Without looking at the display, she pressed the button and jammed it against her ear. 'Hi, Val,' she said as she went inside to pay.

'It's not Val.'

She closed her eyes as she recognized Charlie's voice. 'I'm afraid I'm in a meeting, Charlie, can I get back to you?'

'No, you're not. You're getting petrol and I'm sitting across the road watching you.'

Anna whirled around and saw Charlie sitting on

his motorbike. 'Meet me down at the entrance to the park,' he told her.

'I can't, I'm on my way to a client,' she hissed, as she went into the shop and shoved a 50 Euro note at the attendant.

'I won't keep you long,' Charlie promised. 'It's your choice. You can meet me or I can follow you back to the office and come in. I think Mark would be very surprised that you didn't want to talk to your knight in shining armour.'

Anna sighed as she took her change and came back out to the car. 'Five minutes, Charlie,' she said, meeting his eyes as she got into her car.

'Great.' Charlie roared off down the road and Anna followed him more slowly.

When she pulled in beside him, Charlie had already removed his helmet and was climbing off his bike. She got out of the car, realizing that it would be a mistake to let him get in beside her.

Charlie grinned knowingly. 'What's the matter, Anna, don't you trust yourself?'

Before she could answer, Anna's mobile rang. This time it was Val.

'I'm afraid you can't take those photos after all, love,' she told Anna. 'They have a skip in the drive-way today, they're doing a good clear-out. It should be collected before noon tomorrow so you can do it then or leave it until Monday.'

'Oh, right. Thanks, Val.'

'No problem. See you later.'

'I have to go,' Anna told Charlie, when she'd rung off.

'Liar.' He settled back against the bonnet of her car. 'Val has a very loud voice. It sounds to me like you have plenty of time.'

'I've a mountain of work waiting for me back at the office.'

'Then the sooner you talk to me, the sooner you can get back to it.'

Anna tossed her phone back into the car and went to perch on the low wall nearby. 'What do you want, Charlie?'

'You know what I want,' he murmured.

'That night was a mistake. I was upset and I was drunk . . .'

'And you wanted me,' he finished.

'So, what if I did? That's just sex, Charlie. It doesn't mean anything.'

'You're lying again.'

'Please,' she begged. 'Just leave me alone.' She looked around nervously as a car drove past. 'I can't stay here – anyone might see me.'

'We're not doing anything,' he said, crossing his arms. 'Yet.'

'Oh, and what did you have in mind? A roll in the grass?'

He threw back his head and laughed. 'I'm game if you are, but after that rain last night, it might be a bit damp.'

Anna had to smile.

'That's better,' he murmured. 'Now – how are you?'

She nodded. 'I'm fine.'

'That's great. How's your mother-in-law?'

'Okay.'

'And your husband?'

Anna looked away. 'He was waiting for me when I got home that night.'

'What? But I thought he was staying with his mother.'

'He was – he is – but he'd called over to see me. He'd been waiting ages.' Anna closed her eyes as she remembered the expression on Liam's face.

'What did you tell him?'

'The truth – well, some of it. I told him about the attack and that you'd discovered me in the filling station and brought me for a pizza.'

'And?'

She shrugged. 'He was upset about the attack and that I hadn't called him.'

'So, it's okay then.'

'You mean we got away with it?'

'We didn't do a whole lot,' he reminded her.

Anna studied her hands. She wasn't going to admit to him that she was guilty as hell in her head. They may not have gone the whole way, but she'd wanted to. Just then, he came to sit beside her, very close but not actually touching. Anna could feel his breath on her cheek and smell his cologne. Desire rose up in her and she had to steel herself not to turn her head and kiss him.

'You want me as much as I want you,' he said, his mouth close to her ear.

'I'm married,' Anna said, moving away.

'Not happily.'

'What would you know?' she retorted.

'Don't deny it, Anna.'

'We're going through a bad patch,' she admitted, 'but we'll be okay.'

'Really?' Charlie tucked a tendril of hair behind her ear and she shuddered at his touch.

'Really.' Anna stood up and went back to her car. 'Please leave me alone, Charlie. My marriage won't have a chance if you don't.'

'Maybe it's already over,' he suggested. 'Maybe it's time you both moved on.'

'How can you say that? You don't know anything about us!'

'I know that you're here with me.'

'Yes, but now I'm leaving.' And before he could say another word, Anna slid behind the wheel, shut her door and drove away.

When she got back into the office Anna threw herself into her work, making it clear to Val that she had no time to chat. Val, to her credit, left her alone, but put a strong cup of coffee and two chocolate biscuits by her elbow and patted her shoulder. Anna smiled her thanks and went back to work. She was in the middle of trying to write some creative prose about a particularly nondescript house when Jill phoned. Unlike Rachel, Jill knew all about the attack. She also knew that Anna was showing a property today.

'How did it go?' she asked.

For a moment, Anna thought she meant her meeting with Charlie and then realized what her cousin was talking about. 'No problem, Jill.'

'Great, I'm glad. Listen, I won't keep you, I know you're busy but I wanted to organize a night out with you and Rachel. I have some news.'

'Well, I'm going over to Rachel's for tea tomorrow. Why don't you come too and we could go for a pint after Alex goes to bed?'

'That's perfect. I've a few things to do tomorrow but I should be with you by about seven. Byee!'

'Aren't you going to tell me—' Anna asked, but Jill had already hung up. She'd just have to wait until tomorrow to find out Jill's news. Maybe there was a new man in her life or, better still, maybe Andy was back on the scene. Anna felt relieved that the spotlight would be on Jill and not her. She didn't want to talk about Liam and she certainly didn't want Jill asking any awkward questions about Charlie.

Anna had told Jill that Charlie had taken her out on Monday, just in case it ever came up in a future conversation with Liam. Jill hadn't said much but she'd given Anna a funny look. Anna had prattled on about the attack and Jill had let it go. Anna didn't want to revisit the subject. Jill was too sharp and

Anna was way too vulnerable. She'd have to sip mineral water tomorrow night. A few glasses of wine and she would probably spill the beans. She could just imagine her sister's face.

'Anna? A word please?'

She jumped as Mark stuck his head out of his office. 'Coming.'

Chapter 35

The sound of Alex chattering excitedly down in the kitchen woke Rachel early the following morning. She opened one eye and groaned as she saw it was only eight o'clock. She had been awake half the night, as usual, and was hoping that she could at least have a lie-in. Still, now that she was awake she might as well go down for a cup of tea. When she walked into the kitchen, Gary was making a pile of sandwiches and Alex was stuffing toys into his schoolbag. 'Hi, Mum. We're going camping!'

'You are?' Rachel looked from her son to his father.

'We're going up to Cavan fishing with Gus and his little lad. They have a cabin up there so we'll probably stay the night.'

Alex hopped around the kitchen, his eyes shining. 'It's going to be a real adventure!'

'When was this decided?' Rachel said, her mouth turning down in disapproval. Alex will catch his death sleeping in some damp, draughty cabin.'

'He'll be fine,' Gary assured her. 'Gus called last

night and asked us did we want to come along, Rache. I thought you'd be glad of the break.'

'Oh.'

'Alex is looking forward to it, aren't you, buddy?'

'Yeah. Oh please, Mum, say I can go. Pleaaaase?' He wound himself around her leg, and stared up at her.

Rachel smiled. 'Well, okay then, but I want you to bring a change of clothes.'

'Already packed.' Gary nodded towards the holdall by the door. 'I was just going to make a flask of soup and then we're ready to go.'

'I'll do it.' Rachel reached into a cupboard and pulled out two Thermos. 'How about I make some coffee for you?'

'Thanks.' Gary smiled at her and Rachel smiled back.

'I had asked Anna over for tea this evening.'

'Well, she can still come, can't she? You two can have a nice girls' night in.'

'Mmnn, I suppose. When will you be back?'

'Lunchtime tomorrow, I should think. Is that okay?'

'Fine.'

Gary finished the sandwiches, parcelled them up in tinfoil and put them in the holdall. Rachel filled the flasks and gave them to him and then went to make up a first-aid pack. He stood patiently while she put Band-Aids, antiseptic cream, Paracetamol capsules and Calpol sachets into a bag.

'I don't think I've got anything for diarrhoea or constipation,' Rachel murmured.

'We're only going for one night, Rache!'

'Still, you never know. What about pyjamas? And extra socks, have you got extra socks for Alex?'

'Muuuum!' Alex protested. 'We've got to go.'

'You get your coats on and I'll finish packing your bag,' she told them.

'Yes, Mum.'

'Come on, Alex.' Gary steered his son out of the kitchen. 'We'll get the fishing gear sorted.'

When she was alone, Rachel pulled the bag apart and sighed at the clothes Gary had packed. And he'd forgotten Alex's toothbrush! Going upstairs she pulled out vests, socks and heavy sweaters for both her husband and her son. Then she gathered together the basic toiletries that they'd need and hurried back down to cram the much larger bundle into the bag. She zipped it up with difficulty and could imagine Gary's reaction when he picked it up. 'All ready,' she said as they came back in.

'Yes!' Alex punched the air.

'Give your mother a hug,' Gary told him, 'and let's hit the road.' As the boy ran to his mother, Gary lifted the bag and groaned. 'What the hell's in here, the kitchen sink?'

'Just a few necessities,' Rachel said as she held her son. 'You'll thank me for them when you're shivering in your little cabin tonight.'

Gary kissed her cheek and put an arm around her in a brief hug. 'I'll have the mobile. Call if you need me.'

'I'll be fine.'

Gary patted her bump. 'And don't you give your mother any trouble, do you hear me? Why don't you have a nice relaxing day, sweetheart? Catch up on some sleep.'

She nodded and smiled. 'I think I might just do that. You two have a great time.'

'Bye, Mum. We'll bring you back dinner!'

'I hope not.' Rachel shuddered at the thought of gutting a fish.

Gary laughed. 'Bye, Rache.'

'Drive carefully,' she said, following them to the door. 'And you be careful, Alex, and do what Daddy tells you.'

'I will, Mum. Bye.'

Rachel waved until they were out of sight and then went to make a cup of tea. Carrying it upstairs she decided to take Gary's advice. A nice bath would help her relax and then she would go back to bed for a while. It might be quite nice to have a day to herself. She went into the bathroom, set her tea down and turned on the taps. Now, somewhere she had a lavender-scented candle that Jill had bought her. Where the hell had she put it?

Rachel returned to bed after a pleasant soak. Propping herself up with plenty of pillows, she read her book, dozing off now and then. It was a very pleasant and indulgent day and every so often she went down to make a cup of tea or a sandwich. Around four, she thought that she should think about getting up. Anna would be here soon. Rather than make a meal for just the two of them, Rachel was going to suggest a visit to the bistro in the village. It would save her cooking and conversation wouldn't seem quite as stilted in the noisy restaurant.

Hauling herself out of bed, she went to the wardrobe to check through her clothes to see if she possessed anything that would make her look less like a mountain. It was as she was rummaging through her clothes that something struck her. She hadn't felt the baby move in ages. Usually, Baby was at its most active when she lay down, and it absolutely loved bathtime. But, she realized, fingers of fear reaching in and curling around her heart, there had been nothing. Sitting down on the side of the bed, she gave her bump a gentle prod. There was no answering kick. 'Baby? Come on, Baby, wake up. You're scaring me.' She prodded herself in a few different places but there was nothing. 'Oh shit,' she muttered and went to the wardrobe, pulling out the first pair of maternity trousers and top that came to hand. She was just coming down the stairs when the doorbell went. 'Oh, thank God!' She hurried to open it, grabbing her coat off the hook in the hall. 'Come on, we've got to go to the hospital,' she told Anna, who was standing on the step with a bouquet and a bag of sweets in her arms.

'Hospital? Are you in labour?' Anna put down her gifts on the hall table as she watched her sister squeeze her feet into a pair of pumps.

'No, but the baby hasn't moved in ages.'

'What does that mean?' Anna asked.

'I don't know.' Rachel was reluctant to voice her fears. 'I think I need to go for a scan. Will you take me? Gary and Alex are in Cavan.'

'Of course I'll take you. Now have you got everything? Bag, phone, purse?'

Rachel looked in her bag and nodded. 'Yes, you start the car while I set the alarm.'

Within minutes, Anna was driving them towards the city. She shot her sister a sidelong glance. 'I'm sure everything's going to be fine. The baby's probably just having a sleep. They do sleep a lot, don't they?' she added. Her knowledge of pregnancy and babies was sketchy to say the least.

'Yes, that's probably it,' Rachel murmured, staring out of the window, her arms protectively around the bump. 'Please hurry,' she added.

Anna put her foot down on the accelerator and overtook the car in front. 'No problem.' Traffic was light and they were making good time until they hit roadworks as they neared the city centre. A truck was manoeuvring back and forward and the traffic was blocked both ways.

'Oh, come on!' Rachel cried out, banging on the dashboard. 'Come on!'

Anna took one look at her sister, did a U-turn and

sped down a side road. 'I know a way round,' she told Rachel. 'There are speed ramps up here so hold tight.'

Rachel did, and as they bumped down the road, tears coursed down her cheeks. All this jogging up and down and still she hadn't felt as much as a flutter.

Anna reached out a hand and squeezed her sister's. 'It will be okay, Rache.'

Rachel just shook her head, unable to reply. When they got to Holles Street, Anna abandoned her car on a double-yellow line and ran to help Rachel out.

'My sister needs help,' she called to the receptionist as they came through the door.

'Take a seat and I'll get a nurse,' the receptionist said, picking up the phone.

'You go and move the car, I'll be fine,' Rachel said shakily.

'No, I'll wait.'

'You'll get towed, Anna. I'll be fine.'

'Right. I'll be back in a minute.'

Rachel had just finished giving her details to the receptionist when a nurse arrived down. 'Hello, love. You're having problems?'

'I haven't felt the baby move in ages.'

'Right.' The nurse took her arm and steered her towards the lift. 'When was the last time you felt the baby move?'

'During the night.'

'Nothing when you woke up this morning?'

'I don't remember anything, but I was rushing around – my husband and son were going on a fishing trip.'

'That's nice.'

'Do you think there's something wrong?' Rachel asked, the tears welling up again.

'Let's get you upstairs and we'll do a scan,' the nurse said, patting her arm.

Rachel was lying on a bed in a cubicle waiting for the doctor when she heard Anna outside asking for her. 'In here,' she called, pulling the curtain to one side.

'Any news?'

'The doctor is coming in a minute.'

Anna perched nervously on the edge of a stool. 'Do you want me to stay or will I wait outside?'

'Please stay. I've never been so terrified in my life.'

Anna immediately hopped up on the bed and grabbed her sister in a tight hold. 'I know you are, Rache, but it will be fine.'

'What if it isn't? What if, what if . . .' Rachel couldn't bring herself to say it.

'Your baby is going to be just fine.'

'Hello, Rachel.' A dark, solemn-faced young girl pulled open the curtain and stepped into the cubicle. 'I'm Dr Rourke.'

'Hello, Doctor,' Rachel whispered, stretching out on the bed and pulling up her jumper.

Anna moved back to her stool but kept a tight hold of her sister's hand. She watched as the doctor felt Rachel's bump and then turned to get some gel.

'This might be a little cold,' she said before squeezing it on to Rachel's tummy.

Rachel said nothing as the doctor spread gel across the bump and turned to the screen, tapping at the keyboard. '*Get on with it!*' Rachel wanted to scream. It seemed like forever before the doctor took the probe and held it to Rachel's tummy. She moved it around a little and then stopped. Rachel craned her neck to see the screen but it was turned slightly away from her.

'Can I see? Is my baby okay?' she said, hoarsely.

Anna shot her a worried look and then looked back at the screen. She couldn't make out any baby.

'Please try and hold still, Rachel,' the doctor was saying. Then she turned the monitor so Rachel could see it.

'I don't know what I'm looking at,' Rachel wept.

'It's harder as the baby gets bigger. This is his back and that's his thigh.' She repositioned the probe. 'And there's his head.'

As Rachel looked, the baby lifted his hand and stuck his thumb in his mouth. 'Oh! Look! Look what it did! It's okay. Isn't it okay?' She looked from the monitor to the doctor.

'Your baby looks fine,' the doctor agreed. 'Now I'll just take some measurements to make sure everything is as it should be, and then we'll have a listen to the heartbeat.'

When the measurements were taken, the young

woman produced a Doppler and placed it on Rachel's tummy. Within seconds, they could hear a strong, steady beat and Rachel started to laugh, tears running down her cheeks.

'Sounds healthy enough to me.' Dr Rourke smiled.

Rachel beamed at her sister, noticing that Anna too was crying.

'It sounds wonderful,' Anna said, smiling through her tears.

Rachel squeezed her hand before turning back to the doctor. 'But I don't understand. Why didn't I feel any movements?'

The young woman shrugged. 'Perhaps you were busy and just didn't notice. Also, sometimes when the baby changes position, the movements aren't as strong. And sometimes, they're just asleep.'

'I was busy this morning,' Rachel admitted. 'And I've been dozing most of the day.'

The doctor cleaned the gel off Rachel's stomach and pulled off her gloves. 'Well, everything seems to be just fine, Rachel.'

'I'm sorry for wasting your time.'

Dr Rourke shook her head. 'Don't say that, you did exactly the right thing. If ever you're worried, just phone or drop in, that's what we're here for.'

'Thank you, Doctor,' Anna said, helping her sister to sit up. 'Can I take her home now?'

'You certainly can. I'd say you're in for an active evening, Rachel, if he's had that much sleep.'

'I'll never complain about sore ribs again,' Rachel

said with feeling. 'I don't care how many kicks—wait a minute.'

'What's wrong?' Anna looked at her worriedly.

Rachel looked from Anna to the doctor. 'You said "he".'

Dr Rourke bit her lip. 'Did I?'

'Is it definitely a boy?'

'Are you sure you want to know?' the girl hedged.

Rachel nodded fervently.

'Yes, you're having a boy, Rachel.'

'Oh!' Rachel grinned broadly at her sister. 'Another little boy!'

Anna smiled back. 'Alex will be pleased. Come on, missus, let's go home.'

Rachel made a face. 'No, let's go and eat, I'm starving!'

'Another little boy,' she marvelled later as they sat over dinner. 'I'm so glad. A girl would have been fine too, mind you, but a little brother will be nicer for Alex.'

'You know, you're completely different on this pregnancy than you were the last time,' Anna said, emboldened by their sudden closeness.

'What do you mean?'

'Well, the first time you were reading all the books, doing up the nursery, spending a small fortune on baby clothes and you never talked about anything else. You were quite boring, to be honest.'

'I was, wasn't I?' Rachel laughed. 'I suppose

you're always more excited about your first, and of course—' she stopped suddenly.

'Go on,' Anna urged.

Rachel looked across at her sister. 'I didn't really want this baby.'

Anna gaped at her. 'I didn't realize. Oh Rachel, I'm so sorry. But why not?'

'I just knew that I'd be back to square one – tied to the house with no life of my own. I'd be little more than a milk machine. I suppose you must think I'm a selfish bitch.'

Anna shook her head. 'Not at all. It must be hard having something so tiny, dependent on you all of the time.'

'It's wonderful, it's terrible, it's very hard and very fulfilling, it makes you want to scream and it makes you want to weep with joy.'

'That was very poetic,' Anna teased. 'You don't still feel that way though, do you?' Anna would never forget the joy on Rachel's face when she'd seen her baby move on the monitor today.

Her sister put a loving hand on her bump. 'Oh no. Now I feel lucky – very, very, lucky.'

Anna reached out a hand and touched Rachel's bump. 'And I'm very, very jealous.'

Rachel's mouth fell open. 'What? You want to get pregnant?'

'There's no need to sound so amazed.'

'Sorry, I just thought you were a dedicated career woman.'

Anna shrugged. 'I love my job and I'd like to continue it, but if I had children I'd be quite happy to work part-time.'

Rachel sighed. 'Oh, yes, that would be the best of both worlds. You know, there are times when I'd kill to dress up in a nice business suit?'

Anna laughed. 'And there are mornings when I wish I could stay at home and slob around in an old tracksuit.'

Rachel bristled. 'I don't slob around.'

'And I didn't say you did.' Anna said affectionately. 'Now don't you dare get touchy on me. This is the closest we've been in years.'

'It is, isn't it?' Rachel murmured. 'What happened to us, Anna?'

'I suppose we went in completely different directions and didn't have anything in common any more.'

'No, it was really my fault. I was jealous of you,' Rachel admitted.

Anna paused, her glass halfway to her mouth. 'Jealous of me? Why?'

'I was at home playing ring-a-ring-a-roses and making fairy cakes with only a child to talk to, and you were swanning about town in sexy suits, with a successful job and making potloads of money. You know, I really would love to earn my own money,' she added.

'I had no idea you felt like this. I thought you were dying to give up work.'

'I was dying to get out of that job,' Rachel agreed. 'But it was a mistake to give up work completely.'

'You could still go back to work and put the baby in a crèche or with a childminder.'

'I may have to,' Rachel said gloomily.

'What do you mean?'

Rachel pushed her plate away. 'I think Gary is having an affair and if he is then it's over and he'll have to go, but I'm terrified of being on my own and it's not fair to the kids and—'

'Hey, hey, slow down.' Anna reached across and took her hand. 'Take a few deep breaths, have a drink and then tell me.'

Rachel did as she was told, beginning with the night of Alex's operation.

'I can't believe it,' Anna said when she finally stopped talking. 'What are the chances?'

'What do you mean?' Rachel frowned.

'I think Liam's been at it too,' Anna admitted, her eyes filling up.

'No!'

Anna nodded. 'With Tara Brady.'

'Tara Brady?' Rachel goggled at her. 'No way! Are you sure?'

'No,' Anna admitted. 'But I know they've been seeing a lot of each other since Liam lost his job.'

'And does he know that you know?' Rachel asked, her own problems forgotten for the moment.

'Oh yeah.' And Anna told her sister about walking in on Tara. 'You should have seen her,' she fumed, 'wandering around my kitchen as if she owned the place!'

'And where are things at now?'

Anna sighed. 'We were supposed to sit down and have a talk the day I got back from Spain but then Josie had her accident and that was the end of that.' She broke off as her mobile started to ring and she scrambled around in her bag searching for it. 'Hello?' she said when she'd finally found it.

'Where the hell are you?' Jill exclaimed.

'Jill? Oh, shit, Jill, I completely forgot about you!'

'Yes, well, I kind of figured that out. And I wouldn't mind, but Rachel isn't home either.'

'She's here with me. We're in the bistro in the village.'

'Oh right, thanks for waiting for me.' Jill retorted.

'I'm sorry, but we had a bit of a crisis. Come on down and I'll buy you a glass of wine and explain everything.'

'What was all that about?' Rachel asked.

'I forgot to mention that Jill was meeting us at your house. She has something to tell us, apparently.'

'Well, at least it can't be about her fella being unfaithful,' Rachel joked.

'So tell me, how are things with Gary now?'

'They were fine when I got back from Spain, he was being really nice to me, and then he dropped this bombshell about wanting to go out on his own. Well, I have to tell you, I completely flipped. So it's been frosty to say the least since then, although he was quite pleasant this morning.'

'So what are you going to do?'

'Mam and Jill think I should confront him.'

'Mam and Jill know?' Anna looked hurt.

'I told Mam last week and, well . . . I told Jill a few months ago.'

'I see.'

'Don't look like that,' Rachel warned. 'I was hardly likely to confide in you the way things were between us. Anyway, I bet you told Jill about Liam and Tara.'

Anna's lips twitched. 'I did, yeah.'

'And Mam?'

'Last week,' Anna admitted.

'And we went out there to check that *they* were okay,' Rachel said with a wry smile. 'We're a fine pair, aren't we?'

'Terrible. And what about Jill? She must be sick of the both of us.'

'Believe me, I am!' Jill stood grinning down at them as she took off her coat and flung her bag on a chair. 'Now where's my drink?'

Chapter 36

Anna asked the waiter for another glass and Jill flashed him a flirtatious smile as he poured her wine. '*Merci*.'

'Would you like a menu, Mademoiselle?' he asked.

'No, I'm not really hungry.'

'Oh no, you're not on a starvation diet, I hope,' Anna protested.

'I'm not on any diet,' Jill said firmly. 'I've given all that up. And the funny thing is that I don't seem to be as hungry any more. Anyway, what have you two been up to? What's this "crisis" that made Anna forget all about me?' Jill looked from one sister to the other.

'We had to go to Holles Street,' Rachel told her. 'I thought there was something wrong with the baby but there isn't. It's absolutely fine, and it's a boy!'

'Oh, that's wonderful!' Jill hugged her cousin. 'Are you thrilled?'

'Over the moon.'

'About the baby anyway,' Anna added.

'Yeah,' Rachel agreed.

'What does that mean?' Jill asked.

'I've told Anna everything, Jill.'

'Oh?' Jill's expression was guarded.

'And vice-versa,' Anna chipped in.

'I see.'

Rachel and Anna looked at each other and burst out laughing.

'What?' Jill asked.

'It's safe to talk, Jill, honest,' Anna told her.

'Yeah, well, it's hard to break the habit of a lifetime.'

'We've behaved like idiots,' Rachel said, 'but we're both very grateful to you. You've been a great friend.'

'Amen to that.' Anna nodded.

'My pleasure,' Jill said. 'It's nice to finally see you two like this. I look forward to a lot more threesomes. No going back to the old days,' she warned.

'No more secrets,' Anna said, meeting her sister's eyes.

'No more secrets,' Rachel echoed.

'So, bring me up to date.' Jill settled herself more comfortably.

'No, not yet. I think it's time you did the talking,' Anna replied.

'Yes, you're right.' Rachel nodded enthusiastically. 'Tell us your news.'

Jill looked from one to the other and took a long drink. 'Right. Okay. Well, er . . .'

'Come on, Jill. You know you can tell us anything. Good heavens, you know everything there is to know about us!' Rachel smiled at her sister, but Anna was rummaging in her bag for a tissue.

'Right, okay then. I'm going to live in Spain.'

Rachel slopped her wine on to the tablecloth. 'What!?'

'Spain?' Anna repeated.

Jill nodded. 'I pretty much decided when I was down in Benalmadena. I'm going to work for Kitty.'

Anna held up her hands. 'Hang on a minute. You only met Kitty a couple of weeks ago and you're going to throw in a brilliant job to go and work behind her bar?'

'Well, I'm going to manage the place, but yeah, that's about the size of it.'

Rachel looked bemused. 'I don't know what to say. I thought you loved your job.'

Jill shrugged. 'I used to, but the last few months I've been pretty miserable.'

'I knew that Vinny character was getting to you but I didn't realize it was that bad,' Anna marvelled.

'We were too caught up in our own lives to notice,' Rachel murmured.

'I can understand you wanting to leave your job, Jill, but why Spain?' Anna asked.

'Why not? I really like Kitty, I think her business has a lot of potential and it's not like I have any ties to Ireland.'

'What about your folks? What about us?' Rachel cried.

'Ma and Da have each other and you guys have your families and now,' Jill took their hands and smiled, 'you have each other. Maybe if I was in a relationship I'd stay but there's been no one since Andy. I think I really messed up there, girls! But that's history now. You know, I like the idea of making a fresh start.'

'Then go for it,' Anna told her. 'It's time you put yourself first. And think about it, Rache – we can go down and visit whenever we need to escape.'

'The way my life's going I might end up coming with you. How would you feel about sharing with a single mum and two kids?'

Jill laughed. 'Well, as I'm going to be living over the shop, it might be a bit cramped but you're always welcome.'

'Why are you going to live there?' Anna looked horrified. 'It will be noisy and smelly and—'

'Free,' Jill interjected. 'I don't want to buy a place until I'm certain that Benalmadena is the place for me. Kitty and I have agreed that we'll review the situation in six months, but if I'm happy there and we're getting on okay, then I'll become a partner in the business.'

'Wow!' Rachel stared at her. 'I can't believe this. You've really thought this all through, haven't you?'

'Pretty much,' Jill laughed. 'But you know me. Once I make a decision, I don't hang about.'

'So when are you going to go?' Rachel asked.

'The week before Christmas, so I will still be here for the birth.'

'Christmas?' Anna gasped. 'But you'll be all alone out there on Christmas Day, surrounded by strangers.'

'I'll have Kitty and Pepe and Juan and anyway, I'll be too busy to be lonely. Kitty says the restaurant is quite full at Christmas. And she's open on Christmas Day itself, doing the full roast turkey, minced pies and pudding lark. I think it'll be fun and it certainly beats sitting watching ancient sitcoms while Dad snores and Aunty Vi lashes through the sherry and quizzes me about my lovelife!'

'We are going to have one hell of a party before you go,' Anna announced.

'But when?' Rachel looked down at her bump.

'After the baby, as soon as you feel up to it.' Anna patted her hand.

Rachel rolled her eyes. 'It doesn't really work like that, Sis. Babies eat every three hours. What should I do, strap him to my back while I jig around the dance floor?'

Anna scowled. 'Hey, this is Jill's party we're talking about. Baby can have bottles for one night and Gary can babysit.'

'If he's around.'

'What's happening?' Jill asked her. 'Have you talked?'

Rachel shook her head. 'I was all ready to have it

out with him but . . . well, I won't go into all the details. Suffice to say it didn't happen.'

Jill looked over at Anna. 'And what about you? Have you talked to Liam?'

Anna shook her head. 'No. First Josie broke her ankle and he moved in with her, and then there was the attack . . .'

'What attack? What are you talking about!' Rachel exclaimed. 'And how come we've been together for the last four hours and you never mentioned it?'

'Calm down, Rache, it's okay. It wasn't really a proper attack. This guy tried to grope me, I gave him a knee in the balls and ran – end of story.'

'But when did this happen?'

'Last Monday,' Jill told her.

'You should have called, Anna,' Rachel told her.

'I didn't call anyone, not Liam, not Jill, not you.'

'Is that because you had Charlie to look after you?'

'Charlie? Who's Charlie?' Rachel looked from her cousin to her sister.

Jill sighed. 'I thought you'd told her everything.'

Anna glared at her cousin. 'There's nothing to tell.'

Jill ignored her and turned to Rachel. 'He's a customer.' Jill drew quotes in the air. 'And he fancies the pants off Anna.'

'Jill!'

'And he came riding in on his white charger, or Kawasaki motorbike, to save her on Monday.'

'It wasn't like that.' Anna protested. 'I bumped

into him in the filling station.' And he was in his car, if you must know.

'And then he took her out to dinner.' Jill couldn't stop herself. She'd had a bad feeling from the moment she met Charlie Coleman. He'd come into Anna's life at a time when she was feeling low and unloved, and she felt her cousin was dangerously close to walking out on Liam on the basis of a bit of extra-marital romance.

'Pizza! We went for a bloody pizza!' Anna grabbed the bottle of wine and filled up her glass. 'And Liam knows all about it, for your information.'

Jill held up her hands. 'Hey, sorry I spoke.'

Rachel looked at her sister's angry expression. 'We're getting sidetracked here. This pervert who attacked you, Anna, did he hurt you?'

'No, honestly. I got a fright, that's all.'

'I'm sorry, Anna.' Jill reached out a hand to her cousin. 'I'm not having a go at you. I just think you and Liam are perfect for each other and I'm terrified that Charlie will get in the way of you two sorting things out. It would be a terrible shame if you gave up on your marriage without a fight. You have to talk to Liam.' Jill gave the table a decisive thump. 'In fact, that goes for you too, Rache.'

'What?'

'You need to talk to Gary.'

'Yeah, I will.'

'When?' Jill demanded, looking from one to the other.

'When Liam moves back in, I suppose.' Anna felt cornered.

Jill shook her head. 'No, that's not good enough. The two of you need to get your lives sorted once and for all. Tomorrow.'

Rachel looked at her. 'Tomorrow?'

'Four o'clock tomorrow. You are both going to do it.'

'Liam will be looking after his mother,' Anna said.

'Alex will be there,' Rachel pointed out.

'Someone could come and sit with Josie for a couple of hours and Alex can go to play with a friend. No more excuses, ladies. Get on your phones and set it up. Four o'clock tomorrow.'

Anna and Rachel looked at each other.

'She's right,' Anna said finally. 'We've been running away from our problems for long enough. I don't know about you, Rache, but I'm fed up having arguments with Liam in my head. At least if I have them with him face to face, he gets to answer and maybe we'll actually get somewhere.'

Rachel stared at her then nodded slowly. 'You're right. It's time.'

Jill looked from one sister to the other. 'Halleluiah,' she breathed.

'There's just one condition,' Anna said suddenly.

'What's that?' Jill asked, taking a sip of wine.

Anna winked at her sister. 'You call Andy.'

Jill choked. 'What? Why would I do that?'

Rachel nodded furiously. 'Great idea! You were obviously mad about him.'

'What rubbish!'

'Liar,' Anna said calmly. 'Well, that's the deal. If you won't call Andy, then we won't call Liam and Gary.'

Rachel nodded again.

'But it's not the same at all. I dumped him.'

'So? Give him a call, ask him out for a drink and if he says no, so be it. All you've got to lose is your pride.'

'But I'm going to Spain,' Jill wailed. 'I've made my decisions, I'm moving on.'

Anna shrugged. 'He can always come and visit you, and if he doesn't want to know, you can go, knowing that you gave it your best shot.'

'Take your own advice, Jill,' Rachel urged. 'Call him.'

Jill stared at them for a moment and then nodded, resigned. 'Okay.'

'Yes!' Anna grinned in triumph at Rachel.

'So how do we do this?' Rachel looked nervously at her mobile.

'We'll go outside one at a time and make the call,' Jill told them. 'You first, Anna.'

'Oh, why me?' Anna wailed, but she obediently pulled out her mobile and stood up. 'Order another bottle of that wine. I'm going to need it.'

'I'm going to the loo,' Rachel said. 'Order some tea as well, would you, Jill?'

Jill ordered wine, tea and a large cappuccino for herself. If she was honest, she was excited at the idea of hearing Andy's voice again and grateful that her cousins had pressed her to contact him. Her stupid pride wouldn't have allowed it otherwise. And as she'd pushed them to the edge, it was only fair that she should be willing to take that jump herself. But what the hell would she say to him? Oh, why was she worried? She probably wouldn't even get to talk to him – it was Saturday night, after all. He was sure to be in some noisy club or else having a cosy night in with someone, with his phone switched off. If she did get hold of him, he'd probably turn her down flat. The way she'd treated him it would hardly be surprising.

Rachel returned from the loo and eased herself back into her chair. 'I'm not so sure about this.'

'Yeah, maybe we should just forget it,' Jill agreed immediately.

'I did it,' Anna announced, flopping back into her chair and grabbing her glass. 'Four o'clock tomorrow.'

Jill and Rachel stared at each other in panic. 'You next,' Jill said.

Rachel stood up, her mobile clutched in her hand. 'Right.'

'What did he say?' Jill asked Anna as Rachel made her way through the crowded restaurant.

'I didn't really give him a chance to say anything. I just told him to meet me at the house at four and he said "okay".'

'Anna, I'm sorry about what I said earlier. You know, about Charlie.'

'That's okay.'

'Have you two done . . . anything?'

Anna shook her head but she couldn't look Jill in the eye.

Jill sighed. 'You really like him, don't you?'

Anna nodded. 'Oh Jill. Everything has become so complicated.' She dragged her hair back off her face and turned sad eyes on her cousin. 'I don't know what I want any more.'

'Or who?'

Anna nodded dumbly.

'Maybe tomorrow will help to clarify your feelings.'

'I hope so—' Anna broke off as Rachel returned to the table. 'Well?'

'I don't know if he understood me,' Rachel replied. 'He's in Cavan, fishing,' she explained to Jill. 'The line was terrible.'

'Send him a text to confirm,' Anna suggested. 'Even if he doesn't get it straight away, he'll read it on his way back tomorrow.'

'Good idea.' Rachel began to punch in the message. 'I called Alex's friend's mother and she's going to take him for the whole afternoon.'

'So that just leaves you, cuz.' Anna raised an eyebrow at Jill.

Jill stood up. 'Wish me luck.'

'Good luck,' Anna and Rachel chorused.

'How do you feel about this, Rache?' Anna said as they watched her walk away.

'I'm terrified of confronting Gary, but I know I have to. I'll be no use to Alex or my baby until I do.'

Anna squeezed her hand. 'I think you're very brave and I also think you're wrong about Gary. I'm sure he still loves you.'

Rachel stared into the distance. 'Maybe he does but I also sense that there's someone else, or was. I can't explain it, I don't have any real evidence, I just feel it. Do you know what I mean?'

Anna nodded miserably. 'Yes, but I wish I didn't.'

'We'll be fine.' Rachel forced a smile.

'Yeah, you're right. And we have so much to look forward to. This baby is going to have an aunt who'll spoil him rotten.' She sighed. 'I was sort of hoping that he'd have a little baby cousin to play with and it would be just like it was for us when we were kids.'

'I still can't believe that you want a family,' Rachel said. 'I thought between your career and your social life that you would never have time for kids.'

Anna laughed. 'Well, I wasn't planning on giving everything up and chaining myself to the kitchen sink!'

'Neither was I, but that's pretty much what happened. It's like I didn't exist any more. The old Rachel was gone and I was just Alex's mummy, Gary's wife and the general dogsbody who did the cooking, the cleaning and the ironing.'

'But why didn't you go back to work?' Anna asked simply.

'Easier said than done. What would I do? I was never clever like you.'

'That's bullshit, Rache. You gave up work as soon as you got pregnant. You never gave yourself a chance to find out what you were good at. Look at me, for God's sake. I'm thirty-one and on my sixth job. I've been working since I left school and this is the first time I ever felt really good at something.'

'But you've always been so confident,' Rachel protested.

'No one is always confident,' Anna assured her. 'Certainly not me.'

Rachel sipped her tea as she absorbed this piece of information. 'If you had a choice, Anna, between the job and children, which would you pick?'

'Children,' Anna said without hesitation. 'Mark could fire me tomorrow if he wanted and there's not a lot I could do about it. But children? They're for ever.'

'Tell me about it,' Rachel said with feeling. 'But take it from me, Anna, it's not as easy as it looks. Children can be really hard work.'

'I do realize that.' Anna rolled her eyes.

'You don't,' Rachel assured her. 'And you won't until you've been there. But . . .' She held up her hand as Anna went to interrupt. 'It's worth it. It's worth every second of tiredness, every minute of pain, every hour of worry, every day of frustration. It's worth it.' Rachel pulled out a tissue and blew her nose. 'And the sooner this child is born the better because I must be dehydrated on a permanent basis with the amount of crying I do.'

'I never realized how you felt,' Anna admitted. 'I thought you were a terrible moan.'

'Huh, thanks a bunch!'

'Sorry, but I couldn't understand what your problem was. You had Gary, you had Alex and you seemed to do nothing but have coffee mornings and PTA meetings. I couldn't see what you had to complain about.'

'Nothing on the front of it,' Rachel agreed, 'except that was all it was, a front. Gary and I have been growing steadily apart since Alex was born. I don't know whether that's because I became a boring housewife or whether he was just meeting too many other, more exciting girls. The reasons aren't important any more. The fact is that the only thing we have in common now is Alex and, of course, the baby.'

'Oh Rache, I'm so sorry.'

Rachel shrugged as she dabbed at her wet cheeks. '*C'est la vie*. My situation is probably true of a lot of women. When you're working, the job, the company, the deal, it all seems so important. Once you're at home with kids you think, So what? So I know that when Gary came home and told me about his problems at work I probably didn't seem interested. Hell, I wasn't really interested! I can't complain if he went elsewhere for company, can I?'

Before Anna could reply, Jill was back. 'It's no use, I can't get through to him. He's not answering his mobile or his house phone. Sorry, girls, but it looks like I won't be able to keep my part of the bar—' She broke off as her mobile trilled in her hand. She looked at the display and then back at her cousins. 'It's him.'

'Answer it,' Anna urged.

Jill pressed the button and jammed the phone against her ear. 'Hello? Yeah, Andy, hi, how are you?' she stood up as she talked and made her way back outside.

'Sorry, Jill, I was in the shower.'

Jill closed her eyes, imagining him naked, wet, dark hair glistening and damp on his chest . . .

'Jill? Are you still there?'

'Yes! Yes, I am. Oh look, Andy, tell me to get lost if you want to, I'd understand perfectly, but I was wondering if you'd like to come out for a drink tomorrow.'

'Okay.'

'You'll probably tell me where to go and, like I said, no pressure but—'

'Jill, I said yes.'

'Oh! Right! So, how about four o'clock in the bar at the Yacht?'

'See you there,' Andy replied.

Going back inside, Jill was confronted by two expectant faces.

'Well?' Rachel asked.

Jill nodded. 'Sorted.'

Anna reached out and grabbed her hand and Rachel put her hand over theirs. They sat still, staring at each other, silenced for the first time that evening.

Chapter 37

Anna paced the small sitting room, occasionally pausing to look out of the window. It was five to four and her stomach was in a knot as she waited for her husband to arrive. She felt exhausted as she'd had precious little sleep. To compensate for the amount of wine she'd consumed last night, she'd started drinking coffee and when she finally climbed into bed in the small hours of the morning, she was wide-awake.

Jill had stayed the night and Anna had smiled as she'd listened to her cousin snore in the next room. She was hoping her reunion with Andy would be successful. Certainly, of the three of them, Anna thought that Jill was the most likely to have a successful outcome today. Talking to Rachel, Anna had been shocked at how bad things had got between her and Gary, and as for her and Liam – well, Anna just didn't know.

Leaving the window, she went to the fireplace and stared at her reflection in the mirror over the mantel. She felt she'd aged ten years in the last couple of weeks, and looking at her sunken eyes and white face, she looked every day of it. Anna jumped as she heard Liam's key in the door. Going to the sofa, she sat down and waited for him to come and find her. She clasped her hands in her lap, aware that her palms were sweaty, and tried some deep breathing to try and settle her nerves.

'Anna?' she heard him call from the kitchen.

'In here.'

He came into the room and stood there, looking awkward and out of place. He was wearing the camel-coloured sweater that she'd bought him last Christmas with clean, faded jeans. His face was clean-shaven and he smelled faintly of cologne. He looked gorgeous. 'Hi.'

'Hi.'

'How are you?' he asked.

'Fine.'

'Good.'

Anna took a deep breath. 'Why don't you sit down?' When Liam was sitting opposite her on a sofa, she spoke again. 'We were supposed to talk about Tara when I got back from Spain and I know you've tried to have that conversation with me a few times since . . .'

'Yes!' Liam nodded eagerly.

'Right, well now I'm ready to listen.'

'Okay.' Liam hesitated for a moment and then began, looking her straight in the eye as he talked. 'Well, it began when I was made redundant and

I started calling over to Mum more in the daytime. We'd pass the time of day at the garden gate, just chit-chat, the usual thing. Then one day, Tara asked me to take a look at a tap in her bathroom.'

Anna rolled her eyes. 'That was a bit obvious, wasn't it?'

'Probably,' he admitted, 'but then you know I'm not good at picking up on these things. Anyway, I fixed the tap, drank my coffee and left. Honestly. After that, I had coffee with her from time to time. Just coffee,' he emphasized. 'I enjoyed her company. She's a very good listener and as a businesswoman she was able to give me some sound advice as well.'

Anna felt a lump in her throat. It seemed Tara had been doing all the things for Liam that she had wanted to do.

'Things were getting worse between you and me,' Liam continued, 'and I suppose I just wanted someone to talk to.'

'But why didn't you talk to me, Liam? I was there, remember? I wanted to talk, wanted to listen. But you didn't want to know.'

Liam moved over beside her and took her hand. 'I know, love, and I'm sorry. I suppose you were just too close.'

Anna shook her head. 'I don't understand that. I'm too close so you go off with another woman.'

'I did not go off with her,' Liam objected.

Anna put her head back and looked him straight in the eye. 'Tell me you didn't fancy her.'

Liam held her gaze. 'I can't.'

Anna slumped back in the chair and closed her eyes. 'Well, thanks for your honesty, I suppose.'

'I did fancy her, Anna, and I was very flattered by the attention – any man would be. But I don't want her, I want you.'

Anna raised her eyes to his. 'Did you have sex with her?'

'No, I didn't.'

It was on the tip of Anna's tongue to ask him if he'd been tempted and then she thought of Charlie and said nothing.

Liam lifted her hand to his lips and kissed it tenderly. 'I love you, Anna. Tara actually did us a favour. Spending time with her made me realize just how much I love you. I'm sorry, Anna. Sorry for not talking to you, sorry for shutting you out. But losing my job was the scariest thing that's ever happened to me. I felt completely worthless and useless. As the time went on and I still couldn't find a job, I got more and more afraid and, to be honest, I felt I was letting you down. I felt too ashamed to even look you in the eye sometimes. I knew how much you wanted a family and because of me, that had to wait.'

'But I didn't mind that, Liam,' Anna protested. 'And I don't believe I ever said anything to make you feel ashamed. I love you!'

'You didn't do anything to deserve any of this, Anna. I'm afraid I was just torturing myself.'

'So it was easier to be around Tara?'

He nodded. 'Yes. And I have to admit something else.'

'Oh?' Anna braced herself.

'I was jealous of you going off to work every day. And I hated taking money from you.'

'But that's ridiculous! We're a team, we work together and we get through the bad times together. When you have money, you pay the bills, when I have it, I do. That's always the way it's been.'

'Yes,' he agreed, 'but this time you were the one who *always* had the money and I was the one with nothing. I'm sorry, love, but I don't like taking hand-outs, even from you.'

'Then what hope is there for us? The reality is I'm working and you're not. I'd change places with you tomorrow if I could, Liam, but I can't.'

He smiled at her. 'It's not going to be a problem any more.'

Anna searched his face. 'What do you mean?'

'You're looking at the new Factory Manager of Elektrix. I start next Monday.'

Anna flung her arms around him. 'Oh Liam, that's wonderful! Oh my God, I can't believe it!'

He hugged her tightly. 'Neither can I. And as for those bills, I'll be able to pay my share again. The salary is thirty thousand a year more than I was earning in Patterson's.'

Anna drew back from him, her eyes like saucers. 'Thirty thousand! Jesus, you're rich!'

'I don't know about that. Aren't babies very expensive?'

Anna blinked. 'Babies? You want to start a family?'

Liam gazed at her, his eyes tender. 'I seem to remember that being the plan before all hell broke loose.'

Anna turned away slightly, letting her hair fall across her face. 'Oh Liam, I don't know what to say. This is all a bit much to take in.'

'Take your time, love. I'm not trying to rush you into anything. I just want you to know that I'm back and I'm sorry for everything that's happened.'

'I'm sorry too,' Anna replied, allowing him to fold her into his arms and shutting her eyes tight.

'I have my bag with me,' Liam said into her hair. 'Is it okay if I stay?'

'What about Josie?' Anna asked, pulling back to look at him.

'She's flying about on the crutches now, no problem, and her neighbour's agreed to keep an eye on her and do any shopping she needs.'

'Which neighbour?' Anna couldn't stop herself.

Liam made a face. 'The other one.'

'You're still going to be bumping into Tara all the time, Liam. I don't know if I can handle that.'

'You don't have to worry. She's moving.'

'What? Where? When?'

'I don't know the details but a For Sale sign went up yesterday.'

Anna looked into his eyes. 'Had you something to do with that?'

He nodded. 'Yes, I think so. I think she believed that we had some kind of future together. I told her I still loved you and always would. Let's say she didn't take it very well.'

'I suppose that's why she didn't ask Donnelly's Real Estate to sell her property,' Anna joked lamely as relief washed over her. She looked up into her husband's handsome face. 'Is this really what you want, Liam?'

Liam nodded. 'I've never been more certain of anything in my life. And now I want to do something that I haven't done for way too long.'

Bending his head, Liam kissed her and Anna returned the kiss hungrily, enjoying the familiar feel of his lips against hers and his hands in her hair. After a moment, she reluctantly pulled away. 'Sorry to do this to you, Liam, but I have to go out for a little while.'

Liam frowned. 'Is everything okay?'

Anna kissed him again. 'Very okay, but I have to go and meet Rachel and Jill. I'll explain everything when I get back.'

As Anna drove, she chewed over what Liam had told her and realized that they'd both gone through a similar crisis; while he had turned to Tara for comfort, she had turned to Charlie. Anna shivered at the thought of Liam and Tara together. Though she believed him when he told her they hadn't had sex, she knew first-hand that things could still get pretty hot and heavy without actually going all the way. She felt sick with shame when she thought of that night in Paul Brennan's house. Making a sudden decision, Anna pulled over to the side of the road and dialled a number. 'I need to see you,' she said as soon as the phone was answered.

'This is a nice surprise.' Charlie was at the door waiting for her when she stepped out of the car.

Anna looked nervously around as she approached him.

'It's okay, Paul isn't about to jump out of the bushes. I'm the official owner now.'

'Congratulations.' Anna turned her head so that his kiss landed on her cheek.

Charlie grinned and led her into the hallway that was crowded with boxes. 'I'm afraid it's a bit of a mess. My stuff was delivered yesterday but I haven't made much headway with the unpacking. Come into the kitchen. I think I can put my hands on a bottle of wine.'

'Not for me,' Anna said quickly, determined to remain in full control.

'Coffee?' he offered.

'No, thanks, I can't stay long.'

'Oh?' Charlie leaned casually against the worktop and watched her.

'No. I just wanted to tell you, face to face, that

Liam is home. We're back together. Properly,' she added, when his expression didn't change.

'Is that it?'

Anna nodded.

'Hey, don't look so worried. I completely understand.'

Anna smiled with relief. 'Oh good, I was afraid that you'd be . . .' She was about to say 'upset' but that sounded big-headed.

'Annoyed? Upset? Look, Anna, it's okay. I'm a realist. I didn't really expect you to walk out on Liam.'

'You didn't?'

'No, of course not; you obviously love the guy.'

Anna nodded dumbly, relieved that he was making this so easy.

Charlie moved towards her and looped his arms loosely around her. 'As long as we're careful it will be fine.'

'Sorry?'

He chuckled. 'Well, dining out in the village on a regular basis might not be such a good idea! But now that I own this place, you can come here; no one will know the difference. And Sophie won't be around that much. Between school and her friends, and that pony of hers, I hardly see her these days.' He ran his hands up and down her arms. 'But I kind of like the idea of you coming by for a mid-morning shag. Hey, I'd even make you coffee!'

Anna pushed him away. 'You want me to have an affair with you?'

'Why not? We could have fun, and if we're careful, no one will get hurt.'

Anna stared at him as if seeing him for the first time. 'I don't think so.'

'But Anna . . .'

She backed away towards the door, not taking her eyes off him. 'Goodbye, Charlie.'

He looked at her in confusion. 'But you fancy me, I know you do.'

'I did,' Anna corrected. 'But there's a lot more to a relationship than sex – at least, there is for me. I'm going now, Charlie, and I won't be back. And please, do me one favour. If our paths cross in the future, pretend that none of this ever happened. I sold you a house, end of story, okay?'

Charlie sighed and shook his head. 'We could have had so much fun, Anna.'

'Promise me?' she begged.

'Oh, don't worry, woman, I'm not going to stalk you!' He waved an irritable hand at her. 'Go on, get out of here. Have a nice, safe little life.'

When Anna turned out of the driveway she drove straight to the Grand Hotel. She and Rachel and Jill had agreed to meet here after their encounters. It was nearly six o'clock. She wondered if she'd be the first to arrive.

Rachel had been wandering around in a daze since Gary and Alex had got home. She'd received a one-word reply to last night's text – *OK* – and she had seen from the expression on Gary's face when he walked through the hall door at lunchtime that he knew this was a showdown of sorts. Alex gabbled on endlessly about the fishing trip, oblivious to the atmosphere. Rachel's nerves were stretched to breaking-point and she had found it hard to talk to her son and behave normally. Luckily he was so thrilled to hear he was going over to his friend's house, he spent much of the time leading up to it selecting the toys he would take with him. When Gary returned from dropping him off, Rachel was sitting at the kitchen table waiting. According to the clock on the wall it was 3.55 p.m. Close enough, she decided.

'What's all this about?' Gary took the seat opposite her and started to fiddle with the salt cellar.

Rachel recognized the defensive tone in his voice and her heart sank. 'You're seeing someone else, aren't you?' Well, there was no point in dancing around the subject.

Gary's face drained of colour. 'What? What are you talking about?' he blustered.

'It's true, isn't it?'

Gary said nothing, just sat staring at her.

'I know it's true. I've known for ages.'

'You know nothing,' he ground out, his grip tightening on the salt cellar.

'Are you denying it?' Rachel challenged and then her lips twisted in a bitter smile as he looked away.

'It's not what you think,' Gary said dully.

'How do you know what I think?' she shot back.

'How wouldn't I?' he shouted, standing up so fast that he knocked the chair over. 'You've made it perfectly clear what you think of me. When I'm here, you're nagging me, when I'm not here, you're checking up on me. And don't think I don't know that you go through my pockets.'

Rachel reddened. 'Are you surprised? How could I possibly trust you after that night?'

'That bloody night!' Gary slammed his hand down on the worktop and then turned around to face her, his eyes furious. 'It always comes back to that bloody night. And do you know something, Rachel?' He bent down close to her so that they were eyeball to eyeball. 'Read my lips. Nothing happened that night! I was at a dinner with Dan and some clients and then we went to a club. As God is my witness, that's the truth!'

Rachel nodded slowly. 'I believe you,' she whispered.

Gary picked up his chair, flopped back into it and covered his face with his hands. Rachel should have felt relieved, but it was clear to her that he had a lot more to say. Bracing herself, she cradled her arms around her bump. 'Tell me everything, Gary. Let's get this over with, once and for all.'

Gary took his hands away and looked at her, his eyes tortured. 'I'm sorry, Rache, I didn't mean it to happen.'

She swallowed hard. 'Go on.'

'I wasn't out looking for it, I wasn't in pubs or in

nightclubs, though you probably won't believe that. When I said I was working late, I was. I've worked hard to get where I am, and when I told you that I wanted to go out on my own, it wasn't a vague silly idea. It was a very well-researched plan.'

'Just tell me about Her,' Rachel told him, working hard to keep her voice steady.

'She works in a bookshop around the corner from work. There's a coffee-shop in the back and me and Dan used to have lunch there sometimes.' Gary shrugged. 'She got to know me from going in and out, and we used to say hello. Then one day she asked me for a quote for putting in a conservatory and we had a cup of coffee while I talked her through it.'

'When did all this happen?'

'I don't know, maybe five or six months ago.'

Rachel frowned, trying to figure out why warning bells were ringing loudly in her head. Of course! The receipts she'd found in his pocket. They were for the coffee-bar in the bookshop. 'Egan's,' she breathed.

'Yes. Anyway, we hit it off from the start. She bought a conservatory and I popped in occasionally to check that she was happy with the work. Then we got talking about other things. Before long, I was dropping in for a coffee a couple of times a week.'

'So when did it progress from there?' Rachel forced herself to ask.

'It didn't,' he muttered. 'It hasn't.'

'Right!' Rachel looked at him in total disbelief.

'It's true,' he insisted. 'Not because I'm a good

husband but because she's a good wife and mother.'

'She's married?'

Gary nodded. 'Yeah, with two little girls – they're seven and four.'

Rachel said nothing as she tried to absorb what he was saying. *Married, kids, not a good husband . . .* 'You were seeing her after I told you about the baby?'

He nodded, his eyes closed. 'I'm sorry. I wouldn't hurt you for the world, Rache, but I love her.'

It was like a knife through her heart. 'I see.'

'But you don't have to worry.' He wiped his eyes with the back of his hand. 'She won't have anything to do with me. She says we both have responsibilities and we can't walk away from them.'

'Very admirable.'

'She's a good person,' Gary snapped at her.

'Better than me.'

'I didn't say that.'

'It's what you meant.'

'No! Rachel, I love you and I admire you, you're a great mother. And if you hadn't asked me about this, I would never have told you any of it in a million years.'

'But you would leave me – leave *us* – if she'd asked you.'

Gary looked at her, his eyes sad. 'I didn't mean it to happen, Rache, but I suppose it was only a matter of time. It's obvious that you don't love me any more.'

'What do you mean? Of course I love you!'

'You don't,' Gary insisted. 'Sometimes I wonder if

you ever really did. I think you were more in love with the idea of getting married than actually getting married to *me*.'

'That's not true!'

'Then maybe it's all my fault. Maybe I should have been around more when Alex was a baby. If that's true then I'm sorry, Rache. I'm sorry for all of it.'

Rachel realized she should be throwing a tantrum, hurling dishes at him or, at the very least, crying her eyes out – but she felt surprisingly calm. 'So what happens now?' she asked.

'We start again, I suppose, and get ready for the birth of our baby.'

'How can we start again? You're in love with another woman.'

'I won't see her again,' Gary promised. 'It's over. Look, Rache, I'm willing to work at this.'

'You shouldn't have to work at loving someone,' Rachel mumbled.

'I know I've hurt you, and I'll do whatever it takes to make it up to you. I still care about you. I love Alex and I can't wait to meet the baby.'

'It's another boy,' Rachel told him without emotion.

Gary's eyes filled up. 'That's fantastic! But how do you know? When did you find out?'

Rachel shook her head. 'That's not important right now.' She stood up. 'I have to go out for a while.'

'Out? But where? Rache, you're not going to do anything silly, are you?'

'I have arranged to meet Anna and Jill. I won't be long.'

'Oh, okay. Is there anything you want me to do?'

She turned to look at him. 'Yes, I'd like you to pack.'

'No! Rachel!'

'I need you to pick up Alex and look after him until I get back,' Rachel continued as if he hadn't spoken. 'Then we have to work out what to tell him. Possibly we could say you have to go away on business.'

'But Rache—'

She waved away his protests. 'I don't want him hurt. It's very important that we do whatever it takes to protect him from this.'

'Then let me stay,' Gary begged, tears streaming down his face. 'I'll be a better husband, a better father. We can get through this, Rachel. Don't make me leave Alex, don't make me leave my baby!'

'You love another woman, Gary. Do you honestly think I can carry on as normal knowing that?'

'But nothing happened.'

'And what if she changes her mind? What would happen the day she called you and said, "I want to be with you"?'

Gary looked away.

'Yes, that's what I thought. Look, Gary, I'm terrified of letting you walk out the door but I'm more terrified of letting you stay. And I may not have been the best wife in the world but I deserve more than second-best.'

Gary crumpled into a heap at the kitchen table and buried his face in his hands. 'I'm so sorry, Rache. I'm so sorry.'

Rachel looked at the broken man before her, her eyes bright with unshed tears. 'Me too.'

Jill walked into the Yacht Bar at exactly five past four. Well, it wasn't a good idea to look too eager. Andy was already there, in conversation with the barman. He looked good, Jill thought, taking a moment to admire his chocolate leather jacket and tight black jeans. He'd let his hair grow and it made him look younger and even more gorgeous than she remembered. As if sensing her eyes on him, Andy turned and smiled. Jill smiled back and walked towards him. 'Hi, Andy.'

'Hi, Jill.' Andy bent his head and kissed her lightly on the lips. 'It's good to see you.'

Jill sat up on the bar stool he'd pulled out for her. 'And you.'

'What would you like to drink?'

'G and T, please.'

When the barman had brought Jill's drink, Andy raised his pint of Guinness. 'Cheers.'

'Cheers.' Jill took a sip of her drink. 'I didn't think you'd agree to meet me.'

Andy grinned. 'Ah well, I didn't have anything else to do.'

'Thanks very much!' Jill laughed but she was relieved that the atmosphere was so easy and relaxed.

'So why did you ask me here?' he asked, watching her steadily.

'Nothing like getting straight to the point, eh?' Jill chuckled nervously. Andy said nothing so she took a deep breath and went for it. 'I wanted to apologize. The way I ended things . . . well, it wasn't very nice.'

'You didn't actually end anything. You just got very stroppy, then very cool, and then you stopped taking my calls.'

Jill winced. 'Like I said, I'm sorry.'

He sighed. 'I just couldn't understand what went wrong. We were having such a good time, weren't we?'

Jill nodded. 'The best. I'm afraid I'm a bit of a disaster when it comes to relationships. It's like, once things are going well, I press the self-destruct button.'

'So, why did you call now?' Andy asked.

'My cousins made me,' Jill admitted, making a face.

'Oh, great.'

'No, no, that's a good thing! They know me better than anyone and they thought I'd made a huge mistake breaking up with you.'

Andy frowned. 'I don't remember meeting them.'

'You didn't but they saw the effect you were having on me.'

Andy smiled slowly. 'Oh, I had an effect on you, did I?'

'Oh yes,' Jill murmured.

Andy ran a finger down her cheek and she turned

her head so she could kiss it, her eyes never leaving his. He whispered, 'So you think that maybe we should give it another go?'

Jill smiled. 'I would like that, but there's a small complication.'

Andy took his hand away and picked up his pint. 'There would be, wouldn't there? Go on then. Tell me.'

'I'm leaving my job.'

He shrugged. 'So?'

Jill shot him a sheepish look. 'And I'm moving to Spain.'

Chapter 38

When Rachel walked into the lounge of the Grand Hotel in Malahide, Jill was at the bar getting drinks. 'Anna's in the loo,' she said. 'What would you like to drink?'

'Soda water,' Rachel told her.

Jill studied her cousin's white face. 'You go and sit down, I'll bring it over.'

Anna returned from the cloakroom and went to help Jill with the drinks. 'Oh, Rachel's here! How did she get on?'

Jill shook her head. 'I didn't ask but she doesn't look too good.' Picking up her drink and Rachel's she led the way to the corner table where Rachel was sitting.

'Hi,' Anna said to her sister. 'Are you okay?'

Rachel's smile was shaky. 'Not really.'

'What did he say?' Jill asked.

'He's in love with someone else.'

'Oh, Rache!' Anna moved closer and slipped an arm around her sister's shoulders. 'I'm so sorry.'

Jill reached across to take Rachel's hand. 'Me too.'

'So you were right about all those nights that he was supposed to be working late,' Anna fumed.

'No, actually, I was wrong about most of it. He only met her six months ago. It was probably the fact that I didn't trust him that drove him away in the end.'

'You can't take the blame for this,' Anna protested.

'Anna's right,' Jill said angrily. 'It's not your fault. Who is he having the affair with? Is it someone he works with?'

Rachel laughed but there was no humour in it. 'He isn't having an affair. He's in love with a woman who works in a bookshop. She's married, has kids and won't have an affair with him or leave her family. They meet for coffee and talk and hold hands—' She broke off, pressing her hand to her mouth. 'I think it would have been easier if it had all been about sex.'

'So what happens now?' Jill prompted gently. 'What are you going to do?'

'I've told him to leave.'

Anna and Jill exchanged looks.

'It might be an idea for you to have some time apart, right enough,' Jill said carefully.

'No, it's over,' Rachel said with finality, her voice remarkably calm.

'But,' Anna looked at her sister's bump, 'what about Alex, the baby . . .'

'I won't be the first woman to bring her kids up alone. Anyway, Gary will still be in their lives. I would never keep his children from him.'

Anna leaned her head against her sister's, tears streaming down her face. 'You'll never be alone, Rachel,' she promised. 'I'm going to be there for you every step of the way.'

'And you'll always have a second home in Spain,' Jill said, squeezing Rachel's hand.

'Don't cry, Anna, you'll set me off.' Rachel took a drink of her water and cleared her throat. 'Well, that's my sorry little story. What about you two? Please tell me you got on better than I did. Jill?'

Jill nodded and smiled. 'Me and Andy are back together again.'

'Oh, that's wonderful!' Anna beamed at her cousin as she mopped at her tears with a tissue.

'Yeah, I'm delighted for you, Jill.' Rachel also managed a smile.

'But have you told him about Spain?' Anna asked.

'Yes. He wasn't too impressed but he's promised to come out for a long weekend in February.'

'I really hope it works out for you, Jill,' Anna said.

'So what about you, Sis?' Rachel prompted.

Anna sighed. 'It's going to be okay, I think, but I came so close to screwing things up.'

Jill raised an eyebrow. 'Charlie?'

Anna nodded. 'After Liam and I had talked, I decided to go and see Charlie. I wanted to tell him face to face that Liam and I were back together and that there was absolutely no future for him and me.'

Rachel stared at her sister. 'So there *was* something going on between you two?'

Anna shook her head. 'No, honestly, there wasn't, but there could have been. I fancied him and I was very tempted, but nothing actually happened.' Anna sat on her crossed fingers.

'And what about Tara?'

'She was after Liam, all right, and he enjoyed the attention but he says that her coming on to him made him realize how much he loved me. And he's got a new job, starting tomorrow. He's even talking about babies again!'

For the first time that day, Rachel's eyes filled up and a sob escaped her lips.

Anna put a hand to her mouth. 'Oh Rache, I'm sorry. How bloody tactless of me. This is the last thing you need to hear.'

'No, no, really, I'm happy for you,' Rachel said, between sniffs. 'I know I'm doing the right thing. It's just the children I worry about.'

'They'll be fine – they have a fantastic mother. Hey, would you like me to phone Mam and ask her to come home now?'

Rachel shook her head. 'No. Gary and I need time to sort things out. I was thinking that we should tell Alex that his daddy has to go away on business. At least until the baby is born.'

'That's a good idea,' Anna agreed. 'And you know that Liam and I will be happy to have him to stay any time.'

Rachel shot her a grateful smile. 'It would be great if you could make a bit of a fuss of him after the baby comes along. I don't want him to feel left out but I'm going to have a lot on my hands.'

'Absolutely no problem. And you know Dad will spoil him rotten.' Anna glanced over to where Jill was staring into her drink, her face solemn. 'Hey, what's wrong with you?' she asked.

Jill looked up at her and then turned guilty eyes on Rachel. 'I feel awful. If I hadn't pushed you, you probably wouldn't have said anything to Gary and you two would still be together.'

'Oh Jill, don't be silly – you were right. Things haven't been okay between me and Gary for a long time. All you did was prompt me to do something about it. At least now I know exactly where I stand. Before, I was just lurching from one day to the next, searching pockets and listening in on phone calls. What kind of a life is that?'

'You're really brave,' Anna said, her face full of admiration.

Rachel made a face. 'That makes a change from being a moan then.'

Anna cringed. 'I'm sorry, Rache, I've been a crap sister.'

'Hey, don't start being too nice to me,' Rachel joked. 'It's just not natural.'

'Remember, you're not allowed to fight any more,' Jill reminded them. 'I won't be here to step in.'

'I'm so happy for you, Jill, but God, I'm really going to miss you,' Rachel said, choking up again.

'You just hop on a plane anytime and I'll be

waiting at the other end,' Jill said, fighting to hold back her own tears.

Rachel dabbed at the tears coursing down her cheeks. 'Sorry about the waterworks. I suppose I'm worn out. It's been quite a day.'

'Let's get you home to bed,' Anna said.

'I don't think I can face Gary. I was very controlled earlier, you'd have been proud of me, but I doubt that I can keep it up all evening.'

'Then come home with me,' Anna suggested.

Rachel shook her head. 'No, Alex would be wondering where I was.'

Jill glanced at Anna. 'Then we'll come home with you and stay until Gary's gone.'

Anna nodded. 'Yes, that's a good idea.'

'But you must want to get back to Liam,' Rachel said anxiously.

Anna draped Rachel's coat around her shoulders. 'Don't you worry about Liam, Rache. He'll understand.'

Epilogue

Rachel put baby Jamie down in his cot, leaning over to stroke his dark curls and marvel at the length of his lashes. He was only six months old but he was already an integral part of her little family and she found it hard to remember what life was like without him. Drawing the curtains, she crept out of the room and crossed the lounge to step on to the balcony and breathe in the balmy, Mediterranean air. She smiled at the shrieks coming from the children playing in the pool and imagined Alex and Jamie playing there together next year.

Going into the kitchen, Rachel put on the kettle for some coffee, sat down at the table and opened Anna's laptop. Signing on to *MumSpeak*, she saw new entries on a couple of threads she'd been following and quickly tapped into the first to read the latest news on Daisylee's mother-in-law problems.

Oh girls, she's at it again! She stayed over last night to let me and Hubby have our first night out in months. Very generous, I know, but when I came home, Babs was sweating buckets because she'd put a blanket over her. I'd explained – at least once – that it was important not to use blankets with a sleeping bag on, but of course, she knew better! Don't get me wrong, she's not the worst but she just won't be told. I think I'm going to have to ask Hubby to have another 'little chat'.

Immediately, Rachel tapped in an answer.

Hey, Daisylee, hang in there and try to keep your temper. Just remember, whatever she's like, she loves your little princess and she's still your prime babysitter!

The next thread was one Rachel herself had started. She had looked for views from other mothers about returning to work. There was one new reply.

Hi, Al'sMum, thrilled to hear that you're thinking of taking a part-time job!! Please don't worry about the baby. He's going to thrive in a crèche with the other babies and you'll still have him to yourself in the afternoons. Very best of luck with it, GalwayGal

Rachel smiled and tapped in a reply.

Tnx, GalwayGal, I'll let you know what happens. x Al'sMum

Rachel got up to make her coffee and then carried her mug back to the table. The next thread was one she'd contributed to a few times. It was about separated parents and the best way of handling access and awkward questions from the children. Reading some of the entries, Rachel realized how lucky she was. Gary was still a big part of their lives and he had done everything he could to make the transition as easy for Alex and Rachel as he could. He was currently living in a small apartment in the city and as far as Rachel knew, he wasn't seeing anyone. How she would feel if he did get it together with That Woman or anyone else, for that matter, she didn't know. For now she concentrated all her energies on Alex and Jamie and tried to stay positive.

Bridie had come home as soon as Anna had phoned her and had been in the delivery room by Rachel's side. Anna and Jill had waited outside with Gary. Rachel was happy for her husband to be there but would not agree to him being in the delivery room. That would be asking too much.

Taking a sip of her coffee, Rachel read the latest entry.

Hi, girls. I've been following this thread with interest because I'm trying to work up the courage to throw my other half out. He's been drinking very heavily and coming home at all hours. I don't really care any more if he's seeing someone else, I just wish he'd stop wasting our money. The electricity bill arrived this morning and I've no idea how I'm going to pay it. My eldest is 11 in two weeks' time and I haven't even got a present yet. I've tried talking to him and when he's sober he promises that he'll change but it never happens. I don't think I can go on like this. I suppose I do still love him but how can he love me if he's ready to do this to me and the kids? I only work part-time and I'm not sure how I'll manage but at least if he goes, I won't have to worry about feeding him and supporting his drinking habit. Will I be eligible for any kind of grants? Is there anyone out there who can help me? Vi

Rachel was full of sympathy for the girl. Another mother had replied, giving all the details about helplines and support groups that Rachel didn't know anything about. Thankfully, she'd never had reason to. She thought for a minute before tapping in a reply.

Vi, my heart goes out to you at this very difficult time. No one can really advise you what to do, certainly not me. I broke up with my husband nearly eight months ago and it was the best thing for us all. I had lived with a situation for a long time but finally I realized that if I didn't take action, I would crack up. I think you just have to follow your heart: it won't let you down. I hope this helps. You're in my thoughts and prayers. Good luck. Al'sMum

Rachel signed off and took up the phone to call her son. She smiled at the sound of his voice. 'Hi, Alex, it's Mummy,' she said.

'Mummy!' Alex squealed. 'You won't believe where I was this morning!'

'Where?' Rachel sounded suitably curious.

'Kidz Klub!'

'And who brought you there?' Rachel asked. The adventure playground was Alex's favourite place to go.

'Granny and Grandad. And then we went for ice-cream.'

'Sounds like you're having lots of fun. Maybe I should stay here.'

'No, Mum! I do miss you, honest. Is Jamie okay? Does he miss me?'

'He misses you,' Rachel assured him, 'but he's fine. Are you looking forward to your weekend in EuroDisney with Daddy?'

'I can't wait, Mum, it's going to be ace! Peter and Seán have both been there and they say it's the best place in the world.'

Rachel laughed. If Alex's best mates said so, then it must be true. 'You'll have a wonderful time, darling. I'll call you before you go, okay?'

'Okay, Mum. Do you want to speak to Granny?'

'No, darling, I have to run. Tell her that I'll call tonight. And tell her that I got her card.'

'Okay, Mum, bye.'

'Bye, Alex, love you.'

Rachel hung up, still smiling, and went to start lunch – Anna and Jill would be here in a few minutes. It was going to be a very simple meal of grilled chicken and salad. She'd planned on making a Caesar salad, but remembered that Anna was completely off anchovies, and garlic was out too as her sister turned green at even the smell. Rachel gave up trying to be adventurous and simply tossed the salad in olive oil and wine vinegar. At least she had been able to marinate the chicken pieces in a little soy sauce before grilling them so that would give the salad some flavour. She was just cutting the chicken into bite-size pieces when she heard the girls coming up the path.

'He definitely fancies you,' Jill was saying as they fell in the door laughing.

'Lucky me!' Anna put down her bag and flopped into a chair, fanning her face and smiling at her sister. 'Hi, Rache. Apparently Juan has the hots for me.'

'His glasses mist up whenever she's around,' Jill sniggered.

'That's gross,' Rachel retorted. 'He must be ninety if he's a day.'

'Just turned sixty-five,' Jill replied.

'No!' Anna stared at her in disbelief. 'Jeez, he must have had a bloody hard life!'

'Apparently he was quite a man for the ladies in his day.' Jill leaned across Rachel and took a piece of chicken.

'How's the babs?' Anna asked.

'Sleeping peacefully.'

'He's a wonderful little fella, isn't he?' Anna patted her own tummy. 'I hope this little one is half as well-behaved as its cousin.'

'Are you feeling up to some lunch?' Rachel asked.

Anna made a face. 'Not really, but I suppose I'd better have something. Liam has me driven mad. Every night when he calls, he makes me run through what I've eaten for the day.'

'Ah, I think that's nice,' Jill laughed. 'How's life as a Factory Manager?'

'It seems to be going very well although he's working long hours. He says he wants to put in the time now so that he'll be able to take a few weeks when the baby comes.'

'That's good, you're going to need him then,'

Rachel told her. 'Trust me, you'll need everyone then. By the way, girls, the post arrived.' She nodded towards the card on the table.

'A postcard?' Anna asked.

Jill picked it up and turned it over. There was a large, gaudy green shamrock on the front. 'It's from your mam!'

'Oh, she's a gas woman, isn't she?' Anna said. 'Read it out, Jill.'

My darling girls, This makes a nice change, doesn't it? You're off gadding about in Spain and I'm back in Dublin. As we're still waiting to get a card from you (hint-hint) I thought you'd like one from the Emerald Isle (I picked a nice sentimental one just for you, Jill.). Hope you're enjoying yourselves and that my beloved Jamie is sleeping like the little angel that he is. Alex is fine, Rachel, and I'm going to miss him when it's time for us to go back. But that's weeks away yet, and I intend to enjoy myself until then. Have a wonderful time together, girls, you deserve it. Dad sends his love and the picture below is of the three of you by the pool, courtesy of Alex. Love now and always, Mam (PS, I hope you're keeping my lovely little home clean!!)

'Great little artist, your son,' Jill said, admiring the three stick figures beside the blue blob.

'Leave it to her to send us a postcard from Ireland,' Anna chuckled.

'It's so strange being here and them being back there, isn't it?' Rachel said as she served up their lunch. 'I'm so glad they decided to settle in Benalmadena. They seem really happy and it's great that Jill is near enough to keep an eye on them.'

'I think they keep an eye on me more than I keep an eye on them,' Jill replied.

'This is lovely,' Anna told her sister, as she tucked into her salad. 'By the way, did I tell you Mark called earlier?'

Rachel paused, the fork halfway to her mouth. 'No.'

'He was asking about you.'

Jill looked over at her cousin. 'So, Rachel, are you going to do it? Are you going to take the job in Donnelly's Real Estate?'

Rachel glanced at her sister. 'Well, if there really is a job there . . .'

Anna rolled her eyes. 'Rachel, Mark doesn't hire people out of the goodness of his heart! He's agreed that I can work half days and that he'll take someone on to job share.'

'But does he realize that I don't know anything about real estate?'

Jill laughed as she opened a bottle of wine. 'Every woman knows something about real estate – mainly what she'd like and what she can actually afford!'

'Mark isn't looking for experience,' Anna reminded her sister. 'That would cost too much money and you know what a skinflint he is.'

'So?' Jill prompted Rachel as she munched thoughtfully on a piece of bread.

'Well, as long as Jamie settles into the crèche okay, then yes, I'll take the job.'

Anna beamed at her sister. 'Oh that's wonderful, Rache! The first thing we must do is buy you that sexy business suit you've always wanted.'

'God, don't do that,' Jill warned her. 'Mark will be all over you like a rash.'

Anna laughed. 'You know, this calls for a celebration. Let's go out tonight.'

Jill nodded. 'Fine by me. I'm not on duty again until lunchtime tomorrow.'

'But what about Jamie?' Rachel asked.

'Andy will mind him,' Jill told her. 'You've seen them together – he's a natural.'

Anna shook her head as Jill offered her some wine. 'Who'd have thought it, eh? I can't believe you two are still together.'

'Neither can I, sometimes,' Jill admitted. 'It's the longest I've ever been with a guy. Of course, my mother thinks I'm mad buying Kitty out and going into partnership with Andy but hey, I've got to take a chance sometime.'

'Pat's only upset because she'd prefer you two to get married first,' Anna pointed out.

Jill laughed. 'True, but I'm not rushing into that one.' She looked across at Rachel who was gazing out at the coastline, lost in thought. 'Are you okay, Rache?'

'Yeah, fine. I'm just trying to get my head around the idea of being a part of the workforce again.'

'How do you think Gary will feel about you working?'

'What's it got to do with him?' Anna retorted. 'What Rache does with her life is none of his business any more.'

'It's okay, Anna,' Rachel said, although she was touched by her sister's protectiveness. 'Gary is very happy for me. You know, we're getting on better now than we have in years.'

'So are you getting back together again?' Anna asked, wide-eyed.

'Lord, no!' Rachel was vehement. 'Not a chance.'

'Is he still seeing Her?' Anna asked.

'I don't think so.' Rachel looked from her sister to her cousin. 'Did I tell you I went to see her?'

'No!' Anna stared at her. 'What did you say to her?'

'Oh, nothing. I had no intention of actually saying anything, I just wanted to see what she looked like.' Rachel laughed wryly. 'You'd want to have seen me creeping around the shop – it's a wonder I wasn't done for shoplifting.'

'So, what is she like?' Jill prompted.

Rachel grinned. 'At least a size bigger than me! She looks quite normal and very conservatively dressed.'

'Well, she does work in a bookshop,' Jill pointed out.

'Is she pretty?' Anna asked.

'Not particularly. She's not the sort of person you'd really notice – although Gary obviously did.'

'Gary's a bit like that himself,' Anna said.

'Anna!' Jill shook her head at her cousin's lack of tact.

'Oh, you know what I mean, Rache,' Anna appealed to her sister. 'We couldn't believe it when you took up with him after Eric – talk about opposites.'

Rachel sighed. 'Oh Eric – I haven't thought about him in years. I wonder what would have happened if we'd stayed together.'

'You wouldn't have Alex and Jamie,' Jill said gently.

'True, and whatever would I do without them?' Rachel sat back and sipped her wine. 'Gosh, it's nice to be able to drink again.'

'Rub it in, why don't you,' Anna complained. 'I have got to teach Liam how to make some of those marvellous cocktails Juan has been giving me. They're delicious.'

Jill winked at Rachel. 'Told you he fancied you. Maybe he'll decide to follow you back to Dublin.'

Anna shuddered. 'That's not remotely funny. Oh, I can't wait to see Liam again, although I will miss you, Jill.'

'Remember, I'll be back the week after next for Dad's birthday.'

'Of course – I'd forgotten about that. You know, that's probably going to be the last chance we get to let our hair down for quite some time. It's going to be a very busy year for all of us.'

'I don't mind it being busy,' Rachel said, 'but I could do without the drama we had last year.'

'Amen to that,' her sister agreed.

Jill held up a hand. 'I'd like to say something to you both and this seems as good a time as any.'

'Uh-oh, she's off.' Anna rolled her eyes and Rachel kicked her. 'Ouch, that hurt!'

Jill made a face at her. 'I want to say something serious before I drink any more of this stuff, so no more interruptions, if you please. As Rachel said, there have been many changes in each of our lives in the last year. Some heartache, many hard knocks but, thankfully, much happiness too, not least because of that wonderful little bundle in there.' She nodded towards the bedroom.

Rachel and Anna smiled at each other.

'Regardless,' Jill continued, 'we have come through it all and out the other side, and we've done it together. I am proud of you two – hell, I'm even proud of me! So I'd like to propose a toast, dear cousins. To the three of us and survival. All for one –'

'– and one for all!' Anna and Rachel chorused.

'I have something to say too,' Anna said, smiling at her sister. 'Here's to Rachel joining the workforce.'

Rachel clinked her glass against Anna's. 'And here's to you becoming a mother!'

Jill looked at her two best friends and smiled. 'To you both – changing places!'

Colette Caddle

From This Moment On

Lynn Stephens' life has been tough recently, thanks to Vincent Boland, the manager at the four-star hotel where she works. But, after digging her heels in and standing up to him, she is delighted when she is vindicated.

Now, with the support and love of her partner, parents and friends, she can put this terrible time behind her and find a job in another hotel.

But the consequences of Vincent's actions are more far-reaching than Lynn knows and the after effects are still being felt throughout the small town. The Boland family is powerful and influential, and it's not long before Lynn realizes that this man still has the capacity to destroy her and all she holds dear.

ISBN 978-1-84983-892-4
PRICE £12.99

Paperback August 2013
978-1-84983-893-1
£7.99

Colette Caddle

Every Time We Say Goodbye

What if the past wasn't what you thought it was . . .

It hasn't always been easy, but Marianne has worked hard to give her children a secure and loving home. But then comes the news that changes everything: her husband has been found dead and her future is uncertain.

As Marianne struggles to move on, the past keeps drawing her back. For Dominic Thomson was not the man everyone thought he was. In spite of everything, she's not quite ready to believe the worst of him, and she is determined to discover the truth.

Now, even in her darkest moments, there is one thing Marianne can hold on to: a love that has always seen her through . . .

ISBN 978-1-84739-962-5
PRICE £6.99

Colette Caddle

Always on My Mind

Old flames, new temptations . . .

With only weeks to go until her Dublin wedding, Molly Jackson is happily anticipating married life with Declan. She has everything she ever wanted: her perfect job, as an agony aunt for online magazine *Teenage Kix*; Declan, the love of her life; and, in Belle, Oliver, Rory and Laura, a loving and warm, if slightly eccentric family.

Then Declan drops his bombshell: he has to go abroad, on business. The wedding must be postponed. Hurt, and reeling from the shock, Molly is seeing Declan off at the airport when she bumps into her childhood sweetheart, Luke Fortune.

Luke left the country when they were both eighteen. Seeing him again, Molly realises that she has a window of opportunity, while Declan is away, to put a few of the ghosts in her past to rest.

'If you like Marian Keyes, you'll love Colette Caddle'
Company

ISBN: 978-1-84739-961-8
£6.99

Colette Caddle

The Secrets We Keep

Can you keep a secret?

It has been four years since Erin Joyce left Dublin under a cloud and bought a guesthouse in the remote, beautiful village of Dunbarra. The Gatehouse attracts a strange clutch of guests who, once ensconced, never want to leave. There's Hazel, a shy artist, and her sweet, silent daughter Gracie. Sandra, a brash American, wants to know everything about everyone. Then there's wise old easy-going PJ, who's seemingly part of the furniture.

But Erin's fragile happiness is thrown off-balance by the arrival of A-list Hollywood actor Sebastian Gray. Erin finds herself drawn to this handsome enigmatic man, who used to walk with a swagger but now prowls the country lanes with haunted eyes. What trauma could have brought about this devastating change?

Sebastian isn't the only one in the Gatehouse with a secret. Why is Hazel cast so adrift? Where does PJ go each week without fail, and what really brought Sandra to Dunbarra? As Erin finds herself embroiled in her guests' secrets, she starts to ask herself if she can ever reveal her own . . .

ISBN: 978-1-47112-730-4
Price £7.99

Colette Caddle

Between the Sheets

Dana De Lacey, bestselling romance novelist, has the world at her feet. The words on the page flow easily, an exciting new book deal beckons, and life at home in Dublin is good.

But Dana's self-confidence and success depend on one person: her gorgeous husband Gus. Without him, she has no fall-back. No children, no close family of her own to call upon. When Gus leaves her, she is devastated. The words fail to come. The alcohol flows too freely. She cannot sleep.

Then her estranged brother Ed arrives out of the blue to take care of her and memories that she has kept buried for many years start to rise to the surface. Forced to face up to the past, can she find the real Dana, recover her career, and try to make Gus love her for the person she really is?

ISBN 978-1-47112-731-1
£7.99

Colette Caddle

It's All About Him

If you were given the chance to confront the man who ruined your life, what would you do?

With the health of her son always an issue and bills constantly flooding in, the last thing Dee Hewson needs is to open her front door one day and come face to face with the childhood sweetheart who broke her heart and abused her trust.

Though she was devastated by his betrayal, she has triumphed over all the odds and pulled the pieces of her life back together. Through love and a lot of hard work, Dee has changed adored son Sam from being a delicate toddler into a feisty and fun-loving four-year-old. Her money worries may finally be receding and there are wonderful new business opportunities on the horizon. She has even dared to find love again – with strong and reliable Conor.

So is Dee really prepared to jeopardize all this simply to give Sam the chance of having a father?

With great warmth and an unerring eye, Number One Irish bestseller Colette Caddle makes Dee's dilemma acutely real as she explores the fragility of family and friendship in today's fraught world.

ISBN 978-1-47112-732-8
PRICE £7.99

Colette Caddle

The Betrayal of Grace Mulcahy

Interior betrayals, Venetian blinds; this warm, wise and affecting novels unravels the numerous betrayals we make upon even those we love

The life and marriage of Grace and Michael Mulcahy has all the signs of being a successful and fulfilled one: a daughter; rewarding jobs; plenty of friends. But when Grace discovers that Miriam, her partner in her interior design business, is embezzling her, the seeds are sown for Grace's bind. When confronted with her betrayal, Miriam begs Grace not to tell anyone in order to preserve Miriam's marriage which will fall apart if the truth outs. Grace agrees to keep quiet but finds it leads to all sorts of complications and misunderstandings that put a strain on all of her relationships both professional and personal. By the time she notices how close things are to crumbling, is it too late to piece together the ties that bind her to those she loves?

ISBN 978-1-47112-735-9

£7.99

Colette Caddle

Red Letter Day

Recently married to Dermot and tipped as Ireland's hottest new designer, Celine Moore is relaxed, happy and looking forward to an exciting future. Why then, just five years later, is she barely able to hold her head up high in her local Dublin neighbourhood, at odds with her father and sister-in-law and accepting a job in a second hand clothes shop?

Celine's life changed the night Dermot failed to return from work and his violent death destroyed all her happiness and ambition. Aching loneliness and anger took their place, and without thinking through the consequences, Celine embarked on an affair with a married man. Now, desperate to put some distance between herself and the local gossips, a new start in a new place and a new job seems like the perfect opportunity to start again.

But it's not long before she realizes that however much you try to run away, your past has a habit of always catching up with you in the end . . .

ISBN 978-1-47112-734-2
PRICE £7.99